MIRACLE BOY AND OTHER STORIES

Miracle Boy
and Other Stories

PINCKNEY BENEDICT

Press 53
Winston-Salem

Press 53, LLC
PO Box 30314
Winston-Salem, NC 27130

First Edition

Cover photo Copyright © 2010 by Jake Mahaffy

Cover design by Kevin Morgan Watson & Laura Benedict

Pinckney Benedict photo by Laura Benedict

Jake Mahaffy photo by Yulia Nabutovsky

Library of Congress Control Number: 2010903458

Printed on acid-free paper
ISBN 978-1-935708-01-8

For Laura

CONTENTS

ACKNOWLEDGMENTS

The author gratefully acknowledges these fine publications where these stories first appeared.

"Miracle Boy" first appeared in *Esquire* and was selected for *Prize Stories 1999: O. Henry Awards* and *New Stories from the South 1999: The Year's Best.*

"Buckeyes" first appeared in *Antietam Review.*

"The Butcher Cock" (as "Irish Mountain") first appeared in *Zoetrope: All-Story* and was selected for *Pushcart Prize XXVIII: The Best of the Small Presses.*

"Pony Car" appeared in *Ontario Review.*

"Joe Messinger is Dreaming" first appeared in *Appalachian Heritage* and received the 2007 Plattner Award for best fiction to appear there.

"Mudman" first appeared in *Tin House* and subsequently in the anthology *Best of Tin House: Stories.*

"Bridge of Sighs" first appeared in *Zoetrope: All-Story* and was selected for *New Stories from the South: The Year's Best 2008.*

"The Beginnings of Sorrow" first appeared in *Sonora Review* and was reprinted in *The Mammoth Book of Best New Horror #20* (2009).

"The Angel's Trumpet" first appeared in *Appalachian Heritage.*

"The World, the Flesh, and the Devil" first appeared in *Image* and was selected for *New Stories from the South: The Year's Best 2009.*

"Pig Helmet & the Wall of Life" first appeared in *StoryQuarterly.*

"The Secret Nature of the Mechanical Rabbit" first appeared in *The Journal* and was selected for *Pushcart Prize XXI: The Best of the Small Presses.*

"Mercy" first appeared in *Ontario Review* and was selected for *Pushcart Prize XXXII: The Best of the Small Presses.*

"Zog-19: A Scientific Romance" first appeared in *Zoetrope: All-Story* and was selected for *Prize Stories 2001: O. Henry Awards.*

Miracle Boy

Lizard and Geronimo and Eskimo Pie wanted to see the scars. Show us the scars, Miracle Boy, they said.

They cornered Miracle Boy after school one day, waited for him behind the shop-class shed, out beyond the baseball diamond, where the junior high's property bordered McClung's place. Miracle Boy always went home that way, over the fence stile and across the fields with his weird shuffling gait and the black-locust walking stick that his old man had made for him. His old man's place bordered McClung's on the other side.

Show us the scars. Lizard and Geronimo and Eskimo Pie knew all about the accident and Miracle Boy's reattached feet. The newspaper headline had named him Miracle Boy. MIRACLE BOY'S FEET REATTACHED IN EIGHT-HOUR SURGERY. Everybody in school knew, everybody in town. Theirs was not a big town. It had happened a number of years before, but an accident of that sort has a long memory.

Lizard and Geronimo and Eskimo Pie wanted to see where the feet had been sewn back on. They were interested to see what a miracle looked like. They knew about miracles from the Bible—the burning bush, Lazarus who walked again after death—and it got their curiosity up.

Miracle Boy didn't want to show them. He shook his head when they said to him, Show us the scars. He was a portly boy, soft and jiggly at his hips and belly from not being able to run around and play sports like other boys, like Lizard and Geronimo and Eskimo Pie. He was pigeon-toed and wearing heavy dark brogans that looked like they might have some therapeutic value. His black corduroy pants were too long for him and pooled around his ankles. He carried his locust walking stick in one hand.

Lizard and Geronimo and Eskimo Pie asked him one last time— they were being patient with him because he was a cripple—and then they knocked him down. Eskimo Pie sat on his head while the other two took off his pants and shoes and socks. They flung his socks and pants over the sagging woven-wire fence. One of the heavy white socks caught on the rusted single strand of bob-wire along the top of the fence. They tied the legs of his pants in a big knot before tossing them. They tied the laces of the heavy brogans together and pitched them high in the air, so that they caught and dangled from the electric line overhead. Miracle Boy said nothing while they were doing it. Eskimo Pie took his walking stick from him and threw it into the bushes.

They pinned Miracle Boy to the ground and examined his knotted ankles, the smooth lines of the scars, their pearly whiteness, the pink and red and purple of the swollen, painful-looking skin around them.

Don't look like any miracle to me, said Eskimo Pie. Miracle Boy wasn't fighting them. He was just lying there, looking in the other direction. McClung's Hereford steers had drifted over to the fence, excited by the goings-on, thinking maybe somebody was going to feed them. They were a good-looking bunch of whiteface cattle, smooth-hided and stocky, and they'd be going to market soon.

It just looks like a mess of old scars to me, Eskimo Pie said.

Eskimo Pie and Geronimo were brothers. Their old man had lost three quarters of his left hand to the downstroke of a hydraulic fence-post driver a while before, but that hadn't left anything much to reattach.

It's miracles around us every day, said Miracle Boy.

Lizard and Geronimo and Eskimo Pie stopped turning his feet this way and that like the intriguing feet of a dead man. Miracle Boy's voice was soft and piping, and they stopped to listen.

What's that? Geronimo wanted to know. He nudged Miracle Boy with his toe.

Jesus, he made the lame man to walk, Miracle Boy said. And Jesus, he made me to walk, too.

But you wasn't lame before, Geronimo said. Did Jesus take your feet off just so he could put them back on you?

Miracle Boy didn't say anything more. Lizard and Geronimo and Eskimo Pie noticed then that he was crying. His face was wet, shining with tears and mucus. They saw him bawling, without his shoes and socks and trousers, sprawled in his underpants on the ground, his walking stick caught in a pricker bush. They decided that this did not look good.

They were tempted to leave him, but instead they helped him up and retrieved his socks and unknotted his pants and assisted him into them. He was still crying as they did it. Eskimo Pie presented the walking stick to him with a flourish. They debated briefly whether to go after his shoes, dangling from the power line overhead. In the end, though, they decided that, having set him on his feet again, they had done enough.

~ ~ ~

Miracle Boy's old man was the one who cut Miracle Boy's feet off. He was chopping corn into silage. One of the front wheels of the Case 1370 Agri-King that he was driving broke through the crust of the cornfield into a snake's nest. Copperheads boiled up out of the ground. The tractor nose-dived, heeled hard over to one side, and Miracle Boy slid off the fender where he'd been riding.

Miracle Boy's old man couldn't believe what he had done. He shut off the tractor's power-takeoff and scrambled down from the high seat. He was sobbing. He pulled his boy out of the jaws of the silage chopper and saw that the chopper had taken his feet.

It's hard not to admire what he did next.

Thinking fast, he put his boy down, gently put his maimed boy down on the ground. He had to sweep panicked copperheads out of the way to do it. He made a tourniquet for one leg with his belt, made another with his blue bandanna that he kept in his back pocket. Then he went up the side of the silage wagon like a monkey. He began digging in the silage. He dug down into the wet heavy stuff with his bare hands.

From where he was lying on the ground, the boy could see the silage flying. He could tell that his feet were gone. He knew what his old man was looking for up there. He knew exactly.

~ ~ ~

Miracle Boy's old man called Lizard's mother on the telephone. He told Lizard's mother what Lizard and Geronimo and Eskimo Pie had done to Miracle Boy. He told her that they had taken Miracle Boy's shoes from him. That was the worst part of what they had done, he said, to steal a defenseless boy's shoes. The next day, Miracle Boy's old man came by Lizard's house. He brought Miracle Boy with him. Lizard thought that probably Miracle Boy's old man was going to whip the tar out of him for his part in what had been done to Miracle Boy. He figured Miracle Boy was there to watch the beating. Lizard's own old man was gone, and his mother never laid a hand on him, so he figured that, on this occasion, Miracle Boy's old man would likely fill in.

Instead, Lizard's mother made them sit in the front room together, Lizard and Miracle Boy. She brought them cold Coca-Colas and grilled cheese sandwiches. She let them watch TV. An old movie was on; it was called *Dinosaurus!*. Monsters tore at one another on the TV screen and chased tiny humans. Even though it was the kind of thing he would normally have liked, Lizard couldn't keep his mind on the movie. Miracle Boy sat in the crackling brown reclining chair that had belonged to Lizard's old man. The two of them ate from TV trays, and whenever Miracle Boy finished his glass of Coca-Cola, Lizard's mother brought him more. She brought Lizard more, too, and she looked at him with searching eyes, but Lizard could not read the message in her gaze.

By the third glassful of Coca-Cola, Lizard started to feel a little sick, but Miracle Boy went right on, drinking and watching *Dinosaurus!* with an enraptured expression on his face, occasionally belching quietly. Sometimes his lips moved, and Lizard thought he might be getting ready to say something, but he and Lizard never swapped a single word the whole time.

Miracle Boy's old man sat on the front porch of Lizard's house and looked out over the shrouded western slope of the Blue Ridge and swigged at the iced tea that Lizard's mother brought him, never moving from his seat until *Dinosaurus!* was over and it was time to take Miracle Boy away.

~ ~ ~

Geronimo and Eskimo Pie got a hiding from their old man. He used his two-inch-wide black bull-hide belt in his good hand, and he made them take their pants down for the beating, and he made them thank him for every stroke. They couldn't believe it when Lizard told them what his punishment had been. That, Geronimo told Lizard, is the difference between a house with a woman in charge and one with a man.

~ ~ ~

Lizard saw Miracle Boy's shoes every day, hanging on the electric wire over by McClung's property line, slung by their laces. He kept hoping the laces would weather and rot and break and the shoes would come down by themselves, and that way he wouldn't have to see them anymore, but they never did. When he was outside the school, his eyes were drawn to them. He figured that everybody in the school saw those shoes. Everybody knew whose shoes they were. Lizard figured that Miracle Boy must see them every day on his way home.

He wondered what Miracle Boy thought about that, his shoes hung up in the wires, on display like some kind of a trophy, in good weather and in bad. Nestled together nose to tail up in the air like dogs huddled for warmth. He wondered if Miracle Boy ever worried about those shoes.

He took up watching Miracle Boy in school for signs of worry. Miracle Boy kept on just like before. He wore a different pair of shoes these days, a brand-new pair of coal-black Keds that looked too big for him. He shuffled from place to place, his walking stick tapping against the vinyl tiles of the hallway floors as he went.

I'm going to go get the shoes, Lizard announced one day to Geronimo and Eskimo Pie. It was spring by then, the weather alternating between warm and cold, dark days that were winter hanging on and spring days full of hard bright light. Baseball season, and the three of them were on the bench together. Geronimo and Eskimo Pie didn't seem to know what shoes Lizard was talking about. They were concentrating on the game.

Miracle Boy's shoes, Lizard said. Geronimo and Eskimo Pie looked up at them briefly. A breeze swung them first gently clockwise and just as gently counterclockwise.

You don't want to fool with those, Eskimo Pie said.

Lectrocute yourself, Geronimo said.

Or fall to your doom, one, Eskimo Pie said.

Lizard didn't say anything more about it to them. He kept his eyes on the shoes as they moved through their slow oscillation, and he watched the small figure of Miracle Boy, dressed in black like a preacher, bent like a question mark as he moved beneath the shoes, as he bobbed over the fence stile and hobbled across the brittle dead grass of the field beyond.

~ ~ ~

The trees are beginning to go gloriously to color in the windbreak up by the house. The weather is crisp, and the dry unchopped corn in the field around Miracle Boy and his old man chatters and rasps and seems to want to talk. Miracle Boy (though he is not Miracle Boy yet—that is minutes away) sits on the fender of the tractor, watching his old man.

Soon enough, Miracle Boy will be bird-dogging whitewings out of the stubble of this field. Soon enough, his old man will knock the fluttering doves out of the air with a blast of hot singing birdshot from his 12-gauge Remington side-by-side, and Miracle Boy will happily shag the busted birds for him. When the snow falls, Miracle Boy will go into the woods with his old man, after the corn-fat deer that are plentiful on the place. They will drop a salt lick in a clearing that he knows, by a quiet little stream, and they will wait together in the ice-rimed bracken, squatting patiently on their haunches, Miracle Boy and his old man, to kill the deer that come to the salt.

~ ~ ~

Lizard made a study of the subject of the shoes. They were hung up maybe a yard out from one of the utility poles, so clearly the pole was the way to go. He had seen linemen scramble up the poles with ease, using their broad climbing slings and their spiked boots, but he had no idea where he could come by such gear.

In the end, he put on the tool belt that his old man had left behind, cinched it tight, holstered his old man's Tiplady hammer, and filled the pouch of the belt with sixtypenny nails. He left the house in the middle of the night, slipping out the window of his bedroom and clambering down the twisted silver maple that grew there. He walked and trotted the four miles down the state highway to the junior high school. It was a cold night there in the highlands of the Seneca Valley, and he nearly froze. He hid in the ditches by the side of the road whenever a vehicle went by. He didn't care for anyone to stop and offer him a ride or ask him what it was he thought he was doing.

He passed a number of houses on the way to the school. The lights were on in some of the houses and off in others. One of the houses was Miracle Boy's, he knew, a few hundred yards off the road in a grove of walnut trees, its back set against a worn-down knob of a hill. In the dark, the houses were hard to tell one from another. Lizard thought he knew which house was Miracle Boy's, but he couldn't be sure.

His plan was this: to drive one of the sixtypenny nails into the utility pole about three feet off the ground. Then to stand one-footed on that nail and drive in another some distance above it. Then he would stand on the second nail and drive a third, and so on, ascending nail by nail until he reached the humming transformer at the top of the pole. Then, clinging to the transformer, he imagined, he would lean out from the pole and, one-handed, pluck the shoes from the wire, just like taking fruit off a tree.

The first nail went in well and held solid under his weight, and he hugged the pole tight, the wood rough and cool where it rubbed against the skin of his cheek. He fished in the pouch of nails, selected one, and drove it as well. He climbed onto it. His hands were beginning to tremble as he set and drove the third nail. He had to stand with his back bent at an awkward angle, his shoulder dug in hard against the pole, and already he could feel the strain grinding to life in his back and in the muscles of his forearm.

The next several nails were not hard to sink, and he soon found himself a dozen feet up, clinging to the pole. The moon had risen as he'd worked, and the landscape below was bright. He looked around him, at the baseball diamond, with its deep-worn base path and crumbling pitcher's mound and the soiled bags that served as bases. From his new vantage point, he noted with surprise the state of the roof of the shop shed, the tin scabby and blooming with rust, bowed and beginning to buckle. He had never noticed before what hard shape the place was in.

He straightened his back and fought off a yawn. He was getting tired and wished he could quit the job he had started. He looked up. There was no breeze, and the shoes hung as still as though they were shoes in a painting. He fumbled another nail out of the pouch, ran it through his hair to grease the point, mashed his shoulder against the unyielding pole, set the nail with his left hand, and banged it home.

And another, and another. His clothes grew grimy with creosote, and his eyes stung and watered. Whenever he looked down, he was surprised at how far above the ground he had climbed. McClung's Herefords found him, and they stood in a shallow semicircle beneath the utility pole, cropping at the worthless grass that grew along the fence line. This was a different batch from the fall before. These were younger but similarly handsome animals, and Lizard welcomed their company. He felt lonesome up there on the pole. He thought momentarily of Miracle Boy, seated before the television, his gaze fixed on the set, his jaws moving, a half-eaten grilled cheese sandwich in his fingers.

The steers stood companionably close together, their solid barrel bodies touching lightly. Their smell came to him, concentrated and musty, like damp hot sawdust, and he considered how it would be to descend the pole and stand quietly among them. How warm. He imagined himself looping an arm over the neck of one of the steers, leaning his head against the hot skin of its densely muscled shoulder. A nail slithered from his numbing fingers, fell, and dinked musically off the forehead of the lead steer. The steer woofed, blinked, twitched its ears in annoyance. The Herefords wheeled and started off across the field, the moonlight silvering the curly hair along the ridgelines of their backs.

The nail on which Lizard was standing began to give dangerously beneath his weight, and he hurried to make his next foothold. He gripped the utility pole between his knees, clinging hard, trying to take the burden off the surrendering nail as it worked its way free of the wood. A rough splinter stung his thigh. He whacked at the wobbling nail that he held and caught the back of his hand instead, peeling skin from his knuckles. He sucked briefly at the bleeding scrapes and then went back to work, striking the nail with the side of the hammer's head. The heavy nail bent under the force of his blows, and he whimpered at the thought of falling. He struck it again, and the nail bit deep into the pine. Again, and it tested firm when he tugged on it.

He pulled himself up. Resting on the bent nail, he found himself at eye level with the transformer at the pole's top. Miracle Boy's shoes dangled a yard behind him. Lizard felt winded, and he took hold of the transformer. The cold metal cut into the flesh of his fingers. There was deadly current within the transformer, he knew, but still it felt like safety to him. He held fast, shifted his weight to his arms, tilted his head back to catch sight of the shoes. Overhead, the wires crossed the disk of the moon, and the moonlight shone on the wires, on the tarnished hardware that fixed them to the post, on the ceramic insulators. These wires run to every house in the valley, Lizard thought.

He craned his neck further and found the shoes. Still there. The shoes were badly weathered. To Lizard, they looked a million years old, like something that ought to be on display in a museum somewhere, with a little white card identifying them. SHOES OF THE MIRACLE BOY. The uppers were cracked and swollen, pulling loose from the lowers, and the tongues protruded obscenely. Lizard put a tentative hand out toward them. Close, but no cigar.

He loosened his grip, leaned away from the pole. The arm with which he clung to the transformer trembled with the effort. Lizard trusted to his own strength to keep him from falling. He struggled to make himself taller. The tips of his outstretched fingers grazed the sole of one of the shoes and set them both to swinging. The shoes swung away from him and then back. He missed his grip, and they swung again. This time, he got a purchase on the nearest shoe.

He jerked, and the shoes held fast. Jerked again and felt the raveling laces begin to give. A third time, a pull nearly strong enough to dislodge him from his perch, and the laces parted. He drew one shoe to him as the other fell to the ground below with a dry thump. He wondered if the sound the shoe made when it hit was similar to the sound he might make. The shoe he held in his hand was the left.

In the moonlight, Lizard could see almost as well as in the day. He could make out McClung's cattle on the far side of the field, their hind ends toward him, and the trees of the windbreak beyond that, and beyond that the lighted windows of a house. It was, he knew, Miracle Boy's house. Set here and there in the shallow bowl of the Seneca Valley were the scattered lights of other houses. A car or a pickup truck crawled along the state road toward him. The red warning beacons of a microwave relay tower blinked at regular intervals on a hogback to the north.

Lizard was mildly surprised to realize that the valley in which he lived was such a narrow one. He could easily traverse it on foot in a day. The ridges crowded in on the levels. Everything that he knew was within the sight of his eyes. It was as though he lived in the cupped palm of a hand, he thought.

He tucked Miracle Boy's left shoe beneath his arm and began his descent.

~ ~ ~

When Lizard was little, his old man made toys for him. He made them out of wood: spinning tops and tiny saddle horses, trucks and guns, a cannon and caisson just like the one that sat on the lawn of the county courthouse. He fashioned a bull-roarer that made a tremendous howling when he whirled it overhead but that Lizard was too small to use; and what he called a Limber Jack, a little wooden doll of a man that would dance flat-footed while his father sang: "Was an old man near Hell did dwell, / If he ain't dead yet he's living there still."

Lizard's favorite toy was a Jacob's Ladder, a cunning arrangement of wooden blocks and leather strips about three feet long. When you tilted the top block just so, the block beneath it flipped over with a slight clacking sound, and the next block after that, and so on, cascading down the line. When all the blocks had finished their tumbling, the Jacob's Ladder was just as it

had been before, though to Lizard it seemed that it ought to have been longer, or shorter, or anyhow changed.

He could play with it for hours, keeping his eye sharp on the line of end-swapping blocks purling out from his own hand like an infinite stream of water. He wanted to see the secret of it.

I believe he's a simpleton, his old man told his mother.

~ ~ ~

You think my boy wants anything to do with you little bastards?

Lizard wanted to explain that he was alone in this. That Geronimo and Eskimo Pie were at home asleep in their beds, that they knew nothing of what he was doing. Miracle Boy's old man stood behind the closed screen door of his house, his arms crossed over his chest, a cigarette snugged in the corner of his mouth. The hallway behind him was dark.

I don't necessarily want anything to do with him, Lizard said. I just brought him his shoes.

He held out the shoes, but Miracle Boy's old man didn't even look at them.

Your mommy may not know what you are, Miracle Boy's old man said, and his voice was tired and calm. But I do.

Lizard offered the shoes again.

You think he wants those things back? Miracle Boy's old man asked. He's got new shoes now. Different shoes.

Lizard said nothing. He stayed where he was.

Put them down there, Miracle Boy's old man said, nodding at a corner of the porch.

I'm sorry, Lizard said. He held on to the shoes. He felt like he was choking.

It's not me you need to be sorry to.

Miracle Boy appeared at the end of the dark hallway. Lizard could see him past the bulk of his old man's body. He was wearing canary-yellow pajamas. Lizard had never before seen him wear any color other than black.

Daddy? he said. The sleeves of the PJs were too long for his arms, they swallowed his hands, and the pajama legs lapped over his feet. He began to scuff his way down the hall toward the screen door. He moved deliberately. He did not have his walking stick with him, and he pressed one hand against the wall.

His old man kept his eyes fixed on Lizard. Go back to bed, Junior, he said in the same tired tone that he had used with Lizard before.

Daddy?

Miracle Boy brushed past his old man, who took a deferential step back. He came to the door and pressed his pudgy hands against the screen. He looked at Lizard with wide curious eyes. He was a bright yellow figure behind the mesh. He was like a bird or a butterfly. Lizard was surprised to see how small he was.

Miracle Boy pressed hard against the door. If it had not been latched, it would have opened and spilled him out onto the porch. He nodded eagerly at Lizard, shyly ducking his head. Lizard could not believe that Miracle Boy was happy to see him. Miracle Boy beckoned, crooking a finger at Lizard, and he was smiling, a strange small inward smile. Lizard did not move. In his head, he could hear his old man's voice, his long-gone old man, singing, accompanied by clattering percussion: the jigging wooden feet of the Limber Jack. Miracle Boy beckoned again, and this time Lizard took a single stumbling step forward. He held Miracle Boy's ruined shoes in front of him. He held them out before him like a gift.

Buckeyes

My friends and I head over to the salvage yard to see this crowd of dead Ohioans. My dad drives a wrecker for the yard and he's told me about these people and their car. It's like a curiosity or something to him. He sees a lot, accidents and all. He sometimes brings home items from the wreckage, odds and ends, and he tells me about the really terrible ones, and the ones where there's something funny, like the couple that piled up their car because they were screwing out on the turnpike. When the guys brought up the saws and equipment to cut them out of the wreck, there they were, twisted together in the front seat, and the man's pants were down around his ankles and the woman hadn't got a single stitch on, stark naked in there on top of that guy.

So he tells me about these Buckeyes he brought in, tells me it's something I ought to see. I get some friends together and we walk over there. It's a bunch of kids from my sixth-grade class, like it's a field trip or something. When we get to the yard, the guy that owns the place—Mr. Legg is his name—is sitting in a chair at the gate, and he's got a stick laid across his lap, like a walking stick. When I go up to him to tell him hey, tell him what we want, he pokes the stick in my chest. Gives it a pretty good shove. He's chewing tobacco, got a sizable plug of it hung up in one cheek.

I tell him who I am, I say, "I'm Goody Pettus," and he just looks at me like I'm crazy.

"You go in there, I got a big black dog like to eat up your ass," he says to me. I'm standing in front of my friends. I've told them I know this guy, my dad works here, I'll get them in. So I tell him again who I am, thinking maybe he didn't understand me when I said it the first time. I tell him who my dad is. He just looks at me. I tell him what we're all there to see.

He says, "Little fuckers want to go in there and rip me off."

I tell him we don't.

He says, "Each one of you swipes something, you walk out of here with a whole car just about. Jesus Christ."

The kids behind me are starting to talk like they're going home, but I'm not finished yet. There's a sheet-metal fence all around the place. It's ten, twelve feet high, and no gate but the one that old man Legg has got blocked, so it seems like we aren't getting in any other way. Also I know the dog he's talking about. It's a huge bastard, a bull mastiff that has got to weigh seventy or eighty pounds. My dad has told me the old man beats it pretty regularly with that stick to keep it mean. It hates everybody, even my dad, who is a guy that gets along with most animals.

I say, "We've got fifty cents." I don't actually have that much on me at the moment but I figure we can scrape it up among us. The old man looks at me, spits into the dirt beside his chair.

"Fifty cent apiece?" he says.

"No," I say. "Just fifty cents."

He looks the group over. There are about ten of us. He says, "That makes it a nickel each. Not very damn much."

I say, "It's what we've got. We might could go a little higher."

He says, "What do you think this is? A goddamn carnival? Pay somebody and you can go in and look at the sideshow freaks?"

A couple of the other kids have coasted off by now but I want to get past this fellow Legg. I say to him that my dad told me it was worth it, something you should definitely see because things like this don't come along so often. My dad said it was something like a piece of history. He said it was practically art, those people in that car.

He peers at me. "Who's your father, telling you something like that?" he says. "Do I know him?"

I say yeah. I tell him, "My dad's Conrad Pettus. He drives a wrecker for you."

Legg laughs. "Conrad?" he says. "That sounds like old Conrad. He says some pretty damn strange things from time to time. I guess I could let you in a minute then. Cost you a buck and a half, though, for all of you."

Those of us that are left huddle together, and with all of us pitching in we've got a dollar and thirty cents, something like that. We're a little short. I give it to the old man, a handful of change, and he doesn't even count it, just jams it in his pocket. He says, "You've got ten minutes to look. Don't touch nothing back there, because the troopers are going to be coming by in the morning to look it all over. They say it might be foul play involved. They say that might be the scene of the crime." He pauses to cough a time or two, takes a couple of shallow breaths. "And you got to turn out your pockets when you leave. Nobody gets out with nothing he didn't bring in, hear?"

Then he points into the yard, where there are cars lying on top of one another, sitting on their sides, covered in vines, creeper that goes in at the windows and crawls up the radio aerials.

I'm thinking about snakes, and how this looks to be a pretty good place for them to live, to hide in. Some of those cars look like they have sat there for twenty years, and they're all accordioned, got something wrong with them somewhere. Every now and again, a car will look all right as you come up on it, like a car anybody'd have, but then you see that the other side is mashed where a truck or something barreled into it, and you know nobody walked away from that one. So on into the yard we go.

It's evening, and the sun has gone down behind the line of hills to the west. In the half-light in the valleys between the stacked cars, it takes us a while to find the one we're looking for. All I know from my father is we're hunting a Packard with Ohio plates. He told me the Ohioans were still in it when he dropped it off at the yard, and I'm hoping they're there yet. I keep checking around for the dog, but then I hear it, locked in the little shed the old man's got for an office. It's scraping on the door, whining and screeching to get out and get at us. It gives me the shivers to hear its nails on the metal door of that shed, to watch the tin wall panels shiver when it throws itself against them, and I imagine the others feel the same way.

One of the guys gives a yell when we've been looking about five minutes or so, says he found the car. It's just an old Hudson Hornet, though, that's burned out and empty, nobody in it at all. There is melted blackened windshield glass on the hood, so the fire must've burned pretty hot. I yell at him for wasting our time.

One of the other guys says well, it's been a while, maybe we ought to go before the old man gets tired of waiting and turns the mastiff loose on us. Maybe our time that we paid for is up, he thinks.

I say, "He gave us ten minutes *to look*. We got to find the car before we can look at it." They don't seem convinced, but nobody leaves, and we keep poking around among all these piled-up wrecks, and some of the piles reach up thirty feet or so. They're like little mountains of smashed cars, nothing you would want to climb on. You could put a foot wrong and go through a windshield, break a leg, cut yourself on a jagged edge of sheared steel, bleed to death, catch tetanus. You could slip between the cars, slide down into the dark spaces among the exhaust pipes and the differentials and the cast-off wheels, the rotting tires with the canvas belts showing through. Who knows how far you could fall?

I wonder where all these cars have come from. It seems like more than the people around here could drive, let alone wreck, even in a hundred years. I make up my mind I'll ask my dad about that, when I get home.

I'm beginning to have doubts about the tolerance of Legg and the dog myself, beginning to get itchy like we need to go, and I wish I'd asked my old man a little more about where the car was placed, exactly. Then the same guy, the one who located the Hudson, sings out. He's really found it this time, he says. He's the littlest one of us, and his voice is high, like a woman's echoing off the smashed cars. We all razz him a minute, *oh yeah, what did you find this time, Lou?* but it turns out he has. He's found the Packard full of flatlanders.

The car sits off by itself, right up against the metal fence. It's a bulbous thing with a great long hood, looking as much like an upside-down boat as it does a car. Its finish is completely gone, the bare metal eaten through with rust in any number of places. The tires have vanished, and the Packard rests on its rims now. There is no glass to be seen anywhere on it. The interior looks like it is full of jumbled garbage. I can't bring myself to approach it. No one else goes near it either.

Until yesterday, the Packard sat at the base of a limestone cliff on a mountain to the east of us. No telling how it got there. The cliff is called the Eagle's Nest because they say golden eagles used to live in openings in the rock face. They would cruise the river when they hunted; fold their wings and drop a thousand feet like a rock; hit the water and come up flying, with a speckled trout in their claws. Now it is just noisy black rooks that make their nests in the crevices.

The cliff faces a wide bend in the Allegheny River, with a patch of national forest behind it, and people picnic there all the time, make out on the cliff top at night. The rocks along the edge are covered with graffiti, people's names in bright colors of spray paint, hearts with arrows, little slogans. Sometimes you get a short poem. The crevices up there are stuffed full of old used rubbers, and oftentimes a brassiere or a pair of panties is caught in the branches of a scrubby tree, waving with the breeze like some kind of racy flag. Sometimes but not as often, it's a man's Fruit of the Loom.

All those people coming and going for all that time, and nobody ever saw the car from Ohio down below, sitting at the cliff base like it was parked there. It was in the same place for thirty years or better, from the look of it.

A couple of rock climbers found the car. They had scaled their way down the face, and they were eating lunch at the bottom, sandwiches in plastic bags, drinking from a thermos of hot coffee, getting ready to go back up. They thought it was a boulder that had come loose from the cliff face. There are lots of boulders down there, everything from the size of your head to the size of a trailer house, is what I've heard, and the car was covered in vines and mounds of bird guano, surrounded by trees and bushes. There were trees growing up inside it, right through the floorboards and out through the windows and even through the roof. It was only when they went to climb on it, to start back up the cliff, that they found out it was made of metal, that it was a car and not a natural formation.

It took a crane brought over from a highway contractor in the next county and a team of a dozen men, my father among them, to get the car up the cliff. They lowered the men and their axes and hacksaws and chain saws down to the river bottom in a big basket. I would like to have seen that operation, the car lifting up, riding on the hook of the crane, and a couple of the men scrambling underneath with the chattering saws, cutting away the last few roots that held it. And the car cranking slowly toward the sky, banging now and then against the rock wall, sending stone chips and bits of rust and metal and who knows what else in a shower down on the men who sliced it loose. The stuff probably got in their eyes, them not able to resist watching as it rose into the air and away.

The engine block broke free of its mountings about halfway to the cliff top and dropped out of the bottom of the Packard, trailing the transmission, the metal parts pinwheeling back down the stone wall. The lightened chassis rocketed upward, fouling the crane's steel hawser against a rock outcropping. The men scattered, shouting and pushing each other out of the way, stumbling to get clear. Nobody was really sure which way the falling motor would bounce when it got to the bottom, and the team ended up scattered in a rough semicircle, crouching behind bushes and saplings that could not possibly stop a heavy object falling from that height. The heavy V-8 mill hit a spot of soft ground and didn't bounce at all, just sank deep into the dirt like it had been planted there.

My dad told me they managed to haul the car the rest of the way up in one piece, even with the snarled cable, swung it over the edge with the huge crane, and dropped it onto the back of the flatbed wrecker that he drives, neat as you please, and he chained it down and brought it on to the yard. He said a couple of sparrows burst from the windows when he was winding the chain tight. They were frightened by the rattle of the links against what was left of the car body.

He jumped, thinking it was maybe the spirits of the people who had died in the car finally escaping in the form of those birds.

Why weren't there more? I asked him. *Four people in the car but only a couple birds.*

I don't know, he said. *Maybe there were more birds, and I just thought it was a couple.*

You could still see them in there, he said, dark shapes among the limbs of the trees that had grown up, and the sticks and the trash that the birds had brought, the dried skeleton of the driver propped behind the wheel, the others still in their seats. They were the driver's family that had died along with him, or maybe they were his friends, or business associates. Nobody knew.

A bird flies from the empty windshield now, bursting out with its wings fluttering, a sound like the shuffling of a deck of cards. I'm ready for it, but the others fall back a couple of steps and Lou, the little one, gives a squeak. This is stupid, I think, standing five yards from the thing when we come a pretty good way to see it up close and have spent time searching. We don't have much longer to look. The shadows are getting long and deep, and Legg won't wait on us forever. I go to the car and peer in the driver's window.

At first it just looks like a hedge has grown up in the car, some kind of a thicket, bracken that is green and leafed out. I take a sniff, and the only smell on the air is honeysuckle, and the faint scent of metal. The leaves move in a breeze that has sprung up. Lou stands beside me. He's embarrassed that he yelled at the bird, and he's showing off. He calls back to the others, "Hey, it's a car full of brush." He turns to me and he says, "You brought us out here to see this? This old piece of junk?" He kicks at the fender nearest him, and his boot on the metal makes a hollow clang.

"My old man told me," is all I can think of to say.

"Your old man's screwed up," he tells me. The others have come up close too, and they're standing around the car. Their voices are loud, like they're glad to have found out that the car's got no dead Buckeyes inside it, even though that's what they came to see, what they paid the old man to see. Lou tells me to hand over some money. "You owe me thirty cents," he says, "because that's what I give to get in here, and now it's nothing like what you said." He's leaning against the trunk of the car, pushing against it with his little legs, rocking the whole thing. The car's rotted suspension is giving out these little cries every time he pushes.

"I owe you nothing," I say to Lou, and I take a step toward him, figuring to shake him a little to shut him up. The others are watching us, and I know it is my dad has brought me here, where my friends are mocking me. His jokes. His idea of a joke. An empty car. Lou's still pushing at it, looking at me with this expression on his face, like he thinks I won't hit him, which is an error on his part because I will, I surely will. Somebody else, one of the bigger kids, is shoving at the other side of the car, and they've got a pretty good rhythm going, like they plan to rock the gutted Packard over on its side.

Inside the car, a big mess of sticks, a squirrel's nest or a bird's, gives way with the car's heaving, collapses onto the floor. The screen of brush parts as though a hand is passed through it, and something is gazing out of the back of the car at us. Skin like yellow leather, long lank brittle hair that looks as though the birds have been using it to add to their houses, and dark eye sockets which seem to stare even though there are no eyes in them. It's like an illusion, a magic trick, where at first I couldn't see this thing sitting in the back seat of the car. Now that I know what I'm looking for, I see it perfectly, and I wonder how it could be that I missed it, that we all missed it, before.

It's small, like a child, a girl child, and its hands are folded in its lap. Its clothes have melted away over the years, or been taken away by animals, and it is that same yellow color all over, and wrinkled. It's peering out the window nearest it. At its side is another like it, but this one is even smaller, and its head is missing, maybe rolled off and gone under the seat. Two others, larger, sit in front. They are slumped together, like tired people after a long day of driving. It is a family in there—mother, father, sister, brother—and it must seem to them like they are somehow on the road again after all those years, a rough road that makes the car bounce, and bounce, and bounce.

The others have spotted them, and they back away one by one, until it is just Lou and the larger kid shoving. Then the large kid sees them too, catches them out of the corner of his eye, and it is just Lou. He stops what he's doing, but he thinks we're joking with him. When he looks into the car, he sees nothing. Even when I point things out to him, the bones twined among the tough scrub—"Look, there's the hands, the fingers, lying on the knee. There's the *skull* for God's sake"— he claims it's nothing at all but just weeds and garbage. I don't believe him, that he can't see this family, and I take hold of him, I'm going to shove him in there close where he can feel them, if he won't see.

I'm dragging him to the driver's side door of the Packard when the old man comes into sight around a big pile of loose bumpers. He's got his dog on a rope lead, and the mastiff is straining against him, giving the rope short little jerks. The old man's hand, the one holding the rope, flies out from his body every time the dog leaps forward, and I wonder how strong a grip he has on the thing. It's strangling itself against the knot in the leash, and strings of milky drool hang down off its jowls.

"What the hell?" he says. He seems surprised to see us. "You're still here?" he says. He must be making a last patrol of the place before locking up. "Christ, I said ten minutes, not ten days. Get the hell on out of here."

The others are already making for the gate, Lou at the head of the pack, but I stay where I am for a little longer. It's dark in the yard, dusk getting on to night, and when I look into the car it takes me a minute to make out the little girl, the daughter, in the back seat. Suddenly I'm not sure anymore which is her and which is her brother. I'm not sure what is a bare stick, and what is the bone of her forearm. It's black inside the Packard, no colors showing at all now.

"I said get out," the old man says. His voice is shaking, and he lets his grip on the dog slip just a bit more.

"I heard," I say, and I walk past him. I keep my pace steady.

"I know you heard me," he says. "I know your daddy. He works for me. You better not be stealing nothing. Nothing better be gone from here." I'm out of his sight, but his voice carries to me as I go. "I can check up. I can tell your daddy to smack fire out of you!" He goes on for a while, but it is hard to make out his words, the farther away I get from him.

I walk out of the gate of the salvage yard, and nobody is there. All of them are gone, running to get home, I guess. I wonder what they saw that made them back off from the car. They must have seen the same thing that I did. Or maybe they just saw me seeing it, and that was enough to scare them off. Remembering, I can't tell which way it is, and I know they won't be able to recall either, if I ask them about it at school tomorrow.

All the way home, I make a list in my head of the things my father has brought home from the yard, items that nobody wanted or thought to claim. He's brought home bracelets; two full sets of dentures and an upper plate; a Fuller Brush salesman's sample kit; some tiny atomizers full of cologne that he gave to me, and some miniature bottles of liquor that he kept; a suitcase with a busted handle, full of women's party clothes; several car jacks, with and without handles; spare tires, full of air and flat; packets of bobby pins; a .45 caliber pistol with a broken slide; a crushed box of chocolates; the waxy white hand of a manikin; a barrel full of greasy chain; eyeglasses; sunglasses; empty artillery shells; and a hundred other things that it's impossible for me to remember or that he probably never even showed me.

He keeps these things stacked around the house, or gives them away to people who can't use them either. Our neighbors used to laugh when he gave them stuff, but now they just take the items that he hands over and then carry them away, God knows where to. He never asks about the fate of what he gives.

As I walk, the air grows cool and I wish for a jacket, wondering what prize he figures to bear home from this latest find, what terrible next thing will make its way into our house.

The Butcher Cock

S nag Drum has one of his sick headaches, so his son, fifteen-
year-old Ivanhoe, sits behind the wheel of the station wagon.
He's gunning it along the dirt lane to Pluskat's, down the gauntlet
of ornamental concrete chickens. The unpainted chickens line both
sides of the road, right up to the doors of Pluskat's barn, where the
fights are held. Really, it's the same chicken over and over and over
again. Pluskat poured them himself. The chickens stand better than
two feet tall, their high-combed heads tilted to one side.

Snag groans, half from the nauseating headache, half because they
are late. The back of the station wagon is full of animal cages. The
cages are full of gamecocks. The roosters grab at the wire of the cages
with their hard claws, they drive their beaks against the metal. They're
working to get at each other back there. Snag and Ivanhoe can't afford
to be late for the derby. They can't afford not to fight, not to win. "Go
on," Snag moans, head in his hands. Ivanhoe takes his eyes off the
road, looks over at Snag for a second, and the station wagon plows
into the left-hand rank of chickens.

The sound from outside the car is terrible: rupturing concrete, metal
pulled screaming away from metal, the front bumper dragged loose,
the smash and tinkle of glass as the left headlamp winks out, then the
right; gush of steam as the aluminum grille tilts sharply back, as the
radiator collapses, as the heavy engine block shifts in its mounts. Pathetic
honk of the horn as it goes too. Rumble of shattered decorative chickens
under the tires and floorboards, thundering against the floor panel of

the car as though the pieces will punch straight through. Roar of exhaust through straight pipe as the muffler tears loose and bounds along behind them on the soft dirt surface of the lane. A jagged hunk of concrete jumps up and shaves off the driver's-side mirror, clean as a whistle.

And inside the car: Snag screaming *Watch watch watch!* up front as he lunges for the steering wheel, and the roosters in the back all gone mad. Cages sliding and somersaulting, the cage containing the Kelso Yellow-Leg catching Ivanhoe painfully behind the ear and crashing down onto the bench front seat, cartwheeling from there upside down onto the transmission hump. Ivanhoe's crying out *I'm trying!* for all he's worth as he fights the wheel to the right, but the car will not come over, riding fast and straight as an arrow, chickens going down before it like ninepins. It is as though Ivanhoe is deliberately mowing them under.

The car breaks right at last, and the front left fender kisses a final chicken, spins it neatly in place and tips it over onto its back. They slalom to the middle of the road, slew to a stop.

Silence. A hubcap rolls past and down the road, moonlight flaring from the spinner as it goes.

The roosters gawp around them. Snag crouches in the passenger-side footwell, hands clasped before him as though he's praying. Ivanhoe listens carefully for the beat of his own heart. He's got a pancake heart, delicate organ always threatening to give out, and if it's going to stop on him, it might as well go ahead and do it. *Quit now*, he thinks, but the pancake heart labors on.

~ ~ ~

Ivanhoe wears the fighting cock's long-knife tied to his left ankle. This is the dream he dreams every night, and can never remember. In the waking world, the long-knife terrifies him. His mouth grows dry as he straps those three inches of curving oily steel to a rooster's leg. Here, though, he sweeps his terrible wings back just to hear the crisp rustle of the feathers, he cranes his neck to take in the glitter of the long-knife's keen edge. He's waiting on the pit master, and when the call comes he will rise up, heart hammering his chest into splinters, war cry breaking loose from his—

Not his mouth, not Ivanhoe's mouth, with its soft sensuous lips, a girl's lips. Lips for which he's been taunted all his life: *Sweetboy, Sugarmouth.*

This is a hard beak. Not the wretched pancake heart, either, Ivanhoe's flattened heart that limps along beneath the thin concavity of his breastbone. This rounded pulsing muscle, this conqueror's heart hurls him screaming into the air, the long-knife slashing downward, cutting deep into the dubbed head of the opposing cock.

His burnished feathers curve tight over his body like armor. He doesn't have a name in the pit. He is a wicked feathered glasher, a battle stag waiting on the kill.

He knows the rooster he's pitted against. Sleek black cockerel, a hefty Sumatra Game, with the wide breast and strong feathered shanks of the ground fighter. Tut, his old man's favorite, King Tut, longtime killer, eyes like polished quartz stone. Dream-Ivanhoe strokes upward, he's swift, an air fighter. He lashes down with the cruel long-knife, King Tut gaping up, earthbound, wide-beaked and stiff-tongued with fury as Ivanhoe wings over, the knife strike straight to the cape of feathers at the throat. The black cockerel reels, he's necked, he's finished, he's dead.

~ ~ ~

Snag's out of the car in a flash, pries open the rear of the station wagon and begins pawing through the tumbled cages. "Get the Kelso," he says to Ivanhoe, who leans down to look at the bent and distorted metal crate. No way the rooster could have survived the wreck, but there he is nonetheless, burbling grumpily, full of reproach. He sounds just like a percolator on the boil. Kelso Yellow-Leg, the butcher cock, whom Ivanhoe adores. Blinkered Kelso Yellow-Leg, with his blind and ruptured eye.

"Take the Kelso and go," Snag says. He's found King Tut's crate among the jumbled cages, and he has the black game bird out, he's stroking its rumpled feathers. Champion bird. They're maybe a quarter of a mile from Pluskat's barn, and they can't think about the car now. They have to get their birds to the derby. Ivanhoe drags the Kelso's cage free, knees loose, fingers twitching. The adrenaline of the crash is hitting him hard, and he wants to sit down. He wants to cry.

"Go on, go on," Snag says, and then he pauses. "Will you be okay?" he asks. "Your heart..."

"My heart will do what my heart will do," Ivanhoe says. Suddenly he doesn't want to sit down anymore, he doesn't want to cry. He wants to walk down the road, he wants to disappear into the dark. He wants to forget about the smashed car and the shaken roosters and his worried old man and the line of shattered concrete chickens. He wants to leave them all far behind.

~ ~ ~

In the dream, Ivanhoe's wings turn without warning to heavy sodden cardboard, his fierce green-and-yellow plumage becomes nothing but candle wax, it smears and drips under the heat of the big sodium arc lamps that light the arena, leaving him smooth and pink and naked, a dunghill bird who won't raise his hackles. Leaving him a weeping frightened boy awake in his sweat-soaked bed, a boy with soft pouting lips and a tubby belly and ungainly limbs. Leaving him alone, infused with the squalid flavor of the dream but without its memory. Leaving him dream-haunted Ivanhoe.

~ ~ ~

Headlights from behind as Ivanhoe and Snag struggle along the road. Snag banged his knee against something during the wreck, and it's swelling like a goiter under his gabardines, hot and painful, slowing him dreadfully. The lights come up on them, sweep past, and in the rumble of dual pipes and the red glare of taillights, Ivanhoe recognizes Billy Shoemaker's fancy old Lincoln with the suicide doors. Big Billy Shoemaker, a high roller, arriving late because, for him, there's no need to hurry. The Lincoln halts up the road a way, bangs into reverse, and comes tear-assing backward toward them. Ivanhoe has to leap out of its path. Billy leans out the driver's window like an eager dog.

"Ouch!" Billy says, slamming his hard hand against the door panel of the Lincoln. "Saw what you did back there. Ouch! Ouch!"

"Can we catch a ride with you, Billy?" Snag asks. "Up the barn." He's got Tut's cage braced against his hip. Billy's face is bright, the skin tight and shiny over the bones. There's someone in the Lincoln with him, face indistinct in the dark interior of the car.

"Chicken killers!" Billy says, reaching behind him and throwing open the rear door. "Car killers!"

Snag hustles Ivanhoe before him and they climb into the spacious back seat of the Lincoln. Maneuvering the cages inside the car proves trying, but at last they're settled. Billy's turned backward, looking at them a moment longer, all smiles. The front-seat passenger is a girl—no surprise to see a pretty girl in the shotgun seat of Billy Shoemaker's Lincoln—a girl Ivanhoe doesn't know.

She's staring at him like he's something from Mars, so he feels emboldened to stare back. Light dusting of freckles, broad lineless brow, pale solemn mouth, hair caught up in a red bandanna—but he knows that hidden hair, he knows its springy, coarse, slightly oily texture as though his hands are plunged in it at that moment, he knows its scent, like olives (which he has never smelled, never tasted), its flavor like sea salt. How could he know that? He blinks as Billy throws the Lincoln into gear, sees that the girl in the front seat is laughing at him.

"What a strange bird is the pelican," she says to him.

"Pardon?" he says.

"Her beak can hold more than her belly can."

Snag tends to King Tut. Ivanhoe struggles to come up with a reply.

"She's been saying shit like that all evening," Billy says. Then, confidingly, "She's down from Irish Mountain." He pronounces it like *mounting. Irish Mounting.* He rolls his eyes.

Ivanhoe knows about Irish Mountain and the people who live up there. They aren't like the ones down in the foothills, like Snag and Billy Shoemaker and Ivanhoe, who don't dream, or don't remember their dreams. Up on Irish Mountain, he has heard, their dreams are an ocean. Up on Irish Mountain, they swim in and out of each other's dreams like fishes.

When Ivanhoe wakes in the mornings, he struggles to recall his dreams. Within the dreams hides the answer. It must be there, because it isn't anywhere else in his life, it isn't anywhere else in the waking world. Not in the gamecocks, not in Snag's tremulous attention. If Ivanhoe could remember the dreams, he would know the answer, and from the answer he imagines he might be able to guess at the nature of the question. The question and the answer to the question: it's like the chicken and the egg to him. He keeps turning the thing over in his mind, trying to decide which comes first.

"The pelican in the wilderness," Ivanhoe says, and his mouth feels strange to him as it shapes the words. He feels as though he's giving the second part of some secret code in a spy movie. "The pelican in the wilderness, with nothing to feed her birds, wounds her breast and nourishes them upon her blood."

The girl's eyes widen momentarily. He has surprised her. Good.

"Damn," says Billy. They are at Pluskat's barn, cars and trucks parked at rough angles all around them. "Now you with the pelicans too. I thought you Drum fellows were chicken farmers."

"Gamecocks," says Snag. He hates it when anyone refers to his precious birds as chickens.

~ ~ ~

A petit-pointe picture of Jesus hangs at the foot of Ivanhoe's bed. His mother made it when he was little, not long before she died, but it looks much older than that, it looks like something that has traveled forward from another time. In the picture, Jesus' chest is torn open, blood running down, but his face—you can tell this even from across the room, the detail in the needlework is that fine—is peaceful. He's a skinny little hillbilly Jesus with bandy legs and close-set eyes and a clever, foxy face. He's naked and alone, but he's not afraid. Around the border of the picture runs the legend about the pelican. *The pelican in the wilderness...*Ivanhoe sees it every time he wakes from the dream, when he wakes to the raucous crowing of the gamecocks in the chookyard...*nourishes them upon her blood.* There is no pelican in the picture.

Ivanhoe wishes his mother had lived, a little longer at least. He would have liked to ask her what in the world that hanging might signify. *Questions.*

~ ~ ~

Ivanhoe feels sick in his belly, fixing the long-knife to the left spur of the Kelso Yellow-Leg as the rooster dances and skitters and kicks, sensing what's coming, wattles and comb swelling with hot blood, eyes capturing and holding the light. The next bout is a Welsh main. That means that Ivanhoe will pit his bird against another, and the winner of that bout will stay in the pit against a fresh stag, as will the winner of that bout, and so on, a total of seven fights. Only the gamest bird can stick it out in a Welsh main from the beginning, without going under hack or dying.

The Kelso Yellow-Leg seems terribly old to Ivanhoe. Old as Snag, even older maybe. The Kelso jabs him with the long-knife, drawing blood from the sensitive web of skin between thumb and forefinger, then stands tall and looks at Ivanhoe unabashedly with his one good eye. Ivanhoe loves the Kelso for its game heart and its strong legs and its blinkered eye.

On the ground near Ivanhoe's feet, King Tut gabbles and talks. Ivanhoe thinks he's saying words. What is he saying? *Hogbody.* Is he calling Ivanhoe names? *Sweetboy. Sugarmouth.* Ivanhoe nudges the cage with the side of his foot but doesn't dare kick it.

Snag has gone after the remaining roosters with a couple of the other men. Pluskat was pissed at first when he heard about his ornamental chickens, but Big Billy Shoemaker convinced him that it was really pretty funny after all. He convinced Pluskat that Snag and Ivanhoe got the worst of it, the front end of their car stove in, their birds rattled, Snag's swollen knee. Pluskat, the pit master, can see the humor in that.

"You'll be copacetic," Ivanhoe tells the Kelso Yellow-Leg. He steels his heart. When the call comes, he'll send the Kelso into battle. The bird itself wants to fight. It peers nearsightedly around the barn, searching for an opponent. The barn is tall-ceilinged, filled with sizzling light, with the odors of cigarette smoke and sawdust and sweat and hot feathers, the smell of blood. The crowd sits expectantly on flimsy folding risers or in lawn chairs near the pit's edge, talking together in low tones. From time to time, this man or that one will rise from his place and call to the birds in the pit, shout at the handlers, hands hooked, sawing at the air.

"You've never been much of anywhere, have you?" It's the girl, the one from Irish Mountain. She has come up on Ivanhoe without warning. She eyes the Kelso. "Will he hurt me?"

Ivanhoe holds up his wounded hand. "He might," he says, and she keeps her distance.

It's true that he's never been much of anywhere. Never seen anything, really, except for the room where he lives, the thin-walled clapboard house of his old man's, the patch of land in the foothills with its strutting gamecocks, over which Irish Mountain glowers. Never seen anything but the little tilting chookhouses and fly pens filled with sharp-clawed, empty-headed, gimlet-eyed fighting roosters.

Over the shoulder of the girl, Ivanhoe can make out Pluskat and
Billy Shoemaker and some others gathered together in a tight knot,
arguing, their faces twisted—but they're not angry, they're laughing.
Pluskat claps his hands, and Ivanhoe sees him as if for the first time: a
capering, agitated hobgoblin. The men around him imps and beasts,
their mouths nothing but damp toothy maws, their hair thick and
stinking as pelts, their voices the braying of beasts. It's because of the
girl he can see this, he's sure. She's showing it to him. He's glad that
Snag isn't in sight. He's glad that he cannot see himself.

"I hear you share your dreams," he says. It's not easy for him to talk
to the girl—she's so strange, and so pretty—but he forges on. "Up
where you come from."

The girl nods. "I could show you the Eye of God if you want. Up at
the top," she says.

The Eye of God is an Irish Mountain thing, like the dreams. All his
life Ivanhoe's heard the name, but no one has ever been able to describe
to him what it might be. A wheel in a wheel is all that Snag can tell him.
Like the wheel that took the prophet Ezekiel. A wheel in a wheel, way
in the middle of the air.

"I'd like to see that," he says.

"You see it, and it sees you," she says.

Would he like that? An eye like a great wheel, staring down at him.
He is not much to look at, Ivanhoe knows. For the first time it occurs
to him that he might not like the answer, if he finds it. Might not like
the question either.

"Looks *into* you," the girl says. "Into and through you."

Here and there heads in the crowd turn to assess the girl's slender
form, hard eyes roam over her wide shoulders, down her long back to
her waist—from her waist to her rear to her muscular legs. The hard
eyes glint with appreciation. Ivanhoe wonders how old she might be.
He wonders if she thinks he's older than he is. He's sizable for his age,
and consequently clumsy; his coordination hasn't yet caught up with
his frame.

"My family's up there," the girl says. "They were scared to come
down, but I'm not."

And then Pluskat, the pit master, calls the bout, the Welsh main: no
more time for conversation. Ivanhoe wants to ask her when she'll show

him, how he might get there, to the top of Irish Mountain. If he were to decide to come. He wants to ask why she has come down to the foothills, what her family is scared of. He wants to ask if she was serious, what she said. He casts around for Snag, to get him to corner for the Kelso, give him another minute or two with the girl, but Snag's not back from the wrecked station wagon yet.

"Pit your birds, gents," Pluskat bellows, and Ivanhoe's obliged to climb into the arena, the Kelso Yellow-Leg clutched in his outstretched hands. The butcher cock has seen its opponent now, and it's vibrating, light-feathered body thrumming with tension. The Kelso Yellow-Leg feels like a running motor in Ivanhoe's grip.

~ ~ ~

Irish Mountain was once an island, eons ago. An island thrusting its green bulk up above the savage waters, and the valleys below the mountain nothing more than lightless airless rifts in the ocean floor. The foothills where Ivanhoe lives with Snag and the fighting cocks, these were the heights of the ocean floor. Dwelling place of the unthinkable Leviathan, and God moving dolefully above the gray roiling surface.

At the cement works, the quarriers dynamite the rock, peel it in great slabs from the quarry walls, and fossil-pictures of ancient fish and mollusks and whatnot float mutely to the surface—Ivanhoe has seen them—and then the quarriers grind the rock down to gravel and the gravel down to grit and sand. His old man Snag grinds fish into a rich stinking soupy paste, to feed to King Tut and the other gamecocks. The fish keep them strong, keep their feathers glossy and supple and impermeable. Snag feeds them grit, too, and small stones, for their gizzards, so they can digest their food. Where a man has teeth in his head, a chicken has stones in its gut.

~ ~ ~

Somewhere in the midst of the Welsh main, Snag returns with the other birds—the dignified Harvard Whites, the high-priced Blacksmith Hatch, the scalawag Racey Mugs and Cottontail Shufflers, the single ancient Claret Roundhead, which fights with the gaff—and his breath is bitter, his face distant, features blurred and muzzy. He's been drinking milky potato liquor in the back of the borrowed pickup truck, nestled among his birds in their bent cages, nursing the hurt of his wrecked car, his aching skull, his wrenched knee, the jibes of Pluskat, who won't leave him alone. "Chicken killer!" he calls out from the middle of the pit, must have picked it up from Billy. "Car killer!"

Snag is usually gentle with Ivanhoe, almost courtly; mild toward his stable of battle stags. The pit is life to him, it's the entire world—he's a little man with hardly a possession to his name, but his birds are well known in the foothills, respected and feared, especially the dreaded black cockerel King Tut. If men know him at all, it is because his birds fight until they die, they strike and strike and strike until their hearts give out. But tonight Snag is on fire, he shouts at Ivanhoe, he screams at the Kelso Yellow-Leg as it struggles through the endless numbing bouts of the Welsh main, as it is wounded and comes on strong and is wounded again. "I'll put you in a pie, you whoreson!" he shrieks at the bird. "I'll eat you for my God-damned supper!"

Into Ivanhoe's ear he whispers, in a voice unlike any the boy has heard from him before, "Get your ass in gear, hogbody. You got a car to pay for." He casts a look over at Pluskat. "And a bunch of"—here his speech becomes deliberate, as though he's delivering a message even he does not fully comprehend—"custom handmade ornamental poured-concrete *fowl!*" He spits the last word.

Pluskat laughs, overhearing, and the Welsh main continues. Ivanhoe scoops up the Kelso and blows on his comb to revive him, forces open his beak and spits into it. At the last, it's only a couple of weak dunghill birds that the tired Kelso faces, and the lean old butcher cock takes them down, one after the other, indomitable Kelso Yellow-Leg drives them into the dirt of the pit and crows over their corpses. Snag stands to one side with King Tut (whom he calls Tut-Tut like a pet, Tut the lizard-cold death dealer) cradled in his arms, speaking to the black cockerel in sighs.

~ ~ ~

Ivanhoe hoped to look for the Irish Mountain girl after the Welsh main, but Snag will not let him leave the pit. Ivanhoe has never pitted more than a couple of birds during a derby. Tonight, every bird in their stable passes through his bloody hands. His pancake heart works vainly in his chest, his breath hitches, his vision dims. Sometimes they win. More often they lose.

Ivanhoe stumbles as he follows the birds around the periphery of the little arena, stepping on the roosters in his exhaustion. Pluskat harangues him, mocking him for his short wind. *Sweetboy*, he calls him, and the crowd laughs as though this is an act, as though it's part of the show. *Sugarmouth*, and Pluskat smacks his lips deliciously at Ivanhoe.

The dead dunghills stack up at Snag's feet. Again and again he passes new birds over the pit barrier to an exhausted Ivanhoe. All their roosters are dying now—some tide has turned against them, inexorably against them, and they will be left with nothing. The look on Snag's face is blank. Once he winks at Ivanhoe, who stands with a slender Racey Mug dangling dead from his fist, a long slow wink, as though half of Snag is falling asleep. *Hogbody!* someone in the crowd calls out.

At last, it's the final bout of the night, and Ivanhoe holds out his hands. This time, though, the bird is King Tut, and Snag shakes his head. He will pit Tut himself. He steps over the barrier, and Pluskat comes to assist him, takes his elbow and helps him, even reaches out a hand for Tut when Snag's battered knee threatens to give out. Snag snatches the bird back, finds his footing, and enters the ring with his head down, his shoulders hunched.

The crowd's out of their seats, they press against the barrier, faces dark with desire. "Tut!" they call. They have wanted to see this bird, this legendary Sumatra Game, all evening. They have traveled from all over the foothills to see the black cockerel fight. "King Tut!" they shout. It will be King Tut against one of Pluskat's champions, a rainbow-colored Poland Titan with a spray of wild feathers at its neck and a vivid eye, a young bird that's been making a name for itself.

Ivanhoe, paroled, leaves the pit. He's weaving. He can't make himself care about the final fight. He wants to find the girl. He wants to hear about the dreams. He wants to hear about the Eye of God. He spots Big Billy Shoemaker in the crowd—the girl is not beside him—waves at him to get his attention, ask him where she has gone. But Billy has fixed his handsome face on the fight, his pupils dilated, his jaw moving up and down, his throat working. He's shouting "Tut! King Tut!" like all the rest.

~ ~ ~

Disaster. King Tut is defeated. King Tut is dead.

~ ~ ~

Ivanhoe remembers. For the first time, waking in his room well before dawn, he remembers his dream. Remembers wearing the long-knife, and the strength of his wings, and the power in his heart. He remembers cuppling King Tut with a savage blow to the head, Tut reeling and falling. He knows that he killed Tut. It was not Pluskat's young Poland Titan. It was Ivanhoe.

The hillbilly Jesus looks at him from the petit-pointe sampler on the wall. *The pelican in the wilderness...* He decides then that he will climb Irish Mountain. There, he can leave behind Ivanhoe of the foothills, he can leave Snag and the beast-men of the pit and the stinking chookhouses and *Hogbody* and *Sweetboy* and his pathetic pancake heart behind. He will leave the waking world behind, he will leap and slash and fly, his heart will pound in his chest without pain, without leaving him breathless and weak. He will be whole.

~ ~ ~

Ivanhoe wakes with the first crowing. It's the Kelso Yellow-Leg calling him, always the first. Soon the others will respond, those few that are left, and it will be a small cacophony amongst the chookhouses, but for now it's the lone clarion voice of the Kelso, and it sounds as though the Kelso is calling his name into the glassy morning air: *Ivanhoe! Ivanhoe!*

No worry about Snag rising today, even with the clamor in the yard. Snag was broken, sodden and stumbling, openly weeping when they finally reached home in the back of Big Billy Shoemaker's Lincoln. Snag is flat-backed in his sagging bed. Ivanhoe would be surprised to see him before noon.

He steps from the house, takes his first look of the day at Irish Mountain. It looms over him, steep faces gray in the dawn light, summit wreathed in angry clouds. Between the hill on which he lives and the mountain proper lies a narrow valley with a shivering creek at its bottom. Drum's Valley, they call it, he and Snag, and Drum's Creek, because there is no one around to call it anything else.

He trots across the chookyard. A once-powerful Harvard White lies stiff and dead on the floor of its pen. Poor little man—but that is how it is with these birds when they're wounded, they live or they die, they have a game heart or they don't. The Harvard White's feathers stick out awkwardly in all directions, still glossy, still carrying the deep sheen of a diet rich in shell corn and pulped fish.

The other pens are empty. No fractious Racey Mugs, only a couple of sharp-voiced Cottontail Shufflers remaining. No more Blacksmith Hatch, no aged Claret Roundhead. One chookhouse slightly larger than the rest, its boards more tightly fitted, its floor cleaner: the house of the black cockerel, the brutal Sumatra, King Tut. Empty.

"Ivanhoe!" He whirls, caught—but Snag is not there. His eye falls on the lone occupied chookhouse behind him, and the rooster within. It's the golden butcher cock, the Kelso Yellow-Leg, unblinkered eye fixed on Ivanhoe, neck outstretched, beak wide. The cock trumpets, and this time its voice is just a rooster's voice.

The Kelso Yellow-Leg. The good old Kelso will make the perfect companion on his climb. The bird crows again, and in its cry there is to Ivanhoe's ears the sound of pure delight. It turns a circle in the confines of its cage, waggles its small head, fluffs its feathers so that it looks twice its size. Admirable Kelso Yellow-Leg!

Ivanhoe quickly has the Kelso out of its house and into one of the small carrying cages, slung from his left hand, and they're walking together toward the shallow draw that leads down into Drum's Valley, where he will cross Drum's Creek and begin the arduous trip up Irish Mountain.

~ ~ ~

Ivanhoe reaches the low shoulder of the mountain with surprising ease. His pancake heart, usually so troublesome, vexes him not at all. The Kelso Yellow-Leg shifts its weight from leg to leg to keep its balance in the cage that swings by his side. Ivanhoe glories in the privilege he feels in the spacious understory of the forest. It's all virgin hemlocks in here, friendly creaking

hemlocks, each tree standing in its own little clearing, and all around them thick hedges of waxy rhododendron and blooming wildflowers. Great black bees bobble their workaday way from the bell of one flower to the petals of the next.

Thick green light filters down through the dense canopy of leaves, vegetable light filling the clearings, bathing the air around him. This is what he imagines it must be like to walk along the bottom of a shallow sea. He has rubbed his skin with pennyroyal plant, so mosquitoes do not plague him, though they shrill in his ears and buzz his head, and the sharp singing of their wings makes him wince in anticipation of stings that don't come.

He bats his hands at the swarming insects, and they scatter only to collect again, hanging in the same spot in the air. Pushing through a close-grown rhododendron grove, he steps out into a large clearing. At its center, a vast hemlock, its trunk, its branches twisted and humped and corded with age. A skeleton hemlock stripped of bark and clothed all over in soft green moss. How old must such a tree be, to have grown to such a fantastic size?

"Mister," Ivanhoe says, addressing the tree. He is surprised by the smallness of his voice. The Kelso Yellow-Leg falls silent, and Ivanhoe finds himself desperately hoping that the bird will stay that way. He feels tempted to drop down and kneel before the hemlock, with its green-draped branches thrust out toward him.

"Mister," he says again, and it feels to him like the right form of address. "Do you know the girl who lives up in here somewhere? Talks about pelicans?"

No response. It's too paltry a question. Such a tree must stir itself only over questions of significance. Ivanhoe might care about the girl, but clearly Mister does not. Perhaps Mister does not care about people at all. This place is empty of men, but it's not at all empty—it's the opposite of empty, filled with something that presses invisibly against the eyes, something that begs to be seen.

"Do you know about the Eye of God on top of the mountain?"

No response to this either. Clearly, Mister disdains the Eye. Here in this clearing, among all these lesser trees, Mister is a god himself.

"Mister, do you dream?"

Nothing. Ivanhoe is beginning to feel a bit desperate. The tree is ancient, its roots sunk deep into the unyielding flesh of Irish Mountain, it has eaten the minerals and the water of the mountain, it has breathed this air for—what? A thousand years, or a thousand thousand, it's all the same to Ivanhoe. He can think of only one thing that might break the awful silence of the skeleton hemlock.

He holds out the carrying cage before him. "Mister, do you want my chicken?" he asks.

Still nothing. Ivanhoe gasps with relief. He will not be asked to give up the Kelso Yellow-Leg. Not yet, at any rate.

The earth shifts beneath him, and he stumbles, sinks to one knee. The Kelso gives a startled squawk. The earth continues to roll queasily, and Ivanhoe goes to both knees, drops to all fours like an animal. It's his pancake heart quailing in his chest, it makes him thick and dopey, it causes the world to swim before his eyes. The pancake heart flutters again, and he slips onto his elbows, his belly.

"Mister," he says, and his voice is a whisper. "Can I lay down here a minute? I'm awful tired."

No reply to this request either, but Ivanhoe decides that in this instance he will take silence for assent. He crawls to the tree, wriggling like a newt, sets his cheek against its cool, moss-covered flank, and sleeps.

~ ~ ~

And dreams of the girl. She stands in the clearing, beneath the gargantuan hemlock. At first he thinks that she's wearing a cloak made of some strange, shifting fabric. Then he realizes that she is nude, her body covered with twittering birds. Gorgeous little cedar waxwings, glossy and smooth as water-polished stones, perch on her shoulders, cling to her arms, her hair, her thighs, the taut skin of her stomach. The waxwings push themselves against her. They knead her flesh with their tiny claws.

"Having nothing to feed her young birds, the pelican," she begins, and then falters. She brushes at the birds on her head, her shoulders, her chest, and they cloud around her. She flutters her hands at them. "...Her bill can hold more than her belly can." She bares her bosom, and her face is placid. Ivanhoe's terrified that she's bleeding, that her ribs will be exposed, a terrible rent in her flesh, blood bubbling forth. There's no blood, though. What she offers him is her soft breast. What she offers him is the freshet of her milk.

~ ~ ~

When he wakes, it is afternoon getting on toward evening. The hemlock towers over him, its attitude unreadable in the creeping dusk. He takes stock, finds that his heart seems to be keeping steady rhythm again, and rises, bracing himself against the knobby trunk of the tree. "Thanks, Mister," he says, and goes to the carrying cage where it lies on its side in the clearing.

"You okay?" he asks the Kelso Yellow-Leg, and the rooster gabbles indignantly. It must be hungry, Ivanhoe realizes, but he has nothing to feed it. He feels a bit hollow himself, and for a moment he considers heading back down the mountain, returning to the foothills and the game farm. A mockingbird cries from the branches overhead, its voice the voice of Snag, angry Snag. *Hogbody!*

He will not go back to that. Nothing for it but to continue up. On to the summit. "Goodbye," he says to Mister, touching his forehead respectfully. In the lowering darkness, does the tree make a nearly imperceptible gesture, does it lower one of its limbs in quiet salute? Ivanhoe cannot tell.

~ ~ ~

Staggering through a bog of deep peat, a bowl carved into the mountainside by the movement of some ancient glacier. And what bounty has sprung up in the wake of the glacier's passing! Cranberry vines, thickets of swamp rose and speckled alder, sedges and flowers: swamp candle, damp silky orchids, trilliums, lady's slippers, jewelweed glittering among the tough grasses, even carnivorous sundew, its leaves covered with sticky hairs. The pennyroyal seems to have worn off, the mosquitoes pestering Ivanhoe unmercifully, and he wishes the insect-devouring sundew plants good hunting. The cage bangs painfully against his hip with every step he takes.

"Where are we now, Kelso?" he asks the bird in the cage. A narrow stream winds its way through the bog, and he is thirsty, but the peat has stained the water the deep brown color of strong tea, so he does not drink, following the stream toward its source in hopes that the flow will clear.

Which it does, at the edge of the bog, half a mile on. Golden trout hang nearly motionless in the cool current, their red-veined tails waving lazily to keep them in place. Their lipless mouths gape. Ivanhoe tries to think of a way to catch the nearest of them, its dark bulging eye rolling toward him as he kneels at the bank of the stream but not seeming to take him in.

Even the fish gruel that Snag feeds the game birds would taste good to him. Ivanhoe plunges his arm into the water, wets himself to the shoulder, fingers closing on nothing. The trout and its brothers scatter into the small rapids just downstream.

Ivanhoe makes do with water. Handful after handful of cold water, until his belly is full and tight. He offers a cupped palm of it to the Kelso Yellow-Leg, who refuses even to look at him. The rooster is rumpled, dry, weary, furious. It would die of thirst rather than take a drink from Ivanhoe's hand. Ivanhoe briefly regrets having brought it along, toys with the notion of turning the bird loose to fend for itself on the mountain—but then he would be alone.

Onward, following the stream because he doesn't have any better guide. It's been a wet season, and the stream is high between its steep banks, tumbling over itself in its rush down to the flatlands. "Don't be in any hurry," Ivanhoe tells it. The thorn bushes that grow along the water's course tug at the legs of his pants as he passes.

Soon enough he finds himself at the edge of a wide pool. He is so tired that he actually stumbles into the pool up to his knees, almost sets the cage in the water. He puts it down on the pool's bank. The rooster regards him balefully with its one good eye. "Ah, you're all right," Ivanhoe tells it. He wishes desperately that he had some dry shell corn in his pocket. Anything. Chickens, even stout battle stags like the Kelso Yellow-Leg, cannot go long without food and drink. "You're okay." He ducks his head beneath the surface of the water, to refresh himself.

Under the water, the world is gray and cool and nearly silent, and he stays there a moment, bubbles trailing upward from his nostrils and the corners of his mouth. He floats, his heart straining, his lungs bucking against the pressure that speedily builds in them. If he stays this way, he will drown, or his heart will seize up on him. He waits a long moment, the whistling of his blood's need for oxygen growing in his ears, to see what will happen.

The gray lifeless bottom of the pool. The swift ticking of blood in his ears.

Ivanhoe bursts from the water, nearly weeping with relief as air fills his lungs. He shakes his head, flinging droplets from his hair, and finds himself confronted with a waterfall. Twenty feet high, the cataract drops its riches into the upper end of the pool, cloaked by hepatica and trailing vines. At its apex hang thin tongues of polished sandstone, as sharp as spears, the water that spills off them a shimmering filigree of silver and air. The sound of the falls is more like music than like roaring water.

~ ~ ~

Can Ivanhoe recall his mother at work on the petit-pointe? The needle, darting quick as a dragonfly, pricks her finger, and she brings it to her mouth to suck the pain away. A drop of blood on the point of the needle, blood in the weft of the cloth.

~ ~ ~

The waterfall pounds Ivanhoe. He's underneath the cataract, behind it, and it crashes powerfully down on his shoulders and head. The falls stand before him like a curtain, and he finds himself reluctant to part the milky sheet of water. What lies out there? Vines and clematis, the clear pool, the bog and the hemlock forest beyond—but what if all of that is gone, or changed in some inexplicable way? He's sure that the world has contracted down to this one place, the hollow opening (*like a tomb*) in the rocks behind the waterfall and him within it. He shivers with cold as a shadow, a human shadow, passes ghostlike across the face of the water.

And she comes. He hasn't dared to hope for such a thing, not since he set out in the morning, but there she stands, under the falls with him, the water plastering her hair—it's no longer obscured by the bandanna—to her shapely skull. She's dressed as she was at Pluskat's, dungarees and a workshirt, wringing wet. She smiles at Ivanhoe as though she's unsurprised to find him there. He can make out the pleasing shape of her breasts, her nipples, through the soaked material of her shirt. He thinks of his dream beneath the hemlock, imagines her suckling him, grows excited, his breath short.

Then she is next to him, subjecting him to brutal scrutiny. Her warm breath touches his cheek. They are nose to nose, and as he looks at her he discovers that it's uncannily like looking at himself in a mirror. When his eyes dart to the side, hers do likewise. When he steals a look down at her body, she takes in his. A drop of water depends from the tip of her nose, and he feels a bead forming beneath his as well. He laughs.

"I'm dreaming again, aren't I?" he asks. She shrugs her comely shoulders.

Ivanhoe thinks hard. He stands within the penumbra of the falls, near the top of Irish Mountain. From the falls flows a nameless stream, and the stream must empty into Drum's Creek, which rolls past the game farm into the Seneca River at the mountain's base. The Seneca flows to the Kanawha, which runs to the broad sluggish Ohio. The Ohio empties into the Mississippi. The Mississippi in its turn empties into the Gulf of Mexico, and the Gulf into the Atlantic Ocean. And all the oceans of the world open one into the others.

"I'm dreaming," he says.

And discovers himself clothed in shining feathers, plumage that effortlessly turns aside the water that spills down over him. He feels the battle stag's heart beating within him.

The girl regards him warily. He fixes her with a golden eye, clacks his beak. He is strong and proud and barbarous. She takes a step back. "Will you hurt me?" she asks.

"I might," he says. Her teeth chatter slightly, but she gives no other outward sign of discomfort. Her hands hang at her sides. Her skin, where he can see it, is dotted with a pleasing constellation of freckles. Droplets of water gleam like pearls in her hair.

"Turn around," he tells her, his voice half human, half a bird's croaking caw. She turns and he drinks her in, the athletic set of her shoulder blades (so like undeveloped wings), the aristocratic curve of her spine, the soft, shadowed hollow at the small of her back. He imagines sipping water from that hollow.

This must be the answer. This is why he has climbed the mountain, to be here, to be strong beneath this waterfall with this girl. One leap, one stroke of his powerful wings, and he will be on her, he will pin her, drive her down before him, clasp her to him with his sunset-colored pinions, thrust himself upon her, tear her clothes from her body, force himself inside her. He has seen Snag's gamecocks satisfy themselves on the hens so. How many times has he seen it? And she will deny him nothing.

~ ~ ~

Screaming. Not the screaming of the girl. She has turned entirely around now, she has shown him her whole self, and her mouth is closed. The screaming comes from outside the enclosing waterfall. It is the crowing of the forgotten Kelso Yellow-Leg.

Ivanhoe shudders. The voice of the Kelso comes from without, but it's loud, it comes from within too, it caroms off the stone behind him and the water before, it's coming from somewhere close by, it's coming from him, it's coming from Ivanhoe's own chest. The crowing, on and on, tears itself from his lungs, from his panicked heart, ascends his burning throat, issues from his open, upthrust beak. What a noise! The Kelso Yellow-Leg asks, and Ivanhoe answers.

The torrent of the falls washes the feathers from his body, sweeps them away. Each feather wrenches itself from his flesh with a flare of pain, a flare repeated a hundred, a thousand times over in an instant; they rip themselves free and drop down and float in the water at his feet. Each feather leaves behind it a small, hot bubo, a tiny crater welling with his blood for a moment, before the trickle of blood, too, is washed away. The feathers are going, his head is stripped bare, his shoulders and his back, he watches in horror as his long gangling arms reveal themselves beneath the molting feathers of his once-powerful wings. Down his body the terrible sloughing-off goes, like fire down the trunk of his body, along his limbs, his buttocks, his soft belly, his thighs, his groin, until he is freezing, naked before the girl.

"Keep your eyes open," the girl says. "I want you to see this."

The beak is the last thing to go, the sharp beak, it gives a liquid shift like a loosening tooth, hauls itself awkwardly away from his face, the pain unbearable but somehow beautiful too, as it pulls free of its moorings—agony to feel it go, eyeball-rolling, wailing agony, but he knows there will be relief when finally he sheds it. It hangs sideways for a moment, like a cheap mask whose string has broken, and then at last the beak tears loose entirely, first the bottom half and then the top, splashing into the feather-strewn water at his feet, bobbing obscenely there.

What next? He feels terribly small, terrifyingly fragile. What will go next? He raises his face as the water crashes down on him, fully alert, and waits on the final dissolution, joint separating from joint, bone from bone, sinew from sinew, flesh from flesh, until there is nothing left. The crowing of the Kelso Yellow-Leg continues, but under the waterfall there is only the sound of Ivanhoe's frightened weeping.

~ ~ ~

Looking for his vanished boy, Snag hobbles as far as Drum's Creek. He sits on the bank and, wretched, stares into the purling water. His own strained face looks back at him from the dark rippling surface. Then, crossing his image, a sudden flash of color. And another. A dozen, a hundred. Where could they come from? A raft of brilliant color passing him on the stream, numberless at first, and then fewer, and fewer still, only a couple wheeling past in the swift current, one. Too late, Snag thinks to put his hand out, take up one of the dripping feathers. They are past him, they are gone.

~ ~ ~

Naked under the sky. She has led him here, stripped and frail. She climbed before him, nude, up the foaming cataract, the bird in one hand, cradled against her ribs, her naked feet sure as a mountain goat's on the slick outcroppings. The sharp rocks cut his feet as he climbed, and he was deathly afraid that he would fall.

She has brought him to the glade at the brow of the Irish Mountain, brought him to the very center of the Eye of God. He's stretched out there in the predawn dark, and she's beside him. He wants her with a fierce ache, but his thin hide is unbearably tender with his recent flaying, and for the moment their skin touches only lightly, at the knee and the wrist, along their forearms. The cool breeze that sweeps over the mountain summit blows a strand of her hair across his lips, and he tastes ocean foam.

No way for Ivanhoe to know it, but the Eye of God on which he rests is in fact the ruined hulk of a three-hundred-foot-wide transit telescope, erected on the mountaintop by scientists from the National Radio Astronomy Observatory, to listen to the radio signals that emanate from the energetic cores of quasars and pulsars: imperceptible entities a universe from this deserted place. Abandoned now. He would not care if he did know. All he knows is that it's a gigantic tilting dish of steel, its white paint peeling from almost two acres of surface. It's smooth, and he's lying on it with the girl.

Around them, a couple hundred yards below the peak of Irish Mountain, an unbroken floor of clouds stretches away like the ancient ocean in all directions to the horizon. The foothills are invisible beneath them, as distant as the celestial bodies that the Eye of God was intended to spy out. Undetectable: the chookyard, the foothills, Pluskat's pit, Snag, and all the rest of Ivanhoe's old life, the entire waking world, drowned beneath the cloud sea.

All drowned but the Kelso Yellow-Leg, a bit the worse for wear but apparently in good spirits as it works its way along the scaffolding at the edge of the great radio telescope, ululating and chuckling. It fixes its good eye on Ivanhoe and the girl, who seem to be falling asleep beside each other. Soon they will enter each other's dreams. Soon her family will come, the fearful ones. The others will come in due time, but for now it is only the girl and the half-grown boy Ivanhoe, and that is just fine with the Kelso Yellow-Leg. That is all right by the indomitable old butcher cock, who clings tenaciously to the curved perimeter of the Eye of God, who ruffles his golden feathers, who crows his defiance into the face of the rising sun.

Pony Car

Joyriding in Uncle Rowdy's tricked-out pony car: '70 Dodge Challenger, four-hundred-forty cubic inch hemi, Hurst shifter, Cragar rims all the way around, shaker hood with chrome hold-down pins. The river on one side of the road, C&O tracks on the other. Uncle Rowdy telling a story. *So the Angel of the Lord appears to the farmer.* Looming over Esau in the front seat, Esau young at the time, nine or ten. The skin of Uncle Rowdy's fine-featured face tight and bloodless with fury. Esau keenly aware that this story was in some way about his father, Esau's father, Rowdy's older brother, and listening close.

The Angel of the Lord appears in all his blazing glory, and he says to the farmer, he says, Whatever you ask of me, I'll give that thing to you. Was Uncle Rowdy's wife, was Astrid in the car with them? Sitting pert in the back seat, quiet as always, attentive, dark eyes glittering as the countryside whipped by outside the car. Esau can't remember exactly, but he thinks that probably she was. Astrid never far from Uncle Rowdy, unsmiling, watchful. *But listen to me, says the Angel: Whatever I give to you, twice that will I give to your neighbor.* Uncle Rowdy not seeming to pay any attention to where they're going, forearm laid casually along the top of the steering wheel, all his concentration on the story he's telling Esau, the powerful pony wandering all over the road, engine howling. Esau knew that his father was the farmer in the story, that was plain to see. But who was Uncle Rowdy? Was he the angel? The neighbor? Was Esau in the story? Probably not. Esau was never in the story. It was always Uncle Rowdy and his brother in the story.

So the farmer thinks, and he thinks. And finally he says to the Angel of the Lord, he says, All right then, Angel, do this for me: Put out one of my eyes.

~ ~ ~

Esau, grown now to man-size, sits in the bentwood rocker in his bedroom. In the bedroom that belonged to his father, his parents. He sleeps in their bed at night, and he sits in the rocker before he goes to bed, but he does not rock. He listens. He listens to the sounds the house makes, the groaning sighs as it settles against the foundation, the faint beat of steam rising in the radiators. It's a cold night coming on. He hears these sounds, these familiar sounds, without registering them, the way he hears his own breathing and yet does not hear. He has heard these sounds every day of his life. They are not the sounds he's listening for.

He's got his father's short-barreled coach gun in his lap. He caresses the burled walnut stock, the sturdy triggers, the curving, fluted twin hammers.

Down the hall, in the room where Esau lived as a boy, where he lived when he went joyriding with Uncle Rowdy (and with Astrid? Yes, she was there too, he's sure, he's pretty sure) in the pony car, Slow Joe Crow gives out a premonitory croak. It's the sound he makes before he speaks, like clearing his throat. That's not what Esau's listening for either. He's used to Slow Joe Crow's voice. He's listening for sounds from outside: subtle footsteps, the rattle of dry bones and thin, squealing voices, the voices that call to him in the night, *Come out, Esau! Come out! Come out!*

Esau's listening for walking spirits. He used to hear them only occasionally. Now he hears them all the time, now he hears them almost every night. Soon it will be every night, every single night. He squeezes his eyes shut. Maybe before long they will come in the day too, and he won't have any peace at all, ever.

Down the hall, Slow Joe Crow begins to speak. In his dusty bird's voice he cries, *Ladybug Ladybug, fly away home! Your house is afire, your children will burn!*

They are out there, Esau knows. Secreted. In the dark swift-haunted lofts of the barn, the empty machine shed, the ruined granary, crouching in the damp mossy chill of the springhouse. Waiting on the night, waiting on him. Waiting for the moment when his attention turns from them, for the moment when he stops listening, and then they can creep out, come limping and struggling and jack-legging out of their hidie-holes, out into the open.

They will cross the yard, they will come hobbling up to the house itself, right up to its graying clapboard walls, this house where Esau grew to man-size, this house surrounded by century-old silver maples. Crowding together like ants, they will peer in through the windows, they will climb atop one another's backs, they will run their dry dead fingers over the walls, fingers like the claws of birds, scraping, scraping, feeling for him, probing, searching, listening with cocked attentive heads for the sounds of movement, any movement, for sounds of life— that's what they want, isn't it, what they must want, the dead, what else is there for them to want but life, *more life*—listening for sounds of life within: listening for *him*.

~ ~ ~

Uncle Rowdy won his wife in a poker game. Astrid. Telling it proudly, hand on her narrow shoulder, *I won her*. Said he had a pretty decent hand, aces over eights. The dead man's hand, he said. He had a feeling about that hand. He wagered his car, the pony car. Man he was playing against wagered Astrid. *Hot as a two-dollar pistol and I won her.*

Esau's father said, *Esau, there are three kinds of liars in this world: liars, black liars, and Uncle Rowdy.* He said, *You know how you can tell when Rowdy's lying? Know how?* Esau shaking his head no. *I'll tell you how. His lips are moving.*

~ ~ ~

This morning, Esau came across his Uncle Rowdy sitting at the base of the Memorial to the Confederate Dead. The Memorial stands in a pasture field out north of Mount Nebo, the county seat. He didn't know it was Uncle Rowdy at first, of course. At first he thought it must be his father, a tall lean long-legged man, back straight and stiff as a poker. But the man at the statue didn't wear gabardines and a rough workshirt the way Esau's father always did. This man wore a snazzy wool salt-and-pepper suit. On his head, perched at a rakish angle, was a dark felt hat with a New York brim.

Esau's father never wore a hat like that. Only Uncle Rowdy ever wore a hat like that one. He got it during a brief stint as a Fuller Brush Man, got the suit then too, and never gave them up.

Esau was on his way to town, to the hardware store, to pick up something to keep the spirits out, four-by-sixes and sheets of plywood and bags of nails. Groceries also. It was the first time he'd been out of the house in days, weeks—in who knew how long? He can't bear to leave the house these days, not for anything. It's as though the house has a hold on him. Some days he can't even bring himself to leave his parents' room, can't bring himself to so much as rise from the bentwood rocker. But he'd plundered the last of the preserves in the old root cellar, eaten the last of the watermelon-rind pickles his industrious mother put up before she died. Nothing left, and so he forced himself out, one foot after the other, across the dark dirt of the yard, into the truck, twist the key in the ignition, pump the gas pedal, away he went.

And then the man in the salt-and-pepper suit spread his hands, and the man looked up at the passing truck, he looked right at Esau like he'd been sitting there waiting on him to come by, waiting for years maybe, waiting for ages, getting more impatient with every moment, his face long and gray and hollow-cheeked. The same sharp-nosed face that loomed over Esau in the front seat of the pony car. The sockets of the eyes empty. *You're like a son to me, Esau.* A mean, joking tone, a finger poking Esau in his tender ribs. *Like my very own boy.* No mistaking him. Uncle Rowdy. Uncle Rowdy, in the ground all these years.

Esau turned the truck around and went straight back home, his errands utterly forgotten.

~ ~ ~

They are coming now. Esau distracted by the voice of Slow Joe Crow down the hall—*Fifteen men on a dead man's chest! Dead men tell no tales!* Lines from a children's book long put away and forgotten, something with terrible pictures, a skull's toothy grin on a fluttering flag, murdered men buried with their stolen loot, the face of a murderous pirate leering up snaggle-toothed from the pages, burning smoking tapers plaited into his long greasy hair, pictures best forgotten—the guttural voice of Slow Joe Crow and the quiet shuffle of his scaly feet as he shifts on his perch, that shuffle shading into the subtle shifting of movement outside, of the spirits rising from their dark places and making their stealthy way toward the house.

His father. His mother. His brother, dead in infancy. Dry lips parted, teeth shining grotesquely in the dark. Eye sockets dark and empty. His grandmother, still wearing the quilted nightgown in which she died, the one she was wearing when Esau found her in bed. The nameless others, the little twisted scampering ones that dart from between the outbuildings and whisper among themselves in strangely musical voices. The ones like children. The ones that sometimes go upon two feet and sometimes upon four. The flibbertigibbets. The ones that call to him in their singsong tones, *Come out, Esau. Come out here, to us, to us!*

And Uncle Rowdy. Uncle Rowdy is out there now too.

~ ~ ~

Slow Joe Crow. A great glossy bird, wild, a fiercely intelligent field crow with bleak eyes and a horny yellow beak and a tongue like an agile blue worm, taught to speak through the skillful application of the cut-throat razor. *Loosening the tongue,* Uncle Rowdy called it. Split the tongue along its length. Trim the little wedge-shaped band of tissue below the tongue, the one that holds the tongue to the floor of the mouth. Just nick it a little. A barber's move, to let the blood. *That's all that keeps him from talking. Just a little skin is all, nothing much, a cheap exchange. You'd give up a little piece of flesh to be able to talk, wouldn't you? Eh? Eh?*

How long do crows live? Not this long surely, but there he is, Slow Joe Crow, the cap of feathers at the crown of his head white, thinning like the hair of an old man. His black suit of feathers salted with age, his eyes frosted over with milky cataracts. Slow Joe Crow, sitting chained (the chain thin and bright, gold, decorative, like a necklace chain) by one leg to the wooden perch in the boy Esau's room, with its jolly cowboy bedspread and its sailing-ship wallpaper. Talking, talking, talking, Slow Joe Crow. Who taught him to speak? In whose voice does he speak?

Esau did not teach him.

Uncle Rowdy taught him, loosened his tongue and named him and talked at him, sang to him in rhymes until the crow began singing back. All those years ago. Could it be the same bird?

Of course Esau told all his friends about it, this creature whose tongue his Uncle Rowdy had loosened. He wanted them to see, he wanted them to admire. You would think that kids would love to see a talking bird, you would think that Slow Joe Crow, with his expansive conversational repertoire, would have made Esau a popular boy. You might well think it. Esau brought his friends to see the magnificent talking crow, and Slow Joe Crow performed, he talked with his blue split tongue and his fierce eyes, he talked right to the children who clustered around the perch where he was chained, the children who reached out tentative fingers to stroke his inky plumage, his ruined wing and his good one.

And what did he say to them?

Terrible things. Things that Uncle Rowdy could not have, things that no one could have known, could have taught Slow Joe Crow to say. Things that Esau didn't dare, that none of them dared, to repeat, not even to each other. Dark, sliding, slippery things that, once said, could never be unsaid, once heard could never be unheard. Things that crept into their heads and took up permanent lodging there. After their interview with Slow Joe Crow, Esau's friends headed off, one by one, blundered down the steps alone and out of the house alone and walked home across the fields alone.

An animal shouldn't speak. Esau's father. *It's an offense against God and against nature that an animal like that should possess the power of the human tongue without the power of human reason. Without a human soul.* Knowing this in his gut, it was wrong.

But he couldn't find anything in the Bible against it, so Slow Joe Crow went into the boy Esau's room, chained to the perch, and Esau looked after it, fed it little slivers of raw meat from his fingers (and how many times did that beak jab at him, how many times did Slow Joe Crow taste his blood? And how many times did Esau draw his hand back to strike, how often did he think to slaughter the hateful thing, but then the image of Uncle Rowdy would swim up into his mind, Uncle Rowdy with the cut-throat razor in his hand, Uncle Rowdy laboring to loosen the crow's tongue, the blood and the bird screeching, cruelty enough perpetrated against the animal—and Esau stayed his hand).

Every time Uncle Rowdy came he taught it a new thing to say. *Doctor Foster went to Gloucester.* At night the bird would speak to Esau in Uncle

Rowdy's voice. *Stepped in a puddle up to his middle, and never went out again.* While he lay awake in his narrow bed, under the cowboy covers, staring at the sailing ship wallpaper, waiting for sleep to come, praying for it to come. The bird talking to him all the while that he slept. *Winken and Blinken and Nod.* What did it say to him, Slow Joe Crow, what did you say into his ears while he slept?

Even now, now that he's man-size, when everyone else is dead, when the bird should certainly be dead, should be nothing but a moldering clump of feather and bone in a thin-walled shoe-box buried under the dirt of the backyard (but it has outlived them all!), the croaking voice drifts down the hall: *One shoe off and one shoe on. Diddle diddle dumpling, my son John!*

~ ~ ~

Uncle Rowdy cupped his long-boned fingers around his mouth, made a chamber in which his voice could reverberate. Hidden, crouched amongst the bracken, he closed his eyes, he concentrated, summoning something, summoning the power from deep within his chest, and then warbled breathily into his hands, and the sound that emerged was the sound of a wounded crow:

Urk, urk, urk. A crow caught in a snare, helpless, in distress. A perfect imitation, uncanny. Esau stood by at the edge of the clearing, the glossy little coach gun clutched in his hands, loaded with light number eight shot. His orders: shoot to wound, not to kill.

And here they came, the black shapes stooping from the sky like minor hawks, skimming the forest canopy, rapacious eyes raking the forest floor for signs of the wounded one. *A crow will always come to the sound of a wounded crow.* Uncle Rowdy. *Easy meat.*

Esau raising the coach gun *to wound not to kill,* sliding the bead front sight from coal-colored breast to gleaming beating outstretched wing, the first reckless crow descending into the clearing. The crack of the shell, slight buck of the gun against his shoulder and cheek, and it was done. The other crows fleeing, stroking up into the sky overhead with raucous cries, *a trick, we knew, we knew, we knew,* and Uncle Rowdy rushing into the clearing and lifting up the weakly struggling crow in his hand, the bird pecking at him, plucking at his flesh with its broad beak but to no effect, Rowdy's hands as hard as claws.

Gesturing upward. Shaking the wounded crow in triumph, Esau sick with grief and worry over the blood spilling down the back of Rowdy's fist. He had always been taught to kill clean, he had never done that before: wound, not kill. *Don't worry, he'll live. You did good.* The wounded crow, trapped in Uncle Rowdy's fist, looked at Esau as though it could not believe what it saw. It opened its beak, opened it wider, showed its tongue to him, the tongue a shocking blue. It looked as though it ought to be making a sound, the crow, with its mouth open like that, it looked as though it wanted to make some sort of sound, a cry of protest, of pain. No sound emerged.

~ ~ ~

They are at the windows now, they press feverishly against the walls.

Stepped in a puddle up to his middle, and never went out again.

The little crippled capering ones shouting, *Come out! Come out, Esau! Come out!*

~ ~ ~

Where'd you get the money for a ride like that one, Gustavus, is what Esau's old man wanted to know. Calling Uncle Rowdy *Gustavus*, his given name, that he couldn't bear to be called. *Always coming to me for cash all these years, never worked a lick that I know of, and here you haul up in this creamy ride to see me.*

Uncle Rowdy, grinning that sideways grin at his brother, ungenerous brother, can't turn him away, can't deny him a roof over his head, the ties of blood demand that much of him but nothing more: *I won it in a poker game. Yowza.*

~ ~ ~

Tomorrow. Esau decides that, if he should make it through the night, he will leave the house. Tomorrow. No matter how hard it is to do it. He will drag himself out the front door. He will set his feet one before the other. He will make his way across the yard to the sagging cow shed, the one where the pony car is parked, where it has sat parked all these years. He will throw open the wide doors, he will let the light of day shine in upon the car.

The windows coated thickly with dust. Is there anything *(anyone)* inside it? Of course not. The car is empty. The smell of it, the smell of the metal, the smell of the oil, of the engine, that great mill, that hunk of stilled iron, stinging his nostrils. A scent like deep regret. The tires flat, slumped down over the alloy rims, but that's all right, he can get the compressor from the machine shop and fill them again, fill them with new air, if they aren't ruined with dry rot.

He will pull the hold-down pins and pop the hood (*and what will fly up from that engine well when you do? What will burst out with a raucous cry and fling itself at your face, at your eyes? What has lived in there all these years?*), he will pop the hood, clear out the rodents and the bird's nest that have doubtless collected there. He will tug loose the battery and replace it with the Diehard from his father's truck. He will unscrew the spark plugs and drip an ounce or so of WD-40 penetrating oil into each plug hole. He will clean the distributor and disassemble and reassemble the starter, he will do all the things he has learned how to do to make a stale machine function. All his life on his father's farm he has been preparing for this chore. In short order—perhaps in a day, if he's lucky! if he works fast!—he will return the pony car to running condition. Rough running, maybe, but that's only temporary, it's all he needs. He can do it. He knows he can.

Why hasn't he thought of this before? Of course! In the pony car he can escape. A new beginning.

Dead men tell no tales.

The scraping at the walls, at the windows and doors, has stopped. The little ones are not calling him anymore. No more *Esau, come out to us!* Have they given up? Or have they thought of something else?

No telling. Esau returns to his vision of the pony car restored to glorious life, roaring down the road, Esau at the wheel, rolling through Mount Nebo without stopping, rolling beneath the yellow blinking caution light, rolling past the Memorial to the Confederate Dead (and no looking to see who's sitting at the foot of it this time), rolling across the big levels beside the river, the railroad tracks stitching their way alongside, eighty miles an hour, ninety, one hundred. Perhaps one of the great coal trains will thunder along the tracks beside him, perhaps a train will serve as his escort.

The pony car will carry him away from here, away from this house, away from this dead farm with its walking spirits, away from this valley. The pony car will take him anywhere he wants to go.

~ ~ ~

Astrid was skinny and deep-bosomed. She looked a lot younger than Uncle Rowdy. Esau's mother told Esau that Astrid was not really Uncle Rowdy's wife, as they were never officially married in a church. She told Esau that Uncle Rowdy's real wife killed herself, and looking at Rowdy, who can blame the poor woman? That is what Esau's mother said.

Uncle Rowdy could pull a coin out of his ear or yours. He could pull coins out of ears, coin after coin falling from his long nimble fingers in a silver stream, so that you might believe it was an endless supply of money there in your head, and only Uncle Rowdy able to get at it. It made Esau's mother laugh when he pulled coins out of her ears. She said, Get away from me with that mess, Rowdy, but she didn't push him away. Sometimes, when Esau's father wasn't looking on, Rowdy's hands would linger for just an instant at the nape of her neck, under the fall of her hair, and she would grow quiet.

He could pull batteries out of your ears, too, and keys, and a variety of other small objects, anything you wanted. A little gold heart, one time, that he gave to Esau's mother. A tiny sample bottle of sweet perfume. A slim switchblade knife, with blue mica grips and a Corsican blade, for Esau. Whatever your heart desired.

Uncle Rowdy making his nonsense replies to any question you might ask, leaning back with his legs crossed and his feet propped up and that quizzical expression on his face, saying, over and over again, maddeningly saying *Yowza yowza* like it meant something. Uncle Rowdy could sing Lost Highway just like Hank Williams. Uncle Rowdy could sing Santa Lucia just like old Caruso.

Esau's mother was deep-bosomed but not skinny. *Built like a brick shithouse*, was what Uncle Rowdy said. Then, noticing the sour expression on Esau's father's face as if for the first time, *Oops. I mean* outhouse, *is that better?*

~ ~ ~

How did the pony car come to be in the cow shed? Hadn't there been an accident? Uncle Rowdy racing a train, the way he always did, laughing like a madman, *yowza yowza*, the train laboring up the grade beside the road and Uncle Rowdy's powerhouse of a pony car overtaking it easily, child's play, the train miles long, coal car after coal car after coal car, three enormous diesel locomotives, four, a regular leviathan of a train—and then it hits the big levels and begins to pick up speed, and there's a sense of urgency in Uncle Rowdy now, mashing down hard on the accelerator, his fingers gripping the thin steering wheel tight. The way he liked it, narrow margins, no room for error, *balls to the wall* was the way he always put it. *Only way to live.* Calculating like a scientist how much of the train stretches out before him, how fast it's going, the windings in the road ahead. Can he get to the crossing ahead of the train?

No.

Or yes, but not through it, and the lead locomotive takes the pony car right in the passenger door. Such a massive train, it doesn't even shudder as it picks up the car and folds it double and casts it aside. Glass fanning out in the light of the locomotive's headlamp like a wash of diamonds. The great treble air-horns howling like mad, their voices echoing off the hills that ring the valley. Startling awake all the dogs at all the farms, sending them into paroxysms of barking.

The eyes of the horrified engineer blinking, disbelieving, the smashed car well behind him now: maybe they didn't hit anything after all, one of those mirages you encounter after so many years on the same line, the same identical landscape rushing past you forever and the mind makes something up to keep itself entertained. Disbelieving, but still he'd engaged the brakes, steel shrieking against steel, and the loosely strung cars of the great train were coming together, the couplings slamming shut like prison doors behind him. Slowing, slowing, slowing…It takes forever to stop a train of that size.

The image so clear in Esau's mind. But if the pony car was hit, then how can it be in the cow shed? Esau knows that it's there. That's where Uncle Rowdy always put it when he came to visit, to keep it out of the weather. Esau's seen it there a hundred times, a thousand. He used to go look at it all the time when he was younger, when he knew that his father wasn't around to see him looking, see him dreaming. Dreaming that the pony car might carry him away. It's in there, in the shed, and he'll put it to rights, and he'll be off, he'll be on his way, as he should have been ages ago. Why hasn't he already left?

Stepped in a puddle right up to his middle.

And will he take Slow Joe Crow along with him? He will not.

~ ~ ~

I love you like my own son, my own darling little baby boy. I love you just to death.

~ ~ ~

Uncle Rowdy claimed that half the farm was his. Claimed that half of everything Esau's father had was his. More than half, in some cases. In some cases, all. He said to Esau's father, *You think you got sweat equality, Darius, working the place all these years, but they were my parents too. Nobody ever said nothing about it all belongs to Darius. It's half mine and it's half yours. Let my half go to the Devil, if you want, and just work your half!*

There is envy on Uncle Rowdy's face as he looks around him. What he's thinking is written plainly on his features: All of this, and you can't cede me just one little bit. All of this, house and land and *family*, and you can't let me have what's mine.

Esau's father replied, *I can't work half a farm, Rowdy, you know that as well as I do.* And Uncle Rowdy sat back with this big toothy smile on his face and set his feet in their hobnail boots on Esau's mother's highly polished cherrywood coffee table.

I'll have what's mine, Darius. I'll have what's mine.

That's what was written on Uncle Rowdy's face as he and his brother talked about the farm. *I'll have what's mine.* But what he said was what Uncle Rowdy always said. He just said *Yowza, boss. Yowza.*

~ ~ ~

One day Esau pulled the coin from out of Astrid's ear. This was in Esau's room. Where the light was good for reading, and where she had come with her trashy magazines that she liked to linger over, True Crime and True Confessions.

He'd read in a book how to do it, *sleight of hand,* and he expected to be clumsy about it at first, but his fingers seemed already to possess the skill, and the trick went off without a hitch.

He gave over the coin, a Kennedy half-dollar, warm and moist from the skin of his concealing palm, he gave it over to Astrid. She took him in with her watchful eyes. Then he plucked a necklace from her other ear, a thin gold necklace, a cheap thing but pretty.

When he went to hand the necklace to her, Astrid inclined her head. She wanted him to put the necklace around her throat. He had difficulty

working the clasp, his eyes locked on the back of her slender neck, the
fine colorless hairs there, the hand that held the thick plait of her braid
clear for him. Wondering, Will Slow Joe Crow tell?

You sure you ain't Rowdy's boy? she asked him then. *You sure? You got his
ways about you.*

~ ~ ~

Esau's up in the attic, looking through the old things. He's put the
coach gun down beside him on the raw pine boards of the attic floor.
There's a big turtle up here, a turtle with wheels that he used to ride
along the meandering corridors of the house when he was just little, its
wheels going *squeak squeak squeak,* and a tangle of metal tracks for a
Lionel HO scale train set, and switches, and some little trees and cows
and a man in the pinstriped coveralls and hat of a railroad engineer;
and a pile of Matchbox cars; and a crowd of GI Joe dolls with all their
elaborate military gear. He picks up one of the GI Joes. He remembers
this one. Amazing thing, it talked. Will it still work? Esau pulls the
string that hangs from the GI Joe's back, and GI Joe tells him, *You get
the jeep, and I'll grab the ammo!*

From below him (he's right over his old room now), he hears the
voice of Slow Joe Crow, as if in reply: *Fifteen men on a dead man's chest.*

He puts the GI Joe aside. He's looking for something in particular.
He's looking for the book from which that line comes, he's looking for
the picture book with the pirates. Just thinking about that book gives
him the jimmies. He hasn't seen it since he was a kid. He wants to see it
now, now that he is man-size, he wants to flip open its pages, past the
picture of the murdered men, past the picture of the flapping Jolly Roger
with its skull and crossbones. He wants to open the book to the portrait
of Blackbeard, he wants to look old Edward Teach in the eye and see if
he is still scared. He wants to see if (he can't imagine why he thinks it
might be so) Blackbeard has the unrepentant face of Uncle Rowdy.

He opens a dust-covered box in which he seems to remember that
the book resides, and there it is, a thick red volume with a cracked
leather cover. And on top of it—surprise!—another Matchbox car,
this one in mint condition, still in its blister pack. He picks the car up,
carefully, between thumb and forefinger, turns it this way and that,
peering at it. He doesn't recall getting this one. Was it a present? From

whom? Why doesn't he remember? He remembers all these toys, all these rotting boxes, he remembers every one of them. But he doesn't remember this one.

'70 Dodge Challenger. Chrome hood hold-down pins. Perfect in every detail. If he flips up the tiny metal hood with the edge of his fingernail, he will see the hemi motor.

Then, from outside, the unmistakable sound of the cranking of the engine of the pony car, the crackle of the exhaust through the dual glasspacks, the burr of the fat tires as they spin against the dirt floor of the shed, the grunt as the warming rubber catches hold and catapults the car forward. Uncle Rowdy has started the car. Impossible, the shape that the car is in. No one but Uncle Rowdy ever drove that car. Uncle Rowdy circles the house, the V-8 mill growling. American rolling iron, circling the house, circling.

Esau wonders about Astrid. Is she out there too, with the rest of them? Pretty Astrid. *You got his ways about you.* Sitting beside Rowdy, his arm slung possessively over her shoulders. Leaning toward him, into him, her dark head on his chest. Esau hates to think of it, Astrid out there with the rest of them. She deserves better than that. Better than to have her bared teeth shine like phosphorus in the night. Better than to stare out from empty eye sockets.

Put out one of my eyes.

Ha! The bright burning Angel of the Lord has put them both out.

~ ~ ~

She must have told him, must have told Uncle Rowdy what they did, she and Esau, the half-dollar and the necklace. Esau never told Uncle Rowdy about it, never told anybody. Who told? Was it Slow Joe Crow? Uncle Rowdy took the back of her neck in his hand and squeezed. She looked up at him, wiped her fist across her mouth. Her pupils like pinpricks.

Uncle Rowdy laughed. *You want to play with him? That's fine, that's copacetic. Play with him all you care to.*

~ ~ ~

On one side of the pony car, the telephone poles flicking past like the palings of a picket fence, the landscape blurred with speed. On the other side, the roaring train. Uncle Rowdy's overtaking it, of course, but is he going fast enough? Each loaded coal car emblazoned with the yellow silhouette cat, emblem of the Chesapeake & Ohio railroad. Chessie, that cat is called. Esau remembers that. She had a husband, Chessie did, and he had a cute name too. What was it?

The train cars, marked with the names of cities—Portsmouth, Ohio; London, Kentucky; Newport News, Virginia—cities that he will never visit. He's trying to listen to the story that Uncle Rowdy's telling him, a story about a farmer and the Angel of the Lord, he's straining to make out the words over the gnashing of the pony car's transmission, Uncle Rowdy downshifting furiously for more torque, he's trying to hear over the rattle and clash of the train that they're racing. How far up the road is the crossing? And how fast is the train going? And how hard can Uncle Rowdy push the pony car? It's like a word problem in Esau's math class at school.

Dead men tell no tales.

That's not part of Uncle Rowdy's story, which is about wishes, and eyes being put out. Someone else altogether said that, about dead men. Is Astrid in the back seat of the car, her fist held to her mouth? Did she say it? Is Slow Joe Crow there in the back seat with her?

The pony car slews briefly sideways, tilts up onto two wheels, slams back down onto the road again. They are over the uphill grade now, descending into the levels. Below them is the crossing. The train coming on. Its air-horn splits the night.

The light of the train's headlamp fills the interior of the car, blinding, so bright that for a moment Esau thinks that he can see through Uncle Rowdy's skin, he thinks he can see into Uncle Rowdy as though he were looking at an X-ray exposure of the man. He can see the chalky white bones and the way the muscles lie over and around them. He can see revealed the working of the lungs, like a gray bellows in Uncle Rowdy's chest, and the heart beating like the cams and helves of a mechanical trip-hammer. So steady. He can see all of that, and he can smell the oily heat that boils off the pony car's engine, and burning diesel fuel, and he can sense the powerful electric charge that drives the steel wheeltrucks of the locomotives forward. The electricity makes the delicate hairs on his forearms and along the nape of his neck stand on end.

~ ~ ~

I love you to death. My son.

~ ~ ~

Esau uses the muzzle of the coach gun to thrust open the door of his boyhood room. The pony car has stopped its circling. Outside, all is quiet. From within the room, the croaking voice of Slow Joe Crow: *Doctor Foster. Went to Gloucester.* Esau has decided: he will go into the room, and he will take a deep breath, and he will thumb back the coach gun's hammers, and he will shoot Slow Joe Crow. *To kill, and not to wound. To kill clean.* The way he should have done it in the first place, the way his father taught him. He will put both barrels into the bird. And then he will leave the house. He will go out into the yard, he will go out among them, among the capering dead. And their ranks will part before him. The pony car will be out there, waiting on him as it has always waited, the engine idling, white exhaust curling up from the twin pipes, Uncle Rowdy slouched behind the wheel. Uncle Rowdy will raise a hand in merry greeting. *Yowza yowza!*

The bedroom door swings open under the pressure of the coach gun's barrels, and Esau steps inside. The wallpaper is there, its ships leaning hard over, under full sail. The bedspread too, with its smiling cowboys, their lariats frozen in mid-whirl.

Black shadows lie pooled about the room in unexpected places. Esau slits his eyes, straining to see. He can make out Slow Joe Crow's perch; but the perch is empty.

At last he picks out the bird in the darkness. It's sitting on the bed. Like Esau himself, Slow Joe Crow has grown somehow to man-size. Or has Esau grown smaller?

No. It is not the bird there on the bed at all. It's Uncle Rowdy, in his snazzy suit. Under the brim of his hat, his eye-sockets are empty.

Uncle Rowdy is happy. Uncle Rowdy is overjoyed. Esau has come at last. At last!

Stepped in a puddle right up to his middle, and never went out again.

Uncle Rowdy reaches a hand up to his head. The fingers work, and a coin appears. Uncle Rowdy has pulled a coin from his own ear. The coin falls to the floor, spins noisily there for a moment, and comes to rest. Heads. Another coin follows it, this one rolling off under the bed.

And another, and another, an apparently inexhaustible cascade of coins. Other treasures,

too: a chunk of glittering fool's gold, a thin chain, a toy car, a squarish ignition key stamped with the Dodge insignia.

Yowza.

The pony car is not parked in the shed, has not been parked there in ages. Esau understands this. He supposes he has understood it all along. Of course Slow Joe Crow does not occupy his perch. Slow Joe Crow lies in a box, a collapsing shoe-box, his yellow beak bent upon his coal-black breast, buried in the dirt of the yard.

It doesn't occur to Esau to wonder how he is still here, still in this place, if he was in the car, and the car was struck. There's no reason for him to wonder. Uncle Rowdy was in the car. Uncle Rowdy is here, Uncle Rowdy has come. Come, for him.

Esau drops the coach gun with a clatter. *Uncle Rowdy?* he says. It is not a question, not really. The blind eyes are upon him. Uncle Rowdy's treasures lie spread across the floor of the room.

My boy. My boy. My boy.

Joe Messinger
is Dreaming

T*his is the highest step in the world.*
That's what it says, the hand-lettered sign that the engineers made. They've set it at the bottom of the short flight of metal stairs on the gantry of the cramped gondola of Excelsior III. It's 1960, and Excelsior III is an extreme high-altitude balloon. It's a weather balloon that's been repurposed for carrying out near-space experiments, in preparation for manned space flight by U.S. astronauts. The stairs lead nowhere now. The balloon, with the gondola dangling below it like a sack of groceries, has departed. It departed at five a.m. sharp. It's now just a little past eight in morning. 0800 in military time. Joe Messinger rides in the gondola.

This is the highest step in the world.

~ ~ ~

Joe Messinger, as a boy of nine, stood without trembling at the edge of the great limestone cliff that overhung the Seneca River near his house. His parents lived on a sixty-acre farm nestled in a bend of the broad, shallow river outside of the town of Mount Nebo, the county seat. The rocks that lined the river's bottom, worn smooth by years of the water's running, by decades and centuries of it, shone like coins in the last of the day's light, from where Joe Messinger looked down on them. The cliff was four hundred feet tall.

Joe Messinger, with his toes at the crumbling edge of the cliff, gazed on the river and its gloriously smooth stones, stones lapped one over the other in the river's bed like the scales on a snake's back, and he felt as though he might be four hundred and four and one-half feet tall. He felt like the greatest giant ever to walk the earth.

He could see clear across the Seneca Valley, across his family's place, which sat at the base of the cliff, which looked tiny from so far up, a series of tidily-arranged squares and rectangles, some planted in corn, some in alfalfa, some in succulent timothy grass, some populated by strolling sheep. His collie dog trotted to and fro among the sheep, keeping order. In the smooth air over the valley, suspended between heaven and earth, the great birds, the vultures, went gliding on supple wings.

He could see all the way to the ridges on the western edge of the valley, which he knew marked the county line. Beyond those ridges bulked others that were higher, and others even higher beyond those, in dull-edged rows marching off to the curve of the earth. Above them, the rolling sky, the unbroken clouds as serene and friendly and slow-moving as the sheep in his father's fields.

He was aware that such vistas made other people afraid. He was aware that heights frightened his father, who wasn't frightened of much of anything. It seemed odd to Joe Messinger, who wasn't particularly brave in other ways, that he should feel no fear of falling. It seemed wonderful. He closed his eyes and stretched out his arms and imagined leaning forward into the wind that blew straight into his face, a wind of ten knots, perhaps fifteen, brisk up here at the edge of the precipice, bracing as the flat of a hand against Joe Messinger's cheek. He imagined leaning out into the wind, imagined that the wind would hold him up—that he could lean out, how far? A few degrees? Twenty? Forty? Until his entire body hung hovering over the abyss, and nothing visible to hold him there.

If the wind were strong enough, and if he leaned far enough, could he float? Could he fly? Like a predator bird? Like an angel? He had no thought of dying, and no fear of falling. He had climbed up the narrow trail to the cliff-top by himself, a strong little boy, determined, compact and muscular, with clear, far-seeing eyes.

Joe Messinger's father was the county constable. He wore a big Colt's .44 revolver on his hip when he did the county's business, and a brown, wide-brimmed hat. He wore a badge on the lapel of his long brown coat. In the county, if you had a problem, he was the man to see. But his authority ended at the county line. Past that, he was just a good strong man who lived in a poor little valley in a poor little state in the poorest region of a wealthy nation. Joe Messinger looked to the west. Past that first ridge line was a world that didn't know his father.

Between that first ridge line and the next, he surmised, there must be a valley very much like this one. Maybe there was a man who lived in that valley, like Joe Messinger's father, who was important there and unknown beyond the ridges. Maybe there was a boy there, looking eastward from the ridge's summit. Maybe that boy was looking at the place where Joe Messinger stood at the edge of his cliff. Maybe they were looking at each other. He wished he could see the boy across all that distance. He wished he could hear that boy's voice, which was likely quite like his own, reedy and ready, soon, to break.

This is the highest step in the world.

Step out into nothing, Joe Messinger.

~ ~ ~

Air Force Captain Joe Messinger perches stoic and immobile in the gondola of Excelsior III, his expression serene and deeply serious behind the glare shield of his helmet. He's a handsome fellow, though it's impossible to tell that from looking at him in his bulky environment suit. He looks as ungainly as the Michelin man. He looks comical, but he's never been more solemn in his life. No sane man could do what he is about to do. No sane man, fully awake and aware, could undertake the task that Joe Messinger is about to undertake, to step out of safety and into the air.

Joe Messinger is awake, but Joe Messinger is dreaming.

~ ~ ~

Colonel John Paul Stabb wears his full dress uniform, and he grips the sides of the podium before him, referring liberally to his notes as he speaks.

"I recruited Captain Joseph A. Messinger for Project Man-High five years ago, in 1955," says the colonel. "It's an Air Force endeavor to test the limits of man's endurance in, or at the lower limits of, outer space. At the moment, Captain Messinger occupies the gondola of the

Excelsior III, floating above the earth at its peak altitude of one hundred and two thousand eight hundred feet. It has taken him just over three hours to reach this altitude."

Joe Messinger is dreaming, and in his dream, he can hear the colonel perfectly. He does not need a radio to know what is being said about him on the surface of the earth, unimaginably far below.

"Joe Messinger will stay with Excelsior III at peak altitude for approximately ten minutes. And then he will jump."

Do you hear him, Joe Messinger? He says you'll jump.

Joe Messinger blinks. When a man leaves the congenial atmosphere of Earth behind, apparently, he leaves behind human chronology and physics as well. He can see across the gulfs of time and space. He can hear the voices of those who love him. He can dream without sleeping. Are these the effects of increased radiation at extreme high altitude? These are just the sorts of things that he is here to experience. He will have to report to the colonel on these anomalies. When he reaches the ground, in just a few minutes' time.

"Captain Messinger will free-fall for four and one-half minutes. He will fall eighty-five thousand feet during that time. He will reach speeds of over six hundred miles per hour, nearly the speed of sound. Without an airplane, ladies and gentlemen!"

In Joe Messinger's dream, the colonel sounds remarkably like a carnival barker. Joe Messinger has always liked and admired the colonel, but he finds him faintly ridiculous when he waxes bombastic. "At approximately seventeen thousand feet, he will deploy his main chute, after which—it is profoundly to be hoped—he will float safely to the ground."

Do you hear him? He says you're going to fall.

"Let's all applaud the bravery of this singular man, Air Force Captain Joseph Messinger, shall we, ladies and gentlemen?"

~ ~ ~

Years after he stood at the cliff's verge, on one of his first solo cross-country flight in the little yellow rented J3 Cub, Joe Messinger passed over the rectangles of his father's farm, swung the plane over the boxy farmhouse. With him was his current girl, the beautiful Margaret, who later that night will give herself to him entirely, her body, her spirit. She will become pregnant. They will marry. Margaret had never been in an airplane before, and the sight of the places she knew so far below her thrilled and terrified her, left her helpless and adoring of her pilot, her Joe.

Joe's mother, still lovely, the skin still firm and tight on her bones, looked up from where she knelt digging in her garden plot and waved at him, at them and their tiny wooden plane. Joe waggled the Cub's fabric-covered wings flirtatiously at her.

His father sat in a low chair, his hat—the one he wore when he worked—pulled down over his brow. He had left the valley for the South Pacific, Recon Marines, a few years after Joe Messinger stood on the cliff and looked across the valley, and there he got blown up by a Jap hand grenade. Lost his left leg from the knee down. Couple of fingers off his left hand. His left nut. He waved at Joe too, with his good hand. It made him happy to see the bright yellow plane pass over his place. It made him happy to see a plane that wasn't trying to shoot at him, that wasn't trying to shoot at anybody. Any day where nobody was trying to kill him was a good day. He watched the cruciform shadow of the J3 as it passed over his neat fields on its way to somewhere else.

He was still the constable, Joe Messinger's father, but they had hired a deputy for him. County commission hired the guy. A young fellow, served in the European theater and didn't get blown up. Didn't get a scratch. He was on his way up. He was going to be somebody in the Seneca Valley, someday soon. Joe Messinger's father was glad to have the help.

Joe Messinger pointed his plane to the west, circling and climbing, climbing and circling, until he passed over the ridge that he had spied from the cliff's edge years before. He made sure to pass over it right at the spot where he had imagined that other boy, the one just like him, the one that was looking at him. He wanted the boy to see the airplane. He wanted the boy to see his girl, to see Margaret: the melting expression on her face as they passed through the wisps of cloud, her lush figure, the desire written on her face.

One day Joe Messinger would go to war in an airplane, but that day was not this day. The engine of the Cub strained and whined. The wings thrummed. He was gaining altitude as he departed from his father's county.

~ ~ ~

"You're all clapping for my father, aren't you?" asks Katherine Messinger, called Kitty, sixteen years old and pretty as a picture. Joe Messinger can see her clear as day from the gondola that hangs beneath the converted weather balloon, twenty miles above the earth. He can hear her as clearly as though she were in the gondola and speaking right to him. More clearly, in fact, because her voice is not muffled by the thick helmet of plastic and metal. "People clap for him a lot. I don't know why, exactly. He always tells me that what he does is classified."

She's a painfully good-looking girl, slender as a young birch, with strong slim legs and a narrow waist. Her skirt is prim and swirls stiffly around her calves when she moves. Her face is flushed with excitement and worry. Is she a virgin? Joe Messinger can hardly bear to think about the answer to that question. It's not possible to stay pure for long in this world. He wasn't a virgin at her age, though her mother was, he believes. He was a dashing fellow, a burgeoning pilot, a good-looking kid, the son of a powerful man in the county. Clearly headed for someplace else, clearly going beyond the narrow confines of the Seneca Valley—but where?

If he had told them then, those high-breasted little damsels who gave him what he wanted, if he had told them that he was going to fall to earth from more than one hundred thousand feet in the air, fall from the very edge of space—would they have believed him? They would have laughed and slapped at him in a playful way as he tugged at their clothes, and they would have sighed and gone ahead and surrendered their virtue to him, dreaming (while awake) of something well outside of that place, and never imagining the truth, never imagining how far away the truth would take him. Kitty's mother Margaret had been just such a one. He had been her first. And her only. So he believed.

"When I told my history teacher what my father did for a living," Kitty says, "that he did classified things for the Air Force, he said my father was a hero."

Did you hear that, Joe Messinger? A hero!

"But that's in 1960. You're all living in the future." Who could she be talking to? She's speaking to the future. Her own children, perhaps? He struggles to imagine her married, his innocent little Kitty, imagine her pregnant, imagine her telling stories about him to her children, his grandchildren. Is that who she's speaking to? Or to some posterity that lies beyond the confines of his family? It occurs to him that it may be that, once a man has left the atmosphere, once a man has learned to see through time and across space as he has, perhaps all men are simultaneously freed from the bondage of the standard dimensions. He has been liberated, and his liberation has freed the world. What a discovery!

"You've never heard of my father," she says. "You've never heard of Joe Messinger. Probably by now… Probably in the future everybody's been to outer space. It's probably no big thing anymore."

That's what they promised us, those men in sterile white lab coats and horn-rimmed glasses, unamused under their flat-top haircuts. The men who wrote the sign: *This is the highest step in the world.* They promised us flying cars. Personal submersible watercraft. Robots and ray guns. X-ray glasses, so that we could conveniently see through the clothes of good-looking girls. All the items offered in the ads in the back of the comic books: they were supposed to have come true by now. Where are they, Joe Messinger? Where is my hovercar?

~ ~ ~

"Eight minutes!" cries Colonel Stabb.

And on the earth far below you, Joe Messinger, the earth that hangs like a lamp at your feet, in the year 1960, when your daughter is sixteen and maybe still a virgin: great adversity between the nations, and perplexity, roaring like the sea's mighty waves. Those mountains that seemed endlessly tall when you were a boy, the cliff that it took you hours to scale, the valley that seemed so broad—they are invisible below the clouds that blanket the planet, as far as the eye can see. If you could see those mountains, that cliff, they would barely register in your vision. What is a mountain that's three thousand feet tall, four thousand, five, when you are a hundred thousand feet in the air? That cliff on which you stood, on which you were a giant—it wouldn't make a footstool for you now.

Still the voices come to him. He is dreaming in the air, and they are dreaming of him far below: his daughter, and the colonel. The tops of the clouds—they are so like the cloud bottoms that day on the cliff.

They seem to be moving peacefully across the face of the earth, but he knows that the winds down there are wicked and violent and may well shortly tear him to pieces. Joe Messinger is looking down, and he was looking up on that earlier day, but the view is quite similar. Rising and falling—if the distance is sufficient, they are much the same.

"When I was a kid, there was a war in Korea," says Kitty.

"Joe Messinger will fall through a layer of clouds more than a mile thick!" bellows the colonel.

Fearful sights and great signs will appear in the heavens when the end times come. Do you see them dancing around you, Joe Messinger, where you dangle in the sky? Are you one of them yourself?

"They say there will be another war soon," says Kitty.

The Colonel continues, his stentorian voice nearly drowning out Kitty's soft soprano. If he keeps on shouting, Joe Messinger will awake. Joe Messinger very much wants to remain asleep. "And after returning safely to the surface of the planet, Captain Joe Messinger will fly nearly five hundred missions, in three combat tours of Vietnam. Which is a country where there is not yet a war in which we are involved. That's in the future, like the forgetting of Joe Messinger's name."

Kitty will not give up. She means to be heard. "They say this next war will be fought with nuclear bombs. They say this next one will kill everybody in the whole world."

Famines, plagues, and earthquakes. Much better to be up here, yes, Joe Messinger? Where it's quiet, and calm, and unfrightening, for at least a little while yet. The thought of falling cannot frighten you. What comes after the fall, the return to earth, boots on the ground again and looking into the faces of those who love you—yes, that can make even a man like you afraid. But the sleep before the fall, and the fall itself, those are sweet as milk with honey stirred into it. What you used to drink before bed, warmed by your mother. Before you climbed into the upper bunk in your room, there to sleep until morning and the crowing of the cock.

"Except for the cockroaches, which will survive," says Kitty. "I hate cockroaches. The cockroaches will become gigantic and intelligent, and they'll be the next species to inherit the earth, they will be the next race of men, because they're hardy and they breed so fast." Cockroaches! Where do kids get this stuff? She is describing some movie she has seen, he supposes. She has quite the imagination, his little girl.

He pictures her in the movie house, and it's not the movie house near their suburban home. It's the old Princess Theater in Mount Nebo, the one from the 30s, the only movie theater in Seneca County. Decorated like the tombs of the ancient pharaohs, golden columns and twelve-foot-tall statues of half-nude gods and goddesses, Osiris and Isis and Anubis and Ra—unreadable faces with high cheekbones and mascaraed eyes. It's been shut down for twenty years, but still that's where he pictures her, her figure dimly lit with the flickering of the projector's arc lamp. Is she there with someone? Is there a boy slouching in the seat beside her? Is his arm across her shoulders, is he touching her? Is she resisting or is she yielding?

Recall those nights in the upper bunk, far above the floor of your humble room. Where it is very quiet, and no one can reach you. Where you have a few moments to think.

"Do you imagine cockroaches can fall in love?" Kitty wants to know. Is she asking him, or the listeners from the future? She used to ask him all manner of things, and most often he knew the answers, and when he didn't, he made them up and she was satisfied with what he told her. How to answer this new line of questions? Cockroaches and love. He knows as much about one, he supposes, as he does about the other. "Intelligent mutant cockroaches," she says. "Maybe they wouldn't breed so fast, if they had to love somebody first. Love another cockroach."

"Six minutes!" shouts Colonel Stabb.

"I think I'm in love, Daddy!"

All these are the beginnings of sorrow, Joe Messinger, and the love of many will turn cold.

~ ~ ~

Margaret Messinger isn't out of her bathrobe yet. Eight in the morning and it looks like she has just rolled out of bed. Joe Messinger always rises at first light—sometimes, frequently in fact, before first light—but Margaret likes her beauty sleep. This is how Joe Messinger likes her best, warm from the unmade marriage bed, housecoat barely covering her sumptuous figure. She's not young, but she's still a great tumble.

She snaps a smart salute toward Joe. She can't know where he is, can she? His mission is highly classified. No man can make such a jump when others are watching. It's a private thing, this leap from twenty miles up. Beyond the atmosphere, though, it seems that nothing is private anymore. They can see him, and he can see them, and it's as if there's no distance between them at all.

"Love you, Captain. Love you … Joe," Margaret says. Her voice surprises him. It's full of static and echoes, and there are gaps in the transmission. Data loss.

"He goes to the Air Force Academy, Daddy." Kitty interrupts her mother. It's something she does frequently of late. Sorrow, to those who bear children in those days! "The boy I'm in love with. Mother adores him."

She is still a virgin. He can hear it in her voice. But she won't be for long. He can hear that too. He has the sense that he's watching his own life from on high, watching it repeat itself. The boy, the girl, the Air Force. The leap that's coming.

~ ~ ~

"Joe? Where are you, Joe?" Margaret asks. Why, of all these people, is she the least able to apprehend him, where he is, what he's doing? "I know you're high in the air. You're always high in the air. Can you see me from where you are?" She's calling out as though she's blind. He can barely hear her, barely understand.

Of course I can see you, Margaret. I can see all the world, I can see everything, and you are at the heart of it.

"I know you'll love him too," Kitty tells Joe in a whisper.

Margaret says to Kitty, "A father can't ever really love the man who marries his little girl, you know. He can like him, he can respect him, he can even admire him—but he can never love his rival."

"That's silly, Mother," Kitty says. "Rival?"

"Yes, baby. Don't you know? The man you marry will be your father's greatest rival. His rival for your love. You're the great love of his life, Kitty!"

"But that's you, Mother. You're the great love of his life."

Margaret laughs, and the laughter is tinged with bitterness. Joe Messinger's cheeks burn with shame.

"Captain Joe Messinger will kill many men in his three tours of duty," calls the colonel. "Men who killed that many of their country's enemies—in the old days, they became kings."

"What do they become now, Colonel Stabb?" Kitty wants to know.

"Now? Now, they become... colonels," says Stabb, shooting his cuffs and straightening his shoulders. He is gleaming and magnificent and covered in medals, lean and muscular and fierce as a hawk in his crisp blue uniform. Joe Messinger wears a clumsy suit of canvas and rubber and buckles. "Now," says the colonel, "they become me."

"When you were just a tiny baby girl," says Margaret into Kitty's small pink ear, "I would ask you, I would ask: 'Where do you have your daddy, Kitty-kins? Where have you got your daddy?' And do you know what you would do?"

Kitty holds up her right pinkie and encircles it with the forefinger and thumb of the opposite hand. Margaret grabs her linked hands and raises them high.

"That's right! That's right! Wrapped around your little finger. You were so precocious."

"Five minutes!"

"Five minutes until what, Colonel Stabb?" Kitty asks. She wrests her hands away from Margaret.

Margaret makes a shushing noise. "Don't ask the colonel that, honey," she says. "It's probably classified."

"I'm afraid that information is classified," the colonel admits.

"But I'm his daughter. I think I deserve to know."

"I'm his wife!" Margaret says. "Do you think I ever had him wrapped around my little finger? Joe Messinger the brave? Joe Messinger the stoic? Joe Messinger the hero?"

Joe Messinger is dreaming. The hero is dreaming.

"The killing is all in the future, though," says the colonel.

"Is the future classified?" Kitty wants to know.

"He loves me," says Margaret. "Oh yes, he love me. But not like you, little Kitty-kins! He loves no one the way he loves you."

The colonel resumes his air of professionalism. It is important to remain professional, even in the face of powerful and potentially unsettling emotions. Especially then. "Right now, Captain Joe Messinger is hanging over one hundred thousand feet above the earth, peacefully and contentedly waiting for the moment to come when he will jump from the gondola. He will set a free-fall record that will stand unbroken for nearly fifty years! That's what I can tell you about the future."

~ ~ ~

Joe Messinger dreams about the dog he had when he was a boy. The dog was a great big collie that guarded his father's sheep. It was named Grenadier. He smiles at the thought.

"Do you love my daddy, Colonel Stabb?" Kitty asks.

Margaret flutters her hands in the air. Her peignoir comes slightly untucked, and she moves quickly to fasten it again. "Kitty! What a question to ask."

"No, no, Margaret, that's a very good question," the colonel tells her. His tone is as reassuring as his words. He is not afraid of sincere sentiment, in its proper context. "Let me answer it."

"It's not classified?"

"I honor your father, Katherine."

"Everybody calls me Kitty."

"I honor your father, Kitty."

"But do you love him?"

"I honor him because it's possible for him to do what other men cannot. No one could order another man to do what your father is doing today, right now... in four minutes..."

"Is it possible that he'll be killed?" Kitty's face is strained, but she's prepared for the answer, whatever it might be. It shocks Joe Messinger a bit, to see his daughter so prepared to hear that he will die.

"Yes, is it possible that he'll be killed?" Margaret asks. Joe Messinger cannot hear through the static what her attitude toward the question is. Does she want him to die?

"I have ordered men to their deaths in battle, many times, in more than one war, but I could not order a man to do what Joe Messinger, what your father, what your husband, Margaret, has volunteered to do."

Joe Messinger is dreaming of his great fluffy collie dog Grenadier, he's dreaming that he and his dog are playing out in the great meadow of timothy grass out behind the house where he grew up –

"Should his stabilizing chute fail to deploy correctly," the colonel says, his voice calm, " it's entirely possible that Captain Messinger will enter an irrecoverable flat spin, which could quickly accelerate to as much as two thousand revolutions per minute."

"Oh my!" cries Kitty.

"What then?" The look on Margaret's face is bland, her inquiry practical. The belt of her robe has slacked again. She's a voluptuous woman, and the colonel has a difficult time keeping his eyes on his notes, the bland notes that rest on the podium before him.

"He will be … liquefied."

"Daddy!"

"Joe!"

"Two minutes!"

Joe Messinger dreams that his mother is calling him in from the field, and that a glorious meal awaits him and his mother and his loyal dog Grenadier, a great groaning board laden with all the foods that he loved as a boy. Fried chicken. Green beans. Mashed potatoes. Silver Queen corn, on the cob, dripping with butter.

Joey! Jo-ey! Time to come in now! Supper's waiting!

Best of all, his father will be waiting at the table, and he will hold young Joe's hand, and his father's hand will be whole, as it was before the Japs took his fingers; and he will hold Joe's mother's hand, and they will say grace together before they eat. And afterward young Joe will climb upstairs to his bed, and he will lie down to sleep, and to dream, and it will be peaceful and quiet and he won't have to jump out of anything until morning.

"Should his stabilizing chute fail to deploy correctly, and should he enter such a flat spin as I have described, I imagine he'll return to earth as a light rain, all along the slopes and ridges of the Alleghenies. He will have—even in failure—a glorious return to the land of his beginnings."

"He'll turn into rain?" Kitty asks. It's the sort of transformation a girl such as she can understand and enjoy. Cockroaches into men. Men into rain.

"You know why he loves you best, don't you? Best in all the world?" Margaret again, her voice edged with fury.

"Why will he turn into rain?"

"It's in the best tradition of the military, and in service of the highest calling of science. We must know!"

"What must we know?"

"The answer to the question."

"He loves you best," Margaret says, "because you remind him of me. When we met. When we fell in love. We were just children. Children! He went to the Air Force Academy. He was so handsome in his cadet's uniform. I looked just like you then! I looked just like you, Kitty!"

Kitty ignores her mother. More and more these days. "What question?" she asks.

"The one that your father, Capt. Joe Messinger, is hanging twenty miles above the earth in order to answer."

"Why doesn't he love me that way anymore?" Margaret demands.

"One minute."

Joe Messinger makes his way to the open hatch of the Excelsior III. Below him, the earth is covered in a blanket of clouds. Soon Joe Messinger will be falling through them.

Joe Messinger's fingers drum against his legs.

"He will feel no sense of acceleration as he falls. Only a man who is dreaming could do such a thing." The colonel.

"I was beautiful." Margaret.

"Thirty seconds. Count with me, Kitty. Twenty-nine, twenty-eight…"

Only a man who remembers the prayers of his youth, his bedtime prayers, could do such a thing.

Now I lay me down to sleep—

Kitty and the colonel count together. "Twenty-seven, twenty-six, twenty-five…"

I pray the Lord my soul to keep—

"Come on, Mother. Count with us! Twenty-four, twenty-three, twenty-two…"

If I should… If I should…

All three of them now. "Twenty-one, twenty, nineteen…"

Die.

"Eighteen, seventeen, sixteen…"

If I should die before I wake—

"Fifteen, fourteen, thirteen…"

I pray the Lord my soul to take.

Count with us.

It occurs to Joe Messinger that he could easily just stay where he is.

Distant. Omniscient. Holy. He could stay aloft for all time, drifting from place to place above the globe and dreaming the world. Dreaming it without pain or pleasure. He could become a legend, a ghost. There is no one to insist that he walk through that door.

This is the highest step in the world.

"Five, four, three…"

He must return to the ones he loves. He must fall and fall and fall until he is with them again.

Zero.

Joe Messinger leans forward. The wind once again slaps his face. How can such a thing be? He's wearing the heavy helmet, but nonetheless the stiff cool breeze of his youth touches the flesh of his cheeks, caresses his forehead. It is the current at the top of the cliff, and he can lean into it, and he will be borne up. That evening comes back to him whole. The boy on the opposite ridge—where is he? He must be on the earth. He must be grown. He must be waiting for Joe Messinger, back at the border of Seneca County.

Joe's gloved fingers brush the edges of the doorway. He forces himself to relax, not to grab hold. If he does, he will never let go.

Below him lies the farm. Below him lie the valley and the mountains that surround it. Below him his family has gathered. Below, the return to conventional time, conventional space. His center of gravity shifts forward. His balance, always excellent, suddenly deserts him. Unaware that he's falling from the gondola—it seems to him that the gondola has left him, that it's shooting up into the sky at an astonishing rate of speed—Joe Messinger tumbles head over heels into the great blue void.

Mudman

On another day, Tom Snedegar would have smashed the dirt dauber without a thought, but on this day—an overcast Sunday when thin greenish mist fluttered like cobwebs in the gullies and sinkholes of Snedegar's place—on this day, Snedegar just watched it come.

"You'd bite me if you was to get the chance, wouldn't you?" he asked the wasp. It buzzed its wings. It was only maybe a foot from the steel-capped toes of his boots on the cold concrete floor of the milking parlor. Snedegar decided that he liked the wasp, liked it for its truculence, liked it for its solitary ways. "Bite hell out of me," he said.

He rummaged briefly in the cabinet on the wall until he came up with the measuring cup that he sometimes dipped into the cooling tank, to sample the sweet raw milk. He had used the same cup since he was a boy. The glass of the measuring cup was thick and slightly yellow. He upended the cup and bent to put it down over the wasp, but the wasp was gone.

Snedegar looked over the milking parlor. He had just finished hosing it down after the morning milking, and it looked clean and pleasing to him, with its ranked feed bunks and its overhead network of pipes and its solid concrete block walls. He checked the floor again, the measuring cup dangling by its handle from his fingers. No wasp.

"Slipped me," he said, and the wasp buzzed in response. It had found its way onto the leg of his coveralls, its abdomen bobbing dangerously. Snedegar brushed at it with the back of his hand and it fell to the floor. Snedegar plopped the measuring cup over it. The wasp's wings blurred, their whirring muted.

He got on his hands and knees to look at the trapped wasp. He squinted his weak left eye so that he could focus more sharply with the right and put his face close to the measuring cup. The wasp reared up on its hind legs and returned his gaze between the faded seven-eighths and the full-cup markings. It was a great glossy dauber, and it had extraordinarily long wings.

Snedegar took a minute to admire the gorgeous black-pearl curve of its thorax, which was the size of his pinkie finger's first joint. He examined the neat articulation of the wasp's small body, its oily limbs and agile antennae, the deftness of its armor. Its depthless eyes. He tapped the glass, and the wasp droned. It seemed content to wait.

~ ~ ~

Snedegar wanted a mudman. He needed it to help him out around the farm. He worked the operation alone: two milkings a day, feeding, chopping the corn, maintaining the buildings, the equipment. The list of things to be done was endless, but money was always short, and it was almost impossible to hire anybody to do the sort of work that Snedegar did.

"I'll never get to Heaven," Snedegar said to himself as he dug. He was getting the mud to make the mudman. Sundays were the Sabbath, but Snedegar worked anyway. The cows didn't know what day of the week it was. They had to be milked, they had to be fed. When he had a mudman to help him, he could begin keeping the day holy. He could accompany his wife to the church she attended in the county seat, and on the rounds of pleasant errands and visits she always undertook afterward. She was doing those errands right then, and he couldn't tell when she might be back.

Snedegar's thoughts wandered briefly to the trapped wasp. A wasp didn't get tired. A wasp needed nothing. A wasp never wasted time mooning about what to do. He had watched this particular one for weeks as it built its nest under the eaves of the dairy barn, rolling up little pills of mud at the edges of puddles and then hauling them aloft. Stinging fat spiders and taking them away too to feed its babies, the spiders' long spindly legs dangling as the dauber bore them upward.

Time to get back to digging. Snedegar put the shovel blade into the dirt of the field again. A couple of his Holstein heifers watched him with mild eyes as he burrowed.

Snedegar's wife was town-bred and not made for farm life. She was young and pretty. Sensible shoes, tidy bosom. She worked part-time at a travel agency in the county seat. She worked for a man named Carlson, the youthful guy who owned the travel agency. Snedegar chopped at a stray root that blocked his digging, sank the sharp blade of the shovel deep into the loam, added another wet spade-load to the growing pile. The dirt was rich with fat nightcrawlers.

Without the mudman, Snedegar would never get to Heaven, because he worked on the Sabbath. He did pretty well on the other Commandments, if he said so himself: no strange gods, no cursing, honored his father and mother, both dead for years. Had no reasons to lie, no one to lie to. No murder, and he wanted no woman other than his wife—he wanted her so fiercely that he thought sometimes he would go blind or die with the wanting. Coveted nothing, needed nothing other than this place, these acres that were his and his alone. Couldn't imagine needing anything else. Except the mudman.

Carlson the travel agent would get to Heaven, because he took Sundays off from the office. Carlson was well-scrubbed and he dressed handsomely. Snedegar had no one to work with him, but Carlson had Snedegar's wife. Snedegar laughed to himself, thinking of his orderly wife working alongside him as he grubbed in the dirt of the field.

He was sweating heavily. He had enough dirt piled up to make his mudman, he had plenty, but he kept on going. The hard ground yielded up valueless detritus: a sharp flint spear point, a scattering of hog's teeth, sherds of glazed crockery, a length of greasy chain, a glistening rib. Snedegar's shoulders and arms and back bent eagerly to the task of excavation, as they always had to difficult physical labor, and the dirt flew.

At last the edge of the shovel's blade scraped against bedrock, sending up a flurry of short-lived sparks. Snedegar paused. He was standing in the hole that he had made, and he felt mildly shocked to find how deep it was, only his head rising above the lip. The dark shape of a hawk rode the thermals overhead, cruising, looking to dine on the mice that throve in the dairy barn, or to hook one of the portly groundhogs that populated the farm, that tunneled endlessly through the dirt of the fields.

Snedegar hated the groundhogs because they made their dens in his fields, made craters that were a danger to his livestock and that threatened to damage and destroy his machinery. He killed them whenever he was able, and hung their limp, furry bodies on his fence posts for the crows to pick at. He silently wished the hawk good hunting.

Up to his neck in dirt, Snedegar realized that he had pretty much a groundhog's view of things. Stones loomed like mountains. The horizon was inches away from his nose. He felt like prey.

A cruciform shadow swept over him, and he glanced upward. The hawk cupped its broad wings, stroking its way upward into the flat, colorless sky, and Snedegar closed his left eye so that he could focus the right on it. He saw then, as it flared and circled toward open ground, that it wasn't a hawk at all. It was a horned owl, its curved beak slightly open, its feathers rumpled and dirty-looking. One of its legs was crippled, the claw drawn up and withered. It gave Snedegar the creeps, to see a night bird out in the middle of the day. The owl disappeared over the ridgepole of the dairy barn.

Snedegar bent to his shovel again, but the impulse to dig had left him. He felt tired. He felt so tired suddenly that he thought he might just fall asleep, leaning on his shovel handle. It occurred to him to lie down in the foot of the hole. He could just forget about the mudman, forget about the Sabbath and the wasp in the milking parlor and his wife. He could simply lie down and stare upward. Maybe the hawk (no, the owl, the daylight owl) would return to sail over him, to relieve the monotony of the lowering sky, the deck of clouds that promised more rain to come.

~ ~ ~

Mudmen had once done a lot of the labor in amongst the hills where Snedegar had his dairy. When hardwood was king, a hundred years and more ago. They had worked the clear-cuts, snaking the giant sawlogs out of the woods, dense white oak trees fourteen feet in diameter, logs that could acquire a coltish life of their own when a man chained them and skidded them down the hillsides, into the bottoms where the whining sawmills and the boomtowns squatted. Logs that could turn on a man and stave in his ribcage, smash him to pieces without warning, grind him into the earth like an insect.

You could see them, the mudmen, in the blurry sepia photographs that had come down from Snedegar's grandfather and his great-grandfather. The pictures lined the upstairs hallway of Snedegar's house:

groups of bandy-legged, barrel-chested timber-cutters. Snedegar's grandfather, who had worked the last stands of virgin oaks, had called them "timber apes." The timber apes grinning like boys, teeth gleaming in their pale faces, axes and two-man saws on their shoulders, ranged in a semicircle around the sundered trunk of whatever enormous oak or black locust they'd just brought thundering down.

And in the background, always at the edge of the light, looking as though it might be no more than an awkward-falling shadow, or maybe some hulking, shy, ugly fellow who didn't care to have his picture made: a mudman. Eyes like slits in the broad, flat face, mouth a silent gash above the lantern jaw. Sometimes two of them, or three, standing shoulder to shoulder, close together as though for companionship.

~ ~ ~

Great Caesar's Ghost—that was the name of Snedegar's bull—knew that something was up. As Snedegar, up in the nearly empty hay loft, hammered together the crude mold that had the shape of a man, the bull slammed its ponderous head against the tightly fitted boards of its stall, keeping time with the strokes of the hammer. Even after Snedegar was done hammering, the blows of the bull's head continued on, slow and perfectly rhythmic.

The frame of the dairy barn jolted with every impact, and the chittering swifts in the hay mow left their comfortable perches in the rafters and swept out through the wide north window of the loft and back in again from the west. Snedegar watched the birds as they flashed from daylight into the dusk of the loft. They were marvelous, he thought, better than Chinese acrobats, the way they never so much as touched one another, though maneuvering so close, and in such a confined space.

He left off his hammering for a bit and descended the steep staircase to the ground floor of the barn, went to the stall where Great Caesar's Ghost stood confined. The bull was a monster, well over a ton in his prime, heavier now, bloated, head like a beer keg, chest as broad as a snowplow. It shifted its great shoulders when it caught sight of Snedegar, blew out a vast gust of breath before slamming its skull into the barn wall again.

"Howdy, old man," Snedegar said. The bull had been done with breeding back in the time of Snedegar's father, but Snedegar could somehow never bring himself to do the needful thing, and so Caesar's Ghost continued on here in the half-light of the stall. From where he stood, Snedegar could see the small vacuum-tank of liquid nitrogen where he kept the straws of bull semen he used for breeding his cows. It stood in a corner of the unused stall next to the bull's. Cryo-Bio, read the brightly colored label on the side of the canister. The canister itself was made of burnished aluminum, and the logo on its side bore the cartoon picture of an appealing cow—she looked more like a deer, really—surrounded by snow flakes.

Snedegar knew that if a man stuck his hand into the LN2 and then shook it, his fingers would fall off and shatter like glass. He'd had numerous dreams about just that, dreams in which he slowly, deliberately inserted his hand into the tank. It was like he wanted to do it. In the dream, there was no pain as his hand froze, only a rising numbness and a sense of wonder. When he withdrew it, the fingers and fingernails were a delicate shade of blue, and they glittered like jewels.

In fact, a time or two, he'd had to fight to keep himself away from the canister, fight the impulse to plunge his hand into it, his arm up to the elbow, just to see if it would become numb and beautiful, like the hand in the dream.

Caesar's Ghost bashed its head into the boards again, and Snedegar grabbed the ring in the bull's nose and twisted it fiercely toward him. "Stop it," he said. Something passed from the bull to him, he felt it pass to him through his hand on the nose ring, felt it travel like hot acid up through his arm and into the center of his chest, into the dense muscle of his heart, and from there to his limbs, his cock, his brain, and he saw what he would do when his wife came home that afternoon, that evening: he would pull her close, his hands hard on her shoulders, and she would laugh at his urgency. "Careful," she would say, giggling, "don't muss me," and he would laugh along with her. He would laugh as he jerked her blouse open, laugh as he ignored her protests, frightened of him now, laugh as he rucked her demure skirt above her waist, as he tumbled her to the floor.

~ ~ ~

There had been mudwomen too, at the logging camps and up in the hardwood forests. It was inevitable, so few women in the region, which was a wilderness then, and so many randy, uncouth men. That was what had ended it, finally, the mudwomen. They awakened something that had not previously exhibited itself in the stolid, silent mudmen, who were made exclusively for work, a sort of sympathy. Sympathy that quickly bloomed into what could only be called love.

The unanswerable love of the mudmen, the unrelenting sexual desire of the timber apes: mayhem ensued, deadly violence that spread swiftly and terribly and ineluctably from one teeming sawmill town to the next, swept through the hollers and down the creeks and raced along the ridges. Axes and splitting mauls and whirling bandsaw blades and rotgut liquor and pistols and fire. When it was over, a dozen of the timber apes lay in shallow graves in the stony bottoms, their arms and legs and spines fractured by the awesome, impassive strength of the mudmen, their ears and noses and mouths stopped up with silt, their lungs filled with the suffocating stuff; and the mudmen had been utterly purged from the face of the earth.

~ ~ ~

Snedegar finished cobbling together the form for the mudman out of two-by-fours. He hauled the earth up into the loft bucket by bucket, dumped it into the mold, added water until it achieved what seemed to him an appropriate viscosity, tamped it down, shaped it with his hands. He was covered in it.

He had made the mold large. There wasn't much to it, really, two arms, two legs, heavy body, blocky squared-off head. He was no artist. He had lugged all told probably four hundred, maybe five hundred pounds of earth to fill the mold, but he figured that the mudman would weigh a good bit less when it had dried out some.

He knelt down beside the head of the mold, extended his index finger, poised it over the great flat face. A poke for the left, a poke for the right, and a pair of dark beady eyes stared up at him. He stood back from the mold so that he could observe his handiwork. The mudman's gaze seemed to follow him. Snedegar grinned. Leaning down, he slashed his forefinger across the face a handspan beneath the eyes. A lopsided, unsmiling mouth.

~ ~ ~

Snedegar balanced precariously atop his ladder, jabbing at the delicate pan pipes of the dirt dauber nest with a paint spatula. He worked the thin edge of the spatula under the nest where it adhered to the unpainted wall of the dairy barn, just beneath the eaves of the sharply sloping roof. He wanted the nest, with its sleepily murmuring cargo of baby wasps, to serve as the mudman's heart. The nest began to pull loose, and Snedegar moved too quickly with the spatula.

Bits of the brittle nest broke free and spiraled to the ground thirty feet below, and Snedegar imagined that the muttering within increased in volume and intensity. The dried bodies of garden spiders, the wasps' larder, sifted out like shell corn. He had watched the dauber build the nest and fill it with dauber eggs and paralyzed spiders. The eggs hatched, and—Snedegar's mind did not like to go to what happened next, what happened to the spiders, there in the muddy dark. He was no great fan of spiders, but some things did not bear much thinking about.

"Hush now," Snedegar told the babies, and he crooned a brief lullaby to them. It was a song that he recalled his mother singing, but the memory was a distant one, and it contained no words, so he could only hum the tune as well as he remembered it and hope for the best. He sang in time to the monotonous banging that rose once again from Caesar's Ghost, and Snedegar believed that the wasp babies inside could hear him, that they knew he meant them no harm, that he was going to put them to a good use. He believed that they were humming along with him.

From up near the barn roof, he could see out over the breadth of his operation, with its little clusters of silos and outbuildings, the pole barn and the granary and the machine shop. Along the eastern fence line, a couple of crows did noisy battle over the week-old carcass of a groundhog, spiked to a leaning post. Their screeches floated to him like the voices of bickering children.

The wet soil of the field looked soft as a featherbed. It seemed inviting, as though it wanted him simply to loose his hold on the ladder, to spread his arms, and drop down sprawling onto it. The hole that he had made looked bottomless to him, filled with moving shadows. He glanced around for the cruising owl, thinking that it might be drawn by the squabbling of the crows, but it was nowhere in sight.

There were other wasps' nests under the roofline, dozens of them, decades' worth, but they had been broken open over the years and emptied by the ravenous beaks of barn swifts. This one, the last whole one, would have to suffice. He slowed his breathing and steadied the hand with the spatula, working with the concentration of a surgeon. The ladder wobbled beneath him, and he stopped scraping at the wall for a moment, to brace himself and to get a new grip on the ladder. He had a gallon-size freezer bag with him, into which he planned to drop the nest when he had freed it. He thought that the nest and the baby wasps and the freezer bag all together would make a most satisfactory heart. Growing. Feeding. Tireless.

A swift landed on the edge of the tin roof, fluttering its wings momentarily for balance, its claws clattering like light rain against the slick metal. It turned a bright eye on him. He thought that it looked hungry. "Get your own," he said to the bird, which flicked its head so that it could look at him with its other eye. "These ones are mine." He went back to work.

The dauber nest gave slightly, and the spatula slipped another half-inch beneath it, a full inch, two. Snedegar put his hand on the crumbling surface of the nest, and he could feel the young daubers waking within, ceasing to batten on the still-living spiders, hauling themselves reluctantly over one another's compact bodies there in the trembling dark. In the warm enclosure of its stall, Caesar's Ghost ceased to beat its head against the wooden walls, and the silence was a blessing.

The nest released its hold on the wall with shocking suddenness, and Snedegar went after it as it slipped away from him. The extension ladder rocked and threatened to telescope itself, taking Snedegar down with it. His fingertips recalled the rough terra-cotta exterior of the nest, recalled it so keenly that he felt he could almost will it back into his grasp, but the clatter of the frail mud pipes against the hard ground below told him that the nest was gone.

~ ~ ~

The birds came. They swooped through the air like little fighter planes, the swifts, and they plucked up the struggling young wasps and ate them. They ate the shrunken, quivering spiders too. In their greed they grabbed up bits of the mud nest and flung them down again. Snedegar beat at the birds, and they twittered furiously as they circled his head, avoiding his swatting palms without difficulty. They pecked at the plastic bag, they gobbled wasps, they jabbed at Snedegar's hands, beat their wings against his brow, clung to his back, their tiny claws pricking his flesh through the fabric of the coveralls.

Snedegar crawled on the packed earth, racing against the birds, sweeping the baby wasps and the shattered pipes of the nest and the spiders into the baggie. Sometimes he slipped and his hands or his knees crushed this or that wasp, and the wasps stung him as he saved them. He wanted to cry out but he didn't, swifts caught in his clothes, swifts trapped in the tangle of his hair.

~ ~ ~

Snedegar tapped at the upturned bottom of the measuring cup. "I'll never get to Heaven," he told the trapped wasp. He wondered what his face looked like to it as he gazed in through the distorting lens of the glass. Vast and cratered as the moon. He knew that a wasp's eyes saw differently from a man's.

He wondered if maybe the wasp thought that he was God. What it would be like if he were under the measuring cup. A dirt dauber God leaning over him, poison-filled stinger the size of a man, wings like the sails of a windmill. The notion filled him with horror. *Wasp god.* If God actually was a wasp, then he, Snedegar, was going to be in terrible trouble.

Every now and again, a bird would throw itself against the milking parlor windows with a bone-crunching thump. They wanted more of the wasp larvae. The sound of their bodies smashing into the glass made Snedegar wince. Stunned or dead, they lay on their backs near the barn's foundation, their wings outspread, their dainty claws upthrust.

The wasp turned its back to Snedegar. "Don't you want to bite me?" Snedegar asked it. He held up the baggie, half-filled with baby daubers. "You wanted to bite me this morning. Remember?" He put his lips against the cool glass. "Don't you even remember?"

~ ~ ~

He thrust the plastic bag into the chest of the mudman. He pushed the remains of the dauber nest down deep into the dirt and the muck. Then he waited. He knelt by the mudman's form. From time to time he imagined that he could hear the buried wasp babies stirring in their renewed darkness. The cows were gathering at the wide door of the milking parlor, he knew it by the shuffling of their hooves, their soft lowing at the discomfort of their full udders. He realized with a start that he was, for the first time that he could remember, late for the afternoon milking.

Maybe, he thought, the mudman wasn't moving because it had nothing to do. Snedegar knew that, without the constant nagging of the work, without the terror that something had been left undone, he himself would lie down and never arise again. Maybe the mudman was the same way. It needed a job to do. Snedegar needed to give it a job. He searched the pockets of his coveralls, came across a chewed-up stub of pencil, tore a scrap from a feed sack to write on.

He licked the pencil tip, poised it above the triangular fragment of paper. His needs all crowded into his brain at once. The cows, the preparation of the fields for planting, the repairs of winter damage to the outbuildings, feeding, cleaning, the thousand things small and large that he did during any given day. How to pick one? He could hear the Holsteins shouldering against one another down at the dairy, and his breath grew short at the thought of his tardiness.

At the fence line, the crows continued to caw in harsh voices. It sounded like there were more than two of them now, three, four, a half dozen, screaming and fighting over the mummified remains of the groundhog. KILL GROUNDHOGS, he scrawled on the coarse paper in big block letters. The clamor of the crows increased. How hungry must they be, to fight over such food? Then, inspired, he struck out the word GROUNDHOGS with heavy black strokes of the pencil lead and wrote in another: VERMIN.

At first, he placed the rough triangle of paper on the mudman's inert chest. Then he picked it up, put it down over one of the eyeholes. His wife would be home at any moment. The cows were waiting to be milked. The crows were at war in the lower field. The mudman was waiting for instructions. He took up the paper a third time and thrust it savagely, deeply into the mudman's grim mouth. Outside, the rain that had threatened all day began to fall, the water pooling on the surface of the soaked ground.

~ ~ ~

The upper-floor hallway of his house was ill-lit, illuminated only by a clumsy wall sconce and a narrow slit of a window. The hallway had been dim and full of shadows for all of Snedegar's life. What light there was glinted unhelpfully off the glass that covered pictures of his family. In this picture his grandfather, standing atop the ridgepole of the half-finished dairy barn; in that one his great-grandfather at the center of a newly cleared pasture field; the tilt of their hats jaunty, their faces shaded by the deeply creased brims. They looked much alike, those two men. They looked much like Snedegar.

Snedegar took each one of the photographs from its place on the wall, examined it closely. The pictures left behind them lighter, unsoiled squares of wallpaper. Pictures older than the ones of the farm with its open fields, pictures from the time of the forests, the dark understory and the timber apes, their postures vain as they posed and preened before the toppled corpses of the great trees. Holding up their hands to show where the voracious bandsaws had taken various of their fingers. "There were giants in the earth in those days," Snedegar said to himself.

The shadows in the photographs twisted and slipped, capricious—or were those the shadows in the hall, moving? Shifting with the rain that sheeted across the single window. It seemed impossible to know what anything was for sure.

Downstairs, his wife moved from room to room, the soles of her shoes rapping smartly against the bare floorboards. He had not grabbed her when she had come home, had not wanted to smear her with the mud that covered him. He had twisted the ring in the bull's nose and he had felt the power that still lay within the animal, he knew that he had. He wanted to ravish her. But the notion had come to seem ridiculous with her standing there facing him, her clothes unwrinkled, her makeup fresh. How could he touch her?

"Will you come up?" he called to her. His voice sounded exhausted and weak in his own ears.

"After a while," she replied, her voice light and singsong. "I've got to ret up this mud you tracked in. You go on to bed. Go on to sleep."

He closed his left eye and brought his face close to the photographs, one after another. He wished for a jeweler's loupe. The tones of the photos were muted, and the timber apes swam in his vision, indecipherable blotches of light and dark. They faded even as he peered at them.

The trees were vast, the hillsides steep. The men were small. The mudmen... Where were the mudmen?

He hauled himself into his bedroom. The wasp was there, sitting motionless beneath the measuring cup on his bedside table beside the clock, which he wound and set to wake him for the morning milking. The mudmen were a lie. There would be no mudman for Snedegar. The knowledge grieved him because of the time he had wasted this day. Grieved him, too, because he could no longer imagine how he was going to be able to keep the Sabbath holy, and so he would never get into Heaven. The wasp waved its antennae at him, and he leaned over to it. "Nighty-night," he told it, and the moisture in his breath fogged the glass.

~ ~ ~

Snedegar dreamed of the vacuum canister. In the dream, he carefully unscrewed the top of the tank and set it, just as carefully, to one side. The LN2 was precious stuff and not to be wasted. Wisps of vapor rose from the darkness within, along with a kind of hissing. A buzzing. Putting his ear to the tank, he thought that he could make out the voice of the mudman. The voice spoke to him with the droning of insects' wings. He could make out individual words, longer phrases, but not their meaning. This was an old language, the language of wasps, not meant for human ears, and it filled him with terror.

He stood over the mudman's form, the canister in his hands. The metal of the tank was cold, and he could feel himself beginning to freeze. Freezing was a relief. He welcomed the numbness, but he knew that it could prevent him from doing what he must. From doing his work. He braced himself to resist the creeping cold and raised the canister, tipped it so that the liquid nitrogen ran out, it poured in a heavy stream, seething as it struck the warm earth of the mudman's body, smoking and boiling as Snedegar laved it over the mudman's limbs, the dirt blanching and crystallizing, fracturing under the cascading stuff.

The wasps, grown now to maturity, two inches long and more, began crawling from the mudman's flesh, they pushed their way blindly outward from the buried heart to the surface. They knew that the end was coming, deep within the mudman's chest they felt it coming on like winter. Snedegar deluged them, and there was an astonishing pleasure in it, to see a gleaming wasp, pulling itself free, turn in an instant to blue smoldering glass, the perfect simulacrum of a wasp, before it burst and shattered and crumbled into dust. The mudman was screaming, shrieking imprecations in the voice of the wasp god, but its crude mouth never moved.

The dream shifted, and Snedegar no longer stood over the prostrate mudman. Now it was his own bed that was crawling with wasps. They blundered over the sheets that bore his grandmother's monogram, and over his pillows, and the body of his wife. It was too late to stop the cataract of nitrogen that flowed from the canister, and Snedegar was not at all sure that he'd have called it back if he could. It was a hard job that he was doing, but it was his job, and he would see it done properly. His wife's lithe body writhed and twitched as he bathed her, as he baptized her, and the droplets of nitrogen that went astray and struck Snedegar burned him like fire.

Her breath smoked and she gargled with pain, she tore at the stiff frozen folds of her nightdress and the material collapsed like thinly beaten gold foil beneath her fingers, her delicate fingers which broke loose one joint at a time until she was left with nothing more than stumps. He splashed the nitrogen over her legs, and she howled, and he had never wanted her so much in his life, he was hard as a railroad spike, hard as a diamond. Her voice was gone now, and she arched her back like a gymnast until only the crown of her head and the tips of her toes touched the mattress.

Snedegar stepped back from the bed, in awe of what she had become. What he had made her. Her body was a perfect glimmering bow, of a blue so pure that it pained his eyes to look at it.

He shook the canister, and it continued full. Which meant that his work was not done yet. It was heavy, and the muscles of his arms were tired, but he raised the yawning mouth of the tank, touched its unearthly cold to his blistered lips, and began eagerly to drink.

~ ~ ~

Snedegar woke in the night, thinking that it must be time for the morning milking, but the clock told him that it was not. That was hours off yet. His wife slept heavily beside him. He held his breath, listening for the sound that had brought him out of his dreams. The rain muffled everything. He could hear the settling of the farmhouse on its stone foundation and the ticking of his bedside clock and the slow creeping of the wasp beneath the measuring cup. Round and round the perimeter it went. Then, distantly, the metronomic rapping that he knew to be Great Caesar's Ghost. Snedegar kept track of the strokes until he reached thirteen, and then he left off counting.

~ ~ ~

When his alarm clock rang, Snedegar flung out an arm to shut it off. His fingers connected with the measuring cup, and it flew from the tabletop and thumped to the hooked rug that covered the floor. The wasp sat still for a moment, as though unsure of what to do with its newfound freedom, and Snedegar almost got a hand over it before it spread its impressive wings and darted away. The room was dark and he quickly lost sight of it, but he could still hear it bumbling around up near the ceiling.

Snedegar patted his wife on her warm hip. "You watch out now," he told her as he rose. "There's a wasp loose in the room."

~ ~ ~

Every fencepost along the short lane between the dairy barn and the house bore the body of a groundhog, piniomed like a butterfly in a kid's collection. Crucified, their buck-toothed mouths comically agape, rodent eyes startled and bugging. The sight of them lining the road—ten, fifteen, more and more of them as Snedegar played the beam of his flashlight along the fence—staggered him. It was dark out, time for milking, and the rain was still falling, pattering off his cap and the shoulders of the slicker that he wore, catching like bright beads in the shaggy coats of the groundhogs.

He prodded the pudgy, out-thrust belly of the first groundhog with a forefinger, and the animal twitched and snapped its jaws at him, rolled its eyes, grunted. Still alive. Pinned through the body to the locust post with a square-headed iron nail, a handmade nail that must have been drawn by brute force from the timbers of the dairy barn itself; its spine snapped, its blood staining the post and the ground beneath it; but still living. He shone his light down the row of groundhogs and he could see that others among them—not all, but many—were alive as well, their paws paddling helplessly at the air. Snedegar marveled at the fantastic cruelty of it.

The wasp god.

The mudman.

He came near to laughing. This was the mudman's work. There was such a thing. He himself, Snedegar, had made it. He thought of the despair he had felt the night before with contempt. He wanted to shake that Snedegar, that exhausted Snedegar, and shout into his face, *You see? They were not lies. The stories were not lies.*

He trotted down the lane, sloshing his way through the puddles that had collected in the low places. He tried not to look at the struggling groundhogs, but his eyes were drawn back to them, again and again. He noticed that there were other creatures pinned to the posts as well: a pair of sleek red foxes, squirrels, blacksnakes, copperheads, a wrist-thick diamondback, its rattles still sizzling. On one post alone, two dozen of the little barn swifts, tacked up by their fragile wings. Possums, crows, a feral dog, its eyes shining green in the lamplight. The owl with the withered claw.

Snedegar felt queasy, numbering in his mind the fence posts that bordered the lane. Dozens. How many fence posts on the entire place? Hundreds. Thousands, all set by the hands of the Snedegar men. Spreading out into the darkness on all sides of him, where the beam of his light was too weak to illuminate. The sun would be up soon, already the eastern sky was beginning to pinken with the coming dawn, and then he would see. He knew now the meaning of the alarum from Great Caesar's Ghost in the night, and what would greet him when he reached the barn.

Something passed him in the lane moving toward the house, something massive and cold, something that moved in near silence and so swiftly that he couldn't bring the flashlight beam to bear on it before it was gone. On tottering legs, wishing that he had some other choice but knowing that he did not, he followed.

~ ~ ~

He found the mudman seated on a slight rise on the north side of the house, rain sluicing over its clumsy body. The mudman was smaller than Snedegar had thought it might be. Not much larger than he himself, in fact. Far heavier, though, packed mud denser than flesh, to judge by how deeply sunk it was into the hard ground of the bank. It appeared to be very much at its ease, leaning back on its elbows, its lumpy legs stretched out before it. Snedegar noticed that the liquid nitrogen canister rested on the sod of the bank an arm's length from the mudman, which made a generous gesture, as though to invite him to sit down beside it.

The rise looked in on the windows of Snedegar's bedroom. The mudman's eyes, which were of course nothing more than holes in the blank slate of its face, stayed fixed on the rectangles of light as though there were a particularly fascinating show going on behind them. Snedegar followed the mudman's gaze and was astonished to see his wife, in nothing but her nightie, leaping around the room like a dancer.

As he watched, she jumped up onto the bed, ran nimbly across it, dropped to the floor on the other side, then hopped up onto a chair. Had the mudman not been there with him, he'd have laughed out loud. She gripped a rolled-up magazine in her hand, and she waved it in the air, slapped it against the walls, twirled and squatted. There was an angry red lump on one of her smooth thighs, and another high on her cheek. The asymmetry lent her face a new aspect, a charm that went well beyond mere prettiness, and Snedegar felt again how powerfully he desired her.

"Leave her alone," Snedegar told the mudman. The mudman chortled, a sound like water spattering in hot fat. A wasp crawled from its mouth, and the mudman sucked it soundlessly back in again. Snedegar thought of his dream, thought of going after the nitrogen canister, emptying it over the mudman, watching the mudman's frozen body shatter there on the bank. Even as he considered the notion, the mudman drew the canister close, uncapped it, and took a long draught. Vapor billowed around its head. It offered the canister to Snedegar.

Snedegar considered. How easy, to take the canister and drink. How much easier than enduring what was to come. But Snedegar had never been much of a one for the easy road, and he knew that he could not simply leave his wife to the mercies of the mudman. She sprang over the bench of her vanity, magazine held high above her head, and knocked over a lamp. The room was plunged into darkness.

The mudman spoke for the first time, a low rumbling sentence that Snedegar couldn't make out. Another wasp tried to make its escape from the unmoving mouth and was drawn back. "Come again?" Snedegar said.

The mudman spoke more distinctly this time. "What's she doing?" it asked, and took another swig of liquid nitrogen. The dawn was coming on fast, and Snedegar switched off his flashlight.

"Chasing a wasp," Snedegar told the mudman.

It nodded. A moment later, it began to talk, then paused and seemed to clear its throat. When it spoke again, its words were clearer. It was learning. "She's fucking him," it said.

It was Snedegar's turn to nod. "I know," he said, and he guessed he had known that she was screwing Carlson the travel agent. He guessed he had known it for quite some time.

The light was stronger now, the sun rising and the overcast burning off some, though the storm still spat fretfully on Snedegar and the mudman. Snedegar's wife appeared at the darkened window of the bedroom, peering fearfully out at the two of them. She looked to Snedegar, and then to the mudman, and back to Snedegar again. Her left eye was weepy and nearly closed from the wasp sting, and Snedegar felt his own weak eye throb in sympathy. He figured that she could see them, but she couldn't tell who they were, couldn't tell them one from another in the slanting morning light and the rain: the mudman slouched casually on the ground and Snedegar standing nearby in his wet-weather gear.

The mudman made as if to rise. "I expect I'll go in there," it said. "Not right now. But I will go in there, after a while."

Snedegar balled his fists and squared his shoulders. The mudman regarded him, then motioned toward the fence with its freight of carrion. *Join them if you want*, the gesture said. It reclined on its elbows again, and Snedegar saw that his wife was gone from the window. He was not going to get into Heaven, and his wife was not going to get into Heaven. That much was sure. And one other thing as well: When the time came, the mudman was going to rise and set about his work.

Bridge of Sighs

My father lumbered out into the barnyard, blinking like a baby in the sunlight. It was dark inside the barn. He shaded his eyes with the flat of his hand until he saw the farmer, a fellow by the name of Woodrow Scurry who was standing in the stiff mud of the yard, still as a scarecrow. That was what he looked like, Scurry, a scarecrow, with his too-big overalls and beat-to-shit steel-toe boots, his hair sticking out like straw from under his ball cap.

He was leaning far forward, like whatever was holding him up was about to give. He'd been standing that way since my father went into the barn. He'd been standing just like that for a full five minutes. I was keeping an eye on him. Sometimes they went a little batty.

"I count thirteen head in there, Mister Scurry," my father said. He consulted the clipboard in his hands. "So we're four short." It was always a mystery, how many animals these fellows were hiding. It might be a couple three steers, like Scurry, or it might be a dozen. It was always some, though. They couldn't help it, trying to keep something back. They didn't know how dangerous it was, or they pretended not to know. They were shifty and ignorant, and they were a danger to us all. "Is that right?"

"There is nothing covered that shall not be revealed," I said. It was the first thing I had said since we got there, a thing my father always told me after he'd finished work at a place like this. "Neither anything hid that shall not be known."

"What's that?" Scurry asked. He turned to look at me—I don't think he'd even noticed I was there until that moment—and his cheeks were hollow, the pits of his eye sockets filled with shadow beneath the bill of his cap.

I was sitting on the hood of my father's big black Chrysler Imperial. It was as long as a limousine. Most cars you couldn't sit on the hood for fear of dimpling the metal, but that Chrysler might as well have been armored. We had ridden up here to Scurry's place from the county seat, my father and me, listening to Cowboy Copas loud on the radio and singing along with "Tragic Romance" until we lost the signal among the rocky hilltops. I was tall enough that year that the heels of my Dingos touched the chrome of the wide bumper. The hood ornament, the chrome Imperial eagle that my father had ordered specially, sat serene and solid beneath my hand.

The massive motor poured out waves of warmth, even though it wasn't running. My butt and the backs of my legs tingled from the heat and ran with sweat. The bright light of the sun made my head ache, but it couldn't fill the darkness where Mister Scurry's eyes ought to have been. The metal of the engine block ticked as it cooled. Under that I could hear something else, a soft whispering like many voices. The sound of water running over rocks. I was suddenly violently thirsty.

~ ~ ~

The epizootic was running mad in those days. It was sweeping through the highlands like wildfire, threatening to clean out our valley as well. It was like a charnel house up on those high farms. And we were lucky, where we lived. In other places it had arrived earlier and traveled faster, and there was nothing left. We heard about it on the radio.

Places where there were no cattle anymore at all, no pigs, no sheep. Place where poultry barns, long white windowless buildings holding, some of them, as many as a hundred thousand birds, had simply been set alight and burned flat.

Places where it had wiped out the dogs. I tried to imagine that, a world without dogs, but my imagination just wouldn't frame it. I thought about all our dogs, swarming the Chrysler as they would when we pulled into the yard that evening, barking mindlessly into their own reflections in the bumper, the chrome wheel wells, the hub caps. Standing on their hind legs, grinning in through the windows at us with their tongues out, their spittle flecking the glass. My father would shout at them to get out of the way, he would threaten to run them down if they didn't shift, and they would cheerfully ignore him. A world without dogs. It was impossible.

And in some of those other places, we were now hearing, the epizootic had made the leap over into human beings.

~ ~ ~

"Thirteen," Scurry said, turning back to my father. The corners of his mouth came up in a tight, lopsided smile. There was nothing here for him to smile at. He looked embarrassed. Sometimes they were belligerent, the stockmen, sometimes they were confused, sometimes they were just humiliated and wanted to get it over with. The belligerent ones were easiest, my father said. You didn't mind doing what you had to do when a fellow argued with you. "Do you have to kill them all?" Scurry asked.

My father looked at him, then at me, peering at us out from under the visor of his hand. He had sensitive eyes and was all the time squinting against the light. "I need them all," my father said. He waved the clipboard in Scurry's direction. "That's all I got is right in there," Scurry said. "You can look around the place if you want. All the good it'll do you." He gestured around him, at the barnyard, the barn, the house that stood crookedly, as crookedly as the man himself; at the pastures and the woods that stretched all about us. It was a little lonesome place far up on the scarp.

The sound of running water seemed louder to me now, and I swallowed in a dry throat. There was a creek nearby in the woods. I had spent a good part of the summer looking for a mudpuppy, one of the fat brown mountain salamanders, big as your hand, and I wondered if there might not be one in some shallow cool-water pool along Scurry's creek, lurking among the slick flat stones and the ferns.

"This doesn't give me any pleasure, Mister Scurry," my father said. "I don't do this for the enjoyment of it." He was talking to me, not to Scurry.

~ ~ ~

Some of the extermination men liked their job, and some of them that didn't care for it at first got to like doing it after a while. Not my father, though. He came from a farming family himself, and killing livestock cut pretty close to the bone.

"You know what it is, don't you?" he asked me on the way up to Scurry's farm. "This epizootic, these germs they talk about. It's the Gadarene swine. We've been told this story. We know this story from long past. The demons are leaving the people and infesting the animals. I can hear their voices when we come to a place like this—" He consulted the clipboard that sat beside him on the wide bench of the Imperial. "This fellow Scurry's place. 'Don't kill us, mister,' they beg me in these little wheedling voices. But do I listen to them?"

"You don't," I tell him.

"No I don't," he says. "I'm like Jesus, in a way. I put on the Exterminator—that way the demons can't get out of the animals and back into *me*—and I kill them, and that takes care of the demons. Doesn't it?"

~ ~ ~

I hopped down off the hood of the car and went around to the trunk. My old man had opted for the Flightsweep trunk lid, the one with the shape of a spare tire stamped into it. It was supposed to be fancy, but it looked like a toilet seat to me. He cared for it, though. He got everything extra there was to get on that car. He said he felt like he deserved it, with the work he was doing. He could afford to, I guess, with the bounties from the epizootic. We never had anything like that Imperial before. I popped the lid.

The Exterminator occupied the trunk. It goggled up at me with its opaque glass eyes. It gave me a thrill to look into them. It was like looking at death and seeing myself reflected there. Twice, once in each lens. The Exterminator had a long flexible snout, like an elephant's. Skin like an elephant's, too, thick and gray and wrinkled. No mouth. Massive sausage-fingered hands.

My father didn't do the killing. The Exterminator did the killing. It kept the demons off of him, and it did the killing for him, and it kept him clean and safe inside it, no matter what went on outside.

My father was talking to Scurry in low tones. Explaining to him what was about to happen. Showing him the paperwork on the clipboard. Explaining how it was good agricultural hygiene, and it was the only acceptable way, and it was the law. Scurry just kept wagging his head. I laid hold of one of the Exterminator's legs and dragged it out of the trunk. The rubber was heavy and cool and slick. I put the foot on the ground behind the car. It stood up by itself, folding over at the knee. I got the other leg, stood it beside the first. Then I went after the body, the coverall and the apron. Assembling the Exterminator. That was another one of my jobs.

The Exterminator made my father look like something other than he was, made him look like a giant insect. But really he was a great big sloppy cheerful man, always whistling and humming around the house. My mother loved him, and she was a good, pretty woman, and she would never love anyone bad.

I wouldn't touch the head. That was the one part I wouldn't do. The head just lay there in the well of the trunk, right next to the star wrench and the rear evaporator and the bolted-down spare tire with its sharp crisp tread. The head peered up at me as I worked. It seemed like it wanted to tell me something, but with no mouth there was no way for it to speak. What kind of voice would such a creature have, if it could speak? A voice like the crunch of dead leaves under a boot, I thought, soft and insinuating and brittle. Not like my father's voice at all. My father's voice was loud and boisterous. He was a confident fellow.

"You just sit up there on your porch," my father told Scurry. Scurry stood with the paperwork clutched in his hand. The hot sunlight was getting to him too. He was a thin, dried-out-looking guy, but he had big sweat stains down his back and under his arms, staining the fabric of his shirt. It was hard to believe that such a parched-looking old guy had that much water in him to lose. The papers in his grip were wrinkled and damp. I was still thirsty.

"It's hot as blazes out here in the sun. Be cool," my father advised him. "Be comfortable."

~ ~ ~

They always hid the animals, but they never hid them well. It wasn't in their nature. My father always found them. Usually they just put them in an unused shed or barn. Sometimes we'd find a calf or two bawling and half-crazed, standing knee-deep in the water of a dank stone cistern. I think the farmers knew my father would find them, or somebody, the sheriff if we had to call him, so they didn't go to a whole lot of trouble.

One guy hid a bunch of his treasured angus in an abandoned saltpeter mine at the back of his acreage one time, and it took my father the better part of a day to figure out where they were. Trudging across the fields, peering into empty outbuildings and tilting silos. They were miserable, those half-dozen bulky steers huddled together in that wet, shallow cave. Their moaning sounded like they were trapped in a coffee can.

~ ~ ~

The humane killer stayed in its box next to the jack. I didn't touch the killer either. It was *off limits*. The head of the Exterminator wasn't off limits, I could have touched it if I wanted to. But it gave me the shivers, the way it looked at me. The lack of a mouth. Its snorkel nose. The flat black discs of its eyes.

I would have touched the killer if I'd been allowed. It intrigued me. It looked like a long slender hammer. Stamped into the handle were the words WW Greener London & Birmingham. The Greener company made the killer, and they made shotguns too. Expensive shotguns. Fancy, like the Imperial. My father had started talking about one day buying himself a Greener 12 gauge side-by-side, for bird-hunting. A Greener with a tight choke on it had a long reach, he told me. Pick up those whitewings far down the field, the ones that were always getting away from him.

Below the maker's stamp it said Greener's .455 Humane Cattle Killer. When I was younger I thought it said Human Cattle Killer, and that was an idea that gave me nightmares: human cattle, feedlots packed tight with them, hefty human bodies topped with the blunt groaning heads of steers. Abominations. When you're a kid you'll believe anything is possible.

For a while I saw a lot of people like that. The Fuller Brush man when he came to the door, looking to sell trinkets and kitchen goods and to sharpen knives, he was a sad-eyed Jersey. The man behind us in line at the post office, whose gaze roamed over my mother's body like busy hands. His nostrils flared, his head tossed: a Brahma bull, ready to fight, ready to breed. The men in the barbershop sighed and shuddered and grunted like the gentle Herefords just up the road at Seldomridge's. But then I asked my father, and he explained to me that *humane* just meant kindly. Gentle. After that I didn't see the human cattle so much anymore.

None of the other Exterminators used a killer like my father's. Some of them used what they called captive-bolt pistols, and most of the rest just used a rifle placed behind the ear. One great tall cadaverous man used nothing but an eight-pound Master Mechanic sledge. But my father used the Greener, which seemed like a privilege, since it had come so far and from such a prestigious manufacturer.

A fellow named John Keeper gave it to him. My father had worked with him at the big state abattoir up at Denmar. The slaughter line was the job my father had before he took this one. They recruited almost all the Exterminators from their jobs at the state slaughterhouse, but they never got John Keeper. He just walked off one day, handed the Greener to my father and got in his truck and went. And now the Greener was my father's trademark.

My father struggled into the Exterminator's hip boots and lifted the rubber apron out of the trunk. He nodded at me and I retrieved the disinfectant sprayer, sloshed it back and forth, the gurgle in the canister telling me that we had plenty. That was another one of my duties: spray him down after he had done the job, pump the disinfectant—the sprayer looked just like a big bug sprayer in the cartoons—all over the Exterminator until it was shiny and wet and gave off a smell like ammonia and licorice.

That disinfectant smell, which could beat the odor of contagion, the stench of blood and brain, the smells of shit and terror and ruin— that smell had come to mean the end of the day's work to me. It meant getting in the car and driving back home, back into the valley. Cranking up the air conditioning and turning on the radio and singing along at the top of our lungs as we bulleted along the narrow blacktop, back toward our house and our yard and our dogs. Maybe Pee Wee King would be on the air when we got back in range of the station. I loved good old Pee Wee King.

After we got home, my father would do the job a second time, pin the Exterminator up over the clothesline strung between two big silver maples on our back lot and scrub it down with a long-handled, stiff-bristled brush. The dogs would gambol around his legs. I could almost like the Exterminator then. It looked harmless, pinioned to that line with its gangling arms outstretched, its mute face tilted toward the ground as my father went after it with the brush, sweating and grunting with the effort. It was really getting the treatment then, and I could feel sorry for it.

But right after the job—right then, as I pumped away at the sprayer as hard as I could, working the piston until my arms were sore—then I often pretended that the choking cloud I was soaking it with was acid, that it would melt the Exterminator down, melt it like a lead soldier on the stove and leave just him, leave just my father standing there in the puddle of its remains.

"Keep him company, you hear?" my father told me. He meant Scurry. I lowered the disinfectant sprayer, which I had been holding like I was ready to use it. But the job wasn't done yet, the job hadn't even truly begun yet. To Scurry he called out, "My boy here has some stories he can tell you. He doesn't look like much, but he can spin a tale." Thirteen steers was going to take him a while. After which we would have to find the hidden ones. He touched the side of his nose with one of the Exterminator's gross gray fingers, and I knew the gesture meant that I should find out if I could where the remaining steers were concealed.

And then he pulled on the head of the Exterminator, fumbling a little because the gloves made his hands clumsy. He twisted the head from side to side until it sat comfortably and he could see out through the goggles. He gave the crown of its skull a comical little pat, to show me that he was still in there, shifted his shoulders to loosen them, and then he set off with the Exterminator's sloshing gait toward Scurry's barn.

~ ~ ~

We were sitting around watching TV one evening, about the time my father left the state abattoir, my mother and father and my little brother and me. A cartoon was on, and it was a surprise and a pleasure to be able to watch a cartoon in the evening, because mostly it was just news programs about the war and other things I didn't much care about. The epizootic was just beginning to get a grip around that time. Most people didn't even believe in it yet, I don't think. And the cartoon was funny at first, and I enjoyed it, two men that hated each other fighting in various ingenious ways, ways you'd never think of, with magnets and rockets and matches and rubber bands, hurting but never killing each other. I had the idea it was a very old cartoon of a sort they didn't make much anymore.

We were all enjoying it, even my mother, who hated anything violent or cruel, and my little brother, who was scared of most things. It was the difference my father marked between us, because we were only a year apart in age. Similar in size and appearance, and people often mistook us for twins: I was the one who didn't get scared, and my brother was the one who did.

But then the cartoon changed. It seemed like the two men had run out of inventions and ideas for ways to kill each other, and they just commenced hitting each other over the head. Wham, wham, wham, with these hammers, great wooden mallets. I knew about the man at the abattoir who killed with the eight-pound sledge. This was how that man spent his days, I thought, on the slaughter line. On and on. He had grown a hum, a great swelling of muscle between his shoulders, from swinging that sledge.

My mother and my brother were transfixed. I could see them out of the corners of my vision. My father was sitting in the big chair directly behind me. It seemed to me like the two men hitting each other was going on too long. No TV show lasted this long. I'd been sitting cross-legged in front of the television for hours, watching this one thing over and over. My face ached from smiling at the cartoon, and my lungs hurt from laughing. Maybe it had been going on for days, I couldn't tell. But I was still smiling, and I was still laughing, and so were my mother and brother. Tears were shining in their eyes. Maybe they were enjoying it. The music was strange and full of foreign shouting voices and sounded like it was made out of metal: "The Anvil Chorus," I have since learned it's called, an Italian song I believe. I tried to blink, but my eyes stayed peeled open.

I wondered if my father was trapped the same way I was. Was he watching? I couldn't hear him laughing. If I could get him to understand what was happening—that the cartoon wouldn't end—then he'd figure some way to free me. He'd switch off the TV. Above the metal music that was whamming away, I could hear the wind rising. It was howling around the eaves of the house. The ground started chattering under me, as though it was trembling from the cold. I felt sick, and I was still laughing and grinning.

I cranked my head around. I've never done any harder work than that. The air was as thick as oil. I thought at any second the stacked bones of my neck would crack and splinter. I shifted my gaze over my shoulder, so that I could see my father's chair. Sitting in it was the Exterminator. In its glass eyes I could see the reflection of the television screen: the gaudy colors, the hammers rising and falling in their accelerating rhythm. My own silhouette in the center of each eye, flat like a cardboard cutout. I stopped grinning. I stopped laughing. I screamed.

My mother leaped up. My father—it was him and not the Exterminator at all—gaped at me. My little brother ran from the room. They had not been laughing. I turned back to the TV, and it was easy to turn my head this time. There was no cartoon on the screen. It was the news. On the news, a man with a flamethrower strapped to his back was burning out a bunker while the other soldiers of his squad watched. They were smoking cigarettes. The flamethrower man played the tongue of dull orange flame over the bunker like a kid laving the stream of water from a garden hose over an ant pile. I had flushed out ant colonies in exactly that way. I had done it that morning.

~ ~ ~

"That's a terrible story," Scurry told me.

Bang. And Scurry jumped. It had started and it wouldn't stop. Twelve more times, and I knew Scurry would jump every time. They never got used to it. We sat on his porch. I wanted to ask him for something to drink, because I was thirsty beyond bearing, but I knew it wouldn't be right to ask him for a favor while the Exterminator was killing his cattle.

"You ought not to tell stories like that," Scurry said.

"I made a mistake," I said. "I thought it was a cartoon on, but it was the war. I thought everyone was laughing and enjoying theirselves, but they weren't."

"Do you make a lot of mistakes like that?" Scurry wanted to know.

"I used to do," I said. "When I was little. But I've learned to tell the difference a lot better these days. Between what's happening and what I think is happening. My father helps me with that."

I was pretty sure that this conversation was actually taking place between us. Scurry's words matched up pretty well with the movement of his lips. I could hear voices too, little quiet voices in the distance, no idea what they might have been saying; but they didn't worry me, because they sounded like the voices that come from a radio that was on with nobody paying attention to it, way in the back of the house somewhere. But the radio signals didn't make their way up into this part of the scarp. I knew that, because I'd heard them die out in the Imperial on the way to Scurry's place. It must have been the water I had heard earlier, the creek. I licked my burning lips.

Bang. Scurry jumped again. "What happens next?" he asked.

I didn't know exactly what he meant. Did he mean what happened next in my story? Next my old man picked me up and shook me and my mother cried and my little brother cowered in his room like the scared piss-ant that he was. Next my old man told me, *Don't you ever scream like that again. You're frightening your mother. You're frightening your brother.* That's what happened next: exactly what you might expect.

I didn't say anything about the cartoon, but my father seemed to know. He knew that the world had stopped matching up to itself for a while, and now that I had screamed it was matching up again, rolling along just like it was supposed to. He knew that sometimes it stopped matching up. You didn't need to scream when that happened. You didn't need to look around. You just waited for it to start matching up again.

These were all things my father told me later, when we took to riding in the Imperial together. About the world jumping its tracks, and how you just held on until it came back onto them again. Not to scare the women and the little children. That was half the job, when you were a man and the world got trapped in itself, rolling over and over and seeming like it would never stop. Was that what Scurry meant when he asked me "What happens next?"

Or did he mean what would happen next on his farm? That seemed more likely. He probably didn't know anything about the world coming loose from its moorings. Lots of people didn't, or wouldn't admit that they did. What did he think happened next?

Bang. Jump. That's what.

~ ~ ~

I asked my father what happened to John Keeper after he handed over the Humane Killer and walked out.

"He crossed the Bridge of Sighs both ways," my father said. The Bridge of Sighs was the ramp of steel grillwork that led up onto the slaughter line. It was where the animals came to be slaughtered, sent across by the stock handlers with poles and electric jolts and jeers, shouldering one another out of the way to get to the other side, like they thought they were getting on Noah's ark or something. The metal incline clanged and echoed from the blows of their hooves, and their bellowing and wailing rang off its surface. It was the way the workers came in as well, the men who stood on the slaughter line. They wore rubber hip boots, and their feet made no sound on the Bridge of Sighs at all.

You never crossed the Bridge of Sighs both ways. That was what they said. The animals, because when they went in, they died. And the men, because when they went in, they never left. Maybe their bodies did, but not their minds. Not their souls. They stayed in the state abattoir forever. All except John Keeper, who handed the Greener Humane Killer to my father and strode into the outside and was never seen there again.

"But you left," I said to my father.

"No," he said. "I'm there yet."

I think he meant that he had taken the abattoir out into the world with him. He meant that, when the epizootic had run its course, or when it had been halted by the work of the Exterminators, he would go back to Denmar.

In the meantime, while the government bounties were in place, he would be able to buy himself things like his Chrysler Imperial, that was as long as a limousine. And maybe one day in the not-too-distant future, if the epizootic continued on its present course, a gorgeous Greener shotgun.

~ ~ ~

The water was talking. I couldn't understand what it said, but it was talking all the same. It didn't bother me, because there were lots of times when people talked to me and I couldn't understand what they were saying. I don't think there was anything wrong with my ears. It was my head. I would get confused, but I could usually get along by just looking them straight in the eyes and smiling and nodding and making little noises like I understood and I thought what they were saying was just great. Or if they looked angry or upset, I would pull a face, beetle my brows and bow my head. I got along all right that way.

The voices in the creek sounded pleased to be talking. They never seemed to repeat themselves. I wanted to kneel down and get a big drink. The water was clear, the rocks of the streambed smooth and clean beneath its briskly moving surface, and it looked cool. The sunlight wasn't so bright here in the shadow of the trees that grew along the banks of the creek, broken up as it was by the branches with their hefty load of leaves. I wanted to lean down and cup handful after handful of the cold water into my mouth.

"Do you have mudpuppies along in here?" I asked Scurry. He'd asked if I wanted to go down to the creek. He said he had something he wanted to show me. I hoped he meant a mudpuppy even as I knew it couldn't be. How could he know what I had spent my summer looking for? He had just wanted to get away from what was happening in his barn.

Bang. But this time he didn't jump. I liked him for that. He was getting used to it. "Mudpuppy?" he said. "You mean those big lizards?"

"Salamanders," I said.

"Yeah," he said. "We call them waterdogs up this way. But we've got them. Keep your eyes open and you might see one."

We had followed a little gulley that opened beside his house, followed it as it deepened, became a steep, rock-sided ravine. An easy climb down but a tough climb back up. I wondered how Scurry would handle the exertion. He was winded from the descent. Moss and ferns underfoot, and over the surface of the water lingered dragonflies— what my mother called devil's-darning-needles—with wings as wide as the span of my hand.

I liked the name waterdogs. I kept my eyes on the swiftly moving water. Scurry moved beside me. It was easy going, there alongside the creek, because the trees didn't grow very close to the water, and the bank was solid underfoot. I wondered if the epizootic would get the mudpuppies. The waterdogs. I thought maybe living underwater the way they did would keep them safe. I had heard it said that the epizootic traveled through the air, and that was what made it so dangerous. It could go from place to place, wherever it wanted, borne by the wind. *The wind bloweth where it listeth.*

Salamanders were amphibians. The water couldn't be their shield against anything that was in the wind, because they breathed air and water both.

~ ~ ~

My father jumped out at my little brother and me from behind the front door of our house. We'd just come home from school. He was wearing the Exterminator, the first time he'd put it on, and he thought it would make a good costume to surprise and scare us with. My little brother disappeared for a couple of hours, didn't even make a sound, just vanished back through the door. I stood like I was rooted, this thing, this bug lurching toward me, its arms outstretched.

When it reached me, it swept me up in a great big embrace. It lifted me up high, over its head, and my scalp swept the ceiling, exactly the way it did when my father picked me up. The touch of the Exterminator even through my clothes was clammy and dank, like something freshly dead. It smelled like a public swimming pool. It nuzzled its face against my cheek. I was stiff as a board. I couldn't move. It was trying to kiss me, or eat me, one or the other. It bashed me in the eye with its short, swaying trunk of a nose.

My eyes were near to its eyes. Up close like that, the eyes didn't reflect. I could see through them. I could see inside the head of the Exterminator. I thought I was seeing into its skull, into its brain. And what I saw, behind its blank eyes, were the fond, familiar eyes of my father. He stared out at me. I knew that, behind the snout, he was smiling, but his eyes didn't seem to be smiling. Maybe it was the clouded glass. His eyes looked bewildered. And I suddenly thought, This is what it's like to be a grown-up man. Stumbling like a monster through your own house, scaring your kids. You pick them up but they can't feel your touch. Your skin stinks of disinfectant. You can hardly breathe. You cannot speak and be understood.

My mother swept through then, remonstrating with my father, slapping at him, her hands making wet noises against the slick flabby skin of the Exterminator. "Put the boy down, for the Lord's sake," she said. "Can't you see he's frightened to death?" She swatted at him. I wanted to laugh, but my tongue was still caught against the roof of my mouth. I couldn't say anything. It was just like him. He was a jolly guy, always playing tricks of one kind or another. This was the sort of thing he did. "What gets inside you? I swear I don't know," my mother said to him in exasperation.

Then she noticed that my brother was gone, and the search for him began. We didn't find him until well after dark. Hiding among the foliage of one of the great silver maples in the back, twenty feet off the ground. It took my father another hour and the use of an extension ladder borrowed from the people down the road to finally get him out of the tree.

~ ~ ~

Scurry didn't seem diverted by that story either. It always made my father laugh to think of my brother way up in that tree. He was not much of a tree-climber, my little brother, either before or after that first encounter with the Exterminator. But he sure had gone sky-high that one time. Scurry didn't smile or anything.

"There's not really any mudpuppies down here, are there?" I asked him. He shook his head sorrowfully, like he regretted having told me an untruth.

"There used to be, when I was a kid," he said. "I don't know what happened to them since then."

Bang. Very muted and far-away. I had lost count, but it had to be pretty near the end now. My father would come back out of the barn and he'd be looking for me to have the disinfectant canister out, ready to spray him down and help him get out of the sweaty, foul-smelling Exterminator. He would want me to put it back into the capacious trunk of the Imperial, where it belonged. The trunk would make a solid thump when I closed it. The doors of the Imperial were the same way. When they closed, they closed tight. Good workmanship.

"It's not him that's doing the killing," I tell Scurry. "It's the Exterminator." When he looks at me like he can't tell what I'm talking about, I add, "The suit. The rubber suit."

Scurry shook his head. "No," he said. "It's him. He's doing the killing all right. The suit just keeps the blood and the gore off of him." I decided not to argue with him. We came to a place where the creek shallowed and broadened, parting around a small sandy island in the middle of the current. On the island stood the missing cattle, bunched together and gazing rapt at the sheet of water that passed near their hooves. I should have guessed that they were what Scurry wanted me to see. Sometimes that happened: the farmers just gave in and took us to their hidden animals. They couldn't keep anything hidden for long. I was glad that, thirsty as I was, I hadn't drunk from the stream, downstream from the beasts as we had been. Cholera, diphtheria: it would all be in the water from their waste.

The little group of cattle broke apart when they saw Scurry. They thought he was bringing fodder with him. They were well-fed and sleek, and I knew how much effort it was, bringing feed down to them in this rocky declivity, so far from his house. How hard he was working to keep them alive and safe on their little island.

And I saw that there was something else on the island with them. Something small and terrible in the shifting green shadows beneath the trees. Something that had been hidden behind their bulk. One of the mutants that I had heard the epizootic could bring about. Misshapen: six legs, maybe seven. Grotesquely twisted body. Two heads. My breath stopped in my throat, and I felt the world begin to unhinge. A monster. Time would stop, down here by the island. Who knew how long I would spend in this ravine, with Scurry and his horrible freak calf. An eternity, like that time with the cartoon.

"You see?" Scurry said to me. "They're not sick. These ones aren't. You can see that, can't you?"

The water was talking. Or maybe it was my father, calling out from the barnyard. He had probably wrested the Exterminator's head from his own, his labor done, and he was wondering where I had got to. Me and Scurry. Maybe he was even a little afraid, alone like that.

One of the monster calf's heads wailed, and the other answered it. Their bawling bounced crazily off the rock walls around us and drowned out the voice I had heard. I saw that it was no monster. It was just two spring calves, two little bulls standing twined together, twins and small for their age. One of them trotted down to the edge of the island and sank its muzzle into the water and commenced to drink. My dry throat contracted. I could almost taste the water, the delicious silkiness of it. I wanted that water. The other bull calf stumbled after the first, tripping over its feet, and it too began to drink.

Scurry's voice was loud in my ear. "Nothing," Scurry said. My father would find us soon, the way he had found my little brother, way up in the silver maple. "There's nothing at all wrong with them, is there?" he said to me. He wouldn't be satisfied until I said it. My saying it would avail him nothing, it wouldn't change what had to happen, but he wanted me to witness, he wanted me to testify, to tell him what he already knew. Nothing was wrong. Nothing wrong at all.

The Beginnings of Sorrow

Whoo-oo-oo-oo-hooh-hoo-oo! Oh, look at me, I am perishing in this gateway. ... I howl and howl, but what's the good of howling?
—Mikhail Bulgakov, *Heart of a Dog*

V andal Boucher told his dog Hark to go snatch the duck out of the rushes where it had fallen, and Hark told him *No.* In days to come, Vandal probably wished he'd just pointed his Ithaca 12-gauge side-by-side at Hark's fine-boned skull right that moment and pulled the trigger on the second barrel (he had emptied the first to bring down the duck) and blown the dog's brains out, there at the edge of the freezing, sludgy pond. But that unanticipated answer—any answer would have been a surprise, of course, but this was *no*, unmistakably *no*, in a pleasant tenor, without any obvious edge of anger or resentment—that single syllable took him aback and prevented him from taking action.

Vandal's old man, now: back in the day, Vandal's old man Xerxes Boucher would have slain the dog that showed him any sign of strangeness or resistance to his will, let alone one that told him *no.* Dog's sucking the golden yolks out of the eggs? Blam. Dog's taking chickens out of the coop? Blam. Dog's not sticking tight enough to the sheep, so the coyotes are chivvying them across the high pastures? *This dog's your favorite, your special pet? You wish I would refrain from shooting the dog? Well, sonny, you wish in one hand and shit in the other, see which gets full first.* Blam. Nothing could stop him, no pleading or promises, and threats were out of the question. But that was Xerxes in his prime, and Vandal wasn't a patch on him, everybody said so, Vandal himself had ruefully to agree with the general assessment of his character. So when Hark said *no*, Vandal just blinked. "Come again?" he said.

No.

Well, Vandal thought. He looked out into the reeds, where the body of the mallard he had just shot bobbed in the dark water. That water looked cold. Hark sat on the shore, blinking up at Vandal with mild eyes. It would have struck Xerxes Boucher as outrageous that the dog should balk at wading out there into that cold, muddy mess, the soupy muck at the pond's margin at least shoulder-deep for the dog where the dead mallard floated, maybe deep enough that a dog—even a sizeable dog like Hark—would have to swim.

But damn it if, on that gray November morning, with a hot thermos of his wife's bitter black coffee nearby just waiting on him to drink it, and a solid breakfast when he got home after the hunt, and dry socks— Damned if Vandal couldn't see the dog's point.

"Okay," he said. "This once."

He was wearing his thick rubber waders, the ones that went all the way up to the middle of his chest, so he took off his coat—the frigid air bit into him, made his breath go short—laid the coat down on the bank, set the shotgun on top of the coat, and set off after the mallard himself. The waders clutched his calves as the greasy pond water surged around his legs, and his feet sank unpleasantly into the soft bottom. He considered what might be sleeping down there: frogs settled in for the winter, dreaming their slick wet dreams; flabby catfish whiskered like old men; great knobby snapping turtles, their thick round shells overlapping one another like the shields of some ancient army.

They were down there in the dark, the turtles that had survived unchanged from the age of the dinosaurs, with their spines buckled so that they fit, neatly folded, within their shells; and their eyes closed fast, their turtle hearts beating slow, slow, slow, waiting on the passing of another winter. And what if the winter never passed and spring never came, as looked more and more likely? How long would they sleep, how long could such creatures wait in the dark? A long time, Vandal suspected. Time beyond counting. It might suit them well, the endless empty twilight that the world seemed dead-set on becoming.

Vandal didn't care to put his feet on such creatures, and when his toes touched something hard, he tried to tread elsewhere. The pond bottom was full of hard things, and most of them were probably rocks, but better safe than sorry. He had seen the jaws on snapping turtles up close, the beak on the skeletal face like a hawk's or an eagle's, hooked and hard-edged and sharp as a razor. Easy to lose a toe to such a creature.

When he reached the mallard—it was truly a perfect bird, its head and neck a deep oily green, unmarked by the flying shot—he plucked its limp body up out of the water and waved it over his head for the dog to see. "Got it!" he called.

Hark wasn't paying any attention to him at all. He was sitting next to the tall silver thermos and gazing quizzically at the coat and, cradled on the coat, Vandal's shotgun.

~ ~ ~

"I told him to go get the duck," Vandal said to his wife, who was called Bridie. Then, to Hark, he said, "Tell her what you told me."

No, said Hark.

Bridie looked from her husband to the dog. "Does he mean to tell you no," she asked, working to keep her voice even and calm, her tone reasonable. "Or does he mean he won't tell me?"

No, the dog said again. It wasn't like a bark, which Bridie would have much preferred, one of those clever dogs that has been taught by its owner to "talk" by mimicking human speech without understanding what it was saying. "What's on top of a house?" *Roof!* "How does sandpaper feel?" *Rough!* "Who's the greatest ballplayer of all time?" *Ruth!*

DiMaggio, she thought to herself. *That's the punchline. The dog says* Ruth! *but really it's DiMaggio.*

Vandal laughed. He was a big broad-shouldered good-natured man with an infectious laugh, which was one of the reasons Bridie loved him, and she smiled despite her misgivings. The dog seemed delighted with the turn of events too.

"That's the sixty-four dollar question, ain't it?" Vandal said. He clapped Hark on the head in the old familiar way, and the dog shifted out from under the cupped hand, eyes suddenly slitted and opaque.

No, it said.

Much as she loved Vandal, and much as she had hated his bear of a father, with his great sweaty hands always ready to squeeze her behind or pinch her under her skirt as she was climbing the stairs, always ready to brush against her breasts—glad as she was that the mean old man was in the cold cold ground, she couldn't help but think at that moment that a little of Xerxes' unflinching resolve wouldn't have gone amiss in Vandal's character, in this circumstance. She wished that the dog had said pretty much anything else: *Yes*, or better yet, *yes sir.* Even a word of complaint, *cold, wet, dark. Afraid.* But this flat refusal unnerved her.

"He takes a lot on himself, doesn't he? For a dog," she said.

"Talking dog," said Vandal, his pride written on his knobby face, as though he had taught the dog to speak all by himself, as though it had been his idea.

Hark had begun wandering through the house, inspecting the dark heavy furniture like he had never seen it or the place before. Not exploring timidly, like a guest unsure of his welcome, but more like a new owner. Bridie thought she saw him twitch a lip disdainfully as he sniffed at the fraying upholstery of the davenport. He looked to her for a moment as though maybe he were going to lift his leg. "No!" she snapped. "Bad boy!"

He glanced from her to Vandal and back again, trotted over to Vandal's easy chair with his tail curled high over his back. He gave off the distinct air of having won some sort of victory. "Come here," Bridie called to him. She snapped her fingers, and he swung his narrow, intelligent head, looking past his shoulder at her.

No, he said, and he hopped up into Vandal's chair. Bridie was relieved to see how small he was in the chair, into which Vandal had to work to wedge his bulky frame.

There was room for two of Hark in the seat, three even, so lean was he, slender long-legged retriever mix. Vandal nodded at him with approval. The dog turned around and around and around as though he were treading down brush to make himself a nest, in the ancient way of dogs. In the end, though, he settled himself upright rather than lying down, his spine against the back of the chair, his head high.

"Xerxes wouldn't never allow a dog up in his chair like that," Bridie said. And was immediately sorry she had said it. Vandal had adored and dreaded his brutal, unstoppable old man, and any comparison between them left him feeling failed and wanting. *Xerxes, Xerxes. Will he never leave our house?*

"Xerxes never had him a talking dog," Vandal said. He handed the dead mallard to her. Its glossy head and neck stretched down toward the floor in a comical way, its pearlescent eyes long gone into death. It was a large, muscular bird.

"Not much of a talking dog," Bridie said. She turned, taking the mallard away into the kitchen when she saw the flash of irritation in Vandal's eyes. She didn't look toward Hark, because she didn't want to see the expression of satisfaction that she felt sure animated his doggy features. She wanted to let Vandal have this moment, this chance to own something that his father couldn't have imagined, let alone possessed, but it was—it was wrong. Twisted, bent. It was a thing that couldn't be but was, it was unspeakable, and it was there in her living room, sitting in her husband's chair. "Not much of one, if all it can manage to say is *no*."

~ ~ ~

Hark reclined in the easy chair in the parlor. The television was tuned to the evening news, and the dog watched and listened with bright gleaming eyes, giving every appearance of understanding what was said: Wars and rumors of wars. Earthquakes and famines and troubles. None of it was good at all, it hadn't been good in some little time, but none of it seemed to bother him in the least. He chewed briefly at his own hip, after some itch that was deeply hidden there, and then went back to his television viewing.

Vandal sat on the near end of the davenport, not appearing to hear the news. From time to time he reached out a hand to pet Hark, but Hark shifted his weight and leaned away, just out of reach. It was what Bridie had always striven to do when Xerxes went to put his hands on her but that she had somehow never managed, to create that small distance between them that would prove unbridgeable. Always the hand reached her, to pet and stroke and pinch, always when Vandal's attention was turned elsewhere. And them living in Xerxes' house, and her helpless to turn him away.

About the third time Vandal put his hand out, Hark tore his gaze from the TV screen, snarled, snapped, his jaws closing with a wicked click just shy of Vandal's reaching fingertips. Vandal withdrew his hand, looking sheepish.

"No?" he asked the dog.

No, Hark said, and he settled back into the soft cushions of the chair, his eyes fixed once more on the flickering screen.

~ ~ ~

Over Bridie's objections, Hark ate dinner at the table with them that night. Vandal insisted. The dog tried to climb into the chair with arms, Vandal's seat at the head of the table. Vandal wasn't going to protest, but Bridie wouldn't allow it. She flapped the kitchen towel—it was covered in delicate blue cornflowers—at him, waved her hands and shouted "Shoo! Shoo!" until he slipped down out of the chair and, throwing resentful glances her way, slunk over to one of the chairs at the side of the table and took his place.

He ate like an animal, she noted with satisfaction, chasing the duck leg she had given him around and around the rim of the broad plate with his sharp snout, working to grasp the bone with his teeth, his tongue hanging drolly from the side of his mouth. Always, the leg escaped him. Each time it did, she put it carefully back in the middle of the plate, and he went after it again. From time to time he would stop his pursuit of the drumstick and watch Bridie and Vandal manipulate their utensils, raise their forks to their mouths, dab at their lips with napkins. His own napkin was tucked bib-like under the broad leather strap of his collar, and it billowed ridiculously out over his narrow, hairy chest. Vandal watched this process through a number of repetitions, his brow furrowed, before he put down his knife and fork.

"You can't let a dog have duck bones like that," he said. "He'll crack the bone and swallow it and the sharp edges will lodge in his throat."

Good, Bridie thought. *Let him.* The dog stared across the table at her, his face twisted into what she took to be an accusatory grimace. Hark had always been Vandal's dog, never hers, and she had never felt much affection for him, but he had always seemed to her to be a perfectly normal dog, not overfriendly but that was normal in an animal that was brought up to work rather than as a pet. Restrained in his affections, but never hostile. Lean and quick and hard-muscled, with the bland face and expressions of his kind. And now he looked at her as though he knew what she was thinking—an image of Hark coughing, wheezing, hacking up blood on the kitchen floor swam back into her consciousness—and hated her for it.

Was there an element of surprise there too? she wondered. He hadn't known about the bones. An unanticipated danger, and now he knew, and she could sense him filing the information away, so that such a thing would never be a threat to him again. What else was he ignorant about?

Bridie had never disliked Hark before, had never disliked any of Vandal's boisterous happy-go-lucky hunting dogs, the bird dogs, the bear dogs, the coon dogs, all of them camped out in the tilting kennel attached to the pole barn. They shared the long fenced run that stretched across the barnyard, and they would woof and whirl and slobber when she went out to feed them. Dogs with names like Sam and Kettle and Bengal and Ranger. And Hark. Hark the waterdog, a little quieter than the others, more subdued, maybe, but nothing obvious about him to separate him from the rest of them. They were Vandal's friends and companions, they admired him even when Xerxes fed him scorn, and they were kind to him when even she herself wasn't. She didn't fool with them much.

Something had come alive in Hark, something that allowed him, compelled him, to say *no*, and now he was at her table when the rest were outside in the cold and the dark, now he was looking her in the eye. That was another new thing, this direct confrontation; he had always cast his gaze down, properly canine, when his eyes had locked with hers in the past. He'd regained his earlier cocksureness, and the impression of self-satisfaction that she had from him made him unbearable to her.

Vandal was leaning over, working his knife, paring the crispy skin and the leg meat away from the bone. "Here you go," he told the dog, his tone fond. Hark sniffed.

"If he plans to eat his food at the table like people," Bridie said, "then he better learn to pick it up like people."

Vandal stopped cutting. Bridie half-expected Hark to say *No* in the light voice that sounded so strange coming out of that long maw, with its mottled tongue and (as they seemed to her) cruel-looking teeth. Instead, he nudged Vandal out of his way and planted one forepaw squarely on the duck leg. *He understands*, Bridie thought to herself.

The plate tipped and skittered away from him, the duck leg tumbling off it, the china ringing against the hard oak of the tabletop. The dog looked perplexed, but Vandal slid the plate back into place, picked up the drumstick and laid it gently down.

Just as gently, Hark put his paw on the leg bone, pinning it. He lowered his head, closed his teeth securely on the leg—the chafing squeak of tooth against bone made Bridie squint her eyes in disgust—and pulled away a triumphant mouthful of duck. He tossed it back, swallowed without chewing, and went after the leg again.

"Good dog," Vandal said. The dog's ears flickered at the familiar phrase, but he didn't raise his head from the plate. Bridie bit into her own portion. Duck was normally one of her favorites, but this meal filled her mouth like ashes. Vandal stopped chewing, leaned down close to his plate, his lips pursed as though he were about to kiss his food, his eyes screwed nearly shut. He made a little spitting noise, and a pellet of lead shot, no bigger than a flea, pinged onto his plate, bounced, and lay still.

~ ~ ~

After supper, as Bridie retted up the kitchen, Vandal sat cross-legged on the floor in the parlor, the shotgun broken down and spread out on several thicknesses of newspaper on the floor before him. A small smoky fire—the wood was too green to burn well, hadn't aged sufficiently—flared and popped in the hearth.

Hark sat in the comfortable chair, and his posture had become—she felt sure of this—more human than it had been previously. He was sitting like a man now, a misshapen man, yes, with a curved spine and his head low between his shoulders, but he was working to sit upright. He looked ridiculous, as she glanced in at him from where she was working, but she felt no impulse to laugh. Was he larger than he had been? Did he fill the chair more fully? While she watched, he lost his precarious balance, slipped to the side, thrashed for a moment before righting himself again.

The television was on, the usual chatter from the local news, a terrible wreck out on the state highway, a plant shutting down in the county seat, a marvel on a nearby farm, a Holstein calf born with two heads, both of them alive and bawling, both of them sucking milk. *Who could even take note of something like that in these times*, Bridie wondered to herself as she worked to scrub the grease from the plates. The next day it would be something else, and something else after that, until the wonders and the sports and the abominations (*how to tell the difference among them?*) piled up so high that there wouldn't be any room left for them, for her and for Vandal, the regular ones, the ones that remained.

A talking dog? Was that stranger than a two-headed calf? Stranger than poor old Woodrow Scurry's horses eating each other in his stables a fortnight earlier? Every day the world around her seemed more peculiar than it had the day before, and every day she felt herself getting a little more used to the new strangenesses, numb to them, and wondering idly what ones the next day would bring.

How you use? They were Hark's words, clumsy and laughable, coming to her over the din of the voices on the television. There was another sort of show on, this one a game of some type, where people shouted at one another, encouragement and curses. *That thing*, Hark said.

"So," Vandal said, "you can say more than *No*."

How you use that thing, Hark said again. A demand this time, not a question.

The shotgun, Bridie thought, and she dropped the plate she was washing back into the sink full of lukewarm water and dying suds and hurried into the den, drying her hands on a dishtowel as she went.

"Don't tell him that," she said.

Vandal looked up at her, startled. Just above him on the wall hung a picture that his mother had hung there as a young woman. She had died young. In the decades since it had been hung, the picture, it occurred to Bridie, had taken in every event that had occurred in that low-ceilinged, claustrophobic room. It depicted Jesus, a thick-muscled Jesus, naked but for a drape of white cloth, getting his baptism in the river Jordan. The Baptist raised a crooked hand over his head, water spilling from the upraised palm.

Vandal was fitting the barrels of the shotgun—which had been his old man's but which was now his, like the house, like the farm—back into the stock. The metal mated to the wood with a definitive click. "Why in the world wouldn't I tell him?"

Bridie was at a loss for a cogent answer. It seemed obvious to her that Vandal ought not to impart such information to the dog just for the asking, but he didn't share her worry at all, it was clear. How to explain? The dog looked at her with, she thought, an expression of feigned innocence. "A dog ought not to know how to use a gun," she said.

Vandal chuckled. "He doesn't even have hands. He has no fingers."

"So why tell him how a gun works?"

"Because he wants to know."

"And should he know everything he wants to, just because he wants to know it?"

Vandal shrugged. Bridie felt heat flooding her face. How could he not understand? He thought it was terrific, the way the dog had decided to talk, the way he could sit there with it and watch television, the way it asked him questions, the way it wanted to know the things that he knew. He was happy to share with it: his table, his food, his house, his knowledge. He was treating the dog like a friend, like a member of the family. Like a child, his child.

"What he wants is to have hands. What he wants is to be a man. To do what you do. To have what you have."

She caught Hark gazing at her intently, his eyes gleaming, hungry, his nose wet, his broad flat tongue caught between the rows of his teeth.

"What's wrong with that?" Vandal wanted to know.

He is not your boy, she wanted to tell him. He is not your son. He is a dog, and it's wrong that he can talk. You want to share what you have with him, but he doesn't want to share it with you. He wants to have it instead of you.

The dog wrinkled his nose, sniffing, and she knew suddenly that he was taking her in, the scent of her. A dog's nose was, she knew, a million times more sensitive than a man's. He could know her by her scent. He could tell that she was afraid of him. He could follow her anywhere, because of that phenomenal sense of smell. In prehistoric times, before men became human and made servants out of them, Hark and his kind would have hunted her down in a pack and eaten her alive. Her scent would have led them to her. Hark's eyes narrowed, and her words clung to her jaws. She couldn't bear to speak them in front of the dog. She blinked, dropped her gaze and, under the animal's intense scrutiny, fled the room.

Behind her, Vandal spoke. "This here's the breech," he said. The gun snicked open. "This here is where the shells go." The gun thumped closed.

~ ~ ~

Vandal always wanted her after a meal of game meat: duck, venison, bear, it didn't matter what. It was something about the wild flavor, she thought, and the fact that he had killed the food himself. It made him happy, and when he was happy he always came to her in bed, his hands quick and his breath hot. He was at her now, pushing up her nightgown, slipping the straps off her shoulders, throwing one of his heavy, hairy legs across hers. She shoved at him.

"Don't," she said. "He'll hear."

After supper, after television and the lesson about the gun—he could name all the parts of it now, Hark could, and his speech was becoming rapidly clearer, the words coming to him swiftly and easily; and maybe that was true of his thoughts as well, slipping like eels through that clever brain in its dark prison in the dog's skull—Hark had refused to go outside to sleep in the kennel. He had simply braced his legs at the house's threshold and bared his teeth and muttered at them, *No.*

"For God's sake," Bridie had said to Vandal.

"What's the harm?" Vandal had asked. Plenty of people, he had told her in a patient voice, owned dogs that lived indoors.

"Not you," she said to him. "Never you."

No, he agreed, he'd never owned an indoor dog before. Xerxes wouldn't allow such a thing.

Xerxes. He couldn't understand what was happening to him, to them, because of Xerxes and the shadow he cast, even from the grave. Vandal had always wanted an indoor dog, a pet, and Xerxes wouldn't hear of it.

So Hark became an indoor dog, sleeping in the parlor. Bridie had tried to lay down a couple of old rag rugs on the floor for him, but he had just stared blankly at her from the chair, and she had left him there rather than risking having to hear that flat refusal another time.

"He won't hear anything," Vandal said. Bridie knew how sharp a dog's hearing was. Vandal knew it even better than she did, but he was saying what he imagined she needed to hear, because he wanted to get hold of her. A dog's hearing was like its sense of smell, a million times or more what humans are capable of. "He's downstairs. He's probably asleep," Vandal said. He nuzzled her, took the lobe of her ear between his teeth and nipped. He slid her nightgown down to her waist, his hands on her breasts, his palms and the pads of his fingers tough with callus. Her breathing quickened as he pushed her hard against the mattress and pressed her legs apart. "Who cares if he hears us?"

"I care," she said. She knew that Hark would not be asleep, not on his first night in their house. In his first moments alone and unguarded in a human place. He might not even be in the parlor anymore. She pictured him creeping down the hallways, clambering up the stairs, sloping through their rooms, looking at everything, that keen nose taking in the odors of the house and its denizens, possessing them, filing them away. He might be climbing up on Xerxes' bed—the guest bed, she corrected herself, Xerxes was gone—right now.

"We'll be quiet then," Vandal assured her, and she meant to protest, but he put his hands under her hips and lifted her, and she groaned and opened to him. He gave a sharp cry of delight. She shushed him, but he continued to exclaim as he moved against her, his voice growing louder with every fierce thrust of his hips, until he was calling out wordlessly at the top of his voice. By then she was far gone too, her voice mingling with his, and under it all the sharp metallic crying of the bedsprings.

~ ~ ~

In the night, while Vandal slept, Bridie considered Xerxes. X, as he had told her to call him, all his friends called him X. He had many friends on the neighboring places and in town, the men he hunted with, roistered with, brawny old men like himself who had fought in one war or a couple, men who took no shit from anyone. Terrible X, Mountain-Man X, X the Unknown and Unknowable, his eyes on her always, his hands on her too whenever Vandal was out of the house, when he was out hunting or tending to his dogs in the kennel. Sometimes when Vandal was in the house, too, sometimes when he was in the same room. X wasn't afraid, he wasn't afraid a bit.

Be quiet, he would say to her.

She never told Vandal because she was afraid of what he would do. What was she afraid of, exactly? That he would confront Xerxes, Daddy Xerxes, Daddy X as Vandal called him. Was she afraid that Vandal would challenge Xerxes, fight him, shoot him, kill him? Or was she afraid that he wouldn't? She could imagine no happy outcome to her revelation, and so she chose not to make it.

"No," she would tell Xerxes as he pawed her, plundered her. He didn't even hear her, she didn't believe. She might as well have been speaking another language, or not speaking at all. "No."

When a brain stroke had taken him one wonderful day—he had cornered her in the parlor, was squeezing her breasts, crushing her to him, one great hand pressed hard in the middle of her back so that she couldn't escape him—she had simply stood away from his stumbling, twitching, stiffening body, had watched him topple over like a hewn tree, had watched him spasm and shudder on the floor, his mouth gaping, hands clawing at his own face, one of his eyes bulging grotesquely, rolling upward independent of its twin to take her in where she stood.

She stared back into the rogue eye, in which the pupil was contracting, swift as a star collapsing, until she realized that X's gaze was no longer fixed on her, but on something behind her, above her. She was seized with an awful terror, and the effort of turning left her shaken, exhausted. Nothing. Nothing but the picture on the wall, which was as it had always been since the hand of Xerxes' wife had placed it there: Jesus and, standing over him, John, the Baptist, clothed all in ragged unfinished animal hides. She turned back to the dying man before her.

The eye reeled farther, impossibly far—it was funny to see, really, or would have been in any other circumstance—to fix on the ceiling, until finally the iris and the pupil disappeared altogether and the eye turned over white.

She leaned down to him, breathing hard from the fright he had given her over the picture, and put her mouth right up against his thick cauliflower ear, its whorls filled with stiff gray hair like the bristles of a boar-hog. This time, she wanted to make sure that he heard. "No," she told him.

~ ~ ~

Some folks, the voice said, *have too much life in them to die all the way.*

Bridie snapped awake, sure that the words had come to her in X's voice. That gruff commanding voice, weirdly distorted with wolf-tones and as full of echoes as though it were being broadcast from the moon. *How else should the voice of a dead man sound?* she asked herself. *He's come a long way back to say what he has to say to me.*

The gruff voice, and an answering sound, staccato: Hark's mirthless laughter. The sound of it chilled her. She had never cared much for loud laughter. The bared teeth, the closed eyes, the contorted features of the face, the shuddering, it all looked too much like pain to her, like convulsions or madness. She herself always laughed behind her hand, her eyes down. The voice went droning on below. It sounded like it was giving advice, and Hark's laughter had stopped. She could picture him soaking in whatever notions Xerxes was giving him.

"He's watching TV." Vandal's voice at her shoulder startled her. His eyes glinted in the weak light that filtered in through the window, the moon's final quarter. His good straight teeth glittered. He slid his hands to her breasts, kneaded her flesh. He wanted to go again. "He ain't paying any attention to us, is he?"

"How did he turn it on, Vandal?" she asked him. Another voice was speaking now, this one lighter, quicker, with a peculiar accent. She couldn't make out the words. Was it Hark's voice? Was he having conversation? Vandal urged her over prone, prodded her up onto her elbows and knees. His hands were shaking. He was as eager as a teenager, and rough, too rough. She liked him when he was sweet, and mostly he was, he was sweet, but there was no sweetness in him now. Nothing was strange, nothing was outside the realm of possibility. The television was talking to the dog, and the dog was talking to the television. She pressed her face into the smothering whiteness of the pillow, which smelled to her of her own soap and night sweat. Nothing was too strange to happen anymore.

~ ~ ~

The next day, as he went out the door, Vandal told Bridie that he'd gone colorblind. Hark was sitting in his place at the table, waiting on his breakfast to be brought to him. He looked from one of them to the other with eager eyes.

"You mean you can't tell red from green?" She'd had an uncle with the same problem. Except for dealing with stoplights and some problems matching clothes, it hadn't seemed to bother him much. As far she knew, though, it was a problem he'd had his whole life, not something he'd acquired.

Vandal waved a hand in front of his face, as though he were demonstrating actual blindness. "The whole ball of wax," he told her. "It's all shades of gray out there."

"You've got to see a doctor," she said to him. "This ain't natural."

"Natural," he said. "Ha. I wouldn't know natural these days if it came up and bit me in the ass."

"Seeing colors. That's natural."

"It's winter coming down," he said. "Just winter, and the color goes out of everything. It just looks like it's all an old movie."

She shook her head, and he drew her to him with a hand on her waist, another in the middle of her back. He pressed against her, and she felt the warmth that spread out from him, felt his hardness. His need for her was palpable, and it made her sad and excited all at once. She peeled his hands from her body because the dog was watching, too avidly. There was something in Vandal's touch that wasn't just for her, and wasn't just for for him either, it wasn't just selfishness. There was something in it that was for the dog too, and she couldn't stand that.

Vandal withdrew. "Who has the money for a doctor?" he said. "Who has the leisure?" His brow was furrowed. Already his thoughts had turned from her to his work. Seldomridge, their neighbor to the east, had called to say that a half dozen of his cattle were dead in the night, no telling what had killed them but the condition of their bodies was very strange, and could Vandal bring over the skid-steer and help him plant them? It was a full morning's labor lost from their own place, but there was no way a man could refuse to help in such a situation. No time to worry about little things like the color of the world going away.

His expression cleared briefly. "It's the winter time. That's what's got everything all turned around. Come spring and the color will come back. You watch."

~ ~ ~

After Vandal left the house, Bridie shooed Hark down off the chair and away from the kitchen table, hustled him out the door with gestures and cries. She made as if she might kick him, and he went, but she could tell by the set of his shoulders that he knew no blows were coming, and he went at his own pace. She kept waiting for him to tell her *no* as she drove him across the yard toward the dog run.

She had decided upon rising that morning what she would do if he refused her, if he refused to do anything she told him. She was expecting it, she was waiting for it, she was even hoping for it: reason to take down the choke collar that Vandal kept for training and slip it over

Hark's head and cinch it tight as a noose around his neck. Watch the chain links cut into his thick pelt and the delicate flesh of his throat. Force him to do what she wanted. Hiss her orders into his sensitive ears. Show him what a dog was, and what a human was, and what the proper relationship between them should be.

And if Hark grew angry, lashed out, bit her? Then she should show Vandal the marks on her skin, and he would understand at last how utterly wrong the situation was, how obscene, and he would do what was necessary. She allowed the ball of her foot to come in contact with Hark's rump—was she tempting him?—but he just hurried on ahead, as though he were suddenly eager to enter the dog run. His tail was up and switching when the steel latch of the kennel door clanged down behind him.

That's that, she thought as she went back into the house. The day stretched out in front of her. Plenty to do, as always, and no Vandal, no Hark, no Xerxes to keep her from it. *That's it for him, returned to the place of his beginnings.*

~ ~ ~

All day, the voice issued from the kennel. Answered at first by the growling and defiant barking from the other dogs, and then their cowed whimpering, and then silence. They were good dogs, obedient dogs, conditioned to a man's voice. It pained Bridie to think of him out there among them; but what else to do? She had hopes that their good simple natures would remind Hark of what he had used to be, what he ought still to be.

Better out there than in here anyway, she thought. *A kennel's the place for dogs, and what happens out there is no worry of mine.*

It was dusk getting on toward night when Vandal arrived home again, the skid-steer up on the flatbed, his shoulders slumped with weariness. "It's bad over at Seldomridge's," he told her. "Worse than he said." He washed his hands vigorously under the hot water tap, skinning them hard with the scrub brush and the Lava soap, lathering himself all the way up to the elbows. His face was pinched and drawn-looking.

"It's bad over here too," she said. He didn't seem to hear her.

"I'll be back over there tomorrow," he said. "After that, it's no more cattle at Seldomridge's." He looked around the kitchen, ducked into the parlor to check in there. "Where's he at?" he wanted to know.

She gestured out the window toward the silent kennel, and his face hardened. "I had work to do too, you know," she said.

"I didn't say nothing." He was already in motion toward the door.

"I didn't have the time to babysit your new pet," she called after him. His pet. His changeling child. She watched his large awkward figure cross the yard and enter the chain-link run, kneel down just inside the gate. Her heart quailed. All afternoon the silence had worn at her. It worried her as much as the voice had done. More. A kennel was never a silent place, always some kind of choir going out there, a tussle, an alarm over a rabbit or over nothing. The jolly voices of dogs. Vandal was bent over something, shaking his head, mumbling, his shoulders bowed.

She strained in the failing light to make out what he was doing. She had a moment in which she imagined that the normal dogs had torn the strange one to pieces, and her heart leaped. *It will be my fault, just like the death of Xerxes*, she thought, *and he will never forgive me, and I will bear the blame gladly.*

And then he was coming back to the house, Hark slinking along at his side. When they entered the kitchen together, Vandal's face was wreathed in a great smile. The smell of dog, hairy and primeval and eye-wateringly strong, struck Bridie like a blow. Hark trotted into the parlor and climbed wearily onto the davenport, where he lay draped like a rug, his sides heaving.

"Tell her what you told me," Vandal called in to him. No answer. "Tell her what you been doing all day, while we was working."

Humping, came the voice from the living room, muffled against the davenport's cushions.

"Did you hear that?" Vandal asked her.

"I heard," Bridie said.

"Made them line up for him, and then he humped every one of those bitches out there, one right after the other. He's the king of the dogs now, I guess."

"I guess," Bridie said.

"We got to make sure he eats good tonight," Vandal said. "He tells me he wants to do it all over again tomorrow."

~ ~ ~

When Hark started in to walking on his hind legs, Bridie told Vandal that he couldn't spend his days in the kennel anymore. "I thought you wanted him penned," he said, "to keep him out of your hair."

"It's not right," she said, "a thing that goes on two legs and a thing that goes on four." She couldn't bring herself to call Hark a man. He wasn't a man exactly, not yet anyway. He was like a tadpole, Bridie thought when she looked at him, something in between two other things and not really anything in itself. He was neither man nor dog, and he was both, and he was awful. Nothing could exist for long in that middle condition, she didn't believe. It was unbearable.

"We've got to put him in some clothes too," she said, "to get him covered up." He went around in an excited state half the time, and the sight of him, slick and red, sickened and haunted her.

"Can he wear some of mine?" Vandal asked.

Probably, Bridie thought. He was getting more man-sized and more man-shaped with every day that passed. *And it's probably exactly what he wants to do too.* But she said, "I think we should get him some of his own." *Some coveralls*, she thought, *and a tractor cap to cover that low sloping forehead and the bony ridges above the eyes.*

The more like a man he became, the more he horrified her. She wondered if there was a point at which she would simply be unable to stand his transformation any longer, and what would happen when she reached it? Would she start screaming and be unable to stop? Would he simply turn into another man who lived in their house, like a vagrant brother or an unsavory cousin? Like Xerxes. Would such a creature be possessed of a human soul? Would it be murder to kill him?

~ ~ ~

After a couple of wobbly practice laps around the pasture field in the truck with Hark behind the wheel, Vandal yelled at him to stop the vehicle. "There's no way you can drive on the road," Vandal told him. Hark's head barely poked up above the steering wheels, and his thin legs wavered uncertainly over the pedals. He glared at Vandal. Bridie, who was watching, silently applauded. She was glad to see Vandal denying him something, anything. "You'd kill somebody, or die yourself."

You take me, Hark said. There was very little he couldn't say these days. Occasionally he struggled for a word, a phrase, but mostly his speech was fluid. At times his voice could be silky and persuasive.

He had taken to answering the phone when it rang, which was not often, and even to initiating phone calls in which he carried on long, secretive conversations with they knew not whom. There was no one outside the house, outside the farm, that they could imagine him knowing. When they asked, he simply told them that he was *finding out.* "Finding out what?" they inquired. *Finding what's out there*, he said. "What's out there?" Vandal had asked him. *You wouldn't believe me if I told you,* Hark said, staring straight at Bridie. *But you'll know before too long, anyhow. It'll soon be more of me and mine out there than you and yours.*

In the truck, he repeated his demand. *You take me, if I can't drive.*

"Take you where?" Vandal wanted to know.

Into town, Hark said. When Vandal just kept looking at him, he continued. *To get … fuck.*

Vandal laughed. "You want to get laid?"

Hark shrugged his narrow shoulders. He wore a youth-size denim work shirt and a pair of Levi's, procured at the Rural King store out on the county line, and they fit him reasonably well, adding considerably to the illusion that he was just a slightly misshapen boy or small man. Sunglasses and a one-size-fits-all John Deere cap helped to obscure his hairy forehead and his unnatural eyes. *Everything wants to fuck*, he said.

Vandal shut off the truck's ignition, pulled the key, and climbed out of the truck's cab.

You won't let me go in amongst the bitches no more, Hark said. His voice was less peremptory now, pleading. *It ain't right, keep me from what I want. What I need.*

"You think you'll find women in town to sleep with you?" Bridie called. "A thing like you are?"

Hark laughed, a short bark that went strangely with his hominid appearance. *There's them in town as would be glad to be with me any way I am. Any way I want.*

"That's why we stay far from town," Vandal said. He stalked away from the truck, his face dark and angry, and marched into the house. Hark stayed where he was, behind the steering wheel, glaring balefully through the dirty windshield. The glass was spiderwebbed with fine cracks.

"Get out of there," Bridie said to him. "You're not driving nowhere."

I belong in town more than you do, Hark said without looking at her. *You know it's so. More and more every day. You got no right to keep me out here with you, amongst the cows and the crows.*

She pictured him among people, in some smoky place where she herself would never go, a cigarette tucked in the corner of his mouth, his hat tilted back on his head because he was unafraid of his own peculiar nature, his long teeth gleaming in dim light, his eyes slitted, one of his paws (*his hands,* she corrected herself, *they are much more like hands now*) on the thigh of a giggling, sighing girl beside him. But was she a girl, exactly, this creature in the vision? Wasn't she just a bit too large to be a normal sort of girl, too sleek and well-fleshed, her hair thick and coarse down her neck, her nostrils too wide, her eyes broadly spaced, on the sides of her head, almost? *A pony,* she thought. And the heavily-bristled, barrel-bodied man across the table from them, snorting with laughter, little eyes glittering with nasty delight, his snout buried in his plate…

"Probably you're right," she said, and she followed Vandal into the house, leaving Hark where he was.

~ ~ ~

He found his way into the liquor not long after that. The bottles had belonged to Xerxes. Vandal was strictly a beer man, and Bridie didn't drink at all. It was a holdover from her upbringing, which was hardshell Baptist. Much of that way of thinking and living had left her in the years she had been gone from her parents' house, which had been at once a stern and a gentle place, but her dislike of hard spirits had stayed with her. She found him in the living room, as usual, fixated on the television screen, which was announcing yet another series of nightmares. His eyes were glazed, a half-empty bottle of Knob Hill on the TV tray at his elbow, and he blinked slowly when she entered the room, so that she knew he was aware of her presence. His breathing was loud and stertorous.

This ain't happening just here, you know, he told her. He nodded at the TV, where hail was pelting down from a clear sky, smashing windows, denting the hoods and roofs of cars, sending people scrambling for solid cover, flattening crops. Birds of every description were dropping dead into the streets. *It's happening everywhere.* He burped lightly and covered his mouth with his hairy palm. His tone had sounded mournful before, but now he giggled.

Bridie understood that he didn't mean their own situation, not exactly, not a dog turning into a man, not just (her thoughts turned away, but she forced them back: she had to look at everything that was happening, and not just a part of it) a man turning into a dog, or at any rate something less than a man; but other, equally terrible things, inexplicable things, things that had never happened before. And she knew that he also meant, *There is no stopping them.*

She sat down across from him, close enough that she could touch him. He took his gaze from the television and looked her full in the face, and his eyes were soft and brown, much more like the dog she remembered, and not antagonistic. There was pain written in them— did it hurt, to become a man?—and fear. For the first time, the sight of him didn't fill her with disgust. He sniffed.

It's the foller-man as gets bit. It's the foller-dog as gets bit. His voice was a kind of singsong. Playful. He took another swig from the bottle, waiting on her response. If he had not been what he was, she might have thought he was being flirtatious.

"What's that mean?" she asked him.

You tell me.

She thought a moment. She believed that she had heard a rhyme like it somewhere before. Her girlhood, maybe. A cadence for jumping rope. Was it some kind of a riddle? *The foller-man.* She thought of the head of a snake, then, the dead eyes and the mouth wide, the fangs milky with poison; and she had it.

"It's always the second man on the trail that gets bitten by the snake," she said. Hark nodded, and his head moved so slowly that the gesture seemed wise. "The first man wakes the snake up, and it strikes the second man in the line."

And the lead dog, he said, *judges the distance to get across the road before the car comes. But the dog that comes along just a second later, trailing the first one like he always does, he...*

"Gets hit," she said.

Is it a joke? he asked. *That the first one plays on the second one?*

"Not so much a joke," she told him, "as just not giving it any thought. Always looking forward and there's no looking behind."

I never want to be no foller-dog anymore, he said to her. *Nor no foller-man neither. I'm going to be the firstest one along every trail, and the firstest one across every road.* He took another drink, and the level in the bottle dropped appreciably. He coughed and sputtered. *From now on in,* he said.

In other places, some not so very far away, the television informed them, the dead were said to be rising up from their graves. The recent dead, and the long dead: it didn't seem to make any difference. The ones who came back to life most often found their ways back to their homes, their families, back to those who loved them, and when they found somebody who recognized them—assuming anybody was left who did—they cried aloud at the wonders they had seen in the great lightless cities that they inhabited after death.

Would resurrected people have the vote, the television wondered?

Hark closed his eyes and sighed. *Some folks just have too much life in them to die all the way, I guess,* he said. He looked so sad when he said it that she felt a sudden stab of unexpected sympathy for him, and sorrow.

~ ~ ~

They took to having conversations, short ones, usually, that ended in unsatisfying confusion, because she didn't know the right questions to ask, or he didn't know the right words to tell her what she wanted to know. Sometimes, she swore, he held back his answers, wanting always to get more than he gave. When he asked her about the wider world, outside the borders of the farm, outside the boundaries of the county, she found that she didn't know very much—only what she saw on TV, really, and he saw as much of that as she did; more, in fact—and he quickly became contemptuous of her. Always, though, their exchanges came back to a single question:

"Why wouldn't you go into the water that day?"

There was something waiting for me in that pond.

"What was waiting?"

A spirit. There was a spirit on that water, and it wanted me to come in there with it. The spirit wanted me, the spirit and the water both.

"You were afraid the water would change you?"

I was afraid it wouldn't. I felt the change coming on me that day, and I had the fear that the water might take it off and leave me what I had always been. I wanted to be something else.

"The change didn't feel bad to you? It didn't hurt?"

It felt— exhilarating. He sounded pleased with himself that he had come up with that word, but his face was impossible to read.

~ ~ ~

Hark was still drinking and watching TV, and the liquor was holding out longer than Bridie had thought (had hoped) it might. Vandal had taken to spending long stretches away from the house, out walking the fields or shuffling about in the granary, sitting alone in the loft of the silent barn, watching over the place as it fell fallow without his labor.

Sometimes he went into the kennel, and she didn't care to ask him what he did there. He didn't touch her in their bed at night anymore, wouldn't undress where she could see him. Under his clothes, he seemed to have shrunk, and his gaze, whenever it fell on her, was cool and distant. At that moment, he was upstairs, asleep in their bed. He slept ten hours a night, sometimes more, and still he seemed always to be exhausted.

Hark dropped an empty bottle and it rolled across the parlor floor and disappeared under the davenport. *It could be,* she thought, *that Xerxes had him a stash that I never knew about. But how did he find it?*

"Hark?" she said.

Ain't my name.

"What?" she asked.

Nefas. That's what you call me now. That's my name now. Not that word you give me, that nothing. That Hark.

"I'm not going to call you—"

Nefas! he shouted. His teeth, still pointed, flashed at her. *Baphomet! Marduk, Shahar, Enkidu! Call me by my God-damned name!*

Her hand flashed out, and her open palm cracked against the sharp bones of his face. The sting of the blow traveled up her arm, to the center of her chest, and her eyes filled with tears, but she swung again, savagely backhanded him so that spittle flew from his gaping mouth. His right eye closed and his head twisted to the side. She thought that she wouldn't be able to stand the throbbing of her hand. Her fingers; had she broken them?

He flew at her with a snarl, and the momentum of his small, furious body took them both to the floor. He put his teeth on the swelling of her throat just below her jaw, and his breath was hot against the skin of her neck. *He will kill me now*, she thought, and the flaming agony of her arm, and Hark's noisome weight—or Marduk's, or whatever he cared to call himself, Nefas—on her, and the events of these last days, made that idea not at all an unwelcome one.

Instead, he began to squeeze her breasts with both his hands, and his breathing quickened as he fumbled to open her blouse. He pushed a knee between her legs and worked to part them. *This is how he did it*, he said.

"No," she said.

He gave a throaty little chuckle. There was real amusement in the sound. *It's all fine and dandy to tell someone No*, he said. *But the question has to be: Can you make it stick?* The stench of whiskey filled her nostrils. His teeth and his lips moved from beneath her chin to the hollow of her throat, and from there to her breastbone. He pressed himself avidly against her.

She willed her wrecked right hand into motion, her fingers and thumb searching for his eyes, her palm forcing his blunt head up and back. The stubble on his cheeks rasped against her like sandpaper, and she cried out with the pain and horror of it. She didn't want to hurt him. She had never wanted to hurt anyone in her life.

She caught sight of the picture of the baptism on the wall, hanging high above her—*I am where Xerxes lay*, she thought, *and this is the angle he saw it from at the last*—while her left hand went seeking, almost on its own, along the wall. In the picture, a great crowd of gray figures, cloaked like ghosts, filled the background, lining the far bank of the river. Seen from a distance, it was possible to take them for clouds, or a line of distant cliffs. *How is it I never noticed them before?* she thought, as Hark (*Nefas!*) fastened his eager mouth on her nipple, as her left hand found the set of fireplace tools that stood on the hearth and brought them all clattering down. As left her hand got purchase on the pair of iron log tongs and whipped them around in a hard arc.

The tongs took him up high, on the temple, and his suckling mouth fell away from her, his limbs spasming. She struck him again, on the shoulder this time, and he screeched and tumbled off of her, scrambling to escape, his limbs scrabbling against the floor. He was like an injured insect. She stood and went after him, straddling his body, thumping him on the back of the head, the spine. He squealed, and she wondered if Vandal might hear the sound and come to investigate. "Your name is Hark!" she shouted at him. Her blows rained down on him.

Nefas, he managed to gasp out.

"You will come when we call!"

Enkidu.

"You will do what we say."

Hark scuttled into a corner of the room, behind the easy chair, where Bridie had a hard time getting at him. She stood with the tongs upraised, waiting on a good moment to strike him again. When she saw his eyes on her, she tugged her blouse closed with her injured hand. A couple of the buttons were missing. Crouched in the corner, his spindly arms crossed over his head for protection, Hark indicated the picture with a lift of his snout.

Okay, he said. His ribs were heaving, and blood stained his shirt and his pants. *You got the upper hand of me. You going to make me get down on my knees and worship him the way that you do?* he said. *Bow down to your water man, your dead man? Your foller-man?*

~ ~ ~

Vandal lay next to her in the dark, moaning softly, his legs kicking from time to time beneath the bedcovers. He faced the wall, and when she touched him, she could feel the puckered ridge of his backbone. He had always been a thickset man, but now it was as if the flesh was melting off him, leaving his body a skeletal landscape of edges and hollows. She envied him his sleep. She had taken some aspirin, the last in the house, but her right arm continued to pain her terribly.

"What if we're imagining all this?" she asked Vandal's back. She kept her voice low, because she didn't really want to wake him. She hoped, somehow, that he might awake on his own, and be as he had been before. He shivered and whimpered at the sound of her voice. "What if he never talked or changed at all? What if we're dreaming it?" she asked.

Dreaming the same dream, he said. She closed her eyes at the sound of his voice, which was no longer his, little more than a buzzing or gurgling deep in his throat. Eyes open, eyes closed, she found that it was the same darkness all around her.

"Maybe I'm just dreaming it," she said. "Alone."

Vandal made a small snorting noise that she took to mean assent, and went on, like a being in a fairy story, with his impenetrable slumber.

~ ~ ~

Deep in the night, when she could not tell how long she had been asleep, the voice came to her from outside her bedroom door, whispering in like wind through the crack at the threshold: *The strong will do what the strong will do. And the weak will bear what they must.*

~ ~ ~

When he surprised her in the kitchen, she understood that this time there would be no lucky hand on the tongs, no surprise blow to the head. He wasn't drunk. He was ready. Nefas (she had come to think of him that way—he wasn't Hark anymore, and it seemed foolish to keep calling him by the vanished dog's name) had grown at least as large as she was, and nimbler, and far faster and stronger, with a beast's terrible speed and strength, and a man's cruelty. If she tried to hurt him, he would hurt her far worse in return, she knew. In some deep part of him, she thought, he hoped that she would fight him, because he very much wanted to hurt her.

Her right arm was immobilized in a sling that she had rigged up for it out of a couple of dish cloths, her fingers bruised, the joints blackened. She had a fever. Vandal was still upstairs, in the bed that was now far too large for him. He slept around the clock, wasting away. She would not have been surprised, upon going into the bedroom, to find him gone altogether.

If I had a pot of water boiling, she thought. *If I had a skillet full of sizzling grease, I would fling it in his grinning face.* There was nothing hot. He had placed himself between her and the great wooden knife block. He wasn't stupid. He had the shotgun in his hand, pointing clumsily downward, at his feet.

She found herself hoping that Vandal wouldn't awake, ever, that he would simply sleep through what was coming, for her, for him, for all of them. She hoped that he could go on forever dreaming for himself a world where the sunshine was bright and golden as in the old days, and untamed birds crisscrossed the sky in their lopsided Vs, and cattle drifted in friendly bunches across the pastures, and game, unending phalanxes of game, deer and clever squirrels and bear and swift wily turkeys that could be hunted and brought down but which did not die, which lent themselves again and again to the eternal chase—she hoped that, in his dreams, all of these filled the emerald mansions of the limitless forest.

God be with you, she thought, and then Vandal, like Hark, was gone from her thoughts.

Nefas set the shotgun carefully on the floor behind him and put his hands on her shoulders. His touch was heavy but not painful. His hands were broad and short-fingered. "Please," she said.

Call me by my name, he said.

"Nefas," she said, choking on the word. "Please."

He leaned into her, cradled the back of her head with his hard palm, sniffed deeply at her hair. *Call me by my name*, he said.

She struggled to remember what he had said she should call him. Why did he need so many names? She couldn't recall them all, and she was terrified of what he would do to her if she couldn't name him properly. Her memory leaped. "Baphomet," she said. "Marduk, please."

He bit the lobe of her ear, hard enough to draw blood, and she cried out. She struggled to free her arm from the sling but it was caught fast. *Call me by my name*, he said, his mouth against her ear. His breath was moist, his tone simultaneously intimate and insistent. He cupped her right breast as though he were weighing it, as though it were a piece of fruit that he was considering buying. His weight against her drew agony from her wounded hand, trapped between her body and his.

"Enkidu," she said. She knew that she could not, must not, resist him, and she steeled herself to surrender. Why, she wondered, was it not possible simply to die? To her astonishment, her uninjured hand, her left, hefted a cumbersome iron trivet from the stovetop. It had belonged to Vandal's mother, and Bridie had never cared much for it, but she had kept it for the sentiment she imagined it provoked in Vandal.

She raised the trivet over Nefas' shaggy head. The fingers of her left hand were bloodless, she was holding it so tightly. He followed its ascent with his eyes, but he did not take his mouth away from her ear. He made a sound that she thought might be laughter. His hand went to the skirt that she was wearing, and he tugged the hem up to her waist.

Shall we fuck each other, or shall we kill each other? he asked. It didn't sound like he much cared which. Both were fine with him. With one of his feet he hooked the shotgun and slid it forward, where he could get a hand on it quickly.

"This doesn't have to happen," she said.

No? he asked. His hands were busy, unbuttoning, unclasping. She was nearly nude, and still her hand stayed poised over his skull. The trivet had a number of pointed projections. It had always seemed a peaceable thing, domestic, sitting patiently atop the stove, but in her hand it had taken on the look of some exotic piece of medieval weaponry. He shucked his baggy Levi's, and the buckle of his belt clattered against the linoleum. *Seems to me it's happening already.*

Spare me, spare me, she thought, but she didn't say it because a creature like him wouldn't spare her anything. He was toying with her. He had come an unspeakable distance and waited an unthinkably long time for the pleasures he was planning to indulge. "You were a good dog," she said. "Can't you be a good man?"

He considered a moment, drew fractionally away from her. Her skin where it had touched his was hot, and the small space between them felt deliciously fresh. The trivet was growing heavy, her hand was trembling with the effort of holding it over him. Nefas jerked a thumb upward, and his hand brushed the metal. He could have taken it from her if he had wanted, but he let it stay. *Is he a good man?* he asked her.

She had to struggle to work out who he might mean. Vandal, asleep in the master bedroom overhead. "He was," she said. "I don't know what precisely he is now."

You think it's only me that gets to choose, he said. *He chooses too. Every minute he chooses.*

Vandal, upstairs, choosing oblivion.

You choose too, just as much as him. Just as much as me. He tapped the trivet with a dense fingernail, and it rang like a bell. *You're choosing right now. What is it you're choosing?* "Not this," she said, indicating his nakedness, and hers. His eyes roamed over her body, and she had the impulse to cover herself, but she resisted it. It took her a great deal of will to open her fingers; wearily, she dropped the iron trivet onto the counter, where it thumped and rolled and left a small scar. "Not this either," she said.

Unable to suppress a whimper of pain as she did it, she shucked the sling and flexed the stiffened fingers of her hand.

Nefas returned his gaze to her face. *He ain't fucked you in a while now*, he said. *And you don't want to fuck me. You just planning on doing without it for the rest of your life?*

"That might not be such a very long time," she said. "With the world the way it is."

And yet it might, he said to her. *That's one choice as is not left up to us.*

Stifling her disgust, she reached out and took him by the hand, his broad palm in her swollen fingers. She drew him gently to her, not in the way of a lover, but as a mother might. An expression of shock, unmistakable even on his inscrutable face, crossed his crude features. Slowly he came to her, almost against his will. She gritted her teeth and shut the feel of his hairy hide away from her. He laid his bony head on her bosom, and she embraced him.

With surprise, she felt how meager he was, how slight his frame. *He's made out of a dog's bones, and he's got a man's mind*, she thought. There was no joy in him anywhere, she could feel that plainly, none of the kind of blind infectious joy that even the least of dogs possesses in abundance. "Why do you think he gave his place up to you?" she asked, meaning Vandal. She could see now that that was precisely what he had done. Slipped away from her, away from the world, and left this twisted creature in his stead. "Being a man isn't what you think it is."

Hark began to cry. His hot tears slipped over her breasts. "I've got my teeth in it now," he said. "I can't ever go back. I don't much want to go forward, but I know for sure I can't go back." He put his arms around her and she stiffened in his embrace, but the lust had passed through him for the moment and left him innocent. It would come back, and the old struggle would rise up between them again; and how it would end she didn't care to contemplate. For the present, they could manage to stand together this way, skin to skin and inextricably linked.

Nefas cocked his head. *I can hear him, you know*, he said. *Always hear him.* His voice was quiet. *Listen to him as he comes this way. He's pretty near.*

"Who?"

Him. Him as sent me on ahead.

She recognized the quality of his fear. It wasn't fear for himself, she realized, and the knowledge clutched at her. "Who can you hear?" she demanded. She struggled to keep her own voice even.

I figured you knew, Nefas said. *I figured you knew all along.* He looked up at her with wide eyes. *He's coming along on my heels, but he ain't your foller-man. It's nothing like that. I don't believe he's any sort of man at all.*

Terror bloomed in her, and her vision dimmed. "X?"

He wanted me to tell as soon as I could talk proper, but I found out I wanted you, so I didn't say it.

"Didn't say what?" she asked. "What were you supposed to say?"

He wanted me to tell you that he don't care about what you said. He supposes he should hold it against you, but he don't plan to pay it any mind at all.

The house felt very small and fragile in that moment, and she felt small and fragile inside it, holding onto this creature, this hairy thing that wasn't her husband, that wasn't her dog either. The world was drawing in around her, the broad fields folding up to the size of handkerchiefs, the once-straight fences crowding and jostling themselves crooked, the barn and the granary and the machine shop butting up hard against the house and the dog run and the kennel, the woods and tangled marshes infiltrating the cleared spaces, humans and beasts colliding, the dead and the living spilling over each other; order failing, pandemonium as all the things that had been separate for so very long came rushing together, splintering one another like ships driven before a storm, until there was no way to know what was one and what was another.

Probably, Bridie thought, this has happened at other times, perhaps countless times before, perhaps every age came to its close in just this way, with no one left alive to tell the tale. Her mind went to the pond, and to the turtles huddled under the shivering surface of the water. *Them*, she thought. *They are the great survivors.*

The house was drawing everything into it and down, like a great whirlpool—all the abhorrent things, all the terrible marvels. Bridie stood at the heart of the catastrophe, and so alone was able to see it for what it was: the end of one thing, and the beginning of another that was infinitely worse.

Perhaps, she thought, Nefas could serve her as a guide, she thought, a scout among the ruins, blend of senses and mind that he was, a genius of sorts, and utterly unique. It might be possible for her to lose herself in the shrieking bedlam, to hide herself away in the ruins, but for how long? The world's collapse might never end, and X would never stop his returning. "Can you smell him?" she asked. From outside, a whispering as from the tongues of a thousand snakes.

He shook his head. *Not yet. But soon.*

"Will you take my part?" she asked.

His eyes were wide, and he was shivering against her. *You don't have the least idea what you're asking, or who you're asking it from,* he told her. He shrugged and pulled her closer, and she felt him decide in her favor. He leaned down and scooped up the shotgun, and his grip on it looked so clumsy and unpracticed that she almost laughed. She had the impulse to take it away from him, but she chose instead not to insult his pride. The understanding between them was brittle enough. "I'll do what I can," he said.

They clung to each other in the midst of the hissing, swaying chaos, murmuring useless reassurances as twilight consumed the kitchen. And Vandal, curled deeply into himself, slumbered away in the upper bedroom, twitching from time to time as dreams of the world, full of infinite life as it had never been, and as it would never be, flitted beautifully across the thin translucent scrim of his mind.

The Angel's Trumpet

T*reat Yourself To The Best.*

That's what it said, in letters eighteen inches high, on the wall of the dairy at our place, at the Goins place. *Chew Mail Pouch Tobacco.* You've seen the Mail Pouch signs on the warped walls of old barns that stand tipsily along the roadside out in the country. You've maybe even stopped your car, pulled over to the side of the road, crowded your vehicle against the ditch that's full of trash and weeds and scrubby little trees, in order to take photographs of some tilting granary and its picturesque sign. You likely used a clever little camera no bigger than a pack of cigarettes, thinking to yourself as you did so, "How quaint."

None of us chewed tobacco. But there it was all the same, the sign (there must have been money involved, back when it was first painted; or my father, a worldly man, would never have allowed such a thing), bigger and bolder and more brightly tinted than anything else on the place, the paint just beginning to flake off here and there toward the end of our time; but the slogan continued, declamatory, hanging over our heads as we worked, as we saw to the cattle, repaired the machinery, pumped out the manure, planted the corn and harvested it, cut and raked (those long golden fragrant windrows!) and bailed the hay on our sloping, rocky fields: *Treat Yourself To The Best.*

We didn't smoke either, we Goins men. We didn't drink. We didn't use hard language. We were clean-living people. Right up until we died.

It was the manure pit that killed us. It didn't kill quite all of us, to be honest. Killed all of us but me. The shear pin on the impeller in the pit gave way, was the origin of the tragedy (as the newspapers all called it, *tragedy*, to a one). That's what shear pins are made to do, to snap cleanly when the strain is too great, when something must give way. The shear pin's a sacrificial part, the element of the machine that breaks by design. Every machine must have a weak point, as perhaps you are aware, and you want it to be something inexpensive and easy to replace. In the particular case of a manure storage tank pumping system like ours, you want it to be a cheap metal rod that you slip easily through hub and axle right behind the impeller, rather than a complex and expensive drive train or motor.

The shear pin that secured the pump's impeller gave way when we were nearly finished pumping out the manure tank—some chunk of hard matter in the viscous stuff caught in the spinning blades, most likely—and to fix it my big brother Albertus climbed down into the manure pit located under the floor of the barn; the barn that said so plainly on its broad wall (there were days it seemed to shout at me, that slogan) *Treat Yourself To The Best*.

~ ~ ~

Albertus: What a grandiose name he had! What grandiose names we all bore. My father was a man who read the works of antiquity and who wanted us to have names that spoke to the world beyond the confines of the Seneca Valley where we dwelt, beyond the narrow confines of the age in which we lived. You learn about history, he told us in authoritative tones, so that you have something intriguing to think about while you're milking the cows. I myself am named Athelstan Brunanburh, after the first King of All Britain and his greatest military triumph.

~ ~ ~

From *The Cave of the Bulls*, an illustrated history of the cave paintings in Lascaux, France, a book in my father's collection: one of my favorites, although I am not a great reader of history. The illustration that accompanies this passage—surprisingly, even astonishingly graceful, suggestive of motion, of a life so monstrously vigorous that even now, even nearly two hundred centuries after it was made, it seems to want to come down off the wall—depicts a vast black bull, huge spread of horns like a lyre, eyes rolled back in rage (presumably at the men who are hunting him, tiny foolish clumsy stick figures with crudely-drawn spears in their hands):

> "These caves were sanctuaries for the performance of sacred rituals and observances. The hunt, and the death at the end of the hunt, were profoundly religious activities for paleolithic peoples. Since time immemorial, Man has used his wiles to trap and kill the animals around him, his consumption of those animals always mixed with his respect for them and his praise of the gods for providing them. Likewise, the creation of his art was originally entirely an act of worship, both of the animals he had dispatched and of the divine beings who loved those animals, and who loved Man sufficiently to provide them to him. The frieze of the Great Bull was painted speedily, with a lump of colorful wet clay. The artist/shaman was presumably rapt in a state of spiritual ecstasy and drug-induced euphoria. Having eaten of the locally available *datura stramonium* (jimson weed: also known as moonflower or 'angel's trumpet,' it grows in dung heaps and contains high concentrations of atropine, scopolamine, and hyosyamine, all powerful natural hallucinogens), he descended into the cave gallery where, in utter darkness and completely alone, the primitive priest, caught up in his waking dream, daubed onto the wall with startling exactitude the hunt as it played itself out in his mind's eye: a representation of the past, yes; but also an invocation, a prophecy of an abundant future."

~ ~ ~

We had pumped nearly the last of the liquid manure up into the honey wagon, the Sperry/New Holland manure spreader that my father had purchased (used, but still in excellent condition) for the farm that year. We'd been spreading manure on the fields all that day, a beastly hot one in July, and this was the final load. I was eager to be done with the stinking job, the worst chore on the place to my mind; but Albertus—as always, Albertus was all business, neither keen nor unenthusiastic about what he was doing, but purely methodical, a man who did a thing until it was done, and when it was done didn't think about it again until it once more needed doing. He was nineteen that summer, and I was two years his junior.

The manure went to nourish the fields, which in their turn flourished and fed the cattle, who in their turn defecated onto the floor of the dairy barn, after which their manure was washed down into the pit, where it fermented and decomposed. When the pit was full, it must be pumped out so that the manure could be spread on the fields to keep them fertile. It was a cycle that propagated itself endlessly, like a *perpetuum mobile*; and that, for the health of the operation, must never be allowed to cease. Not one of us—not Albertus, not our father (with the plain name of John: his parents' lack of bravura must have grated on him), not our uncle Joseph, not our younger brothers Ptolemy (whose middle name was Philadelphus) or Cunobelinus (middle name Togodumnus: my father and his fetish for ancient and obscure names! but they were names with power, he claimed, names that carried with them the enduring momentum and substance of the past)—ever thought to complain about the meanness of the work.

Rather, they did not think to complain. I thought of complaint. All day long, my lungs filled with the stench of fermented manure, the tractor bumping and lurching across the rutted, stony fields, the sun beating down, my eyelids heavy, my stomach turning slowly, queasily, over and over: I thought of practically nothing else but complaint. My God, I wanted to ask, how do you people do this day after day, year after year? How will I? But I never spoke a word.

It was less the work that galled me—although I did not much like the physical exertion it required—than the incessant cyclical nature of the thing. Raise the cows to breed them, to artificially inseminate them (there was not a single bull on the place); they calve; we milk them; the calves themselves grow to be bred and delivered and milked. A great continuous line of cows stretching back into the meaningless past, stretching also into the future, far beyond me and my death. There had been a beginning, I knew. The great bull, the beast that predates all the other cattle, the ancient aurochs that the shamans had painted on the walls of their caves, whom they had revered like a god: I had read of him in my father's books. Alone among all the stories in those books, the tale of the aurochs, spread throughout all of human history, and hinting at a lineage that long preceded mankind, that story interested me. The original bull had taught us to hunt. He taught us to walk upright. He taught us to read; our alphabet begins with him. He made us men. He alone, the bull, stood outside the cycle of the farm, and it had been his flesh, his seed, that made it all possible.

We, the Goins men, must accomplish the round of twice-a-day milkings and twice-a-day feedings of over a hundred healthy, gleaming Holstein-Friesian cattle without fail. Likewise, the manure pit must never become full to overflowing. That was unwritten law. In those days, for us, for the oh-so-preciously-named Goinses who lived to the east of the thriving and upright municipality of Mount Nebo, which was the county seat of prosperous Seneca County in the civilized agricultural eastern part of the state, in that place where we were known and where we were respected—perhaps even feared, because we were ruthless in the demands we made of others, as we were ruthless in the demands we made on ourselves—the nonstop round-robin of our jobs was like the axis on which the world turned.

The great bull from time's beginning knew of us, I felt sure; and just as surely, he pitied us.

I say "big brother" when I speak of Albertus (middle name Magnus, as you have likely guessed), but really I am bigger, I was bigger, which is why he went down into the manure pit. It's a tight squeeze to climb into the tank, through a narrow opening and down a short ladder, and then you're standing, when the pumping is nearly done, in eighteen inches or so of liquid muck, in a space that spans perhaps twenty feet on a side and ten feet tall: four thousand cubic feet, which had just recently been full almost to the top with liquid manure. The remaining stuff was warm from the decomposition process, warm as a bath. A short while more and we would have it all pumped out and spread over the fields, and the filling could begin again.

He held the new shear pin in his hand, did Albertus. The metal of it was bright, and as he descended, he clutched it like it was something terrifically valuable. He'd been in the tank dozens of times, to perform tasks exactly like this one: unplug the pipes, replace the shear pin, break up some intractable chunk of nameless matter. We all had, though I went less frequently than the others, because I was as I say larger than the others, in height and in girth. I was an anomaly in our otherwise compact, tightly-muscled family. Tall and wide, but over-fond of food and leisure. I watched him disappear into the pit: his legs, his torso, and finally his square, close-cropped head.

He laughed, once. The laugh echoed momentarily in the confines of the tank before it dried up and vanished. It sounded quite merry.

"Albertus?" I said. It was odd to hear him laugh, Albertus, who was usually as stolid as the stump of a tree. He didn't answer. "Mag?" I called down. It was my pet name for my brother, of whom I was a bit afraid and whom I admired extravagantly. He was a deeply dignified young man and didn't much like me to call him that, I could tell by his expression whenever I said the name, but he permitted it—when he would not have permitted a similar familiarity from Ptolemy, say, or Cunobelinus—because of my strangeness, as he must have thought of it (it went unspoken, unremarked on), my difference from the rest of the family.

I liked to nap, was one of my strangenesses (sleeping in the middle of the day!), and the books that I indulged in—novels, generally— were light and frivolous by comparison to the books that my father read and loved and learned from—substantial histories and useful agricultural tomes—and that he passed on to my brothers, who seemed not to be much interested in either sort. I liked films and television as well, and garish comic books full of monsters and alien planets and big-breasted Amazons. I liked to talk about my dreams, too, and what they might mean: the terrible clutching figures I saw, the booming disembodied voices I heard, the powerful erections with which I awoke. At times they looked at me, my father and my uncle and my brothers, all of them solid and good and kind and grave and pious and dutiful, as though they wondered where it was I might have come from. From one of the weird planets in my science fiction books, maybe.

I was the middle child. Ptolemy and Cunobelinus were twins. My mother had been like me, as I remembered her, large and florid and quick to laugh; but she had been dead for many years by that time, since not long after the birth of the twins, and so without her I was alone among the Goinses.

Dispensations were made for me that were not made for the others, for my siblings. They were instituted by my father, I suppose, these exemptions, these liberties, but they seemed after a time to emanate from all of them, all of the others. In concert, they knew without asking what they could and could not expect from me. I was not made to do the dangerous or the difficult jobs. I was given extra helpings at meals. I was not consulted about agricultural matters. I was allowed to sleep later than the others. Sometimes I woke with the sun high in the eastern sky, and the house empty, and I lay a while imagining that they were not simply at work, the other Goinses, but that they were dead and gone, and that the whole world was dead and gone, and that I was alone, and free to do as I liked.

The other Goins men were hard. They were hard on themselves, and they were hard on others, when those others failed to meet Goins expectations. The merchants with whom we dealt on our infrequent trips into Mount Nebo (which I now know to have been ridiculously small, but which at the time seemed to me vast and confusing and brimming with frantic activity) were always on their very best behavior, their voices reedy with anxiety, their manners obliging.

But the other Goinses were not hard on me. They were gracious to me, and endlessly decent, and they treated me as they might have treated a (mostly) welcome guest from a far country, one with a barbaric and slightly distasteful culture. My father, from his reading, knew of many such countries, ancient and modern, and told of us the unsavory rituals they practiced in them. Widows burned with the corpses of their husbands. One hand for eating and the other for cleaning your behind. Neolithic peoples drilling holes in the skulls of madmen, using the crudest of tools, to let the evil spirits out. Taurokathapsia, the sport of leaping over a charging bull, using its horns for leverage. Ancestor worship. Chewing jimson weed and peyote to commune with the dead. Revering animals as gods. We knew better than to do these things, of course, and felt amused, as tolerantly and as kindly as we could, at the benighted people who didn't.

Frequently I was grateful that I was not held to the standards of the others. Less frequently, I envied the others the profound (as it seemed to me) bond of their shared discipline and self-restraint. Once or twice during our childhood, Ptolemy and Cunobelinus asked for extension to them of the license I enjoyed or complained at some privilege I was granted—an extra hour of leisure, or the price (so cheap!) of a pulp novel with a gaudy cover; or I might be passed over for the monthly visit to the barber in Mount Nebo and allowed to wear my hair long rather than in the traditional Goins buzzcut—and my father took them aside and spoke to them quietly and earnestly, glancing from time to time at me.

The twins soon enough began similarly tilting their blunt, handsome heads to take me in, cocking their brows, seeing me as my father saw me. They wanted to grow up to be modest, virtuous men. They wanted to fulfill their obligations to me, as they fulfilled their obligations to the farm, to the herd of healthy, stupid milk cows that drifted mindless and content across our fields, chewing grass and calling to one another in low, resonant voices. The twins ceased to comment on the differences between us.

Albertus always treated me with an indifferent kindness. My uncle, on the other hand, my father's younger brother, frequently clapped me on the back (the contact never failed to surprise me, because we were not by and large a physically demonstrative family), loudly proclaiming me to the others to be his favorite nephew; by which declaration we all knew him to mean nothing of the sort.

Joseph, my uncle, could be rambunctious, occasionally challenging my younger brothers (never me; and never Albertus, who was his physical equal) to impromptu wrestling matches in our living room, the sparse furniture pushed back against the walls and the thin central rug rolled up for the event.

He would put a record on the record player, something raucous, jazz (stunningly loud in our normally quiet house) or Dixieland from New Orleans, where he had lived for a while, during a transitory and disastrous marriage, about which we were never allowed to ask, though he from time to time made veiled references to it, to the sultry magic of his ex-wife's body, her wicked, cunning tongue, her desire for money and then more money, her relentless cruelty when he wasn't sufficiently forthcoming with the "baksheesh" as he called it, or when there was no more money for him to give. I never heard him speak her name, this bride whom he hated and for whom he still burned with unappeasable lust.

He was relentless on these occasions when he wanted to wrestle, full of strength and the will to dominate, to conquer (an attribute of Goins men throughout the generations, we were given to know, but sadly lacking in this latest batch; but he would instill it by main force if need be, by God he would!). He caused my younger brothers to cry, made them call out "Uncle! Uncle!" which just made him laugh and twist their arms harder, because of course he *was* their uncle! And didn't they see how funny it was?

He would rub their foreheads with the crooked knuckle of his middle finger until the skin there began to shine and grow angry. I longed to ask him to stop—I would have begged if I had thought it would do even the slightest good—but I was afraid, not without reason, that he would then turn his attention to me. My privileged status, I knew, depended on my maintaining the decorous silence of the outsider.

My father looked on, his expression bland, neither critical nor approving, and I wondered if perhaps he had performed this same sort of rough training on his younger brother.

Until one day, when Joseph turned on his music (it was "Basin Street Blues," as I recall, the solo trumpet rising up strident and shrill, screaming over the thumping, straining, pedestrian rhythm section), shoved the furniture to the edges of the room, flipped back the rug, and challenged the younger boys, challenged both of them together at the same time; which was an error on his part, I saw that right away, because they were gaining size, putting on muscle with their arduous and unending farm work.

They teamed up against him, grinning wide and astonished at each other; and they pancaked him immediately and held him helpless against the hard wood of the floor, more than a little shaken (them and him both) at their shocking and unanticipated victory; and they scrubbed his face against the boards until his skin reddened and broke and bled; and they bent his limbs at gruesome angles until he cried out "Uncle!" and they howled in exultation because of course he *was* their uncle, as he had always told them, and at last they did see how funny it truly was. Breathlessly they apologized to him, hissing the words into his ears, one of them to each ear. They apologized profusely for not having understood the humor of it earlier.

I found myself crying and calling out "Stop! Stop it!" and I had to wonder that I had never cried that way before, when Joseph was mauling

my brothers. But I cried out and—shocked to find myself doing it—
stepped forward. I flexed my arms and was suddenly aware of how
long they were, and how thick, how potentially powerful. My feet in
their hobnail boots thudded against the floorboards as I approached
the knot of struggling men, and I felt like a giant among these smaller
people.

I am going to do it, I thought, though I did not know with any certainty
what *it* might be. I was going to do violence, I knew that much. To
whom? To all of them perhaps. Clean cold fury washed through me,
through all my limbs. I trembled, and the tears that flowed down my
cheeks were no longer the tears of fear or sorrow. They were hot tears
of hatred. My hands—they seemed to me to have grown to the size of
baseball mitts—flexed and fisted themselves, the knuckles cracking,
the blue veins on their backs writhing like snakes. I felt a great cry, like
a bull's bellow, bubbling up inside me. This was the force that had
founded the vast bovine herds of the world. Would it make me one of
them, one of the Goinses, this bellow? Or would it separate me from
them further? Perhaps forever? I found that I did not care.

Albertus reached them first. I had thought too long. It was Albertus,
rather than me, who pulled the twins away. He needed to use all his
considerable strength to do it, because they were clinging to my uncle's
back like monkeys, and I thought Ptolemy was about to clench his
teeth on Joseph's left ear. I could already imagine the flesh tearing and
the blood and the stream of curses and recriminations. And Albertus
pushed them back against the wall of the room, their faces scarlet with
jubilation. "He's our uncle!" they cried at Albertus. I stood back, my
flesh cooling suddenly, my arms dangling at my sides, my hands slack
and open. The bull's roar died in my throat, and the taste of it was slick
and metallic and gray.

"I know he is," Albertus told them, right hand flat against Ptolemy's
sternum, restraining him; left hand against the chest of Cunobelinus.
"I know."

~ ~ ~

From Julius Caesar's *Commentarii de bello Gallico*, a prized volume in my
father's collection, a passage concerning the aurochs, primordial ancestor
of present-day cattle, which Caesar encountered on his adventures in

the Black Forest (the passage is circled, almost certainly by my father, in red ink—he did not mark his books lightly):

> "These beasts, known as *uri*, are only slightly smaller than elephants in size, and possess the color and form of a bull. They enjoy tremendous strength and speed. They spare no living thing, neither man nor animal, once they have laid eyes on it. They cannot endure the sight of men, nor can they be tamed, even when captured as calves. Those who trap them in pitfalls diligently destroy them; and young men harden themselves in this labor. Those who have killed a great number obtain considerable honor."

~ ~ ~

"Albertus?" I called again, after his laugh had died away. The silence in the pit was profound. Inside the dairy barn, the cattle moaned. Looking down, I saw that Albertus had fallen. He lay slumped against the near wall of the tank, the manure slopping around his legs, his broad, thick-fingered, work-hardened hands sunk in the foul stuff. His face was calm and relaxed. I might have imagined that he was asleep, but he and I had shared a bedroom all our lives, tidy twin beds barely an arm's-length from each other in the narrow confines of the Spartan room, and I knew that his sleep was never so easy.

Calm and deliberate during the day, Albertus struggled and fought all night long, ground his teeth and gargled and called out in the harsh syllables of some indecipherable language. When we were little boys, I used to wake him from these fits and ask him what he had been dreaming. Always, always he looked at me, puzzlement in his eyes, and swore that he had not been dreaming at all, that his sleep was deep and black and dreamless, and profoundly refreshing. As time went on, I learned to stay asleep through his thrashing and flailing, to retreat back into my own dreams, which were full of sizzling, scalding light, and shame, and the ghosts of strangers.

"Albertus?" No answer.

Methane. It turned out that an accumulation of methane was the culprit, the tank suffused with the stuff, a deadly and oxygen-free atmosphere put out by the ripening manure, gathering in the void between the crusty surface of the liquid and the flat ceiling of the tank. I knew nothing of that at the time, of course.

The pit was dark. The opening was small. Albertus seemed to me to be infinitely far away, there on the floor of the pit, and I seemed to be moving with infinite slowness. I knew—though I would not have used that exact term for it at that moment—that Albertus was dead. *Gone* was the word that reverberated in my brain. I stood at the edge of the pit, the blazing sunlight beating down on me as I gazed into the stinking shadows, at the sprawled, unmoving figure of my older brother. I thought of the laugh he had given just before he collapsed, how happy he had sounded before the sound had been cut off. Albertus, happy.

He's gone, I thought.

The rest of it happened quickly. I went and found my father, who was repairing the haybine on the concrete pad at the front of the dairy. The road that led by our place, the Goins place, was empty of vehicles, as it was almost always empty, the asphalt slick and shiny in the heat. *Treat Yourself To The Best*, the sign told me. I thought of the sign painter up on his scaffolding, slathering bright paint onto the boards. I thought of the priests of the bull-god, laboring away in their lightless caverns, ecstatic and blind, slathered in colorful clay.

My father's feet stuck out from under the steel bulk of the machine. I addressed myself to his knobby work boots. "Albertus is gone," I said. The boots shifted as my father torqued some bolt on the underside of the haybine, thumped at the machinery with the side of a wrench. He didn't reply to me. I thought that he must not have heard me. "Albertus is gone," I said again, more loudly.

"What?" His voice sounded muffled and tinny from beneath the haybine. Far off in the distance, I could see a car approaching on the nine-foot road. It was coming along at a great clip, and the heat rising up from the road's surface caused it to gleam as though it were made of molten glass. It might have been a flaming chariot. In a moment, it would sweep past us, headed west toward Mount Nebo.

I wondered what we looked like—what I looked like, really, because my father was hidden from sight—from the point of view of the driver. I imagined that I looked like a big lonely heavyset kid with a headful of shaggy hair, dressed in manure-stained, ill-fitting coveralls, standing in front of a barn, standing next to a bulky complex agricultural machine. I imagined that my expression (whatever that was) would be rendered unreadable by heat distortion and the bright light of the sun, which shone directly on my face and momentarily blinded my eyes. "What did you say about Albertus?" my father asked.

Albertus is gone, I thought, but I didn't say it aloud.

My father struggled out from under the haybine. He lay on his back on the warm concrete, his coveralls, not at all unlike mine, soaked with sweat. The car whooshed by on the road, and I saw the passenger—a woman, and quite a beautiful one, though I only got a brief glimpse of her: thick lustrous hair swept back from a high forehead, prominent nose, tilted eyes—raise a lazy hand and wave in greeting. I waved back without thinking. Then I realized that she had not been waving to me at all. She had instead been pointing out to the driver the Mail Pouch slogan painted on the side of our barn. The driver was a man, I supposed, probably her husband, probably handsome, probably wealthy, not interested in such things, or too intent upon his navigation to take much notice.

She likely had not seen me at all. Probably she thought that the barn was abandoned, the farm empty and dead, the family that had inhabited it gone extinct ages before.

My father—whose books never spoke about mind-reading or intuition or psychic phenomena (things that my books enthused about endlessly) unless it was to ridicule and lampoon them as savage superstition—came to a swift understanding of the situation. He could not have known what had happened to Albertus, could not have known that the manure pit had proved deadly; and yet he did know. "Albertus," he said, and his face went still.

He looked suddenly old: not old like a man who has lived out the span of his years and soon must die; but old as a mummy looks old, old as a king who has been dead and imperfectly preserved and buried in a carefully hidden underground vault for thousands of years. "Albertus," he said again, and then he set off for the manure pit, loping around the corner of the barn as fast as his stocky legs would take him, shouting for my brothers, shouting for my uncle, shouting for them all at the top of his lungs.

He did not call my name.

My father flung himself into the manure pit, to save his oldest son. They tell me that he was overcome by the methane in an instant. Maybe he managed a brief laugh before he succumbed, as Albertus had. My uncle, who was stacking hay in the loft with my younger brothers, and who arrived at the mouth of the pit only seconds after my father did, followed him without hesitation. Then, selflessly, Ptolemy, the older of the twins by a matter of minutes. Then Cunobelinus. Did any of them, did they all manage a final chuckle at the absurdity of their situation? They inhaled the methane, as unbreathable as the atmosphere of some distant alien planet, and they died, while I stood in front of the dairy barn and watched the car with the beautiful woman in it disappear down the road to the west.

~ ~ ~

In *Hoard's Dairyman*, April 1964, unearthed from my father's vast collection of agricultural and animal husbandry literature, concerning the indomitable aurochs:

> "Hunted by common men and by rulers like the Holy Roman Emperor Constantine in the fourth century and Charlemagne in the eighth, the aurochs (*bos Taurus primigenius* or ur-ox) had by the early fourteenth century been brought to the edge of extinction. Ubiquitous in prehistoric times, this progenitor of all modern cattle survived into the second millennium only in limited regions of Eastern Europe. Residents of the king's game preserve in the Wiktorowski Imperial Forest of Poland were exempted from taxation, their single duty to safeguard the last herd of aurochs. Only the king himself was permitted to hunt the beasts. The killing of an aurochs by anyone but the monarch, even by accident, was a crime punishable by death. These draconian measures proved insufficient, however, to save the breed. By the mid-sixteenth century, there remained only two dozen mature cows, three heifers, six calves, and half a dozen bulls. By that century's end, a mere four bulls and one cow survived. Legend has it that the

aurochs dwindled away from isolation, that they yearned for the once-vast herds that had dominated the continent and expired in order to rejoin them. Eighteen years later there was only a lone bull, which reportedly died at the hands of poachers in 1627."

~ ~ ~

There was plenty of money. Alone among all the farmers in the region, my father had put money away, never indulged in debt, never overextended himself. There was insurance, a great deal of it. The manufacturer of the storage tank pumping unit landed a sizable amount on me, to avoid a lawsuit, I suppose. I dispersed the herd of Holstein-Friesians in a single great auction, under a gaily striped tent next to the dairy barn, beneath the Mail Pouch Tobacco sign. I sold all the equipment as well, the tractors and the skid-steer and the haybine under which my father had been working right before he died, and the New Holland manure spreader, which had not been new but which had been new to us. The auctioneer kept shouting out numbers as the day wore on, and they were marvelous, surprising numbers. People paid more than expected for the animals and objects that had belonged to the men of the Goins family, now dead. Apparently this sort of thing, this weird outpouring of sympathy and interest—avidity, even—happens in cases of murder or shocking tragedy (which is what newspapers across the country and around the world endlessly called it) like ours.

Treat yourself to the best.

We should have been aware, of course, though the condition had never before to our knowledge existed on our place, that a deadly methane concentration in the manure pit was possible. Likely even, in the heat of midsummer. We had even heard of such fatalities on other farms, swine farms, beef farms, anyplace with a manure storage tank under the barn like ours was vulnerable; but those other accidents were always far away, and it was easy to dismiss the deaths of others, of strangers, as being outliers of such remoteness that we need hardly even think of them at all. Still, we should have been alive to the danger.

Many questions were asked in the wake of the event, repeatedly and with great vigor: how could such a thing happen? What could be done to prevent such a tragedy in the future? And, most frequently: What will become of the lone survivor, the last of the Goinses?

In the weeks and months since they died, I have eaten voluminously of the jimson weed, which I have discovered grows wild all around the place, and which can also be cultured in dung; and now I will dream.

I have brought my paints—procured at the local hardware store, where I was treated with the deference due the last surviving Goins— down into the manure pit with me. The tank is clean now, or at least as clean as such a place can ever be, and dry, and empty. It was a bit of a squeeze getting down in here, and I am not, truth be told, looking forward to the trip back up. A little light filters down through the opening around the ladder. I will have to fix that. I plan to record the history of the Goinses in this place, on all the walls, and in this way to summon their spirits, their ghosts, to me. The *datura* will help me with that, and the dark. I have plenty of both. The paint buckets are full, and I have chosen bright colors in which to render them, the Goins men: sign painter's colors.

No light reaches the rear wall of the tank, and so I will begin there. What will I record first? The wrestling matches perhaps: men in motion, men engaged in struggle, one against the other, scrapping until one or the other of them, in unendurable tension and pain, cries "Uncle!" I can do that, I think, though I have never painted a picture before. I will paint quickly, like the shamans of old. I will lay down on the crusty walls that which my mind's eye makes plain to me.

I can see them all so clearly, down here in the dark. John Goins and Joseph Goins and Ptolemy Philadelphus Goins and Cunobelinus Togodumnus Goins: they cluster around me in this place where they died, and they wait—patiently, for the dead are nothing if not patient— to see how I will conjure them, what I will paint. Albertus Magnus Goins waits too, his thick arms crossed; and the expression on his face is fond and not at all condescending. I will paint him, I will bring him back to life on these walls; but that will wait, until I have made use of the others to perfect my technique.

The dark is absolute, here in the farthest reaches of the pit. The stench of the paint is strong and makes my head swim. I expect for a moment to hear the sounds of the dairy cattle above me: their hooves against the hard floor, their sighing, their lowing; and then I remember that the cattle have all gone, and the barn is empty. Behind me in the gloom, the great Black Bull shifts its bulk, and the solid concrete beneath my feet seems to shift with it. He is the bull who bears the world on his back, and his slightest movement sends shockwaves through the planet.

My mind reels, and the vision unspools before me. I will paint the Goins men, and I will paint the bull as well: I will capture each of them in the death-defying act of *taurokathapsia*, grasping the horns of the bull and somersaulting over him, their bodies lithe and graceful as those of circus acrobats, green laurels on their heads, their faces wreathed in grins, laughter escaping their mouths. I heft my brush, and a streamer of paint—what color is it, I wonder?—trickles down my forearm.

The vast bull, well-pleased, pokes me with the tip of one of its sweeping horns. I slash the paint against the wall, and I know I have begun to make something wonderful. The bull pokes me again, harder, in the ribs, and a little blood wells out from my side. It feels warm on my skin. The breath of the bull is likewise warm on the back of my neck. It is very close to me, the black bull, as close as a lover. Again I whip my brush across the surface of the wall, feeling the life in the stroke. Once more. Creation. The bull prods me again. I must hurry. I must hurry.

The World,
The Flesh,
and the Devil

*My knights and my servants and my true children, which
be come out of deadly life into spiritual life, I will now no
longer hide me from you, but ye shall see now a part of my
secrets and of my hid things.*
— Sir Thomas Malory, *Le Morte D'Arthur*

T he aviator had been hearing the howling of the dog pack for
some time. He didn't live on this long ridge high in the
Alleghenies or anywhere near it, so he couldn't know that the
raucous bugling meant that death was on its way. His head was full of
what had just happened to him: the dark bird impacting the canopy of
his Phantom at low altitude, blood and feathers and howling wind and
blindness. Groping for the ejection handle, he had managed to punch
out as the uppermost branches of the trees lashed the fuselage, as the
forest pulled him down. The aviator didn't know what had happened
to his backseater. He felt weak with guilt. He didn't belong on the
ground.

He sat at the edge of a clearing, on one in a squat line of tilting
stone blocks, an archipelago of order in the chaos of the forest. Around
him lay maybe an acre of open ground punctuated by sprawling clumps
of rambler rose. He had been drawn to the clearing by the spikes of
golden sunlight that drove downward through the green forest roof.
They reminded him of the light-shafts that often penetrated the cloud-
cover when he was skimming along in the thin margin between the
cloud bottoms and the mountain ridges.

Fat squirrels dashed among the tree-limbs, chittering, staring down at him with frantic bulging eyes. Overhead, boughs squeaked and grunted and thumped against one another in what sounded to his ears like sober conversation. Insect life burrowed beneath his flight suit, into his skin. He had a growing sense of the forest as a single great organism, one that he imagined was slowly becoming aware of him. *I am here*, he thought, *in the vegetable kingdom.*

He had lost everything in his tumble through the forest roof. When his eyesight cleared, he was already sliding into the tree-tops, the silk of his parachute tangling in the branches. Caught high in a monster oak like a discarded marionette, concussion blurring his vision, he had pulled the razor-sharp Ka-Bar knife out of his belt and, in a sudden access of terror, slashed the shroud lines of his chute, his torso harness, the lanyard that attached him to the seat pan with its survival gear. He had cut himself free and left it all irretrievably behind. Flares, smoke, compass, mirror, radio beacon, flashlight. Gone.

He'd slipped and slid and bumped his way down the many-limbed trunk of the oak, slowing his fall with an outflung arm here, a foot against a bough there, dragging stripped-away branches after him, green twigs snapping and cutting into his neck and cheeks, bark scraping the skin from his palms. When he landed at last with a breath-stealing thump on the thick carpet of decaying leaves on the forest floor, he found himself in the midst of a tribe of shaggy wild mountain ponies, who took a single eye-rolling look at him and dashed off into the undergrowth, tails flying. Knowing of no better direction in which to start the search for the wreckage of his jet and for his backseater, he had stood on shaky legs and followed them. He kept walking into spiderwebs strung invisibly between bushes, seeing their elaborate architecture only in the instant before he was into them, the sticky threads adhering to his eyelids, stretching over his nostrils, across his mouth.

There had once been buildings in the clearing where he now rested, and their half-hidden foundations still divided the open ground into squares and rectangles. The aviator took comfort from the straight lines of them, here where nothing was straight. He could recognize the hand of his kind in such a thing. It didn't occur to him to wonder where they had gone, the people who had laid these foundations, what might have swept them away.

In his fall from the oak, the aviator had twisted his ankle. It ached savagely, and he could feel the hot swelling of the flesh and the soreness in the tendons. The leather on the toes of both his boots had been peeled away by contact with the Phantom's dashboard as he ejected, and the steel toecaps shone dully through. He heard the dogs, but dogs in his experience were pets. They ran and played in the grass. You fed them, you picked up their poop. He himself didn't own a dog, but he knew plenty of people who did. He dismissed the sound.

~ ~ ~

The gray dogs raced like flood water through the undergrowth, fifty of them or more, driven by the coming of spring and by their hunger. Everything alive on the ridge they pushed before them: white-tailed deer, possums, raccoons too terrified to remember that they could escape into the trees. Even a cantankerous old black bear, shaggy and leaned out by the winter, looking for early

berries, heard the murderous howl that rose from their many throats and took to his heels, shambling along beside the humbler animals. Nothing stood against the tide of the gray dogs.

The pack's frontrunner was young and fast on his delicate feet, if not particularly strong. None of the dogs was strong, not alone, all of them stringy feral mutts bound together at the mad edge of starvation. Deep in the frontrunner's brain lay the puppy-memory of a place of regular meals and fences and collars, fragmentary, fragile as a cobweb, of a world away from the ridge where he had answered to a name. His name. What had it been? The wild cry that issued unbidden from him tore the memory to shreds. Now he was as gray as dust, as gray as the rest of them, and crazed with fury and hunger. His dog's heart soared because everything on the ridge fled them.

He slowed minutely to snatch a stick insect from the branch of a bush, swallowed it down without tasting, and the rest of the pack surged around him, pushing him hard from beside and behind, their panting breath hot on his hindquarters. The next swiftest of them, a lanky prick-eared dog, ran at his shoulder, as close to him as a littermate at their mother's teats, as close to him as a brother.

Run run run, he cried, they all cried with one voice. The hunger gnawed at them, the agony of appetite hurled them forward, scrawny backs bowed, bony shoulders hunched, empty bellies drawn up tight as drumskins against their spines, eyes slitted against the wan light that filtered down to the forest floor.

~ ~ ~

In sixteenth century Europe, the legend once bloomed that birds of paradise had no feet and that they never lighted anywhere. Instead, the fabulously plumed birds were said to drift forever on the winds, consuming nothing but the dews of heaven; and they descended to touch the earth only when they died. The myth arose because the lustrous skins of the birds arrived from New Guinea preserved in poison, with the feet removed for shipping, and the men who unpacked them, and the people who bought them, none of them ever saw a living bird of paradise.

The aviator could tell you firsthand, though, that to light nowhere, always to fly, to press forever against the taunting edge of the envelope of flesh and mechanism; to watch and strain and yearn as your engines sucked hopelessly at the thinning oxygen, as your enemies spiraled about you, desiring nothing but to see you vanish in flame and smoke and tatters; as the controls bucked and fought and ceased to respond— To see the leading edges of your wings gleam red as blood against the impossible disk of the sun, to grope upward into the darkened freezing curve of the stratosphere, and then always to fall back... To light nowhere and always to fly: The aviator could tell you that this is paradise.

~ ~ ~

A family of bobwhite quail broke out of the dense thicket of rambler rose near which the aviator sat. They flashed away into the sky, their panicked wings thumping at the warm, still air. A thrill ran through the aviator's barrel chest, a shiver of delight to see them fly. He was twenty-nine years old, and that was what he wanted more than anything, to be able to take to the air in a fraction of a second, like a bird. No ready room, no rush across the hot tarmac, no cinching himself solidly into a fabulous gizmo of metal and plastic and Plexiglas. He was a creature of the sky. Only among the cloud tops did he not feel trapped in his own flightless body, excluded from what he thought of as *the true life*. The time on the ground between hops was endless, dull, insufferable.

The aviator's eyesight was excellent. He made out swift movement, small innocuous animals crossing the creek that bounded the clearing, chipmunks and rabbits and even a frightened fox, scurrying out of the tree-line and crossing the rocky clearing where he sat. The smaller animals channeled their way through the lush spring grass and the patches of flowers, forcing their bodies into gaps between the close-grown stalks of rambler rose. The fleeing creatures were silent except for their desperate gasping and the scrabbling of their little hard feet against the earth. A doe and her spotted fawn flashed by, droplets of creek water flicking from their delicate legs. A mouse skittered over one of the aviator's boots. The howling of the hunters rose behind them.

A bear lumbered through the clearing, smelling of half-eaten fruit. The aviator started—he thought someone, perhaps in the survival training classes to which he now wished he'd paid better attention, had told him to roll up into a ball if he was ever confronted by a bear, to pretend that he was dead—but the old bear kept on without even a sideways glance at him and passed out of the high meadow.

Vague shapes clustered at the edge of the forest. Gray and low against the ground, like a terrible mist, they advanced across the fast-running stream and out of the undergrowth, many of them moving in a single body.

~ ~ ~

The frontrunner had not been alone in—how long? No way to tell. There was that faint sense that he had of the life he'd lived before the gray dogs: the life of plentiful food, the life of lying quiet in a cool place and resting, the life shared with men. And then there was the life of the pack, which was all of his life since. It was a life of riot, of constant noise and hunger, of wolfing down any bit of flesh that came his way, no matter how hard, how bitter, how rotten; of running through the dark, constant running, and of falling down to sleep only when the others fell down around him, curling himself over and against the closest dogs, his nose to his neighbor's tail for warmth, the neighbor's nose likewise digging into him.

He snatched at ragged sleep, in which he would sometimes dream of the life of food and the soft voices that came with it—*good dog, good dog*—but in which more often he would dream that he was running,

running, seeking after something to eat, the world fleeing before him; only to wake and find that he was already pounding along with the pack on the trail of some terrified quarry. The dust raised by their relentless passage settled over their coats until they became a single uniform gray.

He had been slow at first, always in the rear of the pack, struggling to keep up, always at the fringes of the group when they flung themselves down to sleep, always cold, always farthest from the kills. Never full, eating only when the feast was so great that the pack leaders couldn't eat more, when they were so gorged that they couldn't be bothered to chase the starvelings away but instead lay a few yards distant, eyes half-closed, bellies bulging, while their inferiors fought each other for the leavings.

Sometimes he would find dry bones in the foliage, usually small— voles, squirrels, perhaps the partial skeleton of a coyote—and he would suck on them, afraid to bite down because he knew that the sound of the cracking bone would draw the attention of others who would snatch the secret morsel away. Sometimes he would strip berries from nearby bushes, but they made him vomit as often as they nourished him.

Soon enough, though, he found his stride lengthening, his legs growing stronger, his pace quicker, and he took his place in the midst of the surging pack, the foot-draggers left far behind him. The gray dogs never looked backward. Always on the move, eyes searching for the kill, anything to keep the specter of starvation away for yet another night and yet another run. His prospect was a lake of bobbing backs and heads and shoulders, the sweep of the tail ahead of him.

When prey was scarce, the pack at some unfathomable signal would wheel, and a shudder of greed and terror passed through their ranks. This was the moment they all feared and dreaded, when the pack whirled on itself, the leaders sweeping in behind the stragglers and overtaking them, knocking them off their feet. The pack would consume its laggards. The frontrunner wasn't innocent of the cannibalism, when the killing went far enough. As dogs drifted in to join the pack—strays gone feral, lost hunting dogs lost, abandoned mutts—others surrendered their bodies to the multitude. The lame and the halt fed the leaders.

In time, he found the ranks before him thinning. He shoved his way forward in the pack, striving for all he was worth, until there were no dogs in front of him. He flew through the forest, and the frontrunner's howl broke from his throat, and the dogs behind him took it up, adding their voices to the awful wail. They trailed him, matching their pace to his. Down the fern-shrouded hillsides they flew, along the ravines, across the ridges and through the deep forest, pressing behind him so that he was fearful to stop, lest they should bowl him over and, seeing him weak for a moment, devour him. Only when he felt the horde flagging could he slow his pace. Only when they collapsed from exhaustion, their scrawny sides heaving, could he stop.

~ ~ ~

The aviator fled. He wasn't aware of any impulse to run: one moment he was at rest, watching the dogs advance, and the next he was thrashing his way through the rambler roses, which tore at his nomex flight suit, at his skin. The watery light in the undergrowth was confusing after the brilliance of the clearing. His strained ankle protested, the swollen flesh pressing against the tight lacing of the boot, but the closing cry of the dogs kept him moving.

His mind went for a moment to the knife, the Ka-Bar with its seven-inch blade, secure in its sheath on his belt. He was a man, he was fit and strong, in the prime of his life. He had been trained to fight, to survive, to prevail. He had killed other *men*, for heaven's sake, though never at close range. The idea that he might be eaten by a bunch of dogs seemed faintly ridiculous to him. But the reddened eyes, the lolling tongues; the bodies bunched together, clenched like fists and then flexed on the bound, the long legs tirelessly eating up the distance; most of all the fangs, the numberless teeth in the gaping mouths—if he faced them, he would die. The aviator knew himself as prey.

He followed the trail of the other animals. His sharp eyes picked out the brown humped back of the bear, maybe thirty yards ahead of him through the light bracken, lolloping along at its best pace. Why didn't it fight? It struck the aviator as wildly unfair that something as strong and fierce as the bear should be fleeing. The bear should rightly be between him and the dogs.

~ ~ ~

The face comes to the aviator, with its high cheekbones and dark eyes: his backseater, Geronimo. And with the face, a blaze of shame. Had the aviator ordered Geronimo to punch out, or had he left him behind? The altimeter unwinding like a nightmare clock as the forest reached upward.

Outside the scratched Plexiglas bubble of the canopy, before the impact, the sky was bright, and the aviator picked out details on the ground below. A skein of silver lines, rivers, broken here and there with white, where rapids boiled. The carpet of endless forest, which furred the rough outlines of the mountains and made them seem soft as pillows. The thousands of hectares of it spread out on all sides, to the horizon. Behind a dam, one of the rivers blossomed into a lake. He eased the stick forward, and the fighter stooped like a hawk. The aviator wanted to make a low-level run through the mountains.

They were deadly men in a deadly machine, one so fast that, pushed to its maximum, it could outpace the turning of the earth. They could run westward with the sun, and night wouldn't ever fall on them. An endless day. The stink of jet-fuel and rubber and stale air filled the aviator's nostrils, the stench of his own sweat. The seat-pan hard beneath his buttocks. Over the intercom, he could hear Geronimo's breathing, high pitched and stertorous. Strange to have breathing in his ears like that, like a lover sharing a pillow, but in a hundred missions he had grown used to it.

The Phantom descended, the forest rising up to meet it. Suddenly, Geronimo laughed, at some private joke, at something glimpsed on the ground below them, at nothing and the sound distorted over the intercom, came to the aviator as a meaningless blast of sound, flat and crackling, like gunfire. He could picture Geronimo's face beneath the oxygen mask and helmet, the eyes amused. Impossible to know what another man was thinking. No one closer than a pilot and his navigator, and yet they might have been worlds apart, connected only by the slender static-filled line of the intercom. Neither of them could see the other, each in his own universe of panels, instruments, lights, cramped and familiar and homelike.

The dark bird shattered the canopy.

~ ~ ~

The Phantom F4B weighed thirty thousand pounds empty. It carried twelve thousand pounds of fuel in an internal tank. At the time of the bird strike, the aviator's jet was fitted with two drop tanks, which brought its initial fuel load to eighteen thousand pounds. The aviator didn't know precisely how much of the fuel they had burned before the collision. Geronimo would know. The backseater managed mundane tasks like navigation, communication, fuel consumption. Say they had consumed five thousand pounds. At impact, the Phantom had weighed well over twenty tons, counting the twin pods of Zuni rockets slung under the wings.

A turkey buzzard—that was what it had to have been, the wingspread wider than the span of the aviator's arms, the glimpse of that ugly naked head, like something peeled and red—weighed about five or six pounds. It had impacted the canopy at just under four hundred knots. Shards of glass from the shattered heads-up display had gashed the aviator's forehead and the bridge of his nose but spared his eyes. If the vulture hadn't caromed off in some unknown direction, it would have decapitated him.

As he ran, the aviator kept hoping to strike a debris trail, trees sheared at a descending angle, with the twisted hulk of the plane's wreckage at the end. Had the plane burned when it struck? All that fuel, it should have blazed like a torch. No smell of smoke reached him, no flicker of flames to tell him where to go. If Geronimo had ejected in time, then he would search for the wreckage of the Phantom as well. The aviator could imagine the backseater leaning nonchalant against the massive tail section of the smashed plane, amused but unsmiling. What was he, maybe twenty-one? A kid. Everything amused him. The two of them could hold off the dogs. Two men together had nothing to fear from a pack of dogs.

~ ~ ~

The frontrunner made out the shape of the man in front of him, hunched and running but nonetheless upright—*two legs*—and the scent was strong in his sensitive nose, the scent of another carnivore, fat on meat and marrow and bone. He had never pursued a man before. Nothing was forbidden the gray dogs; but this? For a moment, the frontrunner was two dogs, and each dog possessed a separate history. One history was ten thousand years of servitude and loyalty and symbiosis, of corrective blows and caresses and the sweet leavings of the master's table.

The other was the history of a million years, and a million years before that. The history of the timber wolves and, behind them, of the dire wolves that ruled the fantastical prehistoric jungles, too fierce to run in packs, too deadly even to their own breed for any kind of companionship. The lanky dog at the frontrunner's shoulder lunged forward, and the frontrunner pushed hard, to stay out in front.

~ ~ ~

The aviator struggled up out of the ravine, knees quaking, lungs burning. He knew that he was only moments ahead of the dog pack. They were screaming at his heels. He felt that he might almost be able to bear what was going to happen to him—it would at least stop the agony in his ankle, the drowning sensation of the carbon dioxide waste building up in his blood, the unbearable tension of the endless sprint—if it weren't for the awful howling. The howling drove him on. The bear had outdistanced him, and the other animals as well. The aviator was alone with the gray dogs.

He dodged an upright stone, hip-high, skirted another, and a third, topped by a crumbling seraph. Grave markers. He was passing through a cemetery. One great central monument, twice the aviator's height, bore the figure of a bandaged man, twisted, misshapen, propped up on clumsy crutches. Little granite dogs twined around the man's bandy legs. If he'd had the breath, the aviator would have laughed at the coincidence.

The graveyard sprawled out on all sides, vast and full of moving shadows. To the left and right, the suggestion of tilting buildings, bracken grown up around them, trees pushing through shattered roofs, thrusting their limbs through glassless windows. Ahead of the aviator, cloaked in trumpet vine, a crumbling brick wall. And in the wall, nearly hidden in the gloom that spread beneath the encroaching trees, a door. The aviator lunged for the door, thrust downward on the great wrought-iron handle, hauled it toward him. It refused to open, and he tasted death, more surely than he ever had in combat, more surely than he had when the vulture had burst through the Phantom's canopy.

Push. He put his solid shoulder to the upper panel of the door and shoved for all he was worth. The door gave before his weight with a terrible scream of age and disuse, and he spilled inside. He found himself in a high-ceilinged building, dark, dust-coated, disused. A church? He took no time to look around him, but kicked the heavy door shut, leaned his weight against it. His breath came in sobs as the howling dogs flung themselves against the wood.

~ ~ ~

The frontrunner struggled to stop short of the closing door but couldn't manage it. The others were too close and moving too fast. He went headfirst into the hard wood of the door's lower half, stunning himself. The lanky dog at his side screeched and bounded, bounced off the door as well, and fell back into the scrambling horde. They were piling up, two and three deep, those behind shoving those in front, dogs' bodies washing into the doorway like waves against a cliff, legs splayed, tails tucked under. They yowled and squealed and bit one another, rolling over and over, dog after dog piling blindly on, the prostrate frontrunner bottom-most.

~ ~ ~

The aviator recognized the building as a barracks, abandoned for some considerable length of time: long and narrow, with a tall pitched roof and small windows. It was a room in which, he felt sure, many lonely men had passed the loneliest hours of their lives. What had they been? Soldiers? Prisoners? Monks? The building would have sufficed to house any of them. The roof

had given way in places, and pale light filtered through to piles of rubble on the floor, but he noted with relief that the walls appeared to be sound. Sanctuary. Behind him, the door held, despite the pounding and thumping and wailing of the gray dogs.

The dogs began scrambling at the sides of the building, growling and griping, seeking another way in, a way to get at him. He hustled around the periphery of the room as fast as his bum ankle and his short breath would allow, making sure that it was as solid as it had seemed at first blush. He was a practical man. The place had been securely constructed. Here and there lay piles of ruined furniture: smashed bedsteads, half-burned mattresses, wrecked chairs, an empty trunk, the leather that bound it cracked and green with mold. Outside the walls, the dogs bawled their frustration.

Elated, the aviator howled at them in return. He tilted his head full back, closed his eyes, inflated his lungs, and roared. He had never in his life done anything like it. The sound of his voice bounced back to him from the sagging rafters, loud and reassuring, and he kept on, his teeth bared, spittle flying in high arcs. His head ached with the echoes. His nails bit into the palms of his hands, and cords stood out on the sides of his neck, blood vessels began to rupture, but he couldn't bring himself to stop. It felt as though there were a dozen of him, a score, all lifting their voices up in protest against the death outside.

A reply came. Not from the dogs. It came booming from deep within the wilderness, wordless and chthonic. The aviator continued screaming for a moment longer, but the great call from the forest was overwhelming, and he felt how small his own voice was, raised up against it. Even the dogs fell silent. It wasn't a challenge, like one bull elk defying another over a female or territory. This was a declaration of dominion, calm, deliberate, absolute. The bellow came again, vast beyond comprehension: the voice of the forest.

The aviator found himself praying—he who never prayed—praying and begging that he would not have to face whatever it was that he had called up.

~ ~ ~

In the refectory of the military school the aviator had attended as a boy, there was a stained-glass window that he particularly admired. It had been installed to honor the graduating class of 1943. Most of the colorful images set into the window meant little to him, a mishmash of Jesus Christ as a human and as a lamb, King Arthur holding up a clumsy sword, his noble knights arrayed around him, the Grail floating above their bowed heads, shedding rays of light. The central figure, though: as he ate, the boy who would become the aviator often lost himself in contemplation of it, and had to be jostled back to awareness of his surroundings by his classmates.

He found it a little humiliating, to be so entranced by the picture. It wasn't even, he didn't believe, a very good piece of art. A man surrounded by doves descending and ascending, bordered by bursting stars, by smoke and long trails of flame. A man in the garb of an old-time combat flyer: leather helmet, goggles, Mae West, parachute harness, leather boots. His coveralls were gleaming white, and he seemed to float above the ground, his feet pressed tight together, his toes pointed downward, his palms outward in a beseeching attitude. His face was bland, his features frustratingly regular and unmanly, his lips full and lush. His hips were strangely wide, and he appeared to have a little pouch of a belly that thrust his flying suit outward.

The man in the stained-glass window was not heroic. He was a bit silly in his passivity, his apparent gentleness, his androgyny. The boy would have preferred that the doves had been hawks, or eagles, with their cruel talons and their hooked beaks, their all-seeing eyes. The smoke and flames seemed to indicate that the man had been defeated in battle, his plane had gone down, he had died. One of the reprobates at the school—the academy was full of them—had thrown some hard thing at the window at some point in the past, and the flyer's right eye was dark, as though it had been shot out.

The boy would rather have been interested in any of the other martial figures in the window, or none of them, but it was this embarrassing image to which he came back again and again, despite the mockery of his table companions, many of whom would fight and die courageously in wars yet to come. Whatever his flaws, this man in the window, he was a being of the air. He was, as the boy knew himself to be, an aviator.

~ ~ ~

The forest whispered with a million vegetable mouths. The aviator found that he didn't want to sleep. He had discovered in this dormitory setting a kind of calm, a repose of the spirit that was better than sleep. He would be sought out soon by men much like himself, he would be judged on how he had handled the bird-strike and resulting crash, would be either hero or goat—but for the moment, he desired only to exult in the familiarity and solitude of the barracks.

The forest murmured, and the dogs kept their vigil. The aviator wanted to take off his boots, but he didn't dare. He would have had to cut the boot off of his injured foot, so severe was the swelling, and he knew that he would never get it on again. For the first hour or so after hearing the voice from the forest, the aviator had hurled pieces of wood and chunks of masonry from the windows in an effort to get the dogs to leave him be. He had managed to brain one lanky dog, and its body lay unmolested in the leaf-filtered moonlight among the gravestones. The gray dogs were either too weary or too agitated to eat it.

The aviator had ceased to want them to depart. The gray dogs were not company, but they were... What? They were not the forest. There was something terrible waiting out there among the trees—or perhaps it was the trees themselves that were waiting, watching. The aviator could almost bring himself to believe that the patrolling dogs were guarding him from whatever it was that walked in the darkness, that dwelled in the shadowed hollows out beyond their protective circle. He regretted having killed the one, and he was grateful to the others for their noise and their animation

Most of the graves that he could see from the windows were graced with a wretched man of rags and tatters more or less similar to the one on the monument, sometimes crude, sometimes elaborate. The figure was always accompanied by numerous dogs, and it was hard to tell if the dogs were being affectionate with him, or if they were plaguing him. The aviator had worked out, in the hours that he had stood at the window peering out, who the man was: St. Lazarus, the leprous beggar who died outside the rich man's gates, where the dogs licked his sores.

This building and the surrounding graveyard had not been part of a prison, not a monastery or a military installation. It had been a leprosarium. The aviator had heard of such places, stuck far away from population, in the swamps, tucked away in barely habitable regions of the deserts of the southwest. In the mountains, on the high lonely ridges, where contact with the uninfected was nearly impossible. No crime had been committed by those who had lived in this dormitory, but confinement here had been lifelong, without hope of mercy or parole. The forest had been the walls.

He yawned. He knew that, if he had suffered a concussion, he mustn't sleep. Sleep for him could mean death. For the lepers, to enter the forest was death. To try to return to civilization was to perish. The uninfected ones who lived in the valleys and the flatlands away from the ridge, what would they have thought of the lepers? Their features ravaged, fingers missing, feet irretrievably lamed, skin luminous with infection. Monsters. Perhaps banishment was the kindest solution, for all involved.

~ ~ ~

The frontrunner roused himself, the foul dark taste of his own blood on his tongue. Only a moment before, as it seemed to him, all had been noise and fury, the shrieking of his packmates as they piled into the closed door and landed atop him. Then darkness like sleep, and a voice that called to him, a voice that spoke his old name. Now silence hung over the place. He stood and shook out all his limbs, checking for serious injury. There was none.

He saw that the lanky dog that had run along at his shoulder lay unmoving out in the middle of the field of standing stones. The rest of the pack milled about aimlessly in the open space between the building and the nighttime forest. There was a man in the building, he knew, the man he had been chasing. The dogs looked to him, and he knew as well that, were he to begin running, they would follow him. He would once again be the frontrunner, and they would once again be the gray dogs, and everything alive would flee before them.

Instead, the frontrunner lay down on the threshold of the door. He would wait on the man to emerge. Resting his aching head on his paws, he turned over in his simple brain that name, the name by which they had known him in the days before the coming of the pack. He had once been called *Attaboy*.

~ ~ ~

"Dead to the world, be thou alive to God."

The voice woke the aviator, who had fallen asleep, propped in a sitting position in a corner of the dormitory, half-wrapped in a flimsy, scorched mattress. The room had grown cold. Before the aviator stood a man covered in silver scales. He was naked, and he gleamed like a fish in a river. He glistened so brightly that it was difficult to make out any particular details of his appearance. His face was a shining caul, pierced only by his dark eyes. The aviator assumed that it was the silver man who had spoken, but there was nothing to prove it. The aviator couldn't make out whether the man even had a mouth.

In the old days, the aviator knew, the priests had given lepers a full funeral. Put them alive into a coffin, covered it with a pall, hauled them out to the cemetery. When they left the leper alone, to climb out of the casket on his own, forever after unclean, they had said those words over him, like a magical incantation. Dead to the world. Dead to the world.

The silver man turned from the aviator, whom he had been examining, and strode toward the door. His back, his buttocks, his legs—the coin-bright scales covered all. The aviator almost expected him to jingle when he walked. It occurred to him that this must be one of the lepers from the leprosarium's operational days. Surely the institution must have been closed for years? This might be the last leper, then, so far gone in the disease that he wouldn't wish to come down off the ridge even when it was allowed.

The silver man's hands and feet, fingerless and toeless so far as the aviator could tell, seemed to confirm this notion. He walked over the warped board floor of the barracks with a rolling gait, like a sailor in heavy seas. When he reached the door, the aviator struggled to find his voice, to shout out a warning.

And knew, in that same instant, that he had not warned Geronimo. He had punched out and left his backseater alone in the Phantom as the forest drew it down and consumed it. As the aviator floated into the foliage under billows of fluttering silk.

"No," he said. The silver man opened the door. The aviator's throat was raw, and it stung with his attempt at speech. "There's something out there." He meant the dogs, of course, but he also meant whatever was beyond the dogs, out in the forest. The forest itself. His hand found the haft of the Ka-Bar.

"Go home. Go home."

Impossible, again, to know if it was the silver man who spoke. The words echoed in the tall-ceilinged room, and the aviator remembered with discomfort the howling that he had set up in the night, and the intolerable reply that had come. This voice was entirely human, humane. Gentle. The aviator could tell that the words were directed at the dog pack, but he thought that they were perhaps meant for him as well. The silver man stepped into the graveyard.

Home. The antiseptic BOQ at Oceana? The cramped cockpit of the Phantom? The dormitory of the military school? The spartan bedroom in his boyhood home? He couldn't tell what precisely the word might mean, but he felt a strong impulse to rise, to search, to find it out.

~ ~ ~

When the aviator emerged from the barracks at dawn, favoring his injured ankle, only Attaboy awaited him. Tracks in numberless circuits around the building testified to the watch the gray dogs had kept over him during the night, and similar tracks led away, in many directions, winding past the ruined outbuildings of the leprosarium and into the trees. The pack was broken. There was no sign of the silver man, and no prints that looked to have been made by unshod human feet. At the aviator's appearance, Attaboy rose from the door's sill and stretched, head cocked at an attentive angle, as though he were waiting on a word of command.

The aviator slapped his palm twice against his thigh, as he had seen other men do to summon their dogs, and Attaboy trotted over to him, looking up with mild brown eyes. The aviator reached down and stroked the dog's dusty, bony head. "Left you all alone up here, did they?" the aviator asked. The dog pushed hard against the hand.

"All right then," the aviator said. He crossed the graveyard to the body of the lanky dog. The piece of jagged masonry that had broken the dog's skull lay nearby. Overhead, a pair of perfectly matched turkey vultures circled counterclockwise, their wings stiff and still as they rode the thermals, waiting with infinite patience and serenity on their chance to descend and feed. The aviator admired their flight for a moment— so effortless, so unforced—before he knelt and picked up the lanky dog, felt the stiffness in its limbs. He was intent before anything else on finding a place to lay the body where it could lie undisturbed. With the dog cradled in his arms and Attaboy at his heels, the aviator entered, limping, into the green sepulcher of the forest.

Pig Helmet &
the Wall of Life

P ig Helmet needed to see the Wall of Life.
  I call him Pig Helmet because he's the sort of fellow that, in
  olden times, you'd have been one of the Civilized People trying
like hell, with fire and boiling oil and molten lead and such, to keep him
and his kind out, and he'd have been one of the dreaded barbarians,
he'd have been the lead barbarian in fact, climbing over your city walls
by means of an improvised ladder, with his snarling face painted a
furious blue, and something large and heavy and sharp-edged clutched
in his massive fist, and wearing a pig for a hat. The head and hide of a
boar, thick and knobby and naturally tough, hardened further by curing
and the cunning attachment of metal plates and studs and rings, with
the great toothy maw of the feral hog sloping down over his heavy
brow, its tusks like upthrust sabers and its dead piggy eyes glinting dully
above his own. Pig Helmet.

Pig Helmet is a cop. He's employed by the county sheriff's
department, and he lives down at the end of my road with his diminutive,
pretty wife. Before that he was a "contractor" in Iraq and Afghanistan,
where the money was good and the action was better, but his wife
worried too much with him away. We tried to look after her as much as
possible, my own wife and I, but we were no substitute for the
ministrations of Pig Helmet, as you can imagine. He's a dutiful and
attentive husband. Before that work, he was a bail bondsman, a bounty
hunter (he hates that term, silly movie bullshit he calls it), and one time

a guy that had jumped bail threw acid in his face, trying to blind him, to avoid capture.

The acid missed his eyes but crisped him pretty good otherwise, and the left side of his head is kind of a nightmare. The teeth show through permanently on that side, and the flesh is rippled and brown like old melted candlewax. He keeps pretty much to himself, does Pig Helmet, has some acreage and a few animals like we all do around here, following his hobbies in his off-hours, hand-loading cartridges and felling trees on his place and then turning the stumps into sawdust with his stump grinder.

He loves the stump grinder. When I cut down a tree, he'll bring the stump grinder over to my place and grind the stump into the ground, leaving nothing but a hole and a few roots and a mound of soft, warm sawdust. He'll grind stumps for hours with apparent satisfaction. Sometimes in the fall he'll bring over the loin from a deer he's shot, and that's good eating. His wife's vegetable garden always produces plenty of tomatoes for them and for us.

Pig Helmet is not a fellow much given to self-pity, as you can imagine, or even to much at all in the way of self-regard, but he had recently been through a bad experience, and he was feeling down and lost and deeply in need of an encounter with Life that would restore him to a proper sense of himself, which is to say, no particular sense of himself at all, except for a kind of exuberant well-being of the sort that would allow him, as of old, to grind a stump or love his wife or swing a truncheon with a deep-seated sense of pleasure.

The bad experience that he underwent can briefly be described as follows: OxyContin addict, alcohol, family Monopoly game gone bad, shotgun deployed, multiple homicide. Topped off with suicide-by-cop. When Pig Helmet arrived in his cruiser at this lonely place to which he had been called, way out in the wilds of the western end of the county, the OxyContin addict was sitting shirtless and blood-spattered on the porch of the little frame house where he had just killed his brother, a cousin, his grandmother (can you imagine?) and an uncle. The house wasn't an unpleasant-looking place, a neatly tended bungalow, with a pretty trumpet vine twining around the porch railing. The door stood wide open behind the OxyContin addict, the screen door too, the room behind it black as pitch; and he still had the scattergun in one hand, wouldn't turn it loose no matter how loudly Pig Helmet yelled for him to do so. Most people, people even marginally in their right minds, do what Pig Helmet tells them to do when he raises his voice at them.

This guy just smoked his cigarette down to the filter and then kind of lazily (this is how Pig Helmet described it to me) stood up and swung the muzzle of the gun around to cover Pig Helmet. So Pig Helmet took him down, double-tapped him right in the center of his chest with the .45 caliber service pistol he carries, and the guy sat down again, hand still wrapped around the stock of the shotgun, and he died right there on the porch. Pig Helmet wouldn't have felt bad about shooting the guy, he said, if there had been some utility in it; but the people beyond that open door were already dead as it turned out, and so there was nobody to rescue. There weren't even any shells in the shotgun anymore. The OxyContin addict had used them all up on his Monopoly opponents and the grandmother, who hadn't even, to all appearances, been involved in the game at all.

"Fucking mess," Pig Helmet said, and I believe him.

So when he saw the sign for the Wall of Life down at the county fairgrounds, he was in the mood. He didn't anticipate any trouble on account of the shooting, because the homicides in the bungalow had been so brutal, and everybody agreed that the OxyContin addict had needed killing. It was a good shoot. Being on administrative leave pending a formal inquiry, Pig Helmet had the leisure to do what he wanted, and he didn't feel much like hand-loading any ammunition, and he didn't feel like grinding stumps, and he knew that his wife's sympathy and worry, while affectionately meant (she's an affectionate woman, with Pig Helmet at least, though cripplingly shy around others, even those of us who have known her for years) would just make him feel worse. So he took himself off to see what the Wall of Life was all about.

Pig Helmet on duty, wearing his Nomex gloves and his bulky body armor and his brown sheriff's office uniform with its broad Sam Browne belt across his barrel body and his thick utility belt (flex cuffs, pepper spray, billy club, taser on the left side, service pistol on the right, plus radio and tactical flashlight and knife and other assorted gadgetry), can be a pretty unsettling sight. He's a big fellow, as I say, a man mountain, well over six feet tall, two hundred fifty pounds if he's an ounce, with a head shaved bald and gleaming and broad as the Dome of the Rock in Jerusalem. And he's got that nasty confusion of his face on the left side, which a person can grow used to, and even fond of, but not in a short period of time.

Now, you know what the Wall of Life is, even if you don't think you do. It's just like the Wall of Death, the county fair attraction where a rider on an old motorbike roars around the inside of a big wooden cylinder, centrifugal force sticking him perpendicular to the sides. The crowd stands on a catwalk at the top of the cylinder, looking in while the guy on the sputtering motorbike apparently defies gravity below them.

At the bigger, better shows, there are a couple, maybe even three motorbikes on the wall at one time, crossing one another's paths, cutting down toward the bottom of the cylinder and then shooting back up to the top again, to cause the crowd to draw back in alarm, fearful that the biker will shoot out onto the catwalk and knock them over and kill them. Sometimes a pretty girl will stand at the bottom of the cylinder, in its center, gesturing toward the motorcyclists as they circle above her head, showing her faith in them, that they will not come unstuck from the walls and crash down on top of her. That's the Wall of Death.

The Wall of Life was just like that, only it was an evangelical preacher and his family who did the riding, and it was the preacher's daughter who stood in the bottom. The Wall of Life was this preacher's ministry, like an old time tent revival meeting but on motorcycles, and he went from town to town, fairground to fairground, setting up the Wall, running for a couple three days until the crowds let down, preaching at the people that came to see him ride and shout.

When his work in one place was done, he and his family would tear down the Wall of Life into a series of short arcs that stacked neatly one inside the next, and stow them aboard the aged Fruehauf tractor-trailer his ministry moved in. There was a huge portrait of the Wall on the side of the trailer, the great wooden cylinder and crude human figures speeding along on motorcycles inside, with a giant Jesus stretching his hands out on either side, like he wanted to catch the little riders if they flew out. After he packed up his stuff, the preacher and his family would shove off for the next place he felt called to.

Pig Helmet wasn't a particularly religious man. Like most of the rest of us he grew up in a Baptist household, and he had been saved at a certain point in his boyhood because it was expected of him, and he had given testimony at various times for much the same reason, but none of it—as he has told me—touched his heart very much. As soon as he moved out of his parents' house, he stopped going to church, more through indifference than any animosity toward the institution. When he met and started courting the pretty girl who would become his wife, he took up going again, because it was what she wanted, it was one of the few places where she came out of her shyness a little and felt at ease among people; and her beauty and kindness and gentleness toward him did touch his heart, and so he went.

Pig Helmet has told me about a tribe of savage Germans whom he particularly admires, that lived back in Roman times. These Germans, it seems, were converted to Christianity sometime after the reign of the Emperor Constantine. This is the sort of thing Pig Helmet knows about, though to look at him—the truculent set of his jaw, the heavy forehead, the glittering left eye that peers out from within the folds of scar tissue—you would never expect it. He reads a lot of nonfiction books about obscure tidbits and peculiarities of history, and other books about the oddities scattered throughout the galaxy: singularities and quarks and quantum theory and gravitons and the like. He says these things just naturally catch his interest.

In the book about Christianity, when these great big hairy Teutonic warriors were baptized, when the Roman priests led them down into the cold rushing water of the river that ran near their home village up in the Black Forest, they willingly pledged themselves to Christ and dunked themselves under. All except their sword arms. Their right hands, palms horny and hard with callus from years of wielding their long blades, those they kept dry above the fast-flowing current. The rest of them might belong to gentle Jesus, but their strength and their killing skills—they still belonged to the god of battle.

Pig Helmet told me that was what he always felt like: some kind of a half-breed monster, a chimera, part one thing and part another and nothing that was whole. He had felt that other piece of him—the sword arm, held up above the current—when the OxyContin addict brought the shotgun to bear, the muzzle yawning wide and dark, and when Pig Helmet, without so much as thinking or deciding, sent a pair of 230-grain Speer Gold Dot jacketed hollowpoints into the guy's chest at nine hundred feet per second.

He had stood there for a moment, pistol in his hand, the pistol reports, so closely spaced they might have been a single sound, echoing off the clapboard side of the tidy bungalow. He'd been around death plenty of times, working for the creepy little bail bondsman in Craig County, in the Middle East, and while serving mental hygiene warrants and issuing subpoenas and such for the sheriff's office; and he could sense it now, boiling off the punctured corpse of the mutt with his shotgun, percolating out of the dark doorway of the bungalow behind the slumped body.

Death dwelt in the house, he knew, and probably had for years, for decades, just waiting on this day, on this combination of drugs and rage and cheating, to take down everyone inside. He could tell it was there, crouched inside the doorway like a lurking beast, but he couldn't see it.

He said he might as well have been naked out there in that little yard, with a couple of dusty chickens pecking in the thin grass around his feet, and the branches of the trees creaking and talking in the light wind that had sprung up. That empty doorway, with its moronic dead guardian, it called to him. It yearned for him. All of his body armor, his pistol and his taser and his years of training—worth nothing. He knew that, if he walked into that place alone, he was finished. When backup arrived, he would be gone. He could cross the yard and step over the OxyContin addict and past the threshold and on into the dark. He even took a step or two in that direction.

And then—this is his take on it—a miracle happened. A woman called his name. At the time, he thought it was his wife. It was definitely a woman's voice. And it wasn't his regular name that she called, it was his secret name, a name no one knew him by. It was a name that he himself didn't know he owned, or that owned him, until the second he heard the woman's voice speak it. He wouldn't tell me what it was, no man should know that about another man, but he said the moment he heard it, he knew it as inescapably his. It was like she was saying it into his ear. He imagined that his wife must be praying for him, a thing she did regularly throughout the day when he was on duty, and that her prayer was what halted his progress toward the door of the bungalow.

He imagined that the name she called him was how she referred to him when she spoke with God.

So he found himself at the Wall of Life. After the search of the bungalow revealed the extent of the slaughter (Pig Helmet couldn't bring himself to go inside even after other units from the sheriff's office arrived), after the arrival and departure of the county coroner, after the ambulances had borne the body bags away—after all that, as he drove homeward, he passed the county fairground, and he saw the tractor-trailer with its garish illustration on the side, and beyond that the squat cylinder of the Wall of Life itself. That word, *Life*, written in letters of orange flame on both the semi-trailer and the Wall, captured and held his eye. Death clung to him. It was on his clothes, his hands, in his nostrils. *Life*.

He pulled the cruiser into the near-empty parking lot, paid the old lady at the foot of the stairs that led to the catwalk along the top edge of the Wall. As he handed her his money, he thought briefly of the grandmother who had died, cowering in one of the narrow back rooms, her hands held up beseechingly before her. The other deputies had described her to him in almost loving detail. "The show's already in progress," the old lady at the Wall told him in a voice like the chirp of a bird, and he nodded at her. The board stairs under his feet trembled with the unmuffled roar of the motorcycles, and the entire Wall shook with their passing.

There were maybe half a dozen spectators atop the Wall. It was the first show of the day, a light crowd. In the evening, under the unearthly glow of the sizzling sodium lamps, there would be more. The few who were there at the catwalk's railing drew back when they caught sight of Pig Helmet ascending the stairs. He was used to that reaction to his size and his marred face and his uniform, so he hardly noticed. A couple of the people held dollar bills out over the void, so that the motorcycle riders would come up near the edge of the Wall and snatch them. With Pig Helmet's arrival, the dollars and the riders were forgotten. Pig Helmet strode to the edge of the platform and looked down.

Easy enough to imagine what he saw as he looked into the well, which was poorly lighted, just a few strings of dingy Christmas bulbs clinging to the safety railing against which Pig Helmet leaned his weight. What else could a man like Pig Helmet see? The stench of exhaust flooded his nose, but it seemed to him to be the smell of burning cordite. He was looking into the muzzle of a great gun. It was the muzzle of the OxyContin addict's shotgun. It was the muzzle of every gun he had ever stared down. It was the muzzle of his own service pistol, pointed straight at his face.

Easy enough to imagine, too, what it was like for the preacher and his people, his family, when Pig Helmet appeared above them, his Neanderthal head silhouetted against the light of the lowering sky, his exposed teeth gritted, his expression (what they could see of it in the dim light) filled with mortal terror, the other spectators on the catwalk drawing back from him, their offerings suddenly out of reach.

Near catastrophe as one motorcyclist, flames crackling from the straight exhaust pipe of his aging Indian bike, dove unexpectedly low on the Wall, nearly colliding with his younger brother, while their father, the preacher, fought to avoid running over them both. The preacher was shouting out above the roar of the engines the text of the gospel of James—he had just gotten to "There is one lawgiver, who is able to save and to destroy. Who art thou that judgest another?"—and he lost his place momentarily, dread and fascination drawing his attention upward to Pig Helmet's looming head and shoulders, the gleam of his shaved skull, the puckered flesh of his scars. His speed dropped as he braked to avoid his boys, his bike wobbled nauseously, and he nearly toppled off the Wall and to the floor.

Pig Helmet's vision quickly adjusted to the changed light. Now he saw more clearly. In white letters two feet high, just below the lip of the wall all the way around, ran the legend "In my name shall they cast out devils. They shall speak with new tongues. They shall take up serpents." Pig Helmet was standing just opposite the word *serpents*, so he could only see the end and the beginning of the quote, ...*shall take up serpents. In my name they shall...*, but he was a good enough student of the gospels from his youth up to know what was hidden from his gaze. The floor of the well seemed to be alive. It was moving, shifting, shining in the blasts of fire from the motorcycle exhausts: iridescent scales, eyes, flickering tongues. It was a snake pit. Adders, vipers, harmless bright green ribbon snakes like blades of grass, the undulating lozenge pattern of diamondback rattlesnakes, the warning sizzle of their tails drowned out in the cacophony of the bikes.

Standing in the midst of the snakes, ankle deep in them, her feet bare, was a young girl, her face turned upward toward Pig Helmet, her expression delighted as though she was glad to see him. In each of her small, pale hands she grasped, just below the spearpoint head, a struggling pit viper. Her eyes were wide and bright, and Pig Helmet realized that she was not looking at him at all. She was gazing past him at something just over his shoulder with that rapturous look on her face.

Her eyes weren't unfocused or dazed. They had the concentrated aspect of the eyes of someone who has caught sight of something precious and vanishing—a lover who has spotted the ghost of a long-dead darling; a sniper to whom a target has just offered himself up for a head shot—and who can hardly bear the intensity of the vision, but who doesn't dare to look away lest it be lost forever. There was something behind him, above him, Pig Helmet knew, but he couldn't bring himself to turn around, to see what it was. The girl was seeing it enough for both of them.

The men on the motorcycles, the preacher and his sons, had speedily recovered their composure, and they swung back into rhythm, racing their bikes in swift ellipses around the interior of the well, now at the top, now at the bottom, weaving across one another's paths at measured intervals, as though they were performing an intricate dance. They were a handsome family, fine-boned and slender, their faces similar, old, young, younger, like the same man appearing in a series of photographs taken through the years. The preacher found his voice again, this time calling on the psalms, as though perhaps to ward off Pig Helmet with his perpetual unintended sneer, whom the preacher might have suspected of being not altogether human, not altogether benign. "Yea, though I walk through the valley of the shadow of death, I will fear no evil," he called out to the crowd on the catwalk.

Pig Helmet saw that the girl wasn't quite as young as he had first taken her to be. She was exquisite, her head tilted, her hair light as silk, her back slightly arched, her breasts pressing against the thin white cotton of her shirt. From his vantage point above her, Pig Helmet could see down into the neck of her blouse, could see the small hollow at the base of her throat, the sheen of perspiration that collected there. He could see the soft swelling of her breasts, the lacy edges of her bra.

He loved his wife very much. And, in that instant, he wanted simultaneously to protect the girl in the snakepit from all the death that was in the world and to screw her silly. Her lips were moving, revealing glimpses of her healthy gums, her small even teeth, her glistening tongue. He couldn't hear her voice, but he knew that she must be praying. He wondered what her prayer was.

The preacher's voice was still audible, and the crowd had begun offering their dollar bills again. "Thou preparest a table before me in the presence of mine enemies," the old man declared. Pig Helmet had a couple of dollars in his wallet, and he thought about holding them out so that one of the riders would snatch them from his hand, and perhaps his fingers would brush against Pig Helmet's fingers, and in that brief contact Pig Helmet would feel what he needed to feel, would know what he wanted to know. *Life.*

It occurred to him that he might even, under the guise of holding out his offering, grab a passing motorcyclist by the wrist. Who among us, faced with that moment of failed equilibrium, the man teetering on the edge of the icy step, the woman the heel of whose shoe has caught in a steel grating, hasn't entertained, however temporarily, that temptation to reach out and, gently, almost lovingly, *push?* Just to see the expression on the face of the one who might have been rescued but who has been doomed instead. Pig Helmet told me it was like that feeling. Would the rider be jerked from his bike and swing there, dangling by the wrist in Pig Helmet's grasp until Pig Helmet dropped him into the writhing snakes? Would the weight of the man and the hurtling bike jerk Pig Helmet's shoulder clean out of its socket, might he be dragged bodily off the catwalk and into the well?

The motorcycles were running in unison, stacked like the rungs of a ladder as they raced around the Wall, and the girl had begun singing, her voice a thin piping that barely reached Pig Helmet's ears. A woman near him on the catwalk had begun clapping her hands together and shouting "Hallelujah" while the men beside her looked slightly chagrined. The boards thrummed like a vast heart beneath Pig Helmet's feet, and the voice of the preacher, in constant flux from the Doppler effect as he came near and went past and away again, beat at Pig Helmet's ears. "I shall dwell in the house of the Lord forever," he called. The snakes flopped and coiled at the girl's feet.

Pig Helmet no longer felt as though he was looking down, into the cylinder. He suddenly knew himself to be looking up. It came to him that he was staring into the barrel of an incalculably large telescope, one with greater power even than the ones they mount on the high ridges, far from the cities and their polluting lights. He knew himself to be watching through it something distant and ancient, something akin to the circuit of the planets, old, young, younger, near, far, farther, around and around in their endless courses; and the weak little Christmas lights were the surrounding stars; and the girl, the infinitely desirable girl clad in white at the very center of it all, singing and praying, and now she's even laughing, laughing breathlessly, her mouth wide with joy, her eyes half-closed, her nostrils flared, a viper grasped tight in each hand, her feet sunk in the unfathomable twinings of the serpents— At what is she laughing?

At him. At Pig Helmet. He's speaking, he's crying out in the command voice he's been taught to use on suspects, in the irresistible voice with which he directed the OxyContin addict to put down the shotgun. He doesn't understand the words he's saying. They're bubbling out of him like water from a busted spigot. The woman next to him is swaying, gaping at him worshipfully, shouting "Hallelujah! Hallelujah!" for all she's worth.

They're the girl's words that pour out of him, Pig Helmet knows, the words she was speaking earlier but that he couldn't hear. The words of her prayer. Her body is shivering and shaking, pulsing like a quasar in one of Pig Helmet's peculiar books, a quasar at the far distant end of the universe. The girl in the pit, the stout woman on the catwalk beside him, they're dancing the same dance, binary suns, quivering as though they're demented with some awful fever. Pig Helmet's hands are spread wide. He cannot understand the words of the prayer, but in the midst of them he hears her say, once, clear as a bell, his secret name. It wasn't his wife at all who called him. He tries to make it be his wife, who has known him in his most intimate moments, and who wants nothing more in the world than to save him, to keep him safe and beside her forever. But no matter how hard he tries, it is this girl who knows the name, who calls to him in his most secret places.

"Put down the weapon." It was a prayer, what he had said to the OxyContin addict. He knew that. "Lay down on the ground." It was a prayer. There was no way for the OxyContin addict to divine what Pig Helmet truly wanted. Pig Helmet didn't hold the key to his understanding. The words of Pig Helmet's heart must have sounded like gibberish in his ears, and it didn't matter how loudly Pig Helmet spoke them, or how beseechingly he meant them. He couldn't imagine the OxyContin addict's secret name; he couldn't save him. We are so distant from one another, impossible to know. "Don't make me shoot you." An unheard prayer.

Pig Helmet's hands are open. The motorcycles continue to circle above him, hanging precariously over his head—who knows what astonishing force keeps them there?—but the screaming of their engines is muted, it no longer reaches his ears, his brain. He speaks in tongues, and spittle flecks his fleshy lips.

He's reaching outward, upward, straining toward the whirling constellation of men, motorbikes, snakes, voices. He's reaching for the girl who knows his name, and she has stopped dancing. She stretches out her slender arms toward him, her skin shining with sweat. She stands on tiptoe among the snakes. He's a tall man, but she's far away. Faster and faster the motorcycles go, and her prayer rises continuously from his lips, unmediated. The Wall of Life is an intricate machine built by men to show him this girl at the other end of space. The door of the little bungalow yawns behind him, and the slain OxyContin addict is the doorman, he's the concierge with the disconcerting smile, holding the portal wide, gesturing Pig Helmet inside with a generous sweep of the scattergun. It's an easy door to enter, the door to that house.

What lies before Pig Helmet's eyes is likewise a door, a hard entrance, a long narrow tunnel of infinite length. Pig Helmet thrusts his killing hand, his unbaptized hand, out toward the girl. She is far away and getting farther, but she extends her hand toward him as well, and her lips shape his true name. If Pig Helmet is strong enough, if he strains far enough, if the motorcycles spin fast enough, and if he keeps stretching out his unclean hand forever, he will reach her.

The Secret Nature
of the
Mechanical Rabbit

The girl who responds to Buddy Gunn's knock is young, maybe sixteen, maybe not even that old: the age of Buddy's little sister. She is wearing a thin cotton tee-shirt, and Buddy has a difficult time keeping his eyes off her chest. She stands on the other side of the screen door, her posture easy, indolent, as his gaze travels up to her narrow, small-featured face, then back again to her willowy body. She offers him no greeting.

Her tee-shirt is the color of old ivory from the many washings it's been through, a man's short sleeved undershirt. Buddy has on a sweatshirt that advertises a dog-racing track in the next county over. A cartoon rendering of a whipcord-thin greyhound decorates his shirtfront. The greyhound wears sunglasses as it streaks along, its ears pinned with speed to the sides of its long sleek head.

The girl rests a hand on her hip. She is on to me, Buddy thinks. And he thinks, Damn, and at the same time, Good for her.

"You want something," the girl says, and she folds her arms. Buddy breaks into a grin. The smile feels false to him, fixed, uncomfortable. He has seen beauty pageant contestants concoct much the same expression for the television cameras. He puts it on at each new door, hoping that it makes him look friendly, trustworthy, sincere. The girl does not return his smile through the brown doorscreen. "The whelps?" she asks him.

Buddy clears his throat. "Yes'm," he says, very polite. "I come about the whelps, as you say. I seen your ad in yesterday's classifieds." *Free to a good home 5 puppies bordercollie mix 6 wks old 3 boys 2 girls. Very cute, good with kids.* The clipping, along with numerous others more or less like it, is back in the van, in a green cardboard folder. The folder is beginning to tear along its spine. Soon it will be time to get a new one.

The ads have been gleaned from half a dozen newspapers in Shawnee and the surrounding counties. It is Buddy Gunn's job to respond to them. This is the first house he has visited today, but there are many leads in the folder, enough to occupy him for the next couple three days at least. Enough to occupy both him and his partner Willard, who sits hulking behind the wheel of the green Ford Econoline van in the driveway. Willard is large and hairy and unappealing, and he knows to stay with the van.

People are often uncomfortable when Willard is nearby. It is all the hair that turns them off, Buddy believes. The stuff sprouts weedlike from Willard's skin, it grows in stiff dark patches from the backs of his hands, his neck. It protrudes from his ears and from the moist wells of his nostrils. The hair that mats his arms and legs and shoulders is as thick and rank as a bear's pelt. Willard is strong and accommodating, but he is also terrifying to behold, like some forest creature that has risen up on its hind legs and wants to chat.

The girl glances at the van, and Buddy says quickly, "My brother." He immediately regrets the invention, imagining that the girl knows it for a lie. He cannot think why he might have said what he did. He has no reason to explain Willard to her.

There aren't any vehicles besides the van in the driveway, and that is a good sign. It means the girl is in all likelihood alone. The bitch that dropped the puppies no doubt belongs to her, and it is her chore to fob the little dogs off on people who want pets. The house is set well away from the paved state road, sitting aslant the points of the compass on a small lot in the midst of a yet-to-be constructed subdivision.

The footers of six or seven other houses have been set down and poured close by, and lots are staked off among the stunted fruit trees that dot the landscape. Stacks of boards lie near the footers, a lumberyard's worth of boards covered in leafy creeper. The boards on top are weathering, while those underneath them soften with rot. The house from which the girl peers at Buddy is old, idiosyncratic, ramshackle. It must have been the original farmhouse, he thinks, when this place was an orchard.

The girl unlatches the door. At first Buddy imagines that he is meant to come in, and there is a momentary embarrassing struggle between them as she endeavors to emerge from the house, he to enter. His hand brushes her arm, the door bashes him in the chest. He steps away in order to let her through.

"The puppies are in back," she says, and sets off at a brisk pace around the house, not looking to see whether he is following. She wears denim cutoffs that fit loosely around her slim waist. Her feet are bare and tough with callous, and she does not flinch or stumble as she strides over the variety of hard objects—bottle caps, the shards of a broken flower pot, bits of gleaming quartz gravel—that stud the dirt of the yard.

Still not looking at him, the girl says, "We'll have to get them away from the mother somehow." And Buddy thinks to himself, Bingo.

~ ~ ~

Buddy works for a man named Terry Robinson, whom everybody knows as Little Pig. They call him that because his nose turns upward so that you can see unpleasantly far into it and his cheeks are round and red and fat. Little Pig doesn't mind the nickname. He thinks it's funny, and sometimes he grunts and squeals in such a realistic swinish way that it makes Buddy uncomfortable.

Occasionally Little Pig will bump against Buddy with his head, shrieking like a boar hog. Buddy pushes him away at such times, jokingly at first and then more roughly as Little Pig keeps it up, squealing more and butting harder. Often, they end up shoving each other around the metal prefab shed that serves as Little Pig's workplace, Buddy using his hands, Little Pig using his head and shoulders and his thick, muscular torso.

Willard laughs like a wild man whenever Little Pig takes on so. Willard thinks Little Pig is a card, a regular caution. Buddy, on the other hand, would like to quit working for Little Pig. If he ever gets the chance to go back to work at the dog-racing track, back to the job he has lost, he will leave. Buddy loves the dog track, the pungent animal smell of it and the constant racket of excitement, the colorful shower of discarded tickets at the end of a race. He also loves the quiet, deserted feel of the place at the end of a long day of racing.

And he loves the dogs, the fleet greyhounds with their long arched necks and graceful heads and almond-shaped eyes, eyes that survey their surroundings utterly without expression: no greed, no affection, no surprise or dismay. Eyes that look only for the mechanical rabbit that leads the hustling pack around the oval of the dirt track, eyes that constantly search after the lure, even from within the steel crates where the greyhounds spend their time between races. Their training is almost unbearable to Buddy in its perfection. But a racing dog must never manage to catch the rabbit. It is a thing Buddy learned early on at the greyhound track, and he has not forgotten it. Once a dog catches the rabbit, it knows it for a fake and it will never race again.

Buddy feels sure he'll go back to work with the greyhounds one day, when the tracks are doing better, when the owners can afford more help. Until that day comes he will work for Little Pig. Little Pig owns a fighting dog that he has named Moloch, and Moloch keeps Little Pig's enterprise afloat with its astonishing prowess in the dog pit. Buddy Gunn has known a lot of dogs in his life, and Moloch is hands down the worst dog that Buddy has ever seen; or the best. Moloch is a savage, a remorseless killer.

Moloch lives alone in a hutch of plywood and chicken wire, and it never makes a sound of any kind. Little Pig says its silence is proof of its lineage, its priceless dingo blood. It is this Australian heritage that makes the dog such a furious fighter, according to Little Pig. The dogs they have in the Australian desert are much tougher than the regular American dogs, he says, and it's expensive to get the few imports in the U.S. to stand stud.

Little Pig has waited for years to get himself a dingo, and even then what he owns is in reality only a half-breed. Its mother was a thick-pelted fighting bitch named Queen Generator from up in the hills of the western end of the county. Moloch's father, a nameless full-breed dingo, came to rut her in a covered pickup truck with Kentucky plates. Queen G, who all her life had been a death-dealer that never showed fear, was pushed shivering into the dark foul-smelling space under the truck cap, and the tailgate raised and latched behind her.

The dingo's owner leaned casually against the rear of the pickup and rolled himself a cigarette. He didn't offer the sack of strong-smelling tobacco to Little Pig. "You're going to have one hell of a litter there," he said, while Little Pig strained to see through the dark-tinted glass of the truck cap's windows. "If she lives through it."

"You should have heard the sound," Little Pig frequently tells Buddy and Willard. "It was like he was *killing* her in there!" It excites Little Pig to talk about the conception of his champion, his darling. Queen Generator was gashed and bleeding when she emerged from under the truck cap some time later. Both her ears had been bitten through.

When Moloch builds a reputation for itself, as it has begun to in local fights, Little Pig stands to make a pile of money breeding it. He figures to put a fiberglass cap on his own truck and go roving from place to place. Even quarter-dingo whelps are costly and hard to get. "We're going straight to the top together," he tells Buddy and Willard, meaning of course himself and Moloch. He gives the impression that when he gets there, to the top, he will have left people like Buddy and Willard far behind.

Buddy and Willard procure puppies for Moloch, to whet its appetite for battle. They feed the puppies to it in the days preceding a bout, getting its bloodlust stirred up. "A dog's got to make a hundred kills for every time it steps into the fighting pit," Little Pig tells them. "It's just like shoveling coal into a furnace, like stoking a boiler. The dog has to get a taste for blood. It has to kill without hesitating for a moment, an instant."

Moloch never hesitates. It kills whatever they give it. They handle it with thick leather gauntlets and stout wooden poles.

When it was little, they gave it cats, several of them at a time sealed up together in a battered canvas bag. After a few months of that, Moloch graduated to puppies. As it turns out, puppies are easier to get than cats. In the spring, Buddy and Willard can easily fill the van in a few hours. Sometimes they manage to nab a half-grown dog, or a full-grown one, when they see it wandering along the berm, nose to the scattered gravel and hot dust, looking for roadkill.

Little Pig especially likes them to bring in old dogs, with their weak jaws and crumbling teeth, because he knows they will not somehow accidentally injure his Moloch.

~ ~ ~

The girl in the tee-shirt curses when she finds the bitch and puppies gone. A cardboard carton, half-filled with soiled towels, sits against the wall of the house, sheltered from the sun. The girl stirs the nest of towels with the toes of her right foot, as though she might dislodge a pup from the musty folds. "She's gone in under the house," the girl says. "It's a crawl space that she likes for nursing."

The girl's face is a long oval, her skin fine-pored and clear. Her hair is newly washed, and the scent of the soap she uses, like the crushed petals of wildflowers, carries faintly to Buddy. He can imagine pushing his face into that hair, drinking in the fresh stinging smell of it. She gestures at the opening of the crawlspace, not far from the carton.

"You want me to go in after them?" Buddy asks.

The girl looks him over. "No," she says, "I'm littler than you. I'll go." She drops to her knees and slips easily beneath the house. Buddy examines her rear end and her smooth flanks, the taut lines of her legs, half-ashamed of himself and his lewd thoughts but unable to look away. She and your sister probably go to school together, he tells himself. Maybe they share some classes. Maybe they are good friends.

He does not want other men to examine his sister in this covetous way, though he knows they do. He has not been able to resist the impulse himself at times. She is strikingly good-looking, his little sister, tall and lean and high-strung. In the family they call her Baby. She is like a racing dog, he thinks, a thoroughbred. He knows that, with dogs, it is acceptable to mate parents with offspring, but never brother with sister, the breed goes down quickly whenever that sort of thing starts happening.

The girl vanishes up to her trim ankles in the crawlspace. He can hear the sound of her voice. She speaks in a low, soothing tone to the bitch. He makes an effort to understand what she says, but her words come to him only as nonsense syllables.

A moment later she scoots backward out into the open again, blinking in the sunlight. A cobweb has caught in her hair, and her knees and elbows are smudged with black earth. The dirt makes her look like a child. Crouching, she holds out a couple of puppies toward Buddy, one in each hand. They are both males, small spotted dogs struggling and grunting, each one caught by the scruff of its neck. Their rear legs kick uselessly at the air. "What do you think?" the girl asks. She rises to her feet, still extending the puppies. The bitch appears briefly at the crawlspace opening, pokes her muzzle out into the light before retreating.

"They're fat ones," Buddy says. "Is it only these two? I thought there was more." He is disappointed at the meagerness of the haul.

"Just two left is all," the girl tells him. She is silent for a moment. "My Pop was flushing out his car radiator the other day, and he spilled some antifreeze on the driveway. The other pups got into the puddle, the two little girls and the one other boy."

Buddy guesses from the terms she uses for the puppies, *girl*, and *boy*, that she is the one who wrote the newspaper advertisement. *Free to a good home.* He can imagine her composing the lines, sitting at the kitchen table with the stub of a pencil caught in her fist, her face fierce with concentration as she looks to find the right words, words that will somehow, magically, secure her dogs a future. He has seen his sister Baby look so as she labors over her schoolwork.

The girl continues, "They lapped it up like they couldn't get enough of it. It took them a while to die from it, but they did die in the end. These ones here were the only two that didn't get any."

Buddy nods. "They sure do like that antifreeze, dogs. It's sugary to the taste," he says, "like syrup."

"Pop says it shouldn't ought to bother me. He says he'd of had to drown them pretty soon in any case. He says nobody's going to want to take them, and he won't have a pack of worthless hounds growing up around here. He says that's the way trash lives, surrounded by a tribe of mutts." Her voice is low and bitter. She puts the pups on the ground in front of her. They immediately set to work sniffing her bare toes and licking her feet. Their attentions cause her to giggle and kick at them gently.

"It's not so bad, drowning," Buddy tells her. "They say it's just like going to sleep." He thinks he may not have that exactly right, but he wants to provide some small comfort to the girl. He has to remind himself that he is not planning to give these puppies a good home. Soon, a day or two from now at the most, he is going to watch these puppies die.

The girl gestures at them. "So," she says, "do you want one of them? Which?"

Buddy hesitates. "Which? I'll take them both."

"All right," the girl says. She picks up the whelps again, gripping them around their pudgy bellies this time, and hands them to Buddy. They whine in identical voices as he takes them. He holds them against his chest, and the larger of the two nips at his chin with its needle-sharp teeth. "He likes you," the girl says. The smaller pup sits quietly. Its flesh is unhealthily warm against Buddy's hand, and he can feel its heart beating away inside its ribcage. The puppy's pulse seems impossibly fast, like the heartbeat of a bird.

"This one looks sick, don't it," the girl says, indicating the small pup. Its eyes are glassy. "It might be the distemper. Do you still want it?" She sounds almost hopeful that he will return the puppy to her. Buddy doesn't answer. He heads around the house, back to Willard and the van. The girl follows.

Behind them, the bitch emerges cautiously from beneath the house. She is an unsightly spotted dog, like the puppies, with a fringe of long silky hair along her low-hanging belly. She watches after Buddy and the girl until they are out of sight, and then she settles into the carton once again, rearranging the disheveled mass of towels to suit her slight solitary form.

~ ~ ~

When Moloch entered the pit for its first fight, nobody in the watching crowd had any idea what to expect. The dog ambled about, its wedge-shaped, crocodile's head held low. It looked almost comical, with its undershot jaw and greasy, nondescript coat, its powerful forequarters and weak-looking hind end. It snuffed the air absently, nonchalant, and appeared to have no idea where it was or what it might be expected to do there. Buddy waited. A couple of fellows behind him speculated about what sort of a dog this new one might be, or whether it was even properly a dog at all.

"Tear him up," Little Pig said, almost inaudibly. "Tear him up." He was twitching with excitement. He had waited a long time for this night, Buddy realized, perhaps all his life. His small close-set eyes were fixed on Moloch's blocky, smoke-colored form as it drifted around the periphery of the ring. It occurred to Buddy to wonder what Little Pig would do if Moloch were to meet defeat; if Moloch

were to be badly wounded, to be killed. For an instant he felt something
like sympathy for Little Pig, or kinship with him. A long time passed
before Moloch's eyes lit on the opponent dog, which was a tough
little pitbull variety from the Shawnee County highlands, a veteran
fighter. Moloch's stance grew rigid, and its eyes seemed first to darken
and then to blaze with angry light. Its lips drew back in a frozen,
silent grimace, revealing the serrated rows of its teeth, its lustrous
black gums. Buddy felt terror steal over him, as though it were he
trapped in the confines of the pit with the terrible half-dingo, the
basilisk, and not the hapless pitbull. Moloch's hackles stood, the hair
stiff as iron spikes between its hunched shoulders and along the ridge
of its sloping back. It took several short, hopping steps toward the
pitbull, which gamely, naively, swung to face it.

By Little Pig's stopwatch, it took Moloch two minutes and seventeen
seconds to swarm over and destroy the pitbull. In short order it broke
the more experienced dog's front legs and then its spine. By the time
the horrified owner of the pitbull thought to throw in the towel, it was
too late for him to salvage his dog. The dingo had to be driven back
from the body by the use of electrified cattle prods, even then refusing
to be humbled. Moloch stood facing the prods, mutely daring them,
lashing out again and again at the hands that held them, the fingers,
until Little Pig took the foaming dog up in his arms and, whispering
endearments into its ear, carted it away from the ring.

~ ~ ~

"Listen," the girl says as they near the van. Buddy has his puppies now
and he is loath to stop and talk. The girl's tone won't permit his ignoring
her, though, so he slows his pace, finally halting altogether when she
does. Her mouth is distorted, her lips drawn down and quivering, and
he is surprised to realize how close she is to crying. He hopes that she
will be able to control herself. She has her back to the van, facing him,
and she is unable to see Willard, who mouths silent words of
congratulation at Buddy and gives him a thumbs-up. He sweeps the
girl's body with his gaze, and Buddy feels a sudden irrational fury at his
friend: at the hairiness of him, his inhuman size and appearance, his
pitiable ugliness.

"A woman called me on the phone yesterday," the girl says. "She told me she planned to call everybody that was advertising puppies in the paper. She said she was calling to give me a warning."

"A warning?" Buddy's mouth is dry. This is what it is like to be found out, he thinks. He has been waiting for the day when someone, some authority, anyone, will stop him in what he is doing. Lately he has not felt so sure that the day is coming.

The girl continues. "This woman said it was a couple of men going around the countryside gathering up the puppies they see in the paper. They work for a laboratory, and they use the dogs in their experiments. They try out different chemical products on them to see if they'll die. I thought it was a joke at first, but after a while of listening I didn't think that anymore. She sounded like she knew what she was talking about."

Buddy considers. "I believe I've heard of those fellows you're talking about," he says.

"And you're not them. You and your brother." The girl indicates Willard and the van with a nod of her head.

"No," Buddy reassures her. The fixed grin is back in its place. "No, we're not." He joggles the puppies up and down, one in each hand, and they cry out. He resettles them against his chest.

"I guess you wouldn't want a sick dog if you were," the girl says. "Not for science experiments and all." For a moment she looks directly into his eyes, and the strain on her face is easy for him to read: the strain of wanting to believe what he has told her, the strain of being unable to believe it. She knows where these two little dogs of hers are headed, he suddenly realizes, or if she does not know exactly, then she has a pretty strong idea. The realization repels him, and he turns from her, goes to the van, throws open the sliding cargo door. Heat spills from the dark interior of the vehicle, and with it the musk of earlier cargoes of vanished dogs, a heady ghost-reek.

The numerous wire cages that Buddy keeps inside the van are plain to see. He throws open the gate of the smallest, pushes the puppies in, and secures it again. The weaker puppy, the sick one, sprawls on the floor of the cage, oversize paws extended, tail stretched out limply behind. The other, larger puppy stumbles over it, seeking a comfortable place to lie down. Buddy slams the van door on the sight of them before he turns.

The girl is gone. She has disappeared back into the weathered house, or around it perhaps, to the place where the bitch lies curled in its cardboard box. Buddy wonders briefly what the girl has seen, what she makes of the thing he has allowed her to see: all the empty cages stacked one atop another; the cages that will most assuredly be full by evening.

~ ~ ~

This is Buddy Gunn's most vivid memory. He stands at the edge of a shallow ditch in the center of a large hayfield, and the ditch is full of dead racing dogs. The farmer who owns the field stands in the ditch among the bodies of the greyhounds, his rubber hipboots covered to midthigh with white caustic lime, a four-tined manure fork in his hand. His son sits in the cab of a rumbling endloader, ready to tip a bucketful of earth onto the sprawled corpses. Buddy has hauled the bodies of the dogs to the field in the covered bed of a ten-wheel dumptruck.

The farmer comes toward Buddy, clambering out of the ditch like a figure in a dream, waving the manure fork, shouting. "What are you standing around gawking at?" he demanded to know. "What is it you think you're looking at down there, boy?"

Buddy doesn't know why the farmer seems so angry. He's been looking at the greyhounds, of course. What else is there to see out in the expanse of the empty rolling meadow? What but the long clay-sided cut into the carpet of newly mown timothy grass? What but the dogs.

So many of them, he thinks, still taking in the branchlike tangle of impossibly slender legs, the jumble of heads and ears and whip tails. The farmer breathes heavily beside him, no longer speaking. The eyes of the dogs: open, closed, half-shuttered, wholly inscrutable.

He knew this before, of course, that they killed the dogs at the end of their racing lives. Knew the owners bludgeoned them, shot them, poisoned them, and the thought has troubled him; but so many. Until this moment he has been unable to imagine them in their proper numbers. So many.

~ ~ ~

"Nice ass," Willard says of the girl when Buddy climbs into the passenger seat. He backs carefully out of the rutted gravel driveway, mindful of the van's long wheelbase and its clumsy handling. He spent five years working in a slaughterhouse before this, lugging carcasses from place to place like a packmule in the frigid meat lockers, and the job that they are doing seems almost too easy to him. He is terribly happy to be working for Little Pig. He genuinely likes Little Pig. There is no air-conditioner in the van, but that's okay with Willard. He is sweating. Droplets of perspiration catch in the hair that covers him and shine there like jewels, like pearls.

"You're nothing but an animal, Willard," Buddy tells him. "Just a God-damned hairy beast."

"I know you are," Willard says, chortling good-naturedly, "but what am I?" He thinks Buddy is in a bantering mood.

"No, I'm wrong about that," Buddy says to him. "You're not even an animal. Calling you an animal is giving you extra credit. It's like an insult to the animals." He sees the hurt starting to register in Willard's mild eyes, and that only serves to make him angrier. "I don't believe—" He searches for words. "I don't believe I could even tell you what kind of a thing you might genuinely be."

"I know you are," Willard says. He realizes that it's not a funny thing to say, realizes now that it wasn't funny the first time, but it's the best that he can do. He continues helplessly to speak. "I know you are," he says yet again. "But what am I?"

~ ~ ~

Buddy fingers the doorlatch on Moloch's hutch, but he does not open it. Not yet. He flicks the catch once with his forefinger, twice, a third time. It makes a high-pitched musical sound when he strikes it. He is alone in the shed; Willard has departed in the van, driven away without speaking after off-loading the day's take. Little Pig hardly ever shows up before eight in the evening, and that is two hours off yet. Plenty of time.

In his right hand Buddy holds a gallon jug of antifreeze. The jug is more than half full. He retrieved it from the trunk of his aging Chevy Malibu not long after Willard drove off, and he's been standing this way since. He can see Moloch's tin waterdish just inside the door of the hutch. There is only a finger or so of tepid water in the bottom. Moloch is probably thirsty. Buddy pictures himself pushing the latch up, swinging open the door, tilting the jug, directing the thick greenish stream of ethylene glycol into the dish, where it glitters like seawater. He pictures himself using the flat of his hand, shoving the waterdish deeper into the noisome confines of the hutch, back to the place where Moloch reclines, glaring resentfully at him.

The pups in the surrounding cages make a terrible racket. It is late in the day and they are hungry. Perhaps, Buddy thinks, he will feed them, after he has poisoned the dingo.

Right now it is fear, he knows, that paralyzes him, that keeps him from lifting the latch and pouring out the sweet lethal stuff. Curiously, though, he finds that, with every intake of his breath, every breath laden with the stifling odors of the trapped dogs that look down on him from all sides, his fear is waning. His thoughts are taken up instead with a single question: How much antifreeze, to make sure of Moloch's death?

He'll come to the answer soon enough, he thinks, for there is no one to stop him in this act. No one, apparently, to stop him in anything he might care to do. His fear recedes continually before him, it pulls itself away like the feverish sheet of an outgoing tide. He discovers himself calm, and eager to see what exactly the fear will leave behind it, what desires, what neglected cairns of small anonymous bones. In the moment before he opens Moloch's cage, curiosity alone animates Buddy Gunn. It consumes him. It draws him irresistibly on.

Mercy

The livestock hauler's ramp banged onto the ground, and out of the darkness they came, the miniature horses, fine-boned and fragile as china. They trit-trotted down the incline like the vanguard of a circus parade, tails up, manes fluttering. They were mostly a bunch of tiny pintos, the biggest not even three feet tall at the withers. I was ten years old, and their little bodies made me feel like a giant. The horses kept coming out of the trailer, more and more of them every moment. The teamsters that were unloading them just stood back and smiled.

My old man and I were leaning on the top wire of the southern fence-line of our place, watching the neighbor farm become home to these exotics. Ponies, he kept saying, ponies ponies ponies, like if he said it enough times, he might be able to make them go away. Or make himself believe they were real, one or the other.

I think they're miniature horses, I told him. Not ponies. I kept my voice low, not sure I wanted him to hear me.

One faultless dog-sized sorrel mare looked right at me, tossed its head, and sauntered out into the thick clover of the field, nostrils flaring. I decided I liked that one the best. To myself, I named it Cinnamon. If I were to try and ride it, I thought, my heels would drag the ground.

Horses, ponies, my old man said. He had heard. He swept out a dismissive hand. Can't work them, can't ride them, can't eat them. Useless.

Useless was the worst insult in his vocabulary.

We were angus farmers. Magnificent deep-fleshed black angus. In the field behind us, a dozen of our market steers roamed past my old man and me in a lopsided wedge, cropping the sweet grass. They ate constantly, putting on a pound, two pounds a day. All together like that, they made a sound like a steam locomotive at rest in the station, a deep resonant sighing. Their rough hides gleamed obsidian in the afternoon sun, and their hooves might have been fashioned out of pig iron.

The biggest of them, the point of the wedge, raised his head, working to suss out this new smell, the source of this nickering and whinnying, that had invaded his neighborhood. His name was Rug, because his hide was perfect, and my old man planned to have it tanned after we sent him off to the lockers in the fall. None of the other steers had names, just the numbers in the yellow tags that dangled from their ears. Rug peered near-sightedly through the woven-wire fence that marked the border between his field and the miniature horses', and his face was impassive, as it always was.

The teamsters slammed the trailer's ramp back into place and climbed into the rig's cab, cranked up the big diesel engine, oily smoke pluming from the dual stacks. The offloaded horses began to play together, nipping at one another with their long yellow teeth, dashing around the periphery of the field, finding the limits of the place. Cinnamon trailed after the others, less playful than the rest. Rug lowered his head and moved on, and the wedge of heavy-shouldered angus moved with him.

Another livestock van pulled into the field, the drivers of the two trucks exchanging casual nods as they passed each other. I was happy enough to see more of them come, funny little beggars, but I had a moment of wondering to myself how many horses, even miniature ones, the pasture could sustain.

More of the midgets, my old man said. What in hell's next? he asked. He wasn't speaking to me exactly. He very seldom addressed a question directly to me. It seemed like he might be asking God Himself. What? Giraffes? Crocodiles?

~ ~ ~

This valley was a beef valley from long before I was born. A broad river valley with good grass, set like a diamond in the center of a wide plateau at twenty-four hundred feet of altitude. For generations it was Herefords all around our place, mostly, and Charolais, but our angus were the sovereigns over them all. My grandfather was president of the cattlemen's association, and he raised some trouble when the Beefmasters and Swiss Simmentals came in, because the breeds were unfamiliar to him; and my old man did the same when the place to our east went with the weird-looking hump-backed lop-eared Brahmas. But they got used to the new breeds. They were, after all, beefers, and beef fed the nation; and we were still royalty.

Then the bottom fell out of beef prices. We hung on. Around us, the Charolais and Simmentals went first, the herds dispersed and the land sold over the course of a few years, and then the rest of them all in a rush, and we were alone. Worse than alone. Now it was swine to the east, and the smell of them when the wind was wrong was enough to gag a strong-stomached man. The smell of angus manure is thick and honest and bland, like the angus himself; but pig manure is acid and briny and bitter and brings a tear to the eye. And the shrieking of the pigs clustered in their long barns at night, as it drifted across the fields into our windows, was like the cries of the damned.

Pigs to the east, with a big poultry operation beyond that, and sheep to the north (with llamas to protect them from packs of feral dogs), and even rumors of a man up in Pocahontas County who wanted to start an ostrich ranch, because ostrich meat was said to be low in fat and cholesterol, and ostrich plumes made wonderful feather dusters that never wore out.

The place to our west wasn't even a farm anymore. A rich surgeon named Slaughter from the county seat had bought the acreage when Warren Kennebaker, the Charolais breeder, went bust. Slaughter had designed it like a fortress, and it looked down on our frame house from a hill where the dignified long-bodied Charolais had grazed: a great gabled many-chimneyed mansion that went up in a matter of months; acres of slate roof, and a decorative entrance flanked by stone pillars and spear-pointed pickets that ran for three or four rods out to each side of the driveway and ended there; and gates with rampant lions picked out in gold. That entrance with its partial fence made my old man angrier than anything else. What good's a fence that doesn't go all the way around? he asked me. Keeps nothing out, keeps nothing in.

Useless, I said.

As tits on a bull, he said. Then: Doctor Slaughter, Doctor Slaughter! he shouted up at the blank windows of the house. He thought her name was the funniest thing he had ever heard. Why don't you just get together and form a practice with Doctor Payne and Doctor Butcher?

There was no Doctor Payne or Doctor Butcher; that was just his joke.

Payne, Slaughter, and Butcher! he shouted. That would be rich.

~ ~ ~

The horses started testing the fence almost from the first. They were smart, I could tell that from watching them, from the way they played tag together, darting off to the far parts of the pasture to hide, flirting, concealing their compact bodies in folds of the earth and leaping up to race off again when they were discovered, their hooves drumming against the hard-packed ground. They galloped until they reached one end of the long field, then swung around in a broad curve and came hell-for-leather back the way they had gone, their coats shaggy with the approach of winter and slick with sweat. I watched them whenever I had a few moments free from ferrying feed for the steers.

I would walk down to the south fence and climb up on the sagging wire and sit and take them in as they leaped and nipped and pawed at one another with their sharp, narrow hooves. I felt like they wanted to put on a show for me when I was there, wanted to entertain me. During the first snow, which was early that year, at the end of October, they stood stock still, the whole crew of them, and gaped around at the gently falling flakes. They twitched their hides and shook their manes and shoulders as though flies were lighting all over them. They snorted and bared their teeth and sneezed. After a while, they grew bored with the snow and went back to their games.

After a few weeks, though, when the weather got colder and the grass was thin and trampled down, the horses became less like kids and more like the convicts in some prison picture: heads down, shoulders hunched, they sidled along the fence line, casting furtive glances at me and at the comparatively lush pasturage on our side of the barrier.

The fence was a shame and an eyesore. It had been a dry summer when it went in, five years before when the last of the dwindling

Herefords had occupied the field, and the dirt that season was dry as desert sand, and the posts weren't sunk as deep as they should have been.

They were loose like bad teeth, and a few of them were nearly rotted through. I was the only one who knew what bad shape it was getting to be in. My old man seldom came down to this boundary after the day the horses arrived, and nobody from the miniature horse farm walked their border the way we walked ours. We didn't know any of them, people from outside the county, hardly ever glimpsed them at all.

It wasn't our problem to solve. By long tradition, that stretch was the responsibility of the landowner to the south, and I figured my old man would die before he would take up labor and expense that properly belonged with the owners of the miniature horses.

~ ~ ~

Cinnamon, the sorrel, came over to me one afternoon when I was taking a break, pushed her soft nose through the fence toward me, and I promised myself that the next time I came I would bring the stump of a carrot or a lump of sugar with me. I petted her velvet nose and she nibbled gently at my fingers and the open palm of my hand. Her whiskers tickled and her breath was warm and damp against my skin.

Then she took her nose from me and clamped her front teeth on the thin steel wire of the fence and pulled it toward her, pushed it back. I laughed. Get away from there, I told her, and smacked her gently on the muzzle. She looked at me reproachfully and tugged at the wire again. Her mouth made grating sounds against the metal that set my own teeth on edge. She had braced her front legs and was really pulling, and the fence flexed and twanged like a bow string. A staple popped loose from the nearest post.

You've got to stop it, I said. You don't want to come over here, even if the grass looks good. My old man will shoot you if you do.

~ ~ ~

He surprised me watching the horses. I was in my usual place on the fence, the top wire biting into my rear end, and he must have caught sight of me as he was setting out one of the great round hay bales for the angus to feed from. Generally I was better at keeping track of him, at knowing where he was, but that day I had brought treats with me and was engrossed, and I didn't hear the approaching rumble of his tractor as it brought the fodder over the hill. When he shut down the engine, I knew that I was caught.

What are you doing? he called. The angus that were following the tractor and the hay, eager to be fed, ranged themselves in a stolid rank behind him. I kicked at Cinnamon to get her away from me, struggled to get the slightly crushed cubes of sugar back into my pocket. Crystals of it clung to my fingers. He strode down to me, and I swung my legs back over to our side of the fence and hopped down. It was a cold day and his breath rolled white from his mouth.

You've got plenty of leisure, I guess, he said. His gaze flicked over my shoulder. A number of the miniature horses, Cinnamon at their head, had peeled off from the main herd and were dashing across the open space. What makes them run like that? he asked. I hesitated a moment, not sure whether he wanted to know or if it was one of those questions that didn't require an answer.

They're just playing, I told him. They spend a lot of time playing.

Playing. Is that right, he said. You'd like to have one, I bet. Wouldn't you, boy? he asked me.

I pictured myself with my legs draped around the barrel of Cinnamon's ribs, my fingers wrapped in the coarse hair of her mane. Even as I pictured it, I knew a person couldn't ride a miniature horse. I recalled what it felt like when she had thrust her muzzle against my hand, her breath as she went after the sugar I had begun bringing her. Her teeth against the wire. I pictured myself holding out a fresh carrot for her to lip into her mouth. I pictured her on our side of the fence, her small form threading its way among the stern gigantic bodies of the angus steers. I knew I would be a fool to tell him I wanted a miniature horse.

Yes sir, I said.

He swept his eyes along the fence. Wire's in pretty bad shape, he said. Bastards aren't doing their job. Looks like we'll have to do it for them.

He shucked off the pair of heavy leather White Mule work gloves he was wearing and tossed them to me. I caught one in the air, and the other fell to the cold ground. You keep the fence in shape then, he said. The staples and wire and stretcher and all were in the machine shed, I knew.

Remember, my old man said as he went back to his tractor. First one that comes on my property, I kill.

~ ~ ~

On the next Saturday, before dawn, I sat in the cab of our beef hauler while he loaded steers. There were not many of them; it would only take us one trip. I couldn't get in among them because I didn't yet own a pair of steel-toed boots, and the angus got skittish when they were headed to the stockyard. I would have helped, I wanted to help, but he was afraid I would get stepped on by the anxious beeves and lose a toe. He was missing toes on both feet. So he was back there by himself at the tailgate of the truck, running the angus up into it, shouting at them.

Rug was the first, and my old man called the name into his twitching ear—Ho, Rug! Ho!—and took his cap off, slapped him on the rump with it. Get up there! he shouted. I watched him in the rearview mirror, and it was hard to make out what was happening, exactly, because the mirror was cracked down its length, the left half crazed into a patchwork of glass slivers. The other angus were growing restive, I could tell that much, while Rug balked.

My old man never would use an electric prod. He twisted Rug's tail up into a tight, painful coil, shoving with his shoulder, and the big steer gave in and waddled reluctantly into the van. The truck shifted with his weight, which was better than a ton. The rest followed, the hauler sinking lower and lower over the rear axle as they clambered inside. My old man silently mouthed their numbers, every one, as they trundled on board, and he never looked at their ear tags once. He knew them.

When they were all embarked, when for the moment his work was done, his face fell slack and dull, and his shoulders slumped. And for a brief instant he stood still, motionless as I had never seen him. It was as though a breaker somewhere inside him had popped, and he had been shut off.

~ ~ ~

I made my daily round of the southern fence, patching up the holes the horses had made, shoveling loose dirt into the cavities they carved into the earth, as though they would tunnel under the fence if I wouldn't let them break through it. They were relentless and I had become relentless too, braiding the ends of the bitten wire back together, hammering bent staples back into the rotting posts. The sharp end of a loose wire snaked its way through the cowhide palm of the glove on my right hand and bit deep into me. I cursed and balled the hand briefly into a fist to stanch the blood, and then I went back to work again.

The field the horses occupied was completely skinned now, dotted with mounds of horse dung. Because the trees were bare of leaves, I could see through the windbreak to the principal barn of the place, surrounded by dead machinery. I couldn't tell if anyone was caring for them at all. I don't believe a single animal had been sold. Their coats were long and matted, their hooves long untrimmed, curling and ugly. A man—I suppose it was a man, because at this distance I couldn't tell, just saw a dark figure in a long coat—emerged from the open double doors of the barn, apparently intent on some errand.

Hey! I shouted to him. My voice was loud in the cold and silence. The figure paused and glanced around. I stood up and waved my arms over my head to get his attention. This is your fence!

He lifted a hand, pale so that I could only imagine that it was ungloved, and waved uncertainly back at me.

This is your fence to fix! I called. I pounded my hand against the loose top wire. These here are your horses!

The hand dropped, and the figure without making any further acknowledgment of me or what I had said turned its back and strolled at a casual pace back into the dark maw of the barn.

~ ~ ~

Most days I hated them. I cursed them as they leaned their slight weight against the fence, their ribs showing. I poked them with a sharp stick to get them to move so that I could fix the fence. They would shift their bodies momentarily, then press them even harder into the wire. The posts groaned and popped. I twisted wire and sucked at the cuts on my fingers to take the sting away. I filched old bald tires from the machine shed and rolled them through the field and laid them against the holes in the fence. The tires smelled of dust and spider webs. This was not the way we mended fence on our place—our posts were always true, our wire stretched taut and uncorroded, our staples solidly planted— but it was all I could think of to keep them out. The horses rolled their eyes at me.

And I tossed them old dry corn cobs that I retrieved from the crib, the one that we hadn't used in years. The horses fell on the dry husks, shoving each other away with their heads, lashing out with their hooves, biting each other now not in play but hard enough to draw blood. I pitched over shriveled windfallen apples from the stunted trees in the old orchard behind the house. I tried to get the apples near the sorrel, near Cinnamon; but as often as not the pintos shunted her aside before she could snatch a mouthful.

~ ~ ~

You know why we can't feed them, don't you? my old man asked me. We were breaking up more of the great round bales, which were warm and moist at their center, like fresh-baked rolls. The angus, led not by Rug now but by another, shifted their muscular shoulders and waited patiently to be fed. I could sense the miniature horses lining the fence, but I didn't look at them.

They'd eat us out of house and home, he said. Like locusts.

Behind me, the hooves of the horses clacked against the frozen ground.

~ ~ ~

One morning, the fence didn't need mending. It had begun to snow in earnest the night before, and it was still snowing when I went out to repair the wire. The television was promising snow for days to come. Most of the horses were at the fence, pressing hard against it but not otherwise moving. Some were lying down in the field beyond. I looked for the sorrel, to see if she was among the standing ones. All of them were covered in thick blankets of snow, and it was impossible to tell one diminutive shape from the next. Each fence post was topped with a sparkling white dome.

I walked the fence, making sure there was no new damage. I took up the stick I had used to poke them and ran its end along the fence wire, hoping its clattering sound would stir them. It didn't. Most of them had clustered at a single point, to exchange body heat, I suppose. I rapped my stick against the post where they were gathered, and its cap of snow fell to the ground with a soft thump. Nothing. The wire was stretched tight with the weight of them.

I knelt down, and the snow soaked immediately through the knees of my coveralls. I put my hand in my pocket, even though I knew there was nothing there for them. The dry cobs were all gone, the apples had been eaten. The eyes of the horse nearest me were closed, and there was snow caught in its long delicate lashes. The eyes of all the horses were closed. This one, I thought, was the sorrel, was Cinnamon. Must be. I put my hand to its muzzle but could feel nothing. I stripped off the White Mule glove, and the cold bit immediately into my fingers, into the half-healed cuts there from the weeks of mending fence. I reached out again.

And the horse groaned. I believed it was the horse. I brushed snow from its forehead, and its eyes blinked open, and the groaning continued, a weird guttural creaking and crying, and I thought that such a sound couldn't be coming from just the one horse, all of the horses must be making it together somehow, they were crying out with a single voice. Then I thought as the sound grew louder that it must be the hogs to the east, they were slaughtering the hogs and that was the source of it, but it was not time for slaughtering, so that couldn't be right either. I thought these things in a moment, as the sound rang out over the frozen fields and echoed off the surrounding hills.

At last I understood that it was the fencepost, the wood of the fencepost and the raveling wire and the straining staples, right at the point where the horses were gathered. And I leaped backward just as the post gave way. It heeled over hard and snapped off at ground level, and the horses tumbled with it, coming alive as they fell, the snow flying from their coats in a wild spray as they scrambled to get out from under one another.

The woven-wire fence, so many times mended, parted like tissue paper under their combined weight. With a report like a gunshot, the next post went over as well, and the post beyond that. Two or three rods of fence just lay down flat on the ground, and the horses rolled right over it, they came pouring onto our place. The horses out in the field roused themselves at the sound, shivered off their mantles of

snow, and came bounding like great dogs through the gap in the fence
as well. And I huddled against the ground, my hands up to ward off
their flying hooves as they went past me, over me. I knew that there
was nothing I could do to stop them. Their hooves would brain me,
they would lay my scalp open to the bone.

I was not touched.

The last of the horses bolted by me, and they set to on the remains
of the broken round bale, giving little cries of pleasure as they buried
their muzzles in the hay's roughness. The few angus that stood nearby
looked on bemused at the arrivals. I knew that I had to go tell my
father, I had to go get him right away. The fence—the fence that I had
maintained day after day, the fence I had hated and that had blistered
and slashed my hands—was down. But because it was snowing and all
around was quiet, the scene had the feel of a holiday, and I let them eat.

~ ~ ~

When they had satisfied themselves, for the moment at least, the horses
began to play. I searched among them until finally I found the sorrel.
She was racing across our field, her hooves kicking up light clouds of
ice crystals. She was moving more quickly than I had ever seen her go,
but she wasn't chasing another horse, and she wasn't being chased. She
was teasing the impassive angus steers, roaring up to them, stopping
just short of their great bulk; turning on a dime and dashing away
again. They stood in a semicircle, hind ends together, lowered heads
outermost, and they towered over her like the walls of a medieval city.
She yearned to charm them. She was almost dancing in the snow.

As I watched her, she passed my old man without paying him the
least attention. He wore his long cold-weather coat. The hood was up,
and it eclipsed his face. He must have been standing there quite a while.
Snow had collected on the ridge of his shoulders, and a rime of frost
clung to the edges of his hood. In his hand he held a hunting rifle, his
Remington .30-06. The lines of his face seemed odd and unfamiliar
beneath the coat's cowl, and his shoulders were trembling in a peculiar
way as he observed the interlopers on his land. I blinked. I knew what
was coming. The thin sunlight, refracted as it was by the snow, dazzled
my eyes, and the shadows that hid him from me were deep.

At last, the sorrel took notice of him, and she turned away from the imperturbable angus and trotted over to him. He watched her come. She lowered her delicate head and nipped at him, caught the hem of his coat between her teeth and began to tug. His feet slipped in the snow. Encouraged by her success, she dragged him forward. I waited for him to kill her. She continued to drag him, a foot, a yard, and at last he fell down. He fell right on his ass in the snow, my old man, the Remington held high above his head. The sorrel stood over him, the other horses clustered around her, and she seemed to gloat.

The Remington dropped to the ground, the bolt open, the breech empty. Half a dozen bright brass cartridges left my old man's hand to skip and scatter across the snow. The hood of his coat fell away from his face, and I saw that my old man was laughing.

Zog-19:
A Scientific Romance

Zog-19 is learning to drive a stick shift. He backs up, judders to a stop, and stalls. It's a big Ford F-250 diesel that he is driving, and it's got a hinky clutch. The two shovel-headed dogs in the bed of the truck bark hysterically. On Zog-19's planet, there are no cars and trucks with manual transmissions. There are no motor vehicles at all. Zog-19 shakes his head, flaps his hands, stomps in on the hinky clutch, and twists the ignition key. The Ford rattles back into life. Zog-19 decides that he will sell the Ford at the first opportunity and replace it with a vehicle that has an automatic transmission. In his short time here on Earth, Zog-19 has had about all he can stand of stick shifts.

A woman watches Zog-19's struggles with the truck. She squints her eyes worriedly. She thinks she's watching Donny McGinty fighting the hinky clutch. She is Missus McGinty, she is Donny McGinty's wife. Zog-19 is not in fact young McGinty, but he resembles McGinty down to the most minute detail. Even McGinty's dogs believe that Zog-19 is McGinty. The problem is, Zog-19 does not know how to drive a stick shift, and McGinty does, McGinty *did*.

McGinty knew how to do a blue million things that Zog-19 has never even so much as heard of on his own planet.

The Ford leaps forward several feet, stops, lurches forward again, dies. Missus McGinty shakes her head in disbelief. McGinty has never before, to her knowledge, had a bit of trouble with the truck, though that clutch often defies her. She is a small woman, and her legs aren't long enough or strong enough to manipulate the truck's pedals. Around her, around Missus McGinty and Zog-19, McGinty's little dairy operation—a hundred acres of decent land in the river bottom, inherited upon the death of McGinty's old man, and twenty-five complacent cows—is going to wrack and ruin. In the days when McGinty's old man ran the place, it gleamed, it glistened. No more, though. There are so many things that Zog-19 doesn't know how to accomplish.

Zog-19 waves to Missus McGinty from the truck. He wants badly to allay her apprehensions about him. "Toot toot," he says.

~ ~ ~

On Zog-19's planet, no one communicates by talking. All of Zog-19's people are equipped with powerful steam whistles. Well, not steam whistles exactly, because they sound using sentient gases rather than steam. The Zogs use their whistles to talk back and forth, using a system not unlike Morse code. On Zog-19's planet, "Toot toot" means "Don't worry." It also means "I love you" and "Everything is A-okay, everything is just peachy keen."

~ ~ ~

Zog-19 frets that McGinty's best friend, Angstrom, will notice the substitution. Zog-19 is not so good at imitating McGinty yet, but he is working hard to get better. Zog-19 is a diligent worker, even though he is not entirely sure what it is that he's supposed to accomplish here on Earth, in the guise of the farmer McGinty. He does know that he's supposed to act just the same as McGinty, and so for the moment he's working like heck at being McGinty.

"Goddamn it hurts," Angstrom says. He's got his arms wrapped around his middle, sways back and forth. He looks like a gargoyle, he looks like he should be a downspout on some French cathedral. Angstrom's belly hurts all the time. Maybe it's cancer, maybe it's an ulcer, maybe it's something else. Whatever it is, Angstrom can feel the blackness growing within him. At night, his hands and feet are cold as blocks of ice. The only thing that scares him more than whatever's going on inside him is how bad the cure for it might be.

Doctors killed Angstrom's old man. Angstrom's old man, strong as a bull, went to the doctors about a painful black dot on the skin of his back. The doctors hollowed him out, and he died. So now Angstrom sits on a hard chair in his kitchen and rocks back and forth, looking like a gargoyle.

"Toot toot," says Zog-19. He likes Angstrom. He's glad McGinty had Angstrom for a friend, that Angstrom is by default Zog-19's friend now, but he wishes that Angstrom felt better. He worries that Angstrom will notice that he isn't McGinty. He wishes that he knew just a bit more clearly what his mission might be. He wishes that, whatever it is, someone else, someone more suitable, had been chosen for it.

~ ~ ~

Zog-19's planet is made of iron. From space, Zog-19's planet looks just like a giant steelie marble. The planet is called Zog. Zog-19's people are called the Zogs. Donny McGinty had a magnificent steelie marble when he was a little boy. He adored the slick, cool feel of the steelie in his hand, he loved the look of it, he loved the click it made when he flicked it against other marbles. He loved the rich tautness in the pit of his stomach when he sent his beloved steelie into battle, when he played marbles with other kids. When he was using that steelie as his striker, he simply could not be beaten. He was the marbles champion of his grammar school up in the highlands of Seneca County.

Those were good days for McGinty. McGinty's old man was alive, Angstrom's old man was alive, the little dairy farm shone like a jewel at a bend in the Seneca River, and Angstrom's belly didn't hurt all the time. It seemed, when McGinty held that heavy, dully gleaming steelie in his hand, like they might all manage to live forever.

Zog-19's planet is a great hollow iron ball, filled with sentient gas. Zog-19's people are also made of iron, and they are also filled with sentient gas. When they walk, their iron feet strike the iron surface of the planet, and the whole thing rings just like a giant bell. With all the ringing, and all the tooting, Zog-19's planet can get very noisy.

~ ~ ~

Missus McGinty talks. She talks and talks. She keeps on talking about Angstrom, how she wishes that Angstrom would go to the doctor. He should go to the doctor, she says, or he should quit complaining. One or the other. She talks about Angstrom to avoid talking about McGinty. She has noticed all the changes in him lately—how could she not?—

but she doesn't know that he's been replaced by Zog-19. She just thinks he's very, very sad about the death of his old man.

She has a great deal to say on the subject of Angstrom. He should wash more frequently, for one thing. It worries Zog-19 when she talks so much. On his planet, every time you talk through your whistle, you use up a little of your sentient gas. You've got a lot to start off with, so it doesn't seem to be a big deal at first; but little by little, you use it up, sure as shooting. When all the sentient gas is gone, that's it. Zog-19 watches Missus McGinty's mouth for telltale signs of the gas. He watches to see whether it's escaping. He thinks maybe it is. He does not want Missus McGinty to run out of sentient gas.

"You should wash more, too," Missus McGinty tells him. "You're getting to be just like old dirty Angstrom." It's true, Zog-19 does not wash himself frequently. He is used to being made of iron. Washing frightens him. He has only recently been made into a creature of flesh, a creature that resembles McGinty down to the last detail, a creature that can pass muster with McGinty's dogs, and he has trouble recalling that he's no longer iron. Do you know what happens when you wash iron? It *corrodes*.

"You smell like a boar hog," says Missus McGinty. "I don't even like to be in the same bed with you anymore." Zog-19 knows that she's only saying these things because she loves him. On his planet, no one talks about anyone they don't love. They can't afford to waste the sentient gas. She loves him, and she loves Angstrom too, she loves him like a brother. She and McGinty have known Angstrom all their lives. Zog-19 imagines that, once he is better able to imitate McGinty, once he forgets that he used to be made out of iron, he'll be able to love her as well.

But here's another thing that scares him: when people on Earth touch a piece of iron, he has noticed, they leave behind prints, they leave behind fingerprints. No two people on Earth, he has heard it said, have the same fingerprints. All those fingerprints, and every one different! No one on Zog-19's planet has any fingerprints at all. And these human fingerprints are composed of body oils, they are acid in their content. Unless they are swiftly scrubbed away, they oxidize the iron, they eat into it, they etch its surface with little ridges and valleys and hollows, they make smooth pristine iron into a rough red landscape of rust. Almost nothing could be worse for someone from the planet Zog than the touch of a human hand.

~ ~ ~

In the year 2347, space explorers from Earth will discover Zog-19's planet. The space explorers will leave their rusting fingerprints all over the iron surface of Zog. During their visit, the space explorers will discover that the sentient gas which fills the planet, and which coincidentally fills and animates the Zogs themselves, makes the space explorers' ships go very, very fast. Because they like to go very, very fast, they will ask the Zogs for the gas. They will ask politely at first.

Because the gas makes their planet ring so nicely under their iron feet, the Zogs will refuse it to them. The space explorers will ask again, less politely this time, more pointedly, and the Zogs will explain, with their thundering whistles, their immutable position on the matter.

War. At first, it looks as though the Zogs will easily win. They are numerous and powerful, and the space explorers are few and a long way from home. The Zogs are made of iron (to the space explorers, they look like great foundry boilers with arms and legs and heads), and the space explorers are made of water and soft meat. Their bones are brittle and break easily. "Toot toot," the Zogs will reassuringly say to one another as they prepare for battle. "Toot toot!"

But one of the space explorers will think of a thing: he will think of a way to magnetize the whole iron planet. He will think of a way to use vast dynamos to turn the entire planet into a gigantic electromagnet. He will get the idea from watching a TV show, one where a big electromagnet-equipped crane picks up a car, a huge old Hudson Terraplane, and drops it into a hydraulic crusher.

McGinty used to see this show in reruns every now and again, before he got replaced by Zog-19, and he was always amazed by what happened to that car. Every time the show played, the crusher mashed the car down into a manageable cube, not much larger than a coffee table.

"Look at that," McGinty would say to Angstrom whenever the show was on. "That's my old man's car that's getting crushed."

~ ~ ~

McGinty's old man used to have a car just like that one when he was young, when he was McGinty's age, and he and McGinty's mother (though McGinty had not been born yet) would run around the county in that big old powerhouse of a car, blowing the horn in a friendly way and waving to everybody they knew, which was pretty much everybody they saw. McGinty does not know it, but he was conceived in the backseat of that Hudson Terraplane.

His old man wanted to sire a child, he wanted a son, and McGinty's mother was only too happy to oblige. While they were making love in the backseat of the Hudson, McGinty's mother's left heel caught the hornring on the steering wheel a pretty blow, and the horn sounded, just as McGinty's old man and his mother were making McGinty. And the sound it made? *Toot toot.*

~ ~ ~

"We don't make love anymore," says Missus McGinty, "not since your father died." Zog-19 has never made love to anyone.

On his planet, they do not have sex. They do not have babies. When a Zog runs out of sentient gas, it is simply replaced by another full-grown Zog more or less like it. Where do these new Zogs come from? No one knows. Perhaps the planet makes them. Once, the best thinkers on the planet Zog gathered together for a summit on the matter. They thought that they'd put their heads together and figure the thing out—where do new Zogs come from?—once and for all. But once they were all together, they got worried about losing all their sentient gas in the course of the palaver. They worried that they themselves would have to be replaced by the as-yet-unfathomed process of Zog regeneration. And so they figured, "What the heck?" and they went home again.

Missus McGinty leads Zog-19 into the cool bedroom of their farmhouse. She draws the shades. She does not ask him to speak. She undresses him and sponges him off with cool water. He does not corrode. She undresses herself. She is not built like a foundry boiler. Her pale, naked skin is luminous in the darkened room. She has a slender waist and a darling little dimple above each buttock. When he sees those dimples, Zog-19 says, "Toot toot."

Because she is only made of water and soft meat, Zog-19 is afraid that he will hurt her when he touches her. He is afraid that his dense, tremendous bulk will crush her, like the Hudson Terraplane on the TV show. He is afraid that his iron claws will puncture her skin. When she draws him to her, and when he enters her, he becomes momentarily convinced that he has injured her, and he tries to lift himself away. But she pulls him back again, with surprising strength, and he concedes, for a time, that he too is only made of water and meat.

~ ~ ~

So the space explorers will magnetize the planet, and the feet of the Zogs will stick to it like glue. Think of it! Poor Zogs. All they will be able to do is look up at the sky as the Earth ships descend. They will look up at the sky, and they will hoot at one another with their whistles. They will not say, "Toot toot," because things will not be A-okay, things will not be hunky-dory. Instead, as the space explorers land and rig up a great sharpened molybdenum straw that will penetrate the surface of Zog and siphon off the sentient gas, the Zogs will whistle, "Hoot hoot hoot," all over the planet.

To the Earthmen who are setting up the molybdenum straw, it will seem a very sad sound. It will also seem very loud, and every Earth space explorer will be issued a set of sturdy earmuffs to prevent damage to sensitive human eardrums. And the sound will mean this: it will mean "I'm sad" and "The end is near" and "We are most definitely screwed."

~ ~ ~

The loafers that hang out at the Modern Barbershop in Mount Nebo, where McGinty used to get his hair cut, and where Zog-19 goes now in imitation of McGinty, are convinced that the death of McGinty's old man has driven McGinty around the bend. They chuckle when McGinty says to them, "Toot toot." They try to jolly him out of the funk he is in.

They are by and large elderly fellows, the loafers, and they tell McGinty stories about his old man when his old man was young. They tell him stories about his old man roaring around the county in his big old Hudson Terraplane, a car so well made that, if McGinty's old man hadn't smashed it into a tree one drunken night, that car would still be out on the road today. All the loafers agree that nobody makes cars anymore that are anywhere near as good as that faithful Hudson.

They tell him other stories too. They tell him how, when he was a little boy, he and his old man used to sing a song, to the delight of everybody in the barbershop. McGinty's old man would set young McGinty up in the barber's chair, and the barber would drape a sheet around young McGinty's neck and set to work with his comb and his flashing silver scissors and his long cutthroat razor, and McGinty's old man would stand before the chair, his arms spread like an orchestra conductor's, and he and young McGinty would sing. And the song they sang went like this: it went, "Well, McGinty is dead and McCarty don't know it, McCarty is dead and McGinty don't know it, and they're both of them dead, and they're in the same bed, and neither one knows that the other is dead."

There was a fellow named McCarty who always loafed at the Modern Barbershop, a tough old guy who had been a frogman in the Second World War, so it was like the McGintys were singing a song about themselves and about McCarty. The loafers at the barbershop loved the song when McGinty was a little boy, and remembering it now they love it all over again. They love it so much that they laugh, laugh really hard, laugh themselves breathless, and pretty soon it is hard to tell if it's a barbershop full of laughing old men or weeping old men.

Of course, when McGinty's old man sang the song, back in McGinty's childhood, both McGinty and McCarty were alive, even though the song said they were dead, and that made it all the funnier. But now McGinty really *is* dead, and McCarty really is dead too, carried off by a wandering blood clot a decade before, and they are both buried out in the graveyard of the Evangelical Church of the New Remnant north of town, which is kind of like being in the same bed. None of the song was true before, and now a lot of it is true, and so it isn't all that funny.

"Poor McGinty," says one of the loafers, when they have all thought of how the song is true and not so funny anymore. And nobody knows whether he's talking about McGinty, or McGinty's old man.

~ ~ ~

Before long, the Earth spacemen, with their very, very fast spaceships, will manage to conquer the entire universe. Everywhere they go, the people who live there will ask them, "How in the heck do you make your spaceships go so darned fast?" The space explorers will be tempted to tell them, because they will want to boast about the clever way in which they defeated the Zogs, but they will play it cagey. They will keep their traps closed. They won't want anybody getting any ideas about using the sentient gas themselves.

Before long, also, the sentient gas that fills the planet of the Zogs will begin to run out. There will be that many Earth spaceships! And the space explorers will become very worried, because, even though they will have conquered the entire universe, they will nonetheless continue to think that there might be something beyond that which they might like to conquer as well.

~ ~ ~

McGinty and Angstrom also used to sing a song. They used to sing it when they got drunk. They used to sing it back in the days when McGinty's old man was alive, when Angstrom's old man was alive, back in the days when even McCarty, the tough old frogman, was alive. They would sing it while they played card games, Deuces and Beggar Your Neighbor.

They used to sing it to girls, too, because it was a slightly naughty song. They used to love singing it to girls. And the song they sang went like this: it went, "Roll me over in the clover. Roll me over and do it again."

It was a simple, silly song, but it seemed to be about sex, and that was unusual in a place where almost nothing was about sex. So little was about sex in the Seneca Valley in the days when McGinty's old man and Angstrom's old man were alive that, weirdly, almost everything seemed to be about sex. Anything could make you think about sex in those days, even a silly little song, even a silly little song about clover. Clover is a kind of fodder that cows and sheep especially like. A clover with four leaves is said on Earth to be particularly lucky.

In addition to the hundred acres of decent bottomland, McGinty's old man also accumulated a little highland pasturage to the north of the valley, where he kept a few fat, lazy sheep. These mountain pastures were almost completely grown over in sweet clover. When McGinty and Angstrom sang the song, when they sang, "Roll me over in the clover," McGinty was always thinking about those pastures. He was thinking about rolling over a girl in the mountain pastures. He was thinking about rolling over a girl he knew who had sweet dimples above her buttocks. He was thinking about rolling her over in the cool mountain pastures.

And now Angstrom tries to teach the song to Zog-19. He cannot believe that McGinty has forgotten the song. Zog-19 understands that it's a song that he's supposed to know, supposed to like, and so he makes a diligent effort to learn it, for Angstrom's sake. Angstrom has been drinking, an activity that sometimes eases the pain in his belly and sometimes exacerbates it. For the moment, drinking seems to have eased the pain.

"Roll me over," sings Angstrom in his scratchy baritone voice.

"Over," sings Zog-19, in McGinty's pleasant, clear tenor.

"In the clover," sings Angstrom, waving a bottle.

"Clover," answers Zog-19. He does not know yet what clover is, but he likes the sound of it. He hopes that someone will teach him about clover, about which McGinty doubtless knew volumes, about which McGinty doubtless knew every little thing. He hopes that someone will teach him soon.

~ ~ ~

All this time, while they will have been out conquering the width and breadth of the universe, the space explorers will have kept the planet of Zog magnetized, with the poor old Zogs stuck to its surface like flies stuck to a strip of flypaper.

The Zogs will still manage to talk back and forth among themselves. Mostly, what they will say is "Hoot hoot hoot." Sometimes one among them, a Zog optimist, will venture a "Toot toot," but he will inevitably be shouted down by a chorus of hooting.

~ ~ ~

Zog-19 wants the spinning radiator fan of the Ford F-250 to stop spinning, and so he simply reaches out a hand to stop it. On Zog, this would not have been a problem. The spinning steel fan blades might have struck a spark or two from his hard iron claws, and then the fan would have been stilled in his mighty grip.

On Earth, though, it is a big problem. On Earth, Zog-19 is only made of water and soft meat. The radiator fan slices easily through the water and meat of his fingers. It sends the tips of two of the fingers cartwheeling off, sailing away to land God knows where, slashes tendons in the other fingers, cross-hatches his palms with bleeding gashes. Zog-19 holds his ruined hand up before his face, stares at it in horror. He knows that he has made a terrible mistake, a mistake of ignorance, and one that it won't be possible to remedy. He wants to shout for Missus McGinty, whose name he has only just mastered. He struggles to come up with her name, but the pain and terror of his hand have driven it from his memory. All that he can come up with is this: he calls out, "Hoot hoot hoot," in a pitiful voice, and then he collapses.

~ ~ ~

Probably by this point you have questions. How is it possible to know what will happen to the Zogs in the year 2347? That might be one of the questions. Easy. The Zogs have seen the future. They have seen the past, too. They watch it the way we watch television. Zog science makes it possible. They have seen what happened on the iron planet a million years ago, and what happened five minutes ago, and what will happen in the year 2347. They can watch the present, too, but they don't.

They have seen the space explorers from Earth. They have seen the depopulation of their planet, they have seen it emptied of its precious sentient gas. In fact, that episode of their history—a holocaust of such indescribable proportions that most Zogs can be brought to tears merely by the mention of it—is by far the most popular program on Zog. Every Zog watches it again and again, backward and forward. Every Zog knows by heart all its images—the Zogs stuck helplessly to the planet's iron surface, the molybdenum straw, the descent of the Earth ships on tongues of fire—and all its dialogue. They are obsessed with their own doom.

Another question: What is Zog-19 doing on Earth, in McGinty's exact form, with McGinty's wife and McGinty's dogs, and with McGinty's best friend, Angstrom? And: How was the switch accomplished? And what the heck happened to the real McGinty?

In a nutshell: Zog-19 was sent to Earth by a Zog scientist who was not enamored of the program, who hated what Fate held in store for Zog. His name was Zog-One-Billion, and he was a very important fellow. He was also brilliant. Being brilliant, he was able to invent a device that allowed him to send one of his own people to Earth in the guise of a human being. The device allowed him to examine Earth at his leisure, and to pick one of its citizens—the most likely of them, as he saw it, to be able to put a stop to the upcoming extermination of the Zogs—as a target for Zog replacement.

Zog-19 didn't go willingly. He had to do what Zog-One-Billion said because he had a lower number, a *much* lower number. The higher numbers tell the lower numbers what to do, and the lower numbers do it. It makes sense to the Zogs, and so that's how Zog society is arranged. Zog-19 couldn't even complain. Zog-One-Billion wanted him to be some unknown thing, a farmer named McGinty a galaxy away, and so Zog-19 had to be that thing that Zog-One-Billion wanted.

In all the excitement, the selection of McGinty and the sending of Zog-19 across the galaxy, Zog-One-Billion failed to explain to Zog-19 what precisely he was to undertake in order to avert the Zog apocalypse. It's possible that he didn't really have many firm ideas in that direction himself. There's no way of knowing because, as he sent Zog-19 on his long sojourn, he gave a last great toot of triumph and went still. His sentient gas was depleted.

What is known is this: it's known that, during his surveillance of Earth, Zog-One-Billion came particularly to like and admire human farmers. He saw them, for some reason, as the possible salvation of Zog. It is believed that he regarded farmers thus because many farmers own cows. Cows were particularly impressive to Zog-One-Billion, especially the big black-and-white ones that give milk. These cows are called Holstein-Friesians, for a region in Europe; or just Holsteins for short.

There are no cows on Zog. There are no animals whatsoever. Cows burp and fart when they're relaxed. That's why it's a terrific compliment when a cow burps in your face, or if it farts when you're around. It means you don't make the cow nervous. You don't make all its innards tighten up.

McGinty didn't make his cows nervous. McGinty's cows were always terrifically relaxed around McGinty, as they always had been around McGinty's old man, and it's believed that this reaction in some way influenced the brilliant scientist Zog-One-Billion, that this lack of nerves on the part of the cows of McGinty attracted the attention of Zog-One-Billion from across the galaxy.

Perhaps the great Holstein-Friesians fascinated Zog-One-Billion because they reminded him of Zogs, because they reminded him of himself, with their great barrel bodies and their hard, blunt heads. Perhaps the burps and farts of the Holsteins reminded him of the sentient gas within himself, the sentient gas within every Zog, the sentient gas within the planet of Zog, the gas that made the iron planet ring in such an exotic and charming way. And yet—this would have been particularly impressive to Zog-One-Billion—cows never run out of gas, no matter how much of it they release. They manufacture the stuff! They are like gas factories made from water and soft meat.

And what happened to poor McGinty, the good-looking young dairy farmer with the beloved shovel-headed dogs and the beloved dimpled wife? Sad to say. Like the released sentient gas of Zog-One-Billion, McGinty simply . . . went away when Zog-19 replaced him. Drifted off. Dispersed. Vanished. Zog-One-Billion believed that McGinty's vanishment was the only way to save his beloved planet. If Zog-One-Billion, a very important Zog, was willing to make the ultimate sacrifice for the salvation of his planet and race, perhaps he reasoned, who was McGinty to object to making the same sacrifice? Of course, it wasn't McGinty's race or McGinty's planet, but there was no good way, given the enormous distances that separated them, for Zog-One-Billion to ask him.

~ ~ ~

Oh, McGinty is dead and McCarty don't know it. McCarty is dead and McGinty don't know it. They're both of them dead and they're in the same bed, and neither one knows that the other is dead.

~ ~ ~

Just when it looks like the ships of the space explorers will run out of sentient gas, the planet of the Zogs having been utterly depleted in this respect; just when it looks like the space explorers will have to stop going very, very fast, one of their number (he was the same one who thought of magnetizing the iron planet of the Zogs) will remember a thing: he will remember that the Zogs themselves are filled with the selfsame sentient gas. That gas is what makes the Zogs the Zogs, and each Zog is filled with quite a quantity of the stuff. He will remember it just in time!

~ ~ ~

Zog-19 cradles his wrecked hand against his chest. The hand is wrapped in a thick webbing of bandages. Zog-19 works hard to forget what the hand looked like after he stuck it into the blades of the radiator fan. He tries to think about what the hand looked like before that, the instant before, when the hand was reaching, and the hand was whole. Angstrom has just been by, and he brought the greetings of all the loafers down at the Modern Barbershop, who shook their heads sagely when they heard the news about the hand. Angstrom tried to interest Zog-19 in a rousing chorus of "Roll Me Over in the Clover," but Zog-19 couldn't forget about the hand long enough to sing. It did not take Angstrom long to leave.

Now Missus McGinty is with Zog-19. She holds his head cradled against her breasts. Zog-19's hand stings and throbs too much for him to take interest in the breasts, either. He does not know about healing. On Zog, no one heals. They are a hardy bunch, the Zogs, and usually last for thousands of years before all their gas is gone and they settle into de-animation. And all that time, all that time, the scars that life inflicts upon them gather on their great iron bodies, until, near the end, most Zogs come to look like rusted, pockmarked, ding-riddled caricatures of themselves. Zog-19 has no idea that his hand will not always hurt.

He is working very hard to listen to what Missus McGinty is telling him. She says it to him over and over, the same five words. And what she says is this: Missus McGinty, lovely dimpled Missus McGinty says, "Everything will be all right. Everything will be all right." Zog-19 knows what that phrase means. It means "Toot toot." He wants to believe it. He wants very badly to believe that everything will be all right.

Zog-19 is also working very hard to forget that he is Zog-19. He's not worried about the Zog extinction now. Right now he's worried about Zog-19, and about making Zog-19 believe that he is not made of iron, that he is made of water and soft meat. He is concerned with making

Zog-19 believe that he is actually McGinty. He understands that, if he cannot forget that he is Zog-19, if he cannot come to believe that he is in fact what he seems to be, which is McGinty, he will—by accident, of course, by doing something that water and meat should never do— kill himself dead.

~ ~ ~

And so the intrepid space explorers will begin sticking sharpened molybdenum straws straight into the Zogs and drawing out their sentient gas. The Zogs will make a very good source of the gas, and the space explorers will be able to keep on going very, very fast. There is nothing beyond the universe they have conquered, they will discover that disheartening fact after a while, but they sure as heck won't waste any time getting there.

Drawing out the gas will de-animate the Zogs, of course. Magnetized as they are, the emptied iron Zogs won't seem to the space explorers much different from the full Zogs, except that they will be quiet, which won't be a problem. It will be, in fact, a decided benefit. Once they have de-animated many of the Zogs, the space explorers will find that they can take their earmuffs off. It will be more comfortable to work without the earmuffs, and so productivity and efficiency will both rise. They will go on sticking molybdenum straws into Zog after Zog and drawing out the sentient gas, until there will be only one unemptied Zog left.

This depletion will happen quickly, because once a space explorer hears about Zog and what the sentient gas can do, he will go there as quickly as possible (of course, he will leave much, much more quickly, thanks to the properties of the sentient gas when combined with Earth spaceships) in order to get his share. Most of the space explorers who come to Zog will never have seen the Zogs before they were magnetized, and so they won't be able to imagine why it might be a problem to empty a Zog of his gas. Except for the Zog's subsequent silence, it will seem the same afterward as it did before.

Everyone knows that the gas will run out—how could it not? And how could they not know?—but this knowledge will just make them swarm to Zog faster and faster, in ever-increasing numbers, because they won't want the gas to run out before they get there. What a dilemma.

~ ~ ~

Zog-19 rounds up his cows in the early morning for milking. It's still dark when he does so. Missus McGinty stays in bed while Zog-19 gathers the cows. Later, she will rise and make him breakfast, she will make him some pancakes. But now she is warm in bed, and dawn will brighten the sky soon, and she can hear Zog-19's voice out in the pasture, calling in the cows. He whoops and hollers, he sings out, and sometimes his voice sounds to her like a whistle, and sometimes it sounds like a regular voice.

The cows come trotting eagerly up to Zog-19. They follow him into the milking parlor. They are ready to be milked.

~ ~ ~

The cows are not nervous around Zog-19. Zog-19 is not nervous around the cows. The cows are large and black-and-white, they are noble Holstein-Friesians, and some of them weigh nearly a ton. If they wanted to, they could rampage and smash up the barn and smash up Zog-19 and smash up any of the water and meat people who got in their way, even though they themselves, the cows, are made only of water-and-meat, and not iron. Lucky for Zog-19—lucky for all of us!—that they never care to rampage.

Zog-19's favorite cow burps directly into his face. This is, as previously mentioned, high praise from a cow. A tag in the cow's ear reads 127. On Zog's planet, that number would make the cow the boss of Zog-19, since it is a higher number than nineteen. She would be able to tell him what to do, and he would have to do it, whether he wanted to or not. She would be able to tell him to go to some other planet for some half-understood reason, and replace some poor sap who lived there with his wife and his dogs, and Zog-19 would have to do just what she said.

Here, though, that number doesn't make the cow the boss of Zog-19. It doesn't make her the boss of anything, not even of the other cows with lower numbers. It's just a number. Cows never want to rampage, and they never want to be the boss.

When the cow burps in Zog-19's face, her breath is fragrant with the scent of masticated clover.

~ ~ ~

The last surviving Zog will be named Zog-1049. That is not a very impressive name for a Zog. Zog-1049 will only be more important than a thousand or so other Zogs, and he will be less important than many other Zogs. He will be much less important, for instance, than

Zog-One-Billion, the Zog who sent Zog-19 to Earth to take McGinty's shape. Zog-One-Billion had a very impressive name, even though he didn't really know what he was doing. Zog-1049 will be, as you can see, more important than Zog-19, though not by much.

The space explorer's hand will rest on the big red button that will plunge the molybdenum straw into Zog-1049. He will wonder how much sentient gas the last Zog contains. He will wonder how far his ship will be able to go on that amount of gas, and how fast it will be able to get there.

Zog-1049 will say to the explorer, "Toot toot?" The space explorer will have heard it a million times, from a million Zogs, and still he won't know what it means. He won't know that it means "Don't you love me? I love you. Everything is hunky-dory."

When Zog-1049 realizes that the space explorer means to empty his sentient gas through the molybdenum straw no matter what he says, he will begin to hoot. "Hoot hoot hoot," he will say. He will hoot so long and so hard that he will expend a lot of his own gas this way. The space explorer will hate to hear Zog-1049 hoot so. He will know that it means the supply of sentient gas inside Zog-1049—and thus the supply of sentient gas in the entire universe—is dwindling ever faster. He will decide to stop contemplating Zog-1049 and go ahead and empty him.

The space explorer—whose name, by a vast coincidence that you have perhaps already intuited, will be Spaceman McGinty; he will be the great-great-great-however-many-greats-grandson of Missus McGinty and Zog-19—will take a final glance at this last of all the Zogs. He will take in the great iron foundry-boiler body, the sad, wagging head, the iron feet pinioned to the planet's surface by surging electromagnetic energy. He will take it all in, this pathetic, trapped creature, this iron being completely alien to him and useful to him only as fuel. And he will think he hears, as though they come to him from some realm far beyond his own, the lyrics of a silly song. They will ring in his head.

Roll me over in the clover.

Clover? Spaceman McGinty will never have seen clover. He will have heard of it, though, a family legend, passed down through the generations. Certainly there is no clover on Zog.

Roll me over and do it again.

The song will be a happy one. Looking at Zog-1049, and hearing the clover song in his head, Spaceman McGinty will feel unaccountably joyful. Looking at Zog-1049, Spaceman McGinty will think of cows, another family legend, great wide-bodied Holstein-Friesians, and he will think of clover, of a single lucky four-leaf clover, and of crickets hidden within the clover, and of sheep trit-trotting across mountain pastures, and of dogs at his heel. He will think of a little farm in a bend of the Seneca River, now lost forever. He will think—unreasonably, he will admit, but still he will think it—of McGinty his distant forebear, who for a time could say nothing but "toot toot" and "hoot hoot hoot," but who finally regained the power of human speech.

He will not know why he thinks of these things, but he will think of them. He will feel the joy of reunion, he will feel his family stretching out for hundreds of years behind him, and before him too, a long line of honorable men and women, almost all farmers but for him, but for Spaceman McGinty. And his family, somehow, impossibly, will encompass poor old Zog-1049. What a peculiar family, these McGintys!

And remembering the cows, and the clover, and the farm, and the family, and the happy song, Spaceman McGinty will stay his hand.

Without the sentient gas that resides within Zog-1049, he will think, he will at last be able to settle down, this formerly peripatetic Spaceman McGinty, he will put down roots, perhaps he will find a planet somewhere that will accommodate him, where he can bust the sod like his ancestors and build a little house and even—dare he think it?— have a few cows, maybe some sheep, maybe some dogs. His blood will call him to it. And on this farm he will have the time he needs to think about the dark ringing hollowness at the core of him, the hollowness that has driven him out into the universe to discover and to conquer. And perhaps by its contemplation, he will be able to understand that hollowness, and even to fill it up, just a bit.

~ ~ ~

Zog-19 has discovered McGinty's sheep pastures, high up on the ridges at the northern end of the county. He has driven the Ford F-250 up there. He no longer wants to sell the Ford, because he has mastered the stick shift. He drives the truck as well as McGinty ever did, even though he is missing the tips of a couple of fingers from his right hand, his shifting hand. A lot of other things are coming along as well, but the farm still looks like hell, it still looks like an amateur's running it. McGinty's old man would have a fit if he were to rise up from the grave and have a look at it. Rust everywhere. Busted machinery. Still, progress is progress.

The hand is healing up all right, but at night the thick scar tissue across the palm itches like hell (it's a sign of healing, so Missus McGinty says, and she does not complain about the scar tissue or the missing tips of the fingers when Zog-19 comes to her in their bed), and he can sometimes feel the amputated finger joints tingling and aching. Sometimes, quite unexpectedly, he can feel McGinty in that same way, poor vanished McGinty, he can feel the pull of the man when he is performing some chore, when he's hooking Number 127 up to the milking machine, when McGinty's dogs come dashing up to him, when he runs the wrecked hand over Missus McGinty's dimples.

Sometimes Zog-19 feels as though McGinty is standing just behind him, as though McGinty is looking out through his eyes. Is there any way that McGinty could come back from the void? Zog-19 does not know. Zog-One-Billion didn't mention the possibility, but then of course there are a blue million things that Zog-One-Billion never mentioned, including stick shift automobiles and spinning radiator fan blades.

McGinty's dogs are with Zog-19 now, scrambling and scrabbling across the metal bed of the truck as it rumbles along the rutted mountain road, their nails scraping and scratching, in a fever of excitement as they recognize the way up to the sheep pastures, as they recognize the pastures themselves. It is lonely up here. It makes Zog-19 feel like he's the last creature on the planet when he comes up here.

He parks the truck, and the dogs are over the side of the truck bed and away; they are across the field before he can climb down from the cab. They swim through the clover like seals. Zog-19 shouts after them, he has learned their names, but they ignore him. Zog-19 doesn't mind. If he were having as much fun as they are, leaping out at each other in mock battle, rolling over and over in the lush, crisp grass, growling playfully, he would ignore him too.

He strolls over to a sagging line of woven-wire fence, leans against it, breathes in, breathes out. He watches the sheep that drift across the field like small clouds heavy with snow. He has learned that he will have to shear them before long, that is part of his job, that is part of McGinty's job. He thinks that probably he can get one of the loafers down at the Modern Barbershop in Mount Nebo to tell him how to do such a thing. They seem to know pretty much everything that a man who wanted to imitate McGinty might care to know, and they're always happy to share. Needless to say, nothing on Zog ever needed shearing. Still, he imagines that he can handle it.

He whistles for the dogs, and they perk up their ears at the summons, then go back to playing. He smiles. He knows. After a while, they will tire. After a while, McGinty's dogs will run out of steam, and they will return to him on their own.

~ ~ ~

Spaceman McGinty—the only space explorer still on Zog—will shut down the great dynamos. It will be his final act before leaving the planet behind forever.

And the last Zog, unimportant Zog-1049, the final, last, and only Zog, will find himself his own master again. But how Zog has changed during his captivity! He knew something bad was happening, but trapped as he was, he could not imagine the scope of it, the impossible magnitude of the disaster. He will take up wandering the planet, he will pass through the rows upon rows of deanimated Zogs, empty, inert Zogs in their ranked, silent billions. He will use his whistle, he will release his sentient gas, the last to be found anywhere, in copious, even reckless, amounts, calling out across the dead echoing iron planet for any compatriot, for any other Zog who is still living. "Toot toot," he will call. He will call, and he will call, and he will call.

~ ~ ~

Zog-19 enjoys a hearty breakfast. He's eating a tall stack of buckwheat pancakes just dripping with melted creamery butter and warm blackstrap molasses. He's never eaten anything that made him happier. He cleans his plate and offers it to Missus McGinty, who refills it with pleasure. McGinty always liked his pancakes and molasses, and to Missus McGinty this healthy appetite, this love for something from his past, a forgotten favorite, is a sure sign of McGinty's return.

He's been gone from her a long time, someplace in his head, gone from her in a way that she can't imagine, and she's awfully happy to have him back. What brought him back? She does not know. She cannot venture a guess, and she does not care. She has wept many bitter tears over his absence, over his apparent madness, the amnesia, the peculiarity (small word for it!), but she thinks that maybe she won't be crying quite so much in the days to come. Watching Zog-19 with his handsome young head low over his plate, tucking into the pancakes with vigor, his injured hand working the fork as of old, working it up and down and up again like the restless bucket of a steam shovel, she can believe this absolutely.

~ ~ ~

And what of the planet Zog? Depopulated, hollow Zog? Well, the space explorers, once they have finished with the sentient gas, the space explorers will feel just terrible about what they have done. They will be determined to make amends. And so they will do what Earth people can always be expected to do in a pinch: they will go to work with a great goodwill.

They will send all kinds of heavy moving equipment, bulldozers and end-loaders and cranes and trucks and forklifts, to Zog. They will work, and they will work, and they will work. They will raise up a great monument. They will move the bodies around, they will use the inanimate husks of the Zogs in building their monument (the materials being so close to hand, and free), they will pile them atop one another in great stacks that will stretch up and up into the Zog sky. They will use every deanimated Zog to make the memorial, every single one.

Zog-1049 will almost get swept up and used too, but he will hoot desperately at the last minute, just as the blade of the snorting bulldozer is about to propel him into the mounting pile of the dead. The good-natured fellow who is driving the bulldozer will climb down, laughing with relief at the mistake he's nearly made, almost shoving the last living Zog into the memorial to the Zog dead, and he will brush Zog-1049 off, leaving some acid oil on Zog-1049's sleek iron body, and he will direct Zog-1049 to a safe spot from which to watch the goings-on without getting into any more trouble. The bulldozer operator will shake his head as Zog-1049 totters off across the empty landscape, hooting and tooting. Poor old thing, the bulldozer man will say to himself. He's gone out of his mind. And who can blame him!

Soon enough, the memorial will be finished. And it will be, all will agree, a magnificent testament to the remorse of mankind at their shocking treatment of the Zogs.

The memorial will be this: it will be a single word, a single two-syllable word, written in letters (and one mark of punctuation) tens of miles tall, the word itself hundreds of miles across. It will be a huge sign, the biggest sign ever made, a record-breaking sign in iron bodies, across the face of the iron planet, and, when the planet revolves on its axis so that the sign lies in daylight, so that the fierce sun of that system strikes lurid fire from the skins of the defunct Zogs, it will be visible from far out in space. It will be a word written across the sterile face of the steelie, the face occupied now only by eternally wandering Zog-1049, and the word will be this: the word will be *SORRY!*

~ ~ ~

Spaceman McGinty will, in the end, find himself on a sweet grass planet (plenty of clover there! and the breeze always blowing out of the east, blowing clover ripples across the face of the grass) far out at the raggedy edge of the universe. No one will live on the planet but McGinty and a primitive race of cricket people who communicate solely by rubbing their back legs together. The cricket people will live hidden in the tall grass, and McGinty will never so much as glimpse one of them, not in his whole life on their world. He will hear them though. He will hear them always. Their stridulation will make a soft, whispering, breezy music to which, at night, former Spaceman McGinty will sometimes sing.

And what will he sing?

Sometimes he will sing, "McCarty is dead and McGinty don't know it. McGinty is dead and McCarty don't know it."

And other times he will sing, "Roll me over in the clover."

And still other times he won't sing at all, but will simply dance, naked and sweating and all alone; former spaceman McGinty will dance along on the balls of his bare feet in the soft rustling waist-high grass of that lonely place.

All that, of course, is in the very far-off future.

~ ~ ~

Zog-19 is back in the sheep pastures. He feels relaxed, and he burps. A crisp breeze has sprung up, and he watches it play over the surface of the pastures; he enjoys the waves that the breeze sends shivering across the tops of the sweet clover. So much like water. Water used to frighten him, but he doesn't worry about it now.

McGinty is dead. McCarty is dead. Angstrom is dead.

The dogs are chivying the sheep over in the far part of the pasture. They are pretending that something, some fox or coyote or wolf or catamount, threatens the sheep, and they must keep the sheep tightly packed together, must keep them moving in a tightly knit body, in order to save their lives. The dogs love this game. The sheep aren't smart enough to know that there's no real danger, and they're bleating with worry.

"Hi," Zog-19 calls out to the dogs. More and more these days, he sounds like McGinty without even thinking about it. "Hi, you dogs! Get away from them woollies!" The dogs ignore him.

Let the dead bury their dead. That is what Missus McGinty tells him. There are so many dead. There is McGinty's old man, there is McCarty, there is Angstrom's old man, there is Angstrom, there is McGinty (though more and more these days, Zog-19 feels McGinty in the room with him, McGinty behind his eyes), there are the Zogs. What could Zog-19 do to prevent the tragedies that have unfolded, to prevent the tragedies that will continue to unfold in the world, across the galaxy? He's only a dairy farmer, he's a man who lives among the grasses. His cows like him. They are relaxed around him. They burp in his face to show their affection. What is there that a man can do?

"Toot toot," says Zog-19, experimentally, but it sounds like an expression from an unknown foreign language to him now.

Let the dead bury their dead.

Missus McGinty has come with him to the sheep pastures. Later in the day, they will shear the sheep together. It turns out that Missus McGinty is a champion sheep shearer, Seneca County Four-H, Heart Head Hands and Health, three years running. They'll have the sheep done in no time. Right now, though, they're in the act of finishing up a delicious picnic lunch. They're sitting together on a cheery red-and-white-checked picnic blanket, sitting in the wealth of the wind-rippled field of clover, Zog-19 and Missus McGinty. Around them are the remains of their meal: a thermos still half full of good, cold raw milk, the gnawed bones of Missus McGinty's wonderful Southern-fried chicken, a couple of crisp Granny Smith apples. Yum.

McGinty would have given the dogs the chicken bones, but Zog-19 will not. He worries that they will crack the bones with their teeth, leaving razor-sharp ends exposed, and that they will then swallow the bones. He is afraid that the bones would lacerate their innards. That's one difference between Zog-19 and McGinty.

"Roll me over in the clover," Missus McGinty sings in her frothy alto voice. She's lying on the checked picnic blanket, and she plucks at Zog-19's sleeve. Her expression is cheerful but serious. She's fiddling with the buttons of her blouse. She takes Zog-19's hand and places it where her hand was, on the buttons. Zog-19 knows that it's now his turn to fiddle with the buttons.

The dogs are barking. The sheep are bleating. The buttons are beneath Zog-19's hand. Missus McGinty is beneath the buttons. The crickets are chirring loudly, hidden deep within the clover. McGinty is standing behind Zog-19 somewhere. The sun is hot on Zog-19's head. There is a four-leaf clover in this pasture, he knows. Somewhere, in among all the regular clover, there must be at least one. His head is swimming with the sun. He feels as though, if he does not move, if he does not speak, if he doesn't do something, something, something, and pretty damned quick, he is going to burst into flame.

Zog-19 can't know it, but it is time for him to resume the line that will lead to that far-off Spaceman McGinty, the one who will spare Zog-1049. It is time for him to sire a brand-new McGinty.

"Roll me over and do it again," Missus McGinty sings. The button comes off in Zog-19's hand. It is small in his scarred palm, like a hard, smooth little pill. He tosses it over his shoulder, laughing. He tosses it in McGinty's direction. He tugs at the next button down. He wants that one too. He wants the one after that one. He wants them all. He wants them all.

The wind ripples the clover, the wind ripples Missus McGinty's chestnut hair.

PINCKNEY BENEDICT grew up on his family's dairy farm in the mountains of southern West Virginia. He has published two previous collections of short fiction (*Town Smokes* and *The Wrecking Yard*) and a novel (*Dogs of God*). His stories have appeared in, among other magazines and anthologies, *Esquire, Zoetrope: All-Story, StoryQuarterly, Ontario Review*, the *O. Henry Award* series, the *New Stories from the South* series, the *Pushcart Prize* series, *The Oxford Book of American Short Stories*, and *The Ecco Anthology of Contemporary American Short Fiction*. He is the recipient, among other prizes, of a Literature Fellowship from the National Endowment for the Arts, a Literary Fellowship from the West Virginia Commission on the Arts, a Michener Fellowship from the Writers' Workshop at the University of Iowa, the Chicago Tribune's Nelson Algren Award, a Individual Artist grant from the Illinois Arts Council, and Britain's Steinbeck Award. He is a professor in the English Department at Southern Illinois University in Carbondale, Illinois.

Cover artist JAKE MAHAFFY is a filmmaker and artist whose low-budget films have shown in festivals worldwide. He currently teaches at Wheaton College in Norton, MA.

Some of his work can be seen at www.burnbarrelfilms.com.